P9-DMO-815

WEEKS

MATTERS OF CHANCE

Matters of Chance

Gail Albert

G. P. Putnam's Sons
New York

Published simultaneously in Canada
by General Publishing Company, Limited, Toronto.

ACKNOWLEDGMENTS

Although this is a work of fiction, I have tried to be as accurate as possible about the scientific and medical data I've used; any inaccuracies are my own responsibility. All the characters in the novel are, of course, imaginary, but I owe a specific debt to Drs. Stephanie Matthews-Simonton and O. Carl Simonton for material adapted from their pioneering efforts in the field of guided imagery.

I also thank Boston Phoenix, Inc., for permission to use parts of "The Son Who Died," a short story published in *The Real Paper* in January 1978.

The text of this book is set in 11 point Baskerville.

LIBRARY OF CONGRESS CATALOGING IN PUBLICATION DATA

Albert, Gail, date.
Matters of chance.

I. Title.
PS3551.L257M3 1982 813'.54 82-5368
ISBN 0-399-12747-X AACR2

PRINTED IN THE UNITED STATES OF AMERICA

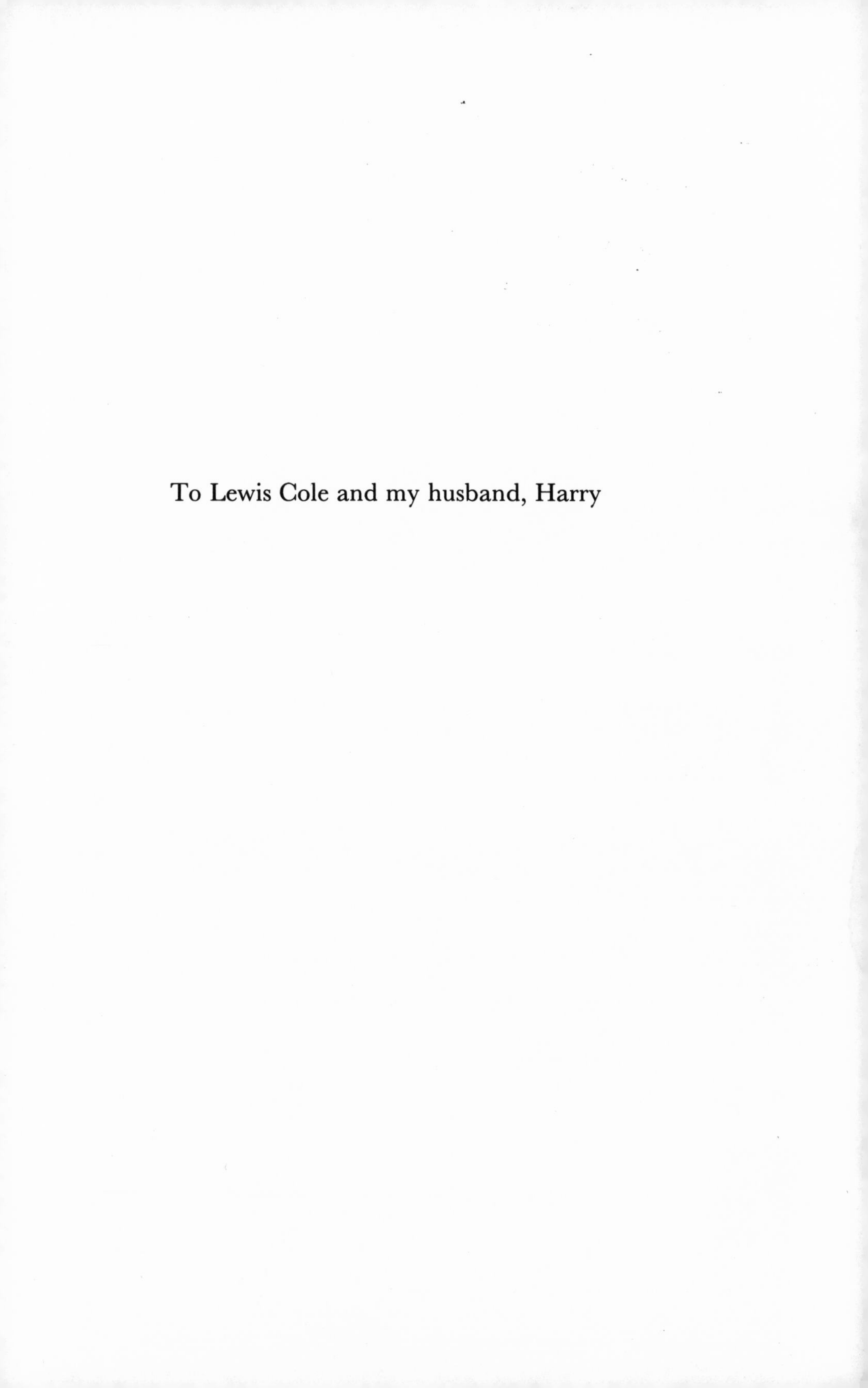

To Lewis Cole and my husband, Harry

I

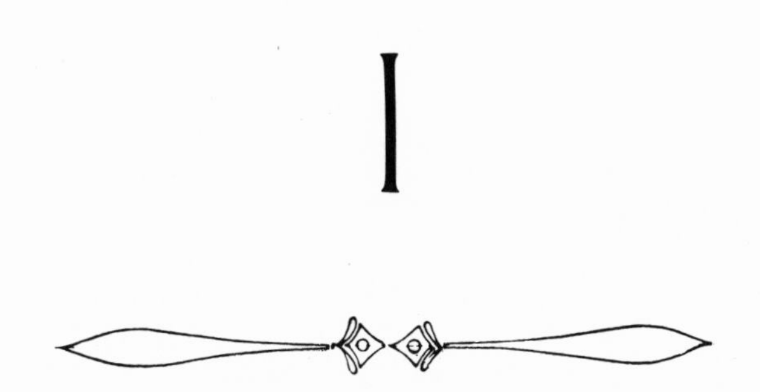

1

HANNAH WAS MY BEST FRIEND UNTIL HER FATHER KILLED HER mother with the bread knife when we were eight. Hannah found the body lying on the kitchen floor late one October afternoon and ran screaming down the stairs into my aunt's arms. Later my uncle said that Hannah's mother had always nagged too much; and he cried because they'd all known each other since before the war.

Hannah's father was sent to prison in upstate New York, and his spinster sister Irene moved in from Philadelphia. A schoolteacher, misplaced in our part of Brooklyn, she never let any of Hannah's friends inside the apartment. I was the only one of us even allowed on the stoop: I'd passed her test.

I stood on the pavement; she looked down at me from her wooden folding chair at the top of the brownstone steps.

"Tell me," she said, "the names of twenty Presidents of the United States. They don't have to be in order." Her mouth was tight, and I felt her eyes on my gypsy hair and scraped knees.

"Franklin Delano Roosevelt, and Theodore Roosevelt," I said, "and Harry Truman and Woodrow Wilson, and Washington and Lincoln, and . . ." Counting on my fingers I slowly ticked off thirteen more. ". . . Did I say Madison?" I asked at last.

"No," she said. "Not yet."

That time Hannah and I played geography and hangman until sunset, while I bit my tongue to keep from spelling m----r for murder or k---e for knife. I loved Hannah and I hated Irene for shutting me out.

I still dream of Hannah twenty-six years later, and wonder what became of her. I see her as unmarried, sometimes living alone and sometimes living with a bent and white-haired Isaac, out of prison at last. I ask if he collects Social Security, unable to remember the rules for convicted murderers.

Indeed, I think that Isaac was actually convicted of manslaughter, although I've never quite seen how stabbing your wife with a bread knife is anything less than murder. The knife had always been there, ready to cut great slabs of the pumpernickel Isaac brought home from work. I can see him using it on Rose instead of on the thick black bread if she pushed him just too far when he already had the knife in hand. And yet I can't, for all the years I've thought about it.

I get angry too; everyone does. With my husband, say, or with my children. When my boys were very little, I'd sometimes slap one of them in a rage, so mad I wanted only to keep on hitting until my child begged me from the floor to stop. But I never gave way to more than those few slaps, no matter what I felt like doing.

Once I even locked myself in the bedroom to protect Daniel from me; he was in the middle of an unending toddler's tantrum and I couldn't make him leave me alone. I locked myself in and covered my head with pillows while Dan screamed and banged and hammered on the door. I was pregnant for the second time; Bob was interning and on duty at the hospital thirty-six hours out of every forty-eight. Huddled on the bed, knowing I'd be alone with Dan for ten more hours, I was afraid I'd kill him if I came out of the room.

Then why did Isaac stab Rose to death? I knew Isaac, I knew Rose, as well as a child knows close neighbors when you're poor together, and sometimes I feel I understand and then again I don't.

We moved from Brownsville to a better part of Brooklyn when I started high school. Hannah moved then too, back to Philadelphia with Irene. We exchanged cards at Rosh Hashanah a few times, but no more than that. We talked so little in the years after Isaac killed Rose; how could we write?

It's Sunday night, almost eleven; Bob and I have been reading in the living room, trying to keep up with this week's journals; the boys are asleep and the room is quiet except for the rumble of buses outside. Remembering that I have to boil an egg for Dan's lunch box, I take the article I'm reading with me to the kitchen, grateful that Adam, at least, eats simple ham sandwiches that need no thought the night before.

Whatever the reason, I picture Hannah as a veterinarian, in white coat, surgical mask perhaps, in her office in some upstate town. Last year it occurred to me that Sing Sing is upstate and that I always see her near her father.

At least the murder must have settled Hannah's life. She is a spinster like Irene. Wanting to marry, perhaps. But unable. I imagine the polite prospective in-laws asking about her absent parents.

"My father killed my mother," she patiently explains. "He's out of Sing Sing now and lives with me. I'm sure you'd like him." But it's too late, they've run out.

"People are peculiar," I announce to Bob when I sit down again in the living room. He looks up, startled, with no context for my observation. Then he grins, the skin around his gray eyes crinkling, and asks what set me off this time.

I am an associate professor of neurobiology at a well-known university. My husband is a doctor, a cardiologist, a Jewish blond from California, with the dazzling smile of a Los Angeles lifeguard hoping to catch the eye of a Hollywood film maker. My marriage is happy, my children normal, and my department voted me tenure a year ago.

At school I teach my students everything I know about the brain, and in the afternoon, after classes, I record nerve impulses from the brains of rats to study precisely how each bit of nerve tissue controls their memory. And the more I study, the more sure I am that I'm not even asking the right questions. I don't know if I've ever asked the right questions.

Why did Isaac murder Rose? Did Isaac know he was going to murder her? Did he even mean to kill her when he did?

It's April 1977, two weeks before my thirty-fifth birthday. Isaac killed his wife over a quarter-century ago. As my father killed my own mother—and himself—in a head-on collision with a truck in the Utah desert four summers ago. My father, who never scratched a fender in thirty-six years of driving on New York City streets, in that empty countryside smashed into a trailer truck on the wrong side of the road. They'd never left New York before; I sent them on that trip, and they died in a gully by the roadside.

Bob has just gone downstairs to walk our dog, McCrae, in Central Park. The cherry trees are blooming; from our windows, the Park looks soft and romantic, its tree-lined winding paths a nineteenth-century vision of an English garden.

We live on the fifteenth floor of a co-op in Manhattan, high above the Central Park Reservoir. Our bedroom overlooks the Park but I see none of it now. With Bob outside, I've gone to bed;

retreating to the warm, king-size, soothing waterbed; ignoring the city and the Park to look up at space and sky, floating in space while the bed makes warm waves beneath me.

On the walls of the room are photographs of the Utah desert; of Canyonlands, Arches, and Cedar Breaks; of rocks red with iron, green with uranium. I float in space on a warm sea, looking at the desert pictures and the sky outside. I've attained the American Dream and it's come near to killing me.

I am thirty-four years old, married, a professor of neurobiology; I have two sons, aged nine and seven. I grew up in Brownsville, and I left it behind, and I was diagnosed as having cancer in January. I know that these facts are connected; I have yet to understand how.

IN BROWNSVILLE, THE WOMAN WHO LIVED ABOVE US WAS A witch. My mother warned me always to be polite to her, to carry her groceries, and to open the door for her. To keep her from giving me the evil eye.

When I was two and my father was in basic training in the infantry, my mother had a second child, a son. In an argument with my mother three months before the birth, Mrs. Goldstein cursed him. My mother was five months pregnant; Mrs. Goldstein had caught her foot in the fire escape upstairs while washing windows. She called down for help, but my mother was afraid to climb the open stairs.

"I was dizzy all the time; I couldn't help her," my mother told me. "She killed your brother because I didn't come."

"Let him choke the way I choke here now," she'd cursed. And when he was born, six weeks early, he turned blue and choked and died. He tried to live, lying in an incubator for ten days of gasping struggle, but in the end the curse was too strong. Or so my mother said.

We lived in an apartment building four stories high, two brick wings around a pink concrete courtyard. The lobby was all marble, floor and walls, and a marble fireplace stood opposite two marble window seats that looked out upon a second weed-filled courtyard in the back. My parents said there had been armchairs in the lobby and a red velvet canopy out front when the building was new in 1923, long before they lived there. The skeleton of the canopy was still standing so I believed them. Now my friends and I roller-skated in the empty lobby on rainy days.

It was still the nicest building on the block; the others had neither courtyards nor lobbies. The block itself was not the best, but it was second best, with three trees and a number of small brownstones across the street; and down the block, a dentist lived in the brownstone that had a white rosebush in front.

We had a two-bedroom apartment one floor up and overlooking the street. My parents slept in one bedroom; I slept in the other with my grandfather.

Isaac and Rose lived just across the street, in the same brownstone as my aunt and uncle, and Mr. and Mrs. Goldstein lived above us. On warm days, I might clamber out my parents' bedroom window to the fire escape, to lie reading on a blanket in the sun; and sometimes I'd climb up the iron staircase one landing to Mrs. Goldstein's window. Careful not to be seen, I could watch her husband put his arms around her, or pinch her as he walked by. At night I heard their bed creak through the ceiling.

Mrs. Goldstein didn't like to bring her garbage to the dumbwaiter for collection every night; often she threw it out the window instead, into the back courtyard, bits of it dropping onto the laundry my mother hung out to dry. My mother said it was people like Mrs. Goldstein who were making the building go downhill. But her own three daughters finished high school and married well, moving out of Brownsville to fairy-tale Long Island suburbs. She had pictures of them on all the flat surfaces of her furniture, posed in front of their suburban homes.

When Isaac killed Rose, many of the neighbors said they understood: Rose nagged too much. But Mrs. Goldstein could never forgive a Jewish man for killing his wife. "In her own kitchen," she raged. "With her daughter to find her dead on the linoleum."

On the other hand, she was glad when Irene moved in, glad to have a schoolteacher across the street, and she took to stopping at Irene's with gifts of homemade noodle puddings and honey cakes.

Irene invited her in when she asked in no one else, and visited with her in turn.

On summer days they sat on wooden chairs around a tiny table on Irene's stoop, sipping iced tea from special thin-walled glasses. One of Mrs. Goldstein's daughters had moved to a suburb of Philadelphia, and Irene would talk about the city while Hannah and I played our endless games of checkers and geography and hangman. I think Mrs. Goldstein approved of me, polite and bookish as I was, and I loved to listen to them talk; but I was afraid of her. She was a witch.

"I don't like you playing over there," my mother said each week. "Not when Hannah's aunt won't even let you inside. And with Mrs. Goldstein over there all the time . . ."

"She doesn't talk to me, she talks to Irene," I answered. But to myself I admitted that she worried me.

"You should get married," Mrs. Goldstein said to Irene when she knew her well enough. Hannah and I must have been ten by then. She smoothed the paper napkin on her lap and waited.

"I'm better off alone," Irene said. "Men are good-for-nothings anyway. And here, who could I meet here? In Philadelphia, there were men with futures. But here? The men who live here are pigs."

She sipped her tea, delicately holding out her pinkie finger. "I met a man at school last week who wasn't bad. We had lunch together in the candy store. But who wants to marry a woman with someone else's child?"

She broke a slice of honey cake in half and swallowed it without dropping a crumb, then wiped her mouth with a napkin. "At least Hannah takes after Isaac instead of her mother."

She paused before beginning the familiar litany, her eyes on the cake still left. "I told Isaac he never should have married her. He was too good for her. You know, he had two years of college. He laughed at me when I told him. When I visit him now, I always remind him how he laughed at his big sister."

Mrs. Goldstein spilled a bit of tea. "Still, a woman needs a man. You're young; my middle daughter is as old as you and she just had another baby."

They looked at us then, aware that Hannah and I had stopped our game to listen. Actually, I thought Hannah looked just like her mother, at least as I remembered her, and not at all like Isaac.

She didn't much like school either, for all of Irene's pushing her and making her do homework. Not that she was dumb. But I knew that Hannah liked boys.

"Can we walk around the block?" Hannah asked. "It's still early." When Irene hesitated, Mrs. Goldstein intervened. "They need a little exercise. They shouldn't sit here listening all day."

Hannah grabbed my hand and pulled me off the steps. "We'll be back in half an hour," she said. "And don't call the cops if I'm a minute late."

She half ran down the block, pulling me along, slowing only as we reached the corner. "You hear that Mr. Goldstein is carrying on with Mrs. Sachs?"

I grinned. "I hear Mrs. Goldstein screaming at him through the ceiling. If he's not careful, she'll put a curse on him."

"My aunt says she's used to his carryings on. She just likes to yell."

"Well, I wouldn't get her mad if I was him." I thought then of my parents and of the coldness so often still between them. "Sometimes I don't know why people get married. My mother says it's a curse that women fall in love." I blinked and changed the subject. "Do you like my new skirt? It's tight."

But that too was a delicate subject. My mother let me pick my own clothes, and she didn't mind them flashy. I was even wearing stockings and sling-back shoes to school, the only girl in the smartest track to wear sling-backs. I had a giant blister on my heel where my left shoe rubbed. I looked at Hannah's saddle shoes and socks. Irene insisted that she dress respectably.

When we turned the corner, Hannah unbuttoned the top two buttons of her blouse. At ten, she was just beginning to get breasts; I could see the nipples through her undershirt and blouse. It was safe enough around the corner: a different neighborhood, where only a few people knew our families. Irene didn't speak to any of them anyway.

"Mr. Goldstein had some beer last week, and he pinched me when my aunt wasn't looking."

I thought of my Uncle Jake and grimaced; he pinched too and he always stank of whiskey. "What did you do?"

"I told him I stuck to boys my own age. It made him laugh."

We stopped then while I bent to fix the Kleenex in my shoe; my blister was getting larger. A few months before I'd had to wear slippers without backs for two weeks to give my feet a chance to heal. But I loved my shoes.

We crossed the street just behind a big red truck, its horn bleating to scatter the crowd of skaters. When I was six, and learning how to skate, I'd turned too fast and fallen in front of a truck that large. I lay in the gutter forever, trying to crawl out of the way, watching the truck bear down on me, everything in slow-motion. It stopped just a few inches from my legs, and the driver jumped out, shouting at me as soon as he saw he hadn't run me over and shaking me by the shoulders when he stood me up; I still couldn't get my legs to move. I'd never told my parents.

I knew that Hannah was looking for some boys to flirt with; I was along for camouflage. To Irene, I was safe company for Hannah in spite of my sling-backs; she'd never gotten over my naming twenty Presidents of the United States. And maybe she even knew I was afraid of boys in spite of how I dressed.

"There's Stanley on his bicycle," I said, hoping to placate Hannah.

"He's a creep."

I knew he was; for me that was the central point. He had a crush on me, and I spent an hour or two each week listening to his baseball talk in return for borrowing his bicycle to go around the block. I'd never owned a bike and I was willing to use him coldheartedly for the privilege. It might have been easier to let him kiss me, but he wasn't interested, or maybe he was even shyer than I was.

He coasted toward us eagerly, the afternoon sun reflected on his glasses. His face was round and soft like his body. A creep.

"Hi, Mona! Hannah. You want to ride my bike?"

I grabbed it before I softened, and left the two of them alone.

I rode terribly, scared and wobbly, too slow or too fast, likely to fall if I had to veer or take a corner. The sidewalk was always crowded too, with carriages, and chairs, and ladies with heavy grocery bags. An old man stood up as I approached and I crashed into the brick wall of the building to avoid him, scraping my elbow and arm, but not the bike. I never came back without a crash.

The old man shouted after me, cursing in Yiddish.

"Drop dead yourself!" I called, hoping he didn't understand me. He didn't know my parents; I was two blocks from home.

My skirt was above my knees, crumpled under me on this boy's bike. Someone whistled. If I looked up, I'd crash again, a good reason not to look. What I needed was my own bike, not a stolen ride once or twice a week. But there was no point asking; we had no extra money. I blushed, remembering how I'd shared spaghetti at Sheila's house last week. I'd eaten without thinking, not noticing that her mother had no plate for herself until it was too late. But I loved her mother's cooking: spicy, with garlic.

The wind blew as I came back around the corner, up the little slopes by the laundromat. The bike veered; I really couldn't ride in this skirt. Ahead of me I saw Hannah and Stanley. I rode right up to them, falling over as I stopped. Stanley caught me; he was stronger than I was, for all his softness. Boys were always stronger than girls.

Hannah glared at me. "We have to keep walking," she said. "You wasted fifteen minutes." She started off; I was grateful as well as embarrassed. Now I didn't have to spend time with soppy Stanley.

"You want to come over here tomorrow afternoon?" he asked. His eyes were damp and shiny, his cheeks pink.

"I'll have to see," I lied. "I don't know if my mother wants me for something."

Hannah called to me from down the block. I thanked Stanley again and ran after her. She was mad.

"That was rotten of you," she said.

"It's the only way I get a chance to ride."

"Well, you started on this walk with me, and then you left me in the middle with that creep. He's not even older than me."

"He's not so bad," I said defensively.

"Then visit him by yourself. You can listen to him talk about his stupid hamster."

"My mother says he's a very nice boy. Not like most of the others."

"Then your mother likes creeps. I never get off that goddamned stoop and you spoil it."

I looked at the sky. "There are no boys out anyway."

"And aren't you just glad," she said bitterly.

I didn't answer and we walked on in silence. I didn't like going home either. I kicked an old bottle cap along in front of me, fearful of scuffing my shoes but needing to do something. At last, I looked sideways at her. "I'm sorry," I said.

She nodded glumly; I was afraid she was going to cry.

"Maybe it will be better when we're grown-ups," I said. So little I could say to her.

She snorted. "Like the people around here?"

She was too direct; I backed off. "Somewhere else, like in the movies."

3

MY MOTHER WAS PLAITING MY HAIR INTO LONG BRAIDS DOWN my back; I was no more than six, watching our reflections in the mirror of her vanity. She was telling me the story of my father's courtship; of their first meeting at a dance at the Henry Street Settlement on the Lower East Side.

"That was when we still had money," she said, "when your grandfather still had his upholstery business. I wore a white dress that I bought at Ohrbach's; it had a yellow rose in the sash. I saw your father watching me across the room and I asked my girlfriends who he was."

I squirmed in anticipation; I loved the answer that was coming. "A bum!" I shouted. "They said he was a bum!"

She nodded, and twisted a rubber band around a braid. "A bum," they said. "Watch out for him. He's always in the pool hall."

"And when he saw you looking at him, he came up and introduced himself," I said.

"He did. And his manners were very fine. He reminded me of Cary Grant, he was so smooth and handsome. He said I was the most beautiful girl in the room and I asked him if he really spent his time shooting pool. I was at City College then and I had no time to waste on men with no future."

My father was poor, and an immigrant, brought here from a farm in Poland when he was ten. My mother's family had reached America when her brother Obbie was four; but she and her older sister were born here.

They all grew up on Manhattan's Lower East Side through the 1920s and 1930s. My mother's mother died while she was still a child, but both her parents had been able to read in several languages, and her father owned a small upholstery business until 1939, when his older brother embezzled the partnership into bankruptcy and fled to South Africa.

By then, my father's father was dead too, after falling down a flight of stairs while carrying a block of ice to a customer in a fifth-floor walk-up. With his mother and a young sister to support, my father left the pool halls, and went to work as a truck driver. My parents met again, at another dance, and this time my mother was interested.

"I had to leave college," she told him. "Now I work at Woolworth's."

"But everyone knows they don't hire Jews," he said.

She laughed and gestured to her pink sweater. "I wear a crucifix around my neck, right here. I told them I was Catholic and they believed me."

My father was shocked; then delighted. He knew immediately he'd marry her.

She knew too, that same night. They left the dance, and walked to the East River, to sit on a bench by the Drive. "I looked out at the river and I told your father that I was going to leave the East Side when I married, and cross over to Brooklyn. He said he was going to open a garage someday; then he asked me to marry him."

They married late in 1940, and my mother talked my father into starting night school for his high school diploma. In Brooklyn, they took a cramped but sunny apartment; when my mother became pregnant a year later, they moved to the two-bedroom apartment in Brownsville that I grew up in.

In December Pearl Harbor was bombed and we went to war; I was born in April 1942, the week U.S. bombers raided Tokyo for the first time. My father read the papers every day; my mother tried to pretend the war didn't exist. The draft notice came at last when I was eighteen months old. My mother was pregnant with their second child, the son who died.

My mother pleaded with my father to ask for a deferment until she gave birth. She argued that he could be deferred indefinitely: he supported a wife, child, mother and sister; at least he could wait until her pregnancy was over. He argued that it was his obligation to defend America, dishonorable to ask for special treatment; anyway, everyone he knew was in the army. They still argued it years later, when I could hear them for myself.

"In Poland, the Gentiles stoned me when I walked to school," my father would say. "Here I'm American, like anyone else. They let us come here, they let us live, they let us vote. It's an honor and a duty to fight."

My grandfather would agree with him. "In Russia, they took us in the Army to clean the boots of Cossacks. They drafted us for fifteen or twenty years; when we came out we were good for nothing, like my father's brother. Here, they treat everyone alike. Sam was right to go as soon as he was called."

My father left for basic training in Florida. In the rural town next to the base he was an oddity, a Jew, and was asked quite humbly, as one should ask a legendary creature, if he really had horns and a tail. He promised to break the nose of the next man who asked.

Then my mother called: she'd given birth early, there was something wrong with the baby. He came home by train on emergency leave.

The initial explanation for my brother's death was Mrs. Goldstein's curse, the evil eye. But there were two others. The last one I heard only after I had given birth to my first child.

"Your father was going into combat," my mother said. "I used to sit with you in the closet in the bedroom, smelling your father's jackets, keeping him alive for us."

She shook her head sadly, watched me change Daniel's Pamper. "I was scared all the time," she said. "I had no room in me for someone else. I killed my son by not wanting him."

That was the final explanation for his death, given to me only when I was grown myself. But they had another explanation in my childhood. When my father returned to Florida to finish basic training, he was put into a different unit, six weeks behind the old one. His first unit shipped out to land in Normandy on D-Day, to be drowned to the last man just off the beach. My father's friend

Dave was in that unit; when he died, his wife stopped speaking to my mother.

My father spent two years in combat, but he missed dying on D-Day because of my mother. Gasping in his incubator, my brother hung onto life and kept my father home for ten days. Dying, he gave my mother power to keep my father with her four days more: long enough to save him.

"I gave my son's life to save yours," my mother said to my father's mother, when they fought so badly years later. "I lost my son so yours would live. Don't talk to me about standing by him now!"

If my brother had a name I never heard it; but I thanked God for his brief existence when I prayed at night; if not for him I might have been sacrificed instead.

In time, my mother asked my grandfather to move in with her, writing my father that she didn't see why they should both live alone, and what was the point when my grandfather ate with her every night anyway. She didn't know for weeks if he got the letter; it took so long for him to answer.

Each morning, we walked down a flight of stairs to the marble lobby and the double row of mailboxes against one wall. She opened the little door with a small gold key, different in shape from the one to our apartment. I watched while she looked through the letters. I was two years old when the ritual began.

If she had a letter, she scanned it while I waited, watching her face go white, her lips pale. If she got no letter, I learned to say "maybe tomorrow," and take her hand to walk upstairs. I learned that any mail was better than none, and that the worst danger came from the special delivery messenger.

"Telegram. Telegram for Mrs. Leiber," he called, and later I heard Mrs. Leiber keening across the courtyard, her apartment dark.

Another day, two telegrams came to different neighbors: one dead, one missing in action. My mother was out with me when the messenger arrived. When we came back, we heard Ruth's husband was missing. My mother's closest friend, twenty-two years old, with two babies, Ruth was at her parents' apartment, half a mile away. My mother ran through the street with my stroller, tears running down her face, crying over and over that it couldn't be. When we got to their building, a smaller one than ours, we saw from the faces of the neighbors outside that it was true.

The other woman whose husband was dead I didn't know, but I could see the black flag from our bedroom window.

I slept in a crib next to my mother's bed; my grandfather took the other bedroom. I'd often wake in the morning to find myself in bed with my mother; she needed to wrap herself around me in the middle of the night.

After a while, I forgot my father, even though I knew I must be bad not to remember him. I pretended to remember, and studied the pictures of him on the dresser: waving from the beach in a skimpy bathing suit; smiling from a bench on the East Side Drive; solemn in a black jacket for his wedding; stiff in his graduation photo from the eighth grade.

I looked at the pictures and listened to the stories my mother told, until I could no longer tell which were stories I remembered and which were real memories.

On Sundays, she'd take me to the movies, often to war films, pointing out how like the hero my daddy looked.

"That's the hero," she would say. "Don't worry about anyone else. Even if they die, the hero lives."

But I was little and easily confused; the soldier I thought was the hero died when a tree fell on him as he lay trapped in a muddy hole, the pointed end of it landing on his upturned face.

I was hysterical; she took me out to the lobby to sit with me and calm me down. By then she was crying too; she ran out of Kleenex and had to bring out toilet tissue from the bathroom.

After that, my grandfather insisted that she stop taking me with her to the films; and when I woke up screaming at night, he took me from her and rocked me in the big armchair in his bedroom.

My mother got thinner each week, and shouted at me for spilling milk, or getting my clothes dirty; she bathed me twice each day and insisted I put a newspaper under me when I sat on the front steps.

My grandpa spent more time with me. He read me stories, making up different voices for each of the Three Bears, and ran down the stairs with me when the merry-go-round on a truck came ringing through each spring and summer afternoon.

He owned a building in Williamsburg, a tenement, all that remained of the partnership with his thieving vanished brother. Often he took me with him to his building in the afternoons, to sit in the kitchen of his super, Selim, and drink coffee with tenants; we'd get there after hour-long train rides on the El through unknown parts of Brooklyn. I explained to a friend that I had two daddies: one in the army and a real one who lived with us. Overhearing, my mother slapped me and cried.

Another day, I watched her get a letter from the mailbox, go white, back off to sit on the stairs, and finally fall forward in a faint. I screamed, and ran banging on Freddy's mother's door across the hall. Irma ran out and slapped my mother's cheeks, then raced back to her apartment and returned with a bottle of ammonia.

My mother revived. Freddy's mother took me inside with her while my mother sat on the stairs, reading and rereading the letter. Freddy was still a baby, and I pretended to be interested in watching him while I waited. After a long time, my mother knocked on the door, and sat down to tea, her face swollen and tear-stained.

"I don't know what happened," she told Irma. "He says, 'Don't worry, I'm beginning to feel better; it's not so bad.' But his letter is written by a nurse. I haven't heard from him in almost two months. I don't know what happened.

"I keep making promises to God, if he'll please let him live. I clean and I take care of Mona, and I don't complain, and I don't buy anything on the black market, not even stockings. And now I don't even know what's happened to him."

She was shivering; Irma put a sweater around her. "Call your mother-in-law first," she said. "If this is your first mail in weeks, maybe she got a letter too, something that tells you what happened."

My mother ran upstairs. Irma wanted me to stay with her but I refused; my mother called back that it was all right for me to go up to her. I heard the phone begin to ring before I reached the landing; my mother had just opened the door. She began shouting into the phone. It was my grandmother, hysterical about the letter she'd just gotten herself. It too was written by a nurse, dated before my mother's, but still without an explanation: "I feel better than last week. Too tired to say more. Sam."

It was the middle of the Battle of the Bulge. January 1945. The newspapers had huge black headlines, pictures of wounded men and bodies even on page one. My father was in Patton's Army, 80th Division, already a veteran of the Battles of the Ardennes and Bastogne. He was an old hand, a survivor, to be sent on patrol whenever the newest lieutenant needed someone who'd come back.

He was wounded twice in quick succession. The first time, the tank in front of him exploded, bloodying his hands with shrapnel. The medics sent him back to combat the same day; men were needed too badly. Two days later, he was crawling through the mud of a hill his battalion had already fought for, won, and lost four times. My father's coat was gone, used to carry down a wounded friend; his toes were numb and infected with a fungus within torn boots; he was fighting with ammunition taken from the bodies of dead soldiers.

The man in front of him was killed, the men on each side of him, and then the man behind. Sure there was no hope of reaching the hilltop unwounded, my father offered God his leg if He'd let him live. He raised his leg out of the mud, as high in the air as he could, watched the bullets go past to churn up the mud around him, but he remained untouched. Once I asked him how he kept climbing, and he said it was easier than turning around. At the top of the hill, he was alone, under God's protection. He stood up and threw a grenade at the Germans, destroying the machine-gun nest. For that, he won a Silver Star.

Within a week, he was thrown from a trench by an explosion, and suffered a concussion. He was sent behind the lines, then shipped to a hospital farther back. With his head in bandages, he dictated letters to a nurse. His first letters were lost in transit; my mother and grandmother got only the later ones.

He was in the hospital for three weeks, long enough to get my mother's mail and write what had happened. Knowing what to expect, he'd been away from combat too long to go back to it. They sent him anyway; he fought two more months to the edge of Czechoslovakia. He and his sergeant were the only men still left of the original unit.

Then he was shelled again, and found half-buried in a hole beneath his sergeant's body. This time he told them he'd desert if they returned him to the front; they compromised and made him an MP two blocks behind the lines. He wrote home that it was wonderful to be so safe.

4

MY FATHER FOLLOWED PATTON'S ARMY AS AN MP THROUGH the spring and summer of 1945, just behind the lines, maintaining law and order in newly occupied territory. He arrested American soldiers for rape and looting, enemy civilians for hiding weapons. With no trust in anyone, he booby-trapped the rooms he commandeered to live in, and slept with his rifle in his bed.

In June he was sent by truck with five other Americans to accept the surrender of a German division: ten thousand German soldiers marched down a hill behind him, silent and frightened, while the truck followed with their weapons. He posed before a photographer from *Stars and Stripes,* but the picture was never printed.

"My division did all the scut work," he said, "and we never got the glory. But it was the best action of the war. All those men following my orders, marching in step with me at the head. It felt like a dream."

Somehow, he was also one of the soldiers to breach the gates of Auschwitz. Inside the death camp, he found a few guards waiting to surrender, two Gestapo agents hiding in an office, and the living skeletons of the survivors. After he vomited, he offered his rifle and bayonet to any inmate strong enough to stand and use them, and with a stolen Leica he took pictures of survivors, of piles of shoes, of gold teeth outside the crematorium. The next day, the Americans made all the people of the nearby town walk slowly through the concentration camp and see what they had allowed. He offered the mayor and his wife the choice of a knife or razor blade to kill themselves.

In talking with the inmates of the camp, he found a woman he had known in Poland, a neighbor whose child he'd played with. She was the only survivor of his town. He wrote my grandmother to arrange for the woman to be transported to Palestine.

In January 1946, he was sent home at last, desperately seasick on the North Atlantic; he said the waves were forty feet high. He docked in Chesapeake Bay, called my mother and grandmother, and came home by train to a street decked with American flags.

I waited at the window with my mother and grandpa, asking each time a soldier approached if it was my father. When he came onto our street at last, we all ran downstairs and I watched him crush my mother against him and cry. He was all bone and muscle, with huge dark eyes circled by deep black shadows. His hands shook when he let go of her, and he hurt me when he picked me up. He looked nothing like the pictures on my mother's dresser and he frightened me.

Upstairs, my father made me sit on his lap while he held my mother against him on the couch. I was rigid with the strangeness of him and the two of them together. After a while, my grandpa took me outside, leaving them alone.

That night I slept in my grandfather's room for the first time, my bed near the door, next to his high iron bed. Through the wall, I heard the springs of my mother's bed creaking. In the middle of the night, I woke to hear my mother screaming and my father shouting. My grandfather ran into their room, with me scrambling after him, afraid to be alone.

My father was kneeling on the floor on one side of the bed; he looked dazed. My mother was on the other side, holding a table lamp as a club.

"You choked me!" she was shouting. "You tried to kill me!"

He was shaking his head, whispering. "It was a dream. I'm not used to anyone sleeping next to me. I thought you were a German."

"Maybe you should keep the light on," my grandfather said from the door. "Helen, Sam needs time to get used to you again."

He turned and took my hand, pulling me back to his room. I was suddenly glad to be sleeping with him instead of my mother.

In his room, he tucked me into my bed, fluffed his pillows, and opened a volume of the Talmud. "Go to sleep," he said. "I'll be up, don't worry. Your father is still a soldier, he needs time to get used to being home again."

"I don't want him home," I said.

"You have no choice," he answered. "God saw fit to spare him when so many died, you have no right to question that. Thank

God you've been safe in America, you don't know what he's seen."

I began to cry, and he put his arms around me. "Mona, we all have to take care of him now, you too. Now go to sleep, tomorrow you're going to your grandma's."

By February, my father was back in his old job as truck driver and delivery man. He began to gain weight, but his eyes still darted above black circles, and he held me too tight whenever he put me on his lap. I learned to be quiet around him, not to make sudden noises or move too quickly. At night, I began to sleep through his muttering dreams and sudden sharp screams.

One night, after my father sprang from the living room armchair to land crouching on the carpet at the sound of a backfire in the street, my mother took me into the bathroom with her and put me in the tub.

"I liked it better when Grandpa was my only daddy," I said, knowing she would be angry.

She scrubbed my back with a sponge and wiped tears from her face. "Your grandpa's not your daddy, he's Grandpa. Your daddy loves you too."

But to my grandfather I heard her say, "He's not the man I married. He doesn't even look the same. Poppa, I'm afraid of him."

My grandfather looked up from his coffee, dark and black and strong, looked down, and blew on it deliberately. "Helen, it's not Clark Gable in a movie. He's seen too much killing, and he's done too much."

"I know, but I'm afraid of him. Every day I prayed for him to come back safe, and now I don't know what to do. If I touch him when he's sleeping, he screams and jumps on me. I stay on the edge to keep away from him."

She put her face in her hands. "Poppa, do you see the way he stares at the wall? Last night, I came into the bedroom and he was staring at the wall and crying. I asked him if there was anything I could do, and he just shook his head and crawled into bed with the covers over him. He said at least there he could be warm enough."

My grandpa looked at his callused hands, ending the conversation as he saw my head peek around the kitchen wall. "I don't have a cure, Helen. But you married him for better or worse."

Then it was March, a month before my birthday. My father asked me what I wanted; I told him I didn't know, I wasn't used to thinking about presents. He walked with me to Pitkin Avenue, to the big toy store I sometimes looked at from the outside with my mother.

"A big box of crayons?" I asked. "Some clay in colors?"

He pointed to the rows of dolls. "Would you like one of these? Your doll is old."

Together we picked out a doll with long black hair like mine, and sparkling eyes; he showed me that she'd cry if pressed along the middle of her back. Then he bought a stroller with pink ribbons on the handle, and let me wheel it all the way home.

"I know your birthday's not until next month," he said. "I wanted to get you something now."

But at home he argued with my mother. Pesach was coming, the celebration of God's rescue of the Jews from slavery in Egypt three thousand years before. I was going to be four years old on the third day of Pesach: instead of birthday cake, my mother would bake a cake of matzoh meal with eggs and honey, flat like the unleavened bread Jews ate in the desert after fleeing from Egypt.

She was scouring the house in preparation for the holiday, polishing even the brass pipes under the sink. Only Pesachdikah food would be allowed, and she tried to use up all our groceries before the first day of Pesach; what was left would be boxed into cartons in the bedroom. Now would come the week of matzoh spread with chicken fat and salt, of matzoh pancakes, of matzoh scrambled with eggs, and my father already complained that his stomach hurt.

We went to my grandmother's for the first night of the holiday. She still lived on the Lower East Side, on an ancient street of smelly tenements, in an apartment that she kept through the Depression by working as the building's janitor, earning a little money on the side by plucking chickens at the market on the next block.

When my father's father died, she went back to what she'd done in Poland while her husband was in America earning money for her passage over. She worked as a healer, selling herbal potions and casting spells. Once she let me watch her heal a child so terrified by something he'd seen that he'd become mute. She closed the curtains, darkened the room, and lit a candle, using its flame to melt a second candle, letting the dripping wax take the form of whatever the child feared. Watching it take shape, he screamed, and began to speak.

Tonight, for the first Seder, I was wearing my new yellow-checked dress with a wide sash tied behind me. I had on new black patent leather sandals too, and yellow socks, and my black braids were tied with yellow ribbon from my mother's sewing box.

I'd hoped to have my ears pierced for my birthday like my friend Marsha, with little golden hoops that I could parade. But my mother said I'd look like one of the Gypsies across the street.

The train to the East Side was crowded. I sat with my grandfather while my parents sat across the aisle. I kneeled at the window to watch the apartments we passed, my knees marked in crisscrosses by the straw seats; on curves I leaned to the center of the car, adding my weight to keep us from tipping off the track. My father saw me leaning over and smiled at me. He stood up and walked across the aisle to me. "I always feel like doing that too," he said.

When we arrived, everyone on the street was in new clothes.

"God always grants us good weather for the Seder," my mother said.

"But He lets them kill us," my father answered. "They stoned me in Poland when I was no bigger than Mona."

"We're lucky to be here," my mother insisted. "So few left."

The halls were dark in my grandma's building, the bulbs on the second floor were broken again. "Even here, I fought with the Irish," my father said. "Although I'll give them credit, in the army they killed Germans. They're good fighters." His eyes were teary.

The stairwells stank of roaches and rancid oil; I ran up the last two flights, retching, and banged on the door for my grandmother to let me in. Picking me up, she hugged me to her fat bosom. She wore a housedress, heavy black shoes with laces, and wrinkled cotton stockings. Even when she was given clothing as a gift, she boxed it for better days.

The table was set with her one white cloth, embroidered by

both daughters over many seasons. Pots of food were everywhere: a chicken on the table; pot roast on the sink; fried matzoh farfel; chicken soup and stewed prunes on the stove.

She had only two rooms: a kitchen with a bathtub on one wall, the toilet in a cubicle at the side, and a tiny bedroom just large enough for a double bed and a wardrobe that I loved to hide in with my cousin Karen. I knew that my grandma shared the bed with her daughter Malkah, my father's younger sister, still unmarried at nineteen.

I hugged Malkah first, then my father's older sister and then her husband Jake. He was already drunk on wine, and pinched me.

My parents and my grandpa came in behind me; they kissed my grandma and her daughters and Karen. My mother was stiff as Jake embraced her, her smile fixed. My grandpa refused the bear hug but shook hands, and my father started to turn away, then turned back, holding his arm straight out for the handshake, as far from Jake as he could get.

"I made your favorite foods, Sam," my grandma said. "Everyone sit down. Sam, you pour the wine."

She spooned soup onto large white china plates, and stood behind my father, one hand on each shoulder.

"Eat, eat everyone."

I stared at my chipped plate helplessly, nauseated by the train ride and wondering why we didn't begin the Seder ritual; by tradition, it fell on my shoulders because I was the youngest at the table, and my grandpa had coached me all week.

"So, Sam, how does it feel to be home?" my uncle asked.

My father shrugged. My mother answered for him. "We're all glad to have him back."

"He's still too thin," my grandma said. "Helen, you have to make him eat more. Sam, try the matzoh farfel. You haven't had a Pesach meal in three years."

My uncle reached for the wine. "Save some for the rest of us," my father said.

"Isn't Mona going to ask the Four Questions?" my Aunt Malkah asked. "She's the youngest here."

I began the three-thousand-year-old ritual, even though it was supposed to come before the meal. "Why is this day different from all other days?"

No one answered. My grandpa took up the response.

Then my father interrupted. "If you're bothering to do this at all, you should have a stranger at the table. That's the law."

"I wanted only us," my grandma said. "It's our first meal with us all together since you're back."

"Your mother's been planning for a month," Jake said. "Every time she phones, she doesn't say, 'How are you, Jake, how are you, Sarah?' All she talks about is you."

"I thank God every day."

"Be glad she didn't have to talk to God about you too, Jake," my father answered. "She only had to worry about you staying sober enough to work overtime. That's a nice suit on you."

Malkah spoke. "He got it wholesale from a friend of mine. I can take you too, anytime you say."

"First he has to put some fat on him," my grandma said.

"Should I ask the questions?" I asked.

"A waste of time. God's turned His back on us," my father said.

"God's ways are not ours to understand!" my grandma cried.

"God's ways are shit! We signed the covenant and He's been persecuting us ever since!"

"I didn't fight because the army turned me down," Jake answered. "But I lost family too, you know. There's no one left."

"With six million murdered, we all lost family. We're marooned here."

"At least it can't happen here," my mother said.

"That's what the German Jews said."

"Can we stop this talk?" Malkah begged.

"If they come for me here, I'll shoot them. No one's taking Mona to a gas chamber."

"Sam, calm down. Not in front of the children." My mother left her chair to reach him across the table.

"When you're done, I'll be downstairs." He walked past her and slammed the door behind him.

My mother started to cry; I joined her. She held me in her lap, rocking back and forth. My grandfather tried to hold us both. I never did ask the Four Questions.

5

THIRTY-ONE YEARS LATER I LIE ON THE WATERBED IN MY OWN apartment remembering my father's homecoming. He was twenty-five then.

When I was twenty-five I had a newborn baby and a Ph.D. in sight. Living in the apartment the medical school supplied, in the compound fenced with six-foot-high steel mesh to divide us from the slums outside; surrounded by other breeding wives with babies and feeling a part of me torn away whenever I left Daniel, I told myself I was lucky to have nursing students to baby-sit while I cut into rats' brains in the lab. Bob was in his last year of school, cramming medicine into every pore of his body, afraid he'd never learn enough, the two of us taking turns walking Dan when he had colic those first three months; I walked Dan while trying to picture the neuroanatomy of the human brain, tracing the twisting patterns of nerve pathways in the air with my free hand, terrified I'd fail my orals. I walked Dan and listened as Bob refused money from his parents in long-distance calls from California, knowing they felt we'd chosen to have Dan too soon; and we took loans from the bank against our future. My parents hadn't offered loans; they knew I'd turn them down.

Now both my parents were dead.

I'd persuaded them to drive cross-country and meet us in California four summers ago. They'd never been outside New York before, and I wanted them for once to see how huge the country was, how little represented by New York; and I wanted them to see the desert that I loved.

I pushed them into going, prodding them with picture books and photographs, poring over maps with my father, deciding the roads he'd drive, holding out the image of them meeting us at last, victorious, at Bob's parents' home in Los Angeles. I pushed them into going and they died in Utah.

They drove away at the beginning of June, and we flew directly to Arizona from New York two weeks later, after the boys' last day of school.

We rented a station wagon and drove slowly in a half-circle toward L.A., across the flat sagebrush lands of Arizona and the red desert of the Mohave, as I felt my soul expand in the desert space. My parents were to spend a week in L.A., at a motel because my mother said she'd be more at home in a rented room than with Bob's rich parents; we'd show them what we could of southern California, and visit Disneyland; then they'd drive back east while we spent another week with my in-laws in their cabin in the Sierras, as we did almost every summer in return for living three thousand miles away from them.

Even with a roof rack, the rented wagon was cramped, stuffed with tents and gear, ice chest and food; and Dan and Adam sat on folded sleeping bags in a tumble of crayons, matchbox cars, and Lego. At not-quite-six and four, they could still stretch out to nap, but Adam complained Dan kicked him when he rolled around, and I wondered how we'd fit when they got any bigger.

We were all to meet for dinner at Bob's parents'; I was surprised not to see my father's car already in the driveway as I pulled in. By the time I turned the engine off, Doris and Jeff were outside the front door. Doris was crying and Jeff held her against his broad chest.

My father, I thought, my father's had a heart attack. I jumped from the wagon and ran to them across the pebbled triangle of yard. Jeff told me as Doris cried: A week ago. Your father crossed the divider and crashed into a trailer truck. No one knew where you were camping; there was no way to reach you. Your father was killed instantly; your mother lived long enough to tell the police to call us. Their bodies were sent back by plane, and they were buried in a cemetery on Long Island.

A year and a half later, I still dreamed of the wreck at night, saw visions of it at odd moments through the day. My father swerved even farther left after crossing the divider, maybe trying to get past the truck. Instead of colliding head-on, they were sideswiped, and their car thrown upside down into a gully. It was my fault for sending them, no matter what Bob said.

It was almost midnight, and we were in bed. I lay on my stomach, face against the pillow, while Bob straddled me, half-kissing, half-massaging knotted muscles in my back and shoulders. His fingers moved across my neck, froze, then moved again, but differently, probing, their touch suddenly delicate and cold.

Rocking the waterbed, he stretched to turn on the table lamp. I squinted at the light and shut my eyes; he prodded my scalp, behind my ears, the back of my head.

"You haven't noticed that before?" he asked. His voice was worried.

I raised my hand to feel what he was feeling. "I'm always having swollen glands," I said. "I never pay attention."

He turned off the lamp, but now I had a medical machine in bed with me, the cogs jammed with potential diagnosis. Most of the time, he refused to look at even a sore throat, contending that a doctor had no judgment for his own family, afraid of making blunders. But he had moments like this, when he diagnosed a fatal ailment out of nowhere and frantically sent me off to be examined.

He went on rubbing my back, his body more knotted than mine had been when he began massaging me. We'd been about to make love, the massage a prelude; I turned over to kiss him and his mouth closed violently on mine. But his lovemaking was distracted, his body still in bed with me but not his mind. Trying to ignore his tension, I pretended to be with someone else, then curled against his back to sleep. When he got out of bed, I opened my eyes and saw him scanning the corner bookshelves in the moonlight. He removed a heavy textbook and took it with him to the living room, shutting the door to our bedroom quietly behind him, not seeing that I'd seen him. When he came back to bed, I murmured sleepily to him. He asked me to call my internist for an appointment the next morning.

Unable to imagine what he had in mind, and not wanting to know, I promised and fell into uneasy dreams. A swollen gland meant nothing to me; still, he'd frightened me.

I saw our internist the next afternoon. His office was in a townhouse off Park Avenue, on the street floor, with its own private bell and entrance. The waiting room was decorated with antiques and English hunting magazines, and filled with elderly, gnarled patients, hunched with multiple and chronic diseases. Denton was a senior physician at the hospital, a consultant to other doctors; he saw simple problems only when a nervous colleague sent in a spouse or a parent. I was embarrassed about bothering him; he thought Bob's rushing me off to his office was funny.

"Bob probably decided you have Hodgkins," he said. "You're thirty-two, you're the right age. I think he should stick to cardiology, but I'll take lab tests to make him happy."

When I called for the results, his nurse said all the tests were negative. Bob seemed puzzled but hugely relieved after I told him, and I didn't even think about it once the node shrank back to almost nothing over the next few months.

Adam began kindergarten and Daniel second grade that fall. With both of them in school all day, either Bob or I could usually be home when they were. Bob had always tried to cover for me when he could, but now we didn't have to count on sitters too; and for the first time I went to work without feeling the tug of a waiting child. I was in my second year as an assistant professor at a New Jersey university. A colleague and I published three more papers on brain processes underlying memory.

The nightmares dropped off month by month as my parents' death receded. At the end of my third year, my department voted me tenure; I was just thirty-four. I'd been losing energy; I didn't notice when it first began. I hiked less when we went to the Sierras with Bob's parents that summer, and began to dread Sunday bike rides in the Park. Wondering why I was so out of shape, I put it down to too much sitting, too little daily exercise. I tried to walk a mile on campus every day, but by December I was so tired I was napping in my office between classes; and I began to pant when I climbed a flight of stairs.

I had a new internist; someone I'd met at a cocktail party: Tom Siegel. He was about my own age and on the staff of the same hospital as Bob. At the beginning of January I made an appointment to see him at his office in the outpatient building without telling Bob; I saw no reason for us both to worry before I knew anything.

I was afraid of emphysema; I'd had bad asthma for a time. I told Tom when he took my history, and he asked more questions about my asthma, and flu, wondered whether I'd ever had pneumonia, and raised a dozen other possibilities that had never occurred to me and still didn't make sense. He was fast, even impatient, interrupting me with another question while I was still struggling with the one before. He cut me off again and again, only to ask me to elaborate on something that seemed trivial.

"Any pain in the left quadrant of the chest?" "Tips of the fingers?" "Nausea on getting up?" "Fever?" "Loss of appetite?" "Weight loss?"

He had no bedside manner, didn't even offer courtesy. Just the naked workings of his mind. The treatment of one doctor toward another, where the computer choice points are obvious to them both. Doctors always thought I knew their business because I did surgery on animals.

At last, he had me strip and lie naked on the examining table under a white sheet, his nurse standing by to protect him from potential accusations of assault. Not that I could imagine his hands as sexual; I was all fright. He listened to me breathe and cough, listened to my heart, and prodded my neck, my chest, my abdomen, and my groin with harsh fingers. I yelped when he tapped my liver, and he volunteered his only comment. "Enlarged," he said.

A few times he asked new questions, but he looked more expressionless with each movement that he made. Finally he felt my ankles, took some blood from my right arm, and turned away to wash his hands at the sink. From his woodenness I knew it must be lung cancer: I'd smoked for a time too.

"I'm sending your blood downstairs for tests," he said, with his back still to me. "If you come back after lunch, they should be ready." He was sending them STAT: on emergency priority.

Watching him dry his hands methodically on brown paper toweling, I asked what he was thinking of.

"I can't tell you until I get the tests back," he said. He smiled apologetically and edged out the door before I pulled myself together to ask again.

My heart was pounding now, and I felt cold and sweaty. I gagged when I sat up; Tom's nurse took orange juice from a small refrigerator and poured some into a paper cup for me. I slowly put my clothes back on.

Outside, the waiting room was decorated in motel modern; shared by all the doctors on the floor, it belonged to no one. I picked a vinyl armchair in a back corner and wondered if he really thought I'd stop for lunch. He'd looked desperate to get away from me. His face told me he meant cancer.

I wanted to call Bob. But it wasn't right to phone him now. In an hour, I'd know what I was afraid of. I gnawed my knuckles, longing for a cigarette for the first time in years. If I had lung cancer, another few cigarettes wouldn't matter. I looked around, but there were no ashtrays. No more ashtrays in doctors' waiting rooms. If I went out for a pack, I'd have to smoke in the bathroom, like a child on the sneak.

If I went outside, into the sun, I could hail a cab before the tests came back. I could pretend I never came. I wouldn't have to tell Bob anything.

I watched the other patients jealously. None of them looked sick. Maybe they were just placed there for effect: plastic mannequins for a plastic waiting room.

Of course I might be jumping to conclusions. I tried to pray, looking up at the ceiling for a sign. But I saw nothing up there besides acoustic tiles.

I couldn't sit still. I had to move around. But I was embarrassed to pace back and forth; it was too public. I bolted for the elevators and pushed the call button before picturing it stuck, myself trapped between floors in an iron box. I walked instead, down five dim flights of narrow metal stairs, with each landing marked by a red bulb over the exit door. Like a Martian spaceship, this the real workings, the waiting room outside a stage set to fool the Earthmen. At the bottom, I leaned with all my weight on the exit door, still afraid of being trapped, and stepped out into the busy plastic lobby once again. I darted across and out the revolving door to the newsstand on the corner, just beyond the cart where the man sells flowers.

In the end, I bought no cigarettes, picking out a *New York Times* instead, for the crossword puzzle. On the walk back I counted my breaths, trying to believe it was all imagination. It was half a block uphill to the hospital entrance; I was panting by the time I reached the door. In defeat, I rang for the elevator, then waited in the same armchair, the *Times* folded neatly to the crossword puzzle, untouched.

I saw Tom come into the waiting room, his face grim as he searched for me. I hurried to him and he smiled nervously but avoided my eyes. Telling me to follow him, he strode ahead of me in the corridor. At his office, he held the door politely, pulled out the chair in front of his desk for me, and sat down on the other side. Slumping, he made a steeple with his hands and faced me at last. The other time we'd sat like this he was half drunk across a dinner table.

"I have bad news," he said. "It's what I was afraid of. It looks like you have a lymphoma."

I didn't know what he was talking about, but it sounded bad. I didn't like the word. I shook my head, gesturing with my own hands open. Again he thought I knew more than I did.

"Do you remember telling me you saw Denton two years ago about a node on your neck?"

I nodded, trying to slow him down so I wouldn't have to understand. What had Denton said that time? My mind wasn't working. My voice cracked. "I have Hodgkins?"

A pause. He didn't want to tell me. That was fine, I didn't want to know. But he cleared his throat, and answered, spewing it out all at once, without a break.

"Not Hodgkins. Something similar but different; I think Denton missed it. There are different lymphomas: I can't tell which you have without a biopsy. Or how far it's spread. I've arranged for you to be admitted this afternoon."

Silence then. Time stopped. There was nowhere to go. He was very far away from me. Smaller, hard to hear. He asked for Bob's number and my voice gave it to him from across a distant space. While he talked to Bob, I turned my head carefully to look at the fingers in my lap; I breathed shallowly. If I didn't move, I might be able to keep this moment from ever giving way to the one ahead. If I held on long enough, I might even find a way to go back through the seconds, might retrace the squares until I could start again at the beginning.

Tom handed me the phone; my throat closed. "Please come fast," I managed, and Tom took it back.

His nurse led me to an empty office and sat me on the couch to wait for Bob. In frozen images, I remembered my mother saying she wished she were a cow, chewing her cud all day with no mail or phones to worry about. A friend of hers, bleeding too often with unending periods: "a woman's problem" was all they told me then. "If I go to the doctor, he'll tell me something I don't want to hear," she said. I nodded stiffly in agreement.

I heard Bob running down the corridor. He knocked, called my name, and pushed the door open all together; crossing the floor with giant steps before I could even find a voice to answer with.

Reaching me, he pulled me to him on the couch, his arms so tight around me it was as though he were trying to pull me into his own body. I was very cold, my arms locked around my chest to keep in what little warmth there was. I burrowed into him, beginning to cry as I warmed up, and he rocked me like a baby, kissing me frantically, repeating the same few phrases over and over.

"It's OK, I'm here. I'm here. Baby, it's OK, I'm here."

He was crying too. So it was as bad as I'd thought. Out of the blue. I spoke with my eyes shut, from the circle of his body, trying to put off the knowledge yet another minute.

"I'm sorry about not telling you I was coming. But I didn't think it would turn out . . . like this."

He didn't answer right away. Was he weighing what to say? When he did speak, his voice was tight, working at control.

"What did Tom tell you?"

"A lymphoma," I recited. "Like Hodgkins but different."

Bob loosened his hold and I moved out from his arms. "But I don't know what that really means," I added. "It was his face and how he sounded. When he wouldn't look at me. And when he said he didn't know how far it's spread." I forced myself to face Bob, silently pleading with him to reassure me.

"You understand it's a malignant disease?" he asked. His skin was ashen in the fluorescent light.

I closed my eyes as though I'd been hit. When I looked again, he was watching me intently, gauging how fast he could go.

"I talked with Tom on the phone," he said. "Tom said he felt a lot of nodes, but there's a chance we might get off with radiation and chemotherapy."

"You mean cured?" I was stunned by the possibility. Then it wasn't as bad as it might be, at least there was a chance.

"Tom says there's always a chance." He stopped, muscles jumping at the corners of his mouth. "But everything depends on the exact diagnosis and how late it is. When I sent you to Denton two years ago . . . I shouldn't have let it go . . ."

I was reeling from the idea there was a chance; I didn't want to hear how much better it would have been two years ago. But I asked because I had to. "Would it have made such a difference?"

"It's over ninety percent curable in the first stage," he said bleakly.

No wonder Tom didn't want to tell me. Ninety percent curable. I couldn't think of that at all.

Bob turned from me to the window, his back a shield. "Tom says we'll know more in three or four days. I don't know how, but we have to wait it out."

When he turned back, the bones of his face showed skull-like through his skin. He smoothed his tie while I combed my hair; his jacket was soaked with my tears. Then we crossed the street to the inpatient building, for me to be admitted.

I was expected; my records were waiting. While Bob filled out forms at the main desk, an orderly took me to my room. Another orderly gave me a green hospital gown and an ID bracelet, and a nurse took my blood pressure and temperature. They were all cool, impersonal and efficient. They saw people die every day. I was just another body, far away, and in another universe from them.

I waited for Bob on the high narrow hospital bed, staring at the ceiling, at the stains of old leaks. The room was old and ugly, like the rest of the building, the paint sickly green where it wasn't flaking off. No pictures on the walls. All to be expected in such a fine hospital: the better the care, the worse the appearance. So Bob believed anyway. At least it was a private room: I didn't have to make small talk with a stranger.

By the time Bob finished all the paperwork, someone else had taken blood and a urine specimen. Later in the afternoon, I was wheeled downstairs for X rays. Residents listened to me breathe; a surgeon came by, said he'd take a node for biopsy the next day. No one was making jokes, no one was even trying.

From my room, Bob called a neighbor for the boys to stay with after school, and called his nurse to cancel all his patients for the next few days. At my insistence that he get something to eat, he went out for half an hour, but spent the time buying science fiction at a drugstore. Pap for escape. Three thick novels, all with the same theme. One man saves the Universe. Only he knows the secret of the ancient Galactic civilization. The stars are in his hands. He pulled his chair close to the bed so we could hold hands; and we tried to read.

At five o'clock I sent him home. We had nothing to say to each other until we knew more. And he had to tell the boys that I was sick. At the drugstore he'd also bought me Valium, knowing the nurses would never give me enough, would hassle me. I floated, and read how Varn-el-Nek saved the Universe. At eight o'clock Bob phoned, and told me the boys knew I was in the hospital, and would be home after a while. He'd left the trouble with me vague, not wanting to frighten them more than we had to. I talked with them for a few minutes, while they each told me about their day. It helped that someone they both knew had just recovered from emergency appendicitis. They didn't seem too worried yet.

When they all hung up, I lay on my belly in the bed, head under the pillow, crying. It was too lonely here, and unnatural to be so alone just when you needed people most. I was trying hard not to think how bad it yet might be. If I expected the worst, I might make it happen.

My grandpa had died in this place, in one of these rooms, turning his back without even saying good-bye to me, dying that night. Nineteen years before, and the peeling of paint looked just the same.

I swallowed more Valium and asked the nurse for a sleeping pill. During the night, I dreamed that someone started World War III, but none of the missiles went off, so everyone turned out all right. When Bob came the next day, he brought more science fiction and an overnight case. He told me he'd called my department and said I was sick; I had at least a week before I had to tell them more. I brushed my teeth with the toothbrush he'd packed, and my own toothpaste, and felt I might get through the day intact.

Three days later, we sat together waiting for the report. My overnight case was packed and I was back in street clothes; no matter what the diagnosis, I was leaving. Bob had the discharge papers with him.

Tom Siegel came in, shook hands, introduced Dr. Blake, the hematologist, and then sat as far away from us as he could, perching on the windowsill across the room. I saw the news was going to be bad.

Blake was a big man, meaty-looking, in his mid-forties. Taking out a purple felt marker, he drew boxes on a long pad of yellow paper. He took forever to get to the point.

"I'm going to show you the new classification," he said. "It's only a few years old."

He divided the page in three. "Lymphomas can be nodular or diffuse. Yours is nodular; that's good."

He drew an X, kept talking; a delaying action. Tom turned away to stare out the window. Anything to keep from catching my eye. He was sweating.

More boxes. Well-differentiated or not. Well-differentiated was good, he said. "We can save almost everyone with well-differentiated nodular lymphomas." I began to pray. He made another X. "However, yours is poorly differentiated."

Wanting to scream, I tried to hurry him along. But he was inflexible.

Four more boxes. Stages, he said. How far the disease had gone.

"That's what most of the tests were for," Tom offered. His first words.

Bob and I took hands. Eons passed while Blake described the stages. He drew three more purple Xs and looked up, triumphant. "There you are. Nodular, poorly differentiated, Stage Four."

Bob's hand jerked in mine; Tom's gaze flickered toward me and dropped. For them, everything had already been said, but to me Blake's words were meaningless. "And the cure rate?" I asked.

He looked suddenly embarrassed; he must have willed himself to forget he wasn't giving a lecture. He coughed. "We can delay," he said. "Not cure."

"There are no cures?"

"Only if you'd come in sooner."

I stared at him, paralyzed.

Bob spoke for me. "How long do we have?"

"Two years. Possibly three." He held Bob's eyes for a few heartbeats, turned toward me, and turned away to look down at his neat boxes. I couldn't think of any more questions.

"You mean that's it?" Bob asked. "Just like that?"

Blake shifted uncomfortably, thighs bulging against his white pants.

Tom shuddered. "I know it's bad news," he said.

Bob walked to the door and wrenched it open. "Out! Get out! Both of you!"

They seemed surprised, as though Bob were being unprofessional, but they stood up. At the door, Tom tried to say something else, but Bob pointed to the hall again. I hoped he'd hit Tom if he didn't leave.

He closed it almost on Tom's heels, leaning back against it to shut them out. On the other side of the room, I crouched in my chair, my face buried in my hands. I finally understood the toast I'd always heard with wine. My grandma's voice: "L'chaim." To life.

I pulled Bob over to the bed with me, and we lay down together, without talking. Two years was nothing.

Blake had said it was curable in the early stages, the node easily removed, one small scar. I saw Denton on a table, tied down, screaming, his gut slowly being cut open.

We finally let go of each other. I washed my face at the bathroom sink and waited for Bob. We walked slowly to the elevator; I was very short of breath. As we shuffled past the other rooms, I looked in at wizened figures hooked to tubes and bottles, breathing raggedly. I had forgotten that hospitals were still for dying.

Bob left me huddled in a lobby chair while he brought the car around. I glared at the receptionist behind the information desk; she was blond and healthy, apparently untouched by pain. I wanted her to tell me all the tragedies she hid behind her social smile; if she had enough of them, I wouldn't have to hate her.

Bob pulled into the circle of the driveway while I was trying to decide how many tragedies would satisfy me. I was surprised at how fast he was before I realized I must have lost track of the time.

"Do you want to go right home?" he asked. "Ellen's with the kids; another hour won't matter."

I shook my head. "It wouldn't help. I want to go home." In two years Dan would be eleven, and Adam nine. They'd never get over my dying.

Using my last Kleenex, I searched the glove compartment for more. I'd gone through untold boxes of tissues these three days, crying whenever I looked up from a science-fiction novel and remembered where I was, and that I wasn't Varn-el-Nek, or Alyssa Superwoman, immortal in the year 3120.

I tried to believe Blake might be wrong. Maybe they'd gotten back someone else's lab report. We'd call another doctor. We couldn't take his word alone. I saw us dancing with relief. A polka. It would all be a mistake.

Bob spoke angrily, interrupting the imagery. "We'll find someone else. I've been reading up on lymphomas; there's got to be more than that asshole says."

I'd guessed he was scavenging the library and reading half the night. He never counted on other people's judgments. But he'd have told me if he found really good news.

"There are new treatments all the time. We'll find another place," he insisted. "There are better hospitals than this."

"But you don't really know."

He turned his head, furious, and riveted me with slitted eyes. "I'm not going to let you leave me. I don't give you the right to die."

He was like a cobra, hypnotic, his words penetrating my skeleton. "And I don't give you the right to leave the children. I won't keep them without you. I'll give them away."

I moved back, against the door, but I couldn't turn my head away. The light turned green and he began to drive again. We reentered the real world. I couldn't believe what he'd said.

"Do you really think I have something to do with this?" I demanded. "You think this is some decision of mine? That I can change it?"

He wouldn't look at me, as though he'd come out of a trance himself, unable to understand his own words. But his face was stubborn, his jaw tight. "I'm a doctor, Mona. I know people can make miracles, because I've seen them."

"You sound like my grandma," I answered, disbelieving. But I felt oddly comforted, his words absorbed by the cells of my body even though they made no sense.

Ten minutes later, we were home, the boys all over me with cards they'd made themselves for my homecoming. It was impossible, I was sobbing again in seconds. Bob pulled two matchbox cars from his pocket for distraction. "Mom has to lie down now," he said. "She's very tired."

Ellen, my best friend, watched our faces. I shook my head. "It's bad."

"I want to call Michael," Bob said. "I trust him a lot more than that prick Blake." Michael, the famous hematologist; he'd been written about in *Time* magazine when he was only twenty-five. He was best man at our wedding.

I held the bedroom phone while Bob dialed from my office behind the kitchen. Michael was in, surprised at the call. Bob began to explain.

Michael interrupted again and again. Bob kept batting him down, but he was going slowly. Michael shouted to interrupt, to ask questions. Then he stopped, sorting references in his head.

"Blake is an asshole. I know him. A pompous asshole."

"Are there cures?"

Another pause. Michael cleared his throat. "No, no, not yet; the most recent reports say seven or eight years. Not two. But more drugs come through every year. You have to buy time, the whole field's in the middle of a revolution."

More thinking. "You need a place with experimental treatments. There are three in the country for you. Stanford on the West Coast. NIH in Washington. Memorial, here in New York." He named names. One doctor at each hospital. He said he'd call back later, he wanted to check references.

Bob came into the bedroom, lay down next to me. We held each other.

"I told you Blake was a prick," Bob said.

"Do you think Michael is right?" I asked.

"When have you ever known him to be wrong about facts?"

"It's funny how long seven years seems now. Suddenly."

"He also said enough to buy us time for more." He stood up, decisive. "Try to get some rest. I'm going to call some other people, get more names."

I read some more. Tried to read. Seven or eight years. Better than two or three. Two or three were nothing. I hoped Michael was right.

Ellen knocked, asking if I wanted to talk. I sent her out and did my calculations. In seven years Dan would be sixteen, Adam fourteen. At least they'd remember me.

But I wouldn't know how they turned out. Bob would be forty-two; someone else would have him. I wouldn't see any of it. Rotting. I could feel my body rotting already. Why didn't I notice? How could I miss the cancer growing?

I was only thirty-four. I didn't even know anyone dead at my age. Except in war. But Michael had said seven or eight years. I would be forty-one or -two. I knew someone who died at forty-six. And my friend Cynthia's mother died when I was a child. She couldn't have been more than forty.

Bob peered in, sat down. Three people had given him the same name at Memorial. Chou. The man was supposed to be decent too, not cold. He left again to make the appointment. The problem was I wanted the Messiah, not a doctor.

I got up eventually. With two more years or even seven, I wasn't going to waste an afternoon locked in the bedroom. Ellen was serving fried chicken. I began to eat, surprised by being ravenous. How could I die if fried chicken made me feel so good? I licked my fingers; Ellen fended off the children. No stories from Mommy today. Bob came back, sat next to me. "We'll see Chou tomorrow at ten. His secretary made a place."

I nodded; there was no way to talk in front of the boys. Seven was almost four times two. Seven years ago the boys were babies, and I'd just finished my dissertation. Another world, an eon past. Who knew what would be in seven more?

6

IN BROWNSVILLE, WE HAD THREE MOVIE THEATERS NEAR enough to walk to. The first was two blocks away, but specialized in Yiddish films. It was always on the edge of bankruptcy, empty even on Sunday afternoons except for two or three old men sitting far apart and coughing.

The second movie was four blocks away, small and undecorated; but they showed real movies in English, and packed the house on weekend mornings for Superman serials, Abbott and Costello, and cartoons.

The third movie was almost a mile away, on the border of East Flatbush, a long walk in even the best weather, the walk itself part of the adventure. The Pitkin Theatre on Pitkin Avenue was smaller than Loew's Palace in downtown Brooklyn, but infinitely more romantic. From the street, the building was rococo: almost a block square, three stories high, the fire escapes on the outside walls intruders on the stone gargoyles at each level.

Inside was a palace, the floor carpeted from the ticket booth to the highest seats in red plush scattered with blue stars. The lobby was huge, with two candy counters, a popcorn machine and four couches; the walls were lined with mirrors.

You could walk right into the orchestra from the lobby. Or you could choose a balcony, climbing a wide spiral staircase guarded at each landing by statues of armored knights with battle-axes. It was all a castle, with the seats in what seemed to be the central courtyard, and the walls around us. The screen took up one wall of the castle; when you looked up from it, you saw blue velvet sky, and stars, and the silhouette of turrets against the night.

Usually, I went to the Pitkin with both my parents. But my father sometimes took me by himself. Once, when I was about seven, he took me with him to a movie of the world championship prize fight. Bored, I began crawling under the seats, and he let me wander off after the fifth round.

I found a staircase inside one of the towers and climbed as high as I could, past the first balcony, and then the second, to new territory and beyond. With each turn of the spiral stairs, the corridor narrowed further, and the candle-shaped lights in wall sconces grew dimmer.

The men in armor at each window loomed over me, their swords and axes shoulder-high, ready to swing down on my neck as I crept past. At the very top, I crawled through a final door into a box on the outside of the castle tower. I lay on the carpet, staring up at the stars while the fighters punched each other in another world.

Hours later, the fight ended, and my father came looking for me; I was afraid to climb down past the armored men again.

"They're statues," he said. "Fakes." He lifted me to the level of a knight's head, told me to peer inside the slitted visor. A hole, empty inside, no eyes. I screamed and grabbed him around the neck, burying my face in his shoulder.

"Look," he said, and put his hand inside the helmet. "See, I can wiggle my fingers. They're only statues."

I watched with half-averted eyes. They didn't bite his fingers off.

"They don't look like statues."

"That's what makes them so interesting." He pulled his hand out from the visor's slit again, and wiggled fingers under my nose. Then he tickled me until I laughed, and, neighing, carried me downstairs on his back.

"They'll want to ride on you if you're a horse," I said, pretending now.

"They can't move," he answered, knowing I pretended. "They're too heavy. When soldiers really wore armor like this, they were lowered on their horses from a winch."

He put me down as we came near the first balcony, but held my hand while we walked the rest of the way out. Across the street, he stopped to buy me a charlotte russe: a ritual in honor of the Pitkin Theatre. The charlotte was made of shortcake crowned with heavy whipped cream and a maraschino cherry, all held on a white cardboard circle in a cardboard cylinder. You pushed the circle up as you ate, until it was all you had left.

They sold it from behind the window of a candy store. In summer, you had to be careful the whipped cream wasn't spoiled; they didn't give your money back once you walked away.

"Why don't soldiers wear armor anymore?" I asked.

"They couldn't fight. You can't run in armor. Anyway, the guns we use now would go right through armor. That's what tanks are, armor you sit inside. They just blow the tanks up."

I nodded and licked more whipped cream. "I saw it in the movies. When Mommy used to take me."

"I don't know why she did," he said. "Sometimes your mother doesn't think."

I didn't understand either, so I waited before going on. "What I like best is Abbott and Costello, or The Three Stooges, or Jerry Lewis. Then I know nothing bad is really going to happen."

"You don't like prize fights either," my father answered. "But that's because you're a girl. Don't tell your mommy, but I bet Ezzard Charles would win this fight and I won fifteen dollars."

I was sorry he told me; my mother hated his gambling. He said it was his money that he worked for, but she said it wasn't his to lose. That was always the problem when I went off with him alone: secrets.

I woke from a dream of the Pitkin Theatre the morning after getting the diagnosis. I was lost again and searching for my father; the pillow was soggy with tears. Bob was gone.

As I lay there groggily, he came back with a fresh cup of coffee. "I thought you'd need it. You had bad dreams all night."

"I don't remember. Just the last one." I turned my head away from him; my breath felt sickening even to myself. His eyes were pouchy. "Did I keep you up? I'm sorry."

"It doesn't matter. I wouldn't have slept anyway."

We were so formal this morning. On different sides of a wall. He looked handsome even with pouches. When I got up to brush my teeth, the mirror showed me puffy-lidded and sallow.

I showered while Bob packed lunch boxes for the boys; I was just in time to kiss them good-bye. At nine, we left for Memorial Hospital, taking our own car for privacy instead of a cab. Not that we talked; we had nothing more to say until we heard Chou out. I was too terrified for speech.

Bob and I used to meet for lunch at the hospital when we were students, and I've worked in the laboratories of two others. But I'd thought of Cancer Memorial as different, less a hospital than a last port of call for the damned. When we arrived, I was shocked at how ordinary the building façades looked; I'd driven by for years without realizing what was behind them.

The building we needed was new, the Arnold and Marie Schwartz International Hall of Science for Cancer Research. I wondered which of the Schwartzes had died of cancer.

While Bob was giving the attendant at the parking lot a deposit, I waited near a man no more than twenty who was leaving with a friend. Pale and scrawny, almost beardless, he looked normal enough from the right side, except for the shaven skull. But when he turned, I saw the patch where his left eye had been removed, the steep incurve of bone behind his forehead and above his ear. Hypnotized and frozen in a space of no-time, I couldn't even blink. I gagged, then saw his friend was calm and matter-of-fact with him. He even touched him, gently helping him into the car.

How to say yes to such mutilation? Even to live? I knew I knew nothing of him. I had no right to judge the cost for him in my own terms. No right at all to judge from outside his skin, never having been within his mind, not knowing what he felt. But I'd rather die than choose as he did.

The boy was gone by the time Bob was ready; he said he hadn't seen him.

"I don't know if it's possible, but you have to let me . . . die . . . if . . ." I stopped, unable to say it, then pointed jerkily to my head. "If it spreads up here. You can't make me live like that."

"It doesn't," he said flatly. "What you have doesn't spread that way."

"But if it does?" My voice was high-pitched, near breaking; his was brisk, doctorly.

"If it did we'd have to decide then. But it's stupid to worry about now."

Taking my arm, he propelled me across the street. We slowly climbed the ramp to the outpatient building; without steps, the entrance was designed for wheelchairs. I felt such a fool, never even to have feared cancer. I'd thought I was too young. Behind my eyes, the skull was laughing at me, grinning at my stupid oversight.

The main lobby was reassuring: cheerful, clean, and bright. No peeling paint in hospital green but white paint and orange, with carpets underfoot and soft armchairs, paintings, and a huge vase filled with yellow roses at the main desk. No shrieks, no stink of despair, and yet it all looked real, not like a movie set.

The receptionist was young, efficient, and comforting all at once. She asked if it was our first time here, wished us well, and told us to go to the fourth floor for the hematology department; hoping we'd hear good news, I didn't hate her. Waiting for the elevator, I shivered in anticipation, afraid of what I might see within; but it was empty. When we reached our floor, it too was cheerful, the vases filled with chrysanthemums instead of roses; and it was crowded.

I pointed to a loveseat toward the back of the waiting room, against a wall of windows looking out on skyscrapers and sky, and as far away from the other patients as I could get. We'd brought doughnuts and orange juice with us; while Bob carried my records to the desk, I began to eat.

In the last few weeks, I got hungry all at once, and ravenous in minutes; but, eating more than ever, I'd begun losing weight. Now I knew why: the cancer cells were starving out the rest of me. As I ate, I felt them gobble up the sugar, pulling it in with little tentacles before my own cells could. They were amorphous microscopic monsters; shape-changers, vampires.

When Bob came back, he pulled two paperbacks from his attaché case. "She said about an hour. He's squeezing us in. You want science-fiction or a mystery?"

He held up a John D. MacDonald and a science-fiction novel on one of my favorite themes: alternate worlds created every nanosecond at each choice point, with each event. In this book, the Armada won against the English, and Spain still ruled the world under the Inquisition. There were no Jews left in this world.

When I was a child, I was told of Isabella's expulsion of the Jews in 1492 as if it had just happened, was like yesterday, and not lost in time at all. When we toured Europe after we married, Bob couldn't understand why I couldn't visit Spain any more than I could go to Germany; but my refusal made my parents happy.

I wondered if there was some other world in which they never let me talk them into driving to the Utah desert, a world in which they were still alive in the narrow confines of Brooklyn. I wiped my eyes and looked cautiously around the waiting room, the science-fiction still opened to page one.

Almost half the patients were younger than I, in their teens or twenties; they'd have Hodgkins or leukemia. Most of them sat with someone, talking quietly; some of them were even laughing. As I watched, a boy on crutches limped into the waiting room to join friends around a coffee table; they shifted seats to give him room. I knew I had ten years on any of them.

Most of the others were older than I, sixtyish. They'd have lymphomas, most of them; older leukemics died too fast to be here many times. The majority of older people were alone, and not ill-looking, but sad and stoical. The man across from me, apparently healthy, stared fixedly at the window until he suddenly began to cry. He stopped almost as abruptly as he'd started, blew his nose, and went back to looking mournfully past my right shoulder until a doctor called him.

Another man dozed in a wheelchair while his wife read a magazine behind him; he was skeletal, dying. I hated him for being where I could see him. I forced myself to count how many wheelchairs. Two more: in one a woman knitted quietly. I looked her over carefully; she still looked human, not a nightmare creature transformed by monsters. And there were a few men who'd lost their hair from radiation and shaven off whatever was still left.

But they looked vigorous, one of them tanned, not unlike Yul Brynner. People lost their hair with chemo as well as radiation; there must be women here in wigs.

I decided the waiting room was no worse than in most other hospitals. It was awful but not unbearable. I wouldn't have to close my eyes against each visit. I prayed to be allowed many appointments; eight years' worth, not two or three. A woman passed me to use the pay telephone, explaining to someone at the other end that the doctor wanted her back for treatments; something was wrong, she didn't know what. I began to cry.

I tried to pull myself together; everyone around me wanted me to stop, everyone was looking somewhere else, anywhere but at me. Even Bob was pretending not to notice. When the nurse called my name, I jumped to my feet, dropping the empty juice can and fragments of plastic-wrapped doughnuts into my purse. Bob followed with our coats, taking my arm with his free hand.

Another nurse took my temperature and blood pressure, in what I'd later learn was an inevitable routine, and walked me to a tiny examination room. She handed me a hospital gown and left the door half open; Bob shut it behind her. I hung my clothing on a wall hook; Dr. Chou knocked just as I slipped the gown on. In his early forties, Chou was short, chunky, and tired-looking; he had thick, ragged straight black hair that looked home cut. His voice was soft, with none of the hard edges that doctors usually develop, and his accent rang of California. I trusted him on sight; anyway, Chinese were smart. Later, I would slowly learn that he was moody, his reactions and his judgment swinging widely with his own internal rhythms.

He talked while examining me, softly said he'd already seen the slides we'd brought. He agreed with the diagnosis: Stage IV nodular lymphoma. While I dressed, he asked how we'd gotten his name, and Bob told him about Michael.

I sat down on a metal chair while Bob perched on the edge of the examining table; Chou spoke from behind a cheap metal desk.

"I can offer two treatments. We have a conventional program, essentially the same as what you've already refused. And we have an experimental program."

"I'd like to hear about the conventional treatment first," I said. "We've been told different things."

He rested his chin on his hands, peering past me to the door. "It's safe, but it won't give you much time."

Michael or Blake? "How much?"

"Two years, three at the most. I'm sorry." His eyes passed over me, toward Bob, and back to the door.

It was less shocking than when Blake first said it. But final now. Chou would know. Michael was wrong. I couldn't think of another question.

Bob looked ready to faint. His eyes were riveted on Chou. "The hematologist who sent us to you. My friend. He said he gets seven or eight years with his patients."

Chou reddened behind his hands and sat straighter. "Dr. Richards, I'm sure your friend said that people sometimes even get cured of this disease. I'm sure your friend is accurate about his patients. But your wife has a very advanced illness. If I'd seen her sooner, I'd say seven years too."

Denton again. If I thought about his blunder, I'd come apart. I tried to locate the next words inside my brain; they kept dissolving before I could speak, like smoke rings. "What are you offering . . . with . . . your other program?"

His answer was intense. "I can probably promise you ten years."

I began to giggle hysterically, rolling the number over in my mind, seeing it from all sides. Two digits, not one; it looked so very different from the number nine. How could adding one to nine make it so much fatter, so much more substantial?

"What are the risks?" Bob asked. His voice was sharp, suspicious; he bit a knuckle.

Chou answered carefully, holding Bob's eyes the whole time. "Your wife will feel sick for a good part of the treatment, she'll probably require hospitalization more than once because of side effects. But we've had no fatalities."

"Out of how many?"

"Twenty-seven."

"How long is the treatment?" I asked.

"More or less two years."

"And no drug fatalities?"

He looked away, then back at me. "None. Although some very serious complications." He paused, his face brightening. "Everyone who's finished is still alive. Several patients are still free of apparent disease three years after the end of treatment."

I turned to Bob; he nodded. The complications didn't matter. Ten years against two or three. Ten years was long enough to have its own name: a decade. Long enough for something else to come along even if this wasn't a cure. All his patients were alive.

"I'll be number twenty-eight."

He smiled broadly, but insisted we think about it a few more days. I needed more tests before beginning treatment anyway. Handing me a copy of the treatment protocol, he pointed out a one-page list of side effects, saying the government required his putting them all in, regardless of their rarity. Shaking hands, he told us to see his secretary about the remaining lab tests, and shut the door gently behind him.

I was soaking wet, and Bob looked drained, his hands icy when he held me. "I don't know how to say this," he said. "I don't know if it will even matter to you. If I could, I'd share whatever years I have left with you."

I buried my face in his shirt, he smelled so good. "Throw the years into one pot and cut them down the middle?"

"I would if I could. You're my other half. I've never wanted another woman."

I kissed him, touched beyond words. This man could lie awake at three in the morning worrying that an immortality drug might come along just after he died. "If you did marry again, I'd haunt you," I whispered, elated by Chou's promise, able to love him for the first time in days. "I'd walk past your bed every night with clanking chains. Worse than the steam pipes banging."

His lips twisted into a half-smile as he teased me back. "If I marry again, I promise she'll be a cow. She'll take care of the boys and cook."

"And when you screw, she'll say moo."

He kissed me on the mouth for the first time since the diagnosis, kissed me hard, opening my mouth with his tongue, exploring, withdrawing, caressing. "It would be restful," he whispered, "but I'd rather keep you."

7

IT WAS ONLY ELEVEN O'CLOCK WHEN WE LEFT THE ROOM. MY stomach rumbled; I was starving again. I wondered if I'd stop being so hungry once I started treatment. While Bob handed Chou's secretary lab slips, I pulled bits of squashed doughnut from my purse.

Their sweetness was life-saving. I began to think I might make it to a restaurant without falling on my face. Ten years, he'd said, maybe more. I beamed at his secretary.

Shaking her auburn hair, she looked brightly at me. "My name's Leila," she said. "How do you like Dr. Chou?"

How did I like him? I couldn't answer. Leila, whom I've never met before, your doctor's just offered me a miracle. He's given me my life back. A decade. I'll pray for him every night from now on. I wish him a Nobel Prize. I'll display myself at conferences if it will help.

"He's very hopeful," I said, watching her closely. Secretaries knew the boss's clay feet. She'd know if he lied.

Her eyes shone. "He's brilliant," she said, adoringly. "You don't know how lucky you are to have him." She lowered her voice, a conspirator. "When I started working here, it was so depressing I thought I'd have to leave. But it's all different since he came."

She crossed the cubicle to a file cabinet. I watched suspiciously. Was it all a crush? Maybe she tossed at night with hopeful dreams of marrying him. Marry brilliant doctor and get transformed into a princess. "He does everything," she said over her shoulder. "He backpacked in Alaska with his family last summer. And you should see his woodcarving!" I saw her wedding ring as she turned around.

I heard my grandpa's voice in memory, thick, chuckling, and telling me the way they always did that the joke couldn't really be translated from Yiddish. "So there's a crash of thunder that picks him up and throws him out of the window into the dung heap. And all the other men stop praying and run out of the shul, pick him up, and start wiping dung off him and off his clothes, his best clothes, and they keep asking what he prayed to make God so angry. And he says, 'I didn't want to bother Him, so I asked only for a little soup for supper.' "

I said good-bye to Leila. If you were going to bother God in the first place, you had to ask for more than a little soup or risk being thrown from the shul. All right. Dr. Chou was the Messiah in Chinese flesh.

Waiting in the lobby for Bob to bring the car, I smiled at a couple trudging up the ramp. I wanted to tell them not to worry, they made miracles inside. It began to rain, a gray January rain under an exquisite leaden sky. I came out to admire the sky, got spattered on my face, and made a retreat. I couldn't stand still, and trotted out again as soon as Bob pulled up.

"Let's go to a nice restaurant," I said. "But near. Before I eat the car seats."

Bob drove as fast as possible, although visibility was terrible, the narrow sidestreet slippery, the construction on Second Avenue blocking the left two lanes. But only two blocks from the hospital we were on the East Side I knew. We passed the movie we'd seen a month before, and the row of singles bars I'd never been in. Bloomingdale's was just ahead.

In Brownsville, we sometimes bought my blouses from the pushcarts on Belmont Avenue, and took the subway four times a year to May's in downtown Brooklyn, where we fought the crowds to buy me skirts and coats. They had no dressing rooms for children, at least not in the section of the store we used, and I tried on clothes on the open floor, putting new clothes over what I was already wearing so that no one would see me in my underwear. It was hard to judge blouses, but skirts were easy; once I had the new one on, I'd drop my own to the floor. At the end of the day, we rewarded ourselves with Hebrew National frankfurters and orange drinks at the corner stand. We were both on edge by then, and my mother's feet hurt; she'd slip off each shoe in turn while we stood at the counter.

She told me all the other frankfurter companies used ground-up rat tails, and I believed her until I moved to Baltimore. I still liked to shop in bargain stores.

I smiled and spoke to Bob. "Did I tell you the last time I was in Bloomingdale's I had to ask the saleswoman why the blouse I was trying on looked so strange, and she told me I had it on backwards?" I'd bought two of them, in different colors, so I wouldn't have to shop anymore that day. She'd looked surprised when I paid with a credit card. Most of the time, I didn't even wear lipstick or eye make-up.

We passed Bloomingdale's and parked in a lot next to a Greek restaurant we knew. Once inside, I was overwhelmed by the number of choices on the menu, wanting everything. Bob told the waiter to begin by bringing me all the appetizers.

I made myself eat slowly, even though I was so hungry, savoring each forkful. I marveled at the fishiness of the tarama, at the garlic in the eggplant, rolling smooth oiled grape leaves on my tongue; it was all glorious. When I finished, I was pinned by the design at the center of the plate, of Narcissus admiring his reflection in a blue pond. Everything had a nimbus about it, from the louvered white ceiling slats, to the leaves of the hanging house plants, to Bob's blond hair against the light behind him. I saw each pore of his skin, each eyelash, the flecks of green in his gray eyes. He told me he'd begun reading about emotional factors in cancer, wanted me to look at Xeroxes he'd made. Watching his intense face, I listened to the rhythms of his voice, to his smooth vowels. It was like hearing the aquarium pump at a friend's apartment when I was high on grass.

In Greece, the sunlight penetrated everything this way, making each detail stand out sharply, illuminated, more than real. When we visited Delphi on our honeymoon, where the oracles spoke first to the Snake Goddess of the old religion and later to Apollo, the olive trees on the hills shone silver, rippling in the sun.

Bob spoke sharply, cutting into my reverie. "You're not listening."

His face was sad and childlike behind the sharpness, to be protected. "No. I was thinking of Greece. Do you remember going to the island of Apollo in that little skiff, trailing our hands in the water, feeling that the sunlight was alive?"

"Delos," he said. "And Mycenae, where the lion gate still stands. You said you could feel the curse on it." He smiled at me, his face softening as he remembered, the sadness receding.

I was about to answer when two women pushed through to the

next table, so close that our chair backs touched when they sat down, their shopping bags from Bloomingdale's almost at my feet. Their voices were nasal and complaining, their faces masks of blue eye shadow and glowing rouge. My mood plummeted, my envy of their health unbearable. My hands began to shake: I pressed them against the table, tracing the veins standing out along the backs. A month ago, I'd covered them with cream, worrying about the first signs of middle age, and turned naked before our bedroom mirror to examine the backs of my thighs for sagging flesh.

As I tried to stop myself from shaking, Bob put his hands over mine. "Do you remember the time you nearly kicked the concierge in Athens, when we got off the cattle boat at the dock, when she said you had straw in your hair? You have the same expression you had then."

I was surprised; I didn't know what my face showed. Bob asked for the check and sent me to the door to wait for him; at the parking lot he took another look at me and shouldered aside two men ahead of us in the rain. "Emergency," he said. "My wife's ill."

In the car, I leaned weakly back against the cushions.

"You looked ready to kill those women," Bob said. "If we had any guns in the house, I'd get rid of them." Then he was a physician again, his voice detached. "You know anger's a good sign."

"Of what?" I asked, thinking I had to get control of myself. I'd gone from hysteria to fury in less than an hour.

"Of resistance. Angry patients do better."

And fuck you too, I thought, the anger spilling out on him; he too was well. Chou had said ten years was likely, but not guaranteed, and he'd added that even ten wouldn't sound so good five years from now.

I wanted to go home, not back to the hospital. I wanted to get in our car and drive somewhere far away, the way I used to drive at night on the empty Beltway when I was studying for orals and afraid of failing. I could see the doughnut stand halfway around the city, with the only lit-up sign for twenty miles, always warm inside, the windows steamy in winter, fresh doughnuts every half hour, filled with cream, jams, chocolate. My stomach rumbled.

At the hospital, we went straight to the second floor, to radiology. Chou's treatment called for radiation of the biggest tumors, as well as drugs. The biggest tumors were drug-resistant, he'd said; only radiation could kill them off completely. So I was to have a dye injected, and pictures taken now for radiation therapy after six or seven rounds of chemo. I didn't understand why not the radiation first, then remembered: I couldn't get as much drug after radiation, it weakened me too much. This was a compromise.

When the technician gave me the injection, I breathed hard on him, trying to wilt him with onions and garlic. He didn't say anything, but I thought I saw him wince. Petty power. I framed a new motto in my head, neatly cross-stitched: "Any power is better than none."

The technician showed me to a special waiting area, reserved for patients. "It may be an hour, probably two or three, maybe more. It depends on how fast the dye penetrates."

I sat on a plastic chair with other patients; we were way in the back, far from the sight of visitors. At first, I thought it was to protect the outsiders, then realized it was probably because we were all half-naked in short hospital gowns. The man next to me kept crossing and recrossing his legs in a tremble of anxiety, exposing his penis every other time and trying with shaky hands to cover himself again. I thought of offering him a magazine for his lap, like the paper bags the perverts used when they jerked off in parked cars near the handball court Hannah and I played in.

It wasn't fair of me. He wasn't like those women in the restaurant, not even like Bob: he was a patient like me. But he looked too well, he probably had nothing really wrong, it would turn out to be a false alarm. Another man was yellow-green, emaciated, terminal. I hated him too, for looking dead.

A nurse wheeled over a stretcher holding a child connected to I.V. tubes. She was tiny, no more than three or four, clinging to a picture book and a small brown teddy bear. She was bald, as all the children here were, her head oversized, huge and domed across the forehead, with a tumor pressing over her right ear. She made grunting noises when she tried to call the nurse, but no words. My hate vanished, humbled by a disaster far worse than mine; I was going to scream if someone didn't take her away.

Another nurse appeared, asking if she felt better. The child nodded, and the nurse took out two lollipops, offering her a choice of red or green. While the child sucked her candy, the nurse took readings off the dials and changed I.V. connections. As she turned away, the child curled up on the stretcher with her teddy bear against her chest, her back against her book, still sucking the lollipop.

Chou said his patients endured more than they thought they were capable of. They had to. I'd kill the child and then myself.

No longer angry, but desperate, I searched my purse for Valium, swallowed two, and looked at my watch for the fifth time in three minutes. I could see the second hand moving, but it didn't seem to add up to anything.

Ellen, with her beautiful clear face, said yoga breathing kept her calm no matter what the stress. I closed my eyes, trying to breathe deeply the way she'd taught me. One, two, three, four and again. Two counts for each, in and out. What day was it anyway? Friday. I breathed in and out, trying to relax the muscles in my neck and shoulders. Bob had a biofeedback machine in his office. I'd practiced with it too. I belched unexpectedly and brought up garlic. I loved Greek food but it was too heavy, not austere enough, not like Greece itself. Greek landscape was like the desert in the West.

With my eyes shut, I could see the Western desert, and my first glimpse of it when Adam was a year old, as I stepped off the plane in Flagstaff, Arizona, into blinding sun that hurt my eyes and went right through my skin. The land was flat to the horizon, stretched out beneath the brilliant light, the sand punctuated with low desert scrub, each plant isolated in its search for water. Arid, struggling, prickly plants that discouraged touching but bloomed once each year with huge and luscious flowers.

The desert was pure, the bones of the earth exposed in rock that jutted through the sand, each plant a testament to endurance. Absorbing the desert heat, I was puzzled that such a strange terrain felt so familiar. Places I'd lived in for two and three years felt stranger. This land was home, known rock by rock already, each plant familiar to a self I didn't know existed. This is my land, I thought. This is home. I wanted to bend and kiss the ground, like the immigrants I'd seen in old pictures.

In Hebrew school they'd said I must believe I lived in the desert, that Moses led me out of slavery in Egypt three thousand years before. At each Seder, my grandpa read the Hebrew words, then translated, "Thus it was not our ancestors alone, whom the Most Holy, blessed be He, then freed, but us also did He redeem with them, as it is said, and He brought us forth from Egypt."

"And so," my mother would add, "we each know what it means to be a slave. That is why we understand the colored people."

And more important, my sins each day could bring on other punishments by God. Each time I broke the Law, I broke the Covenant that God kept only with the Jews.

Each time I broke the Law, turned on a light or brought out my coloring books and crayons on Shabbes, God saw me sin and weighed it on the scales against all other Jews, even the unborn.

"And the wickedness of man was great on the earth, and God was sorry He made him," my grandpa said. "But He found one innocent man, and in His mercy said to him, 'Noah, build an ark and bring in your wife and children and two of each kind of animal, for I will make a flood to cover the earth and all living creatures in it, for all men have sinned and I will destroy all but your seed.' " I'd never realized Noah lived before there were Jews.

All Jews were brothers, the sons of Abraham, God's chosen people, and responsible forever for keeping the Covenant with Him. My Uncle Jake said the Nazis were God's punishment for the German Jews' forgetting they were Jews.

At the Settlement House on the corner, I went to Hebrew school four afternoons a week, after public school, and on Sunday mornings. My teachers were all refugees, rabbinical students, survivors of the Nazis. I couldn't ask them about what my uncle said, but I was little then, still learning not to ask any questions at all.

"Why didn't God let Moses into the Promised Land?" I insisted. "He worked so hard for forty years in the desert."

"He sinned," the teacher answered. "It was God's punishment."

"Well, what about Uzza?" Bobby asked. "He touched the Ark to save it from falling. That wasn't a sin. Why did God strike him dead?"

The teacher shifted uneasily, black curls damp under his yarmulke, his face pale; a ghetto Jew. He crossed his legs and I saw the newspapers stuffed in the holes of his shoes. "He was not of the priestly tribe. He had no right to touch the Ark."

"But he was saving it in God's name!"

"But it was God's will to let it fall. Perhaps a test of his faith. Like Job."

I flinched; I could never understand the Book of Job. How

could God kill all Job's children just to test his faith? I would hate God if He did that to me. And his oxen and sheep? They didn't even know what was going on. I muttered something, and the teacher looked at me with sad brown eyes.

"God rewarded Job for his faith. Remember, Mona?"

I glared at him, half crying. "But what about his children? Or the animals? He *killed* them. It isn't fair."

He stood up, paced around the wooden table to me, taller than before for all his stoop. "Are you so holy that you can question God? Since when are you the Bal Shem Tov? Open your book. I want to hear you read the Hebrew."

How could I press him more? I knew all his family were killed in the concentration camps. I bent my head, began reading the Hebrew letters; when I looked up, he was wiping away tears with the back of his hand. He said we were the hope of Jews everywhere now that so few were left.

My grandpa said this was the Golden Land. Here I could become whatever I wanted. No Cossacks riding through the shtetl during Easter week to kill me, no German neighbor watching me prodded into a cattle car while he drank beer. "But four thousand years are watching you," he said. "You must remember them."

In the waiting room, I shifted on the hard plastic chair. Losing weight these last weeks, my bottom was skinny too; the chair hurt. Today was Friday; tonight, the Sabbath I hadn't kept since I left home. I breathed slowly, remembering.

It was Friday afternoon in Brownsville. All the apartments smelled of chicken boiling in the pot for soup, of chicken roasting in the oven to a dried husk. Upstairs, Mrs. Goldstein was baking challah, the special egg bread of the Sabbath, of Shabbes. My grandmother also baked it herself, but my mother bought it from the grocery. For Saturday's breakfast, I dipped slices of challah into a glass of milk mixed to pale brown with a quarter cup of coffee; the challah left wet ugly crumbs on the inside of the glass, and was my weekly indulgence. I still yearned for it on Saturday mornings and did without, ashamed to let Bob see me.

The women were working hard, preparing not just Friday's meal, but all of Saturday's. From sundown Friday to sundown Saturday, no cooking was allowed. No cooking, no cleaning, no sewing, no shopping. It all had to be done now.

On Saturdays, we couldn't write, or play with crayons, couldn't even carry money to buy an ice cream cone—anyway, all the candy stores were closed.

"It's a day of rest," my mother said, wiping her hands on her apron. "God's gift to the Jews. Even the animals can rest on Saturday."

It reminded me of the signs on the concreted park a block away: NO DOGS, NO BICYCLES, NO ROLLER-SKATING, NO EATING. Spend the day praying and giving thanks to God. Not that all the grownups prayed. My grandpa went to shul, and Isaac, and my grandma, and my Aunt Malkah.

But not everyone. Not my mother or my father. Sometimes my father said, "If I went into shul, your God would strike me dead for blasphemy. Maybe He'd burn the whole shul down just to make sure."

Because of my father, we turned the lights on and off, even lit the stove to make his coffee. My mother said she'd rather risk God's anger than my father's without his morning coffee.

In Hannah's house, they turned on the kitchen light Friday afternoon and kept it on all through Shabbes, sitting around the kitchen table because the rest of the apartment was dark. They had a floor-through apartment, with a windowless living room in the middle; you couldn't read in there even during the day without a light. On Friday night, the Sabbath candles made witch shadows on the walls; Hannah and I dared each other into the living room again and again, only to run right out. Isaac said it would cost too much to keep lights on there too.

"Why is turning on a light called work?" I asked my mother.

She sighed, and looked unhappy. But I had to ask. "Some of the Laws don't make sense anymore. But they're still the Laws until another Talmud is written."

My grandpa kept books of the Talmud in the locked glass cupboard in his room. They held comments on the Bible, on the laws laid down in the Torah, sixty-three books of commentary altogether; he owned as many as he could.

This Friday, Hannah and I were playing in her living room with Freddy. Freddy was bought for adoption on the black market when his mother finally gave up on having children herself; his father hadn't wanted to adopt him. He was the only blond I knew besides the Polish janitor, and Isaac said he was a nice boy even if his blood was goyish.

Freddy had a nervous tic, a twitch around his mouth, worse when his father was near; his father hated it. He was only four and Hannah and I were six, but he played as often at her house as I did. We all liked Isaac.

Now Isaac opened the door, home from work. Soon it would be dark.

"You two here again? You invited yourself over again?" He passed us lying on the rug, glared briefly at our comic books, bent down to kiss Hannah, and bustled off to the bedroom for a change of clothes.

A bookkeeper, Isaac was the only man I knew who wasn't strong, except for my Hebrew teachers. Getting up at dawn each morning to don t'fillin and recite the traditional prayers, he always wore a hat, as the Law required, and left work early each Friday and on each religious holiday to pray at the basement shul halfway down the block. But he shaved his beard, unlike the most religious men, quoting some chapter in the Talmud for authorization. My grandpa said you could always find an excuse for anything if you looked through the Talmud enough.

Isaac worked for Heschie's Pumpernickel Company, a small firm on the East Side with owners as religious as he; they let him make up missed time on Sundays.

"They don't pay enough," he said, "but I know that in this world honor is given only to the dead. At least they make good bread."

Leaving the bedroom, he called us to the kitchen, and cut thick slices of pumpernickel, dropping crumbs all over the floor. With the bread he offered sweet butter, a mound of salt, and scallions for dipping.

"The scallions will keep away the whooping cough, and for the girls, it means no boys will try to kiss you oversoon. Freddy, there is more here if you wish it. Meanwhile I will read to you."

And pulling out the afternoon paper, he turned to the obituary pages. As he read, I struggled with the hard black crust of pumpernickel, afraid I'd break the fillings the dentist had just put in.

"What's the matter, Mona? You are too young for such trouble with your teeth. This is the Promised Land: you must be healthy or you commit a sin." He laughed, not laughing. "Don't you know you can find gold in the streets if you just know where to look? Not silver fillings in the teeth. Look at you, your legs are like sticks. Don't you understand you must be strong to be American?"

I blushed, not knowing what he wanted me to answer. "My mother says we're lucky to be here."

"We are," he said bluntly, turning back to the newspaper. "I would agree with her. And now let me tell you about Daniel K. Neimann, a self-made manufacturer, who has just had the misfortune to die a bit prematurely at the age of fifty-three."

I sat at the enameled table, embarrassed by the silver in my mouth, afraid to eat and afraid to turn the food down. If I used only the same few teeth on the left side, I was probably safe. But my father would be angry if I needed to see the dentist again. His teeth were perfect, he said from growing up on a farm; and he couldn't understand how I managed to have so many cavities.

Meanwhile, Isaac read of Daniel K. Neimann, and Karl Meiner, and all the others recorded as dead that day. Hannah looked impatient, as she often did, while Freddy sat upright with apparent attention. Isaac reached the bottom of the column of names and rewarded Freddy with another slice of pumpernickel.

"Mona, you too know how to pretend to give attention to a grown man, but I think for you what you have on your plate is already sufficient."

I nodded, and tried to look generally appreciative, hoping to get out of there before Rose came into the kitchen. I could hear her heavy footsteps on the staircase.

"Can you help me with these bags?" she called. "God forbid anybody should pay attention to me falling over like a sick horse with my load!"

Isaac plodded to the door. "I'm here, I'm here." He took the bags from her and carried them to the table. "So you spent all my money again? The grocer must thank God every time he sees you down the block."

"You want to eat or you don't? One day, Isaac, I'll surprise you and spend what you give me on a dress for myself instead. At Woolworth's."

I stopped a giggle before it passed my throat. I'd never seen Rose in a new dress. My mother said she wore old clothes to spite Isaac, that they had enough money for her to dress better than she did. She wouldn't even buy a dress for Pesach. And Hannah said she once ate a slice of bread on Pesach instead of matzoh, after a fight with Isaac. But that I couldn't believe: God would kill her with a lightning flash.

"You made a mess in here like always," Rose said, pushing crumbs around the table.

"If I didn't spread out a few crumbs, no one would know I live here. You sweep the table off when I'm still chewing, if I sit down for a rest you pick my legs up like they were sticks of wood so you can sweep under me, and if I let, you'd clean the toilet with me still sitting on it."

His eyes gleamed; I could tell he thought it was a good speech. I did too, but I could see Rose was mad. He shouldn't have said anything about bathrooms in front of us. I stood up.

"Thank you for the bread, Isaac. I have to go now. I'll see you tomorrow, Hannah."

Rose crossed her arms in front of her chest, blocking the way. "You run out as soon as I come in the door?"

I looked her squarely in the eyes; I lied well, my voice earnest. "No, really, my mother told me I had to come home by five o'clock."

Freddy stood up after me, following my lead. "Me too. Thank you, Isaac. Good night, Rose. Good night, Hannah." We ran.

I heard Rose yelling again as we clattered downstairs. "You were talking about me to those babies? Is that why they ran out? Am I some kind of witch?"

I crossed the street with Freddy, wondering why Rose thought we might think she was a witch. "A bitch," my father said, when he thought I wasn't listening, but not a witch. Mrs. Goldstein above us was a witch, everybody knew that, but she wasn't like Rose at all. Rose was always getting mad at Isaac, but she never cursed like Mrs. Goldstein. She said you always had to remember that God was listening and could make a curse come true. Like everyone said.

Suddenly, Bob was standing in front of me, an apparition of the present, while a nurse came angrily toward him from the other end of the hall, shooing him away.

"You can't wait here, sir," she said, her voice British, clipped. "This area is for patients only."

"I'm a doctor," he said.

"I don't care, that's the rule." Was it her accent that gave her such authority?

He turned his back on her, and shoved papers at me. "Here. You might as well look at them while you wait. You look desperate. I'll be waiting for you up front."

He spun on his heel, ignoring her still, and left me in hell. Why was I dreaming of Isaac? His anger? Onions on my breath? Did Rose eat at him like cancer? I turned pages idly while I wondered, reading titles automatically. Half the point of Ph.D. training was the skill you got in wading through jargon no matter how you felt.

The articles had titles like "Cancer and the Mind," "The Cancer-Prone Personality," "Psychological Variables in Cancer Prediction," and all of them were from respectable journals. Several began the same way, with the statement that cancer occurs most often in depressed people, in people whom earlier generations called melancholy. The observation had been made over and over since the Roman physician Galen said it first in the second century A.D. and forgotten only in the last hundred years.

I bit a cuticle and stared into space. My mother's sister died of cancer and she'd been depressed for years, so depressed no one could stand her. She moved when she was widowed and lived in her new apartment for fifteen years without making one friend. At my mother's insistence, I took obligatory lunches with her every three months. Tuna fish on white bread with dead gray talk. I scowled. I had black moods, but not like that.

Scratch paper number one; at least for me.

The next paper was a long-term study from Johns Hopkins by Caroline Bedell Thomas, begun twenty-six years before. I marveled. What an investment of your life. Two-and-a-half decades waiting for results. The longest experiment I ever ran took six months and I thought I'd go batty waiting for the outcome. Unless I counted being pregnant, that took nine months. No, I shouldn't think about time. Not now.

I looked down again, concentrating on the words. It was a study of medical students, with follow-up questionnaires every two years after graduation. Thomas asked what kind of people got which diseases. Who developed heart failure, who became mentally ill, who committed suicide? Cancer was a kind of control: an essentially physical disease. Then a surprise: The subjects who develop cancer have a distinct set of characteristics; their relationships with their parents were unusually cold and distant. They resembled closely the group of suicides.

I shivered, feeling the cancer gnawing at me again from the inside. One part of me turned cannibal, eating the rest. Chou had said all patients struggled with the feeling that they couldn't be separated from the cancer in their bodies, that in some way it was part of them. I thought of phrases: "Cancer of the soul," "Rot," "Eaten up with cancer." I once tried to kill myself.

It was just after I'd left home for college. I was living in a dormitory in Manhattan, alien to the other students but unwilling to go back to Brooklyn even on weekends.

I spent every afternoon in the language lab, taping my voice, trying to hear my accent and change it all at once. If I raised my voice or spoke with any feeling, it came out high-pitched, screechy, and Yiddish. In desperation, I started speaking in a monotone when I spoke at all. My parents didn't like the changes in me, and I couldn't stand the sight or sound of them. We fought and I didn't call for three weeks. Then I phoned; I couldn't bear it anymore and it was almost December. My mother said my father was so depressed by my turning on them that he sat staring at the walls at night, his newspaper forgotten. I was dating a Protestant, the only non-Jewish boy I'd ever been out with; my father said he wouldn't talk to me unless I stopped. I went home that weekend.

Alone in the kitchen, cooking dinner for us all, I turned on the oven fifteen minutes before putting in a roast. When I opened the door, I smelled the gas, and realized my mistake. I remember hesitating, then thinking I didn't care anymore, I was so tired of fighting. I lit a match. A wall of flame came at me, burning off my eyelashes, part of my hair, and the hair inside my nose. I ran screaming out of the apartment, terrified at what I'd almost done. I said it was an accident and prayed for God's forgiveness for months. With six million dead, how did I dare add to it?

But had my relationship with them been cold and distant? I was distant, I'd kept apart to keep my balance; it took too much away from me to see them more than a few times a year. We'd talked more the spring we planned their trip than in the whole year before. But cold? I didn't know. Anyway, what good would it do me now to know?

I skipped to paper number three: angry patients lived longer regardless of the seriousness of the disease. That was what Bob meant. I qualified for that. I checked my watch again. Ten minutes gone. I found my way to a nursing station, told someone I'd waited for two hours and asked if they could see if the dye had been absorbed yet.

She said she'd find out, I should sit down again. I opened the last paper. The summarizing paragraph flew out at me, the letters little black birds nipping at my eyes.

"The development of cancer is commonly associated with a severe emotional loss and with an inability on the person's part to make substitute attachments. . . . In lymphomas, 70% of our group lost a parent or parent-figure within four years of disease development."

My breath caught in my chest; I felt stunned, pinned like a butterfly to the board. When the technician called me into the X-ray room I followed in a daze. She pulled a switch, came back, moved my legs and arms around by fractions of an inch while I lay inert like a doll, and left me again. She told me to wait: they had to see how the films developed.

I lay on the cold glass of the X-ray table, dozing, dazed with shock and Valium. X rays were shooting bullets at me in the compound of a concentration camp. Guards were laughing. I fell on broken glass.

I shifted, and made a phone call to my parents in my head.

My father answered, "Sam's Garage, all car repairs." His voice was sour and resentful.

"It's Mona. Your daughter."

"Daughter," he said. "I have no daughter. She ran away from home."

"I need you. I have cancer."

His voice faded. "Insurance estimates, transmission work."

My mother picked up after him. "Life is hard. Who ever told you God was fair?"

II

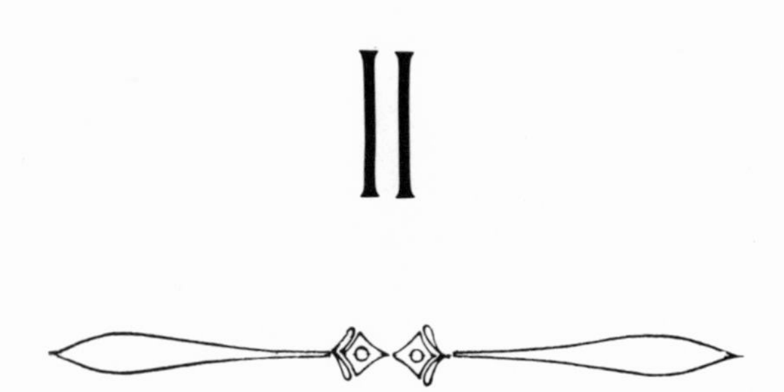

THE NEXT MORNING, I WOKE JUST AFTER DAWN. THE SHADES were up, forgotten last night, and cold yellow light poured through the window. I turned slowly, trying not to rock the bed as I got out; Bob mumbled in his sleep and covered his face with a pillow.

We'd come straight home from the hospital, and I'd gone to sleep right after dinner; even so, my head felt wooly and my eyes burned; I wondered if I'd cried again during the night.

Yesterday's rain had turned to snow by the time we left the radiation department at Memorial; now Central Park was transformed, glistening and virginal in the dawn light, free of footprints. The main road had vanished, the winding footpaths were gone, even the benches were buried to their seats, their slatted backs rising from the snow like ancient monuments.

The Park opened legally at dawn; a small group of skiers were already going in. My friend Barbara was out too, crossing Central Park West with both her dogs, McCrae's best friends, Sarah and Jess. She bent to unleash them as they eagerly strained forward and stood watching while they ran ahead into the Park, chasing each other in joyous circles, leaping into the air, rolling on their backs, churning up the snow. Barbara stamped her feet and zipped the hood of her ski jacket over her face.

I yawned suddenly, widely, and pulled down the shade. Light seeped in around the edges, still too bright, so I drew the yellow curtains too, watching the light turn golden as it filtered through. We didn't have a lot of furniture, but what we had was almost all in tones of yellow and orange. With Bob never working less than sixty hours a week, I'd shopped alone, bringing him in only for the final purchases. So the choices were mine, not his: he liked blue and green. He said a home was always the woman's in the end anyway. I crawled back into bed, thinking I'd have to water all the plants later.

When I woke the second time, I was alone in bed; through the closed door, I heard Bob and the boys in the living room. Bob never slept a lot, he had to be up and active, and he said he'd been sleeping even less the last few nights. I turned on my back and sourly examined the poster over our dresser: a rising sun over the Pacific and California philosophy: "Today is the first day of the rest of your life." It was Bob's choice; I'd told him it was his apartment too.

While I brushed my hair, I heard their shouts in the living room. Was it basketball again today, through the hoop over the door while Bob kept score with a timer? I was grateful Mrs. Bettleheim below us was half deaf; most of our floors were bare wood, and I was sure Daniel and Adam sounded like elephants.

When we moved in, Mrs. Bettleheim told me she'd known the Carrs in our apartment for thirty-two years, and had gone to Miami in winter with the widowed Mrs. Carr for ten. She'd been a widow for sixteen years herself, she said, peering around the empty lobby before bending toward me in confidence. Her lips were pursed, and she whispered in the penetrating tones of the hard-of-hearing. How glad she was that respectable people took Mrs. Carr's apartment. "Not like those two men down the hall," she said, "or those Africans next to me." Gays on one side and tom-toms on the other, I thought, not liking her.

But Mrs. Bettleheim was right about the building changing; the old-timers on the staff lamented it almost as much as she did. Tenants were different, they hinted delicately, and new help deplorable. John, the courtly doorman from the old days, looked like a WASP yacht captain; his manners impeccable, his very appearance calling mine into question; while José, the newest man, muttered insults at every back and called Mrs. Bettleheim a deaf old bitch as he carried in her packages. But José didn't leave me feeling unworthy of the building.

My hair was still silky from washing it yesterday morning; I ran my fingers through it slowly. It hadn't been cut for fifteen years and came to my waist; when I began getting chemo in a few days, it would thin and fall out. I thought I dreaded losing my hair more than any of the other side effects.

Cupping my breasts in my hands, I assessed them in the mirror; after two children, they sagged only a little. Even if my hair fell out, the rest of my body would be the same. I wondered if I could go bare-breasted and cover my balding head with a babushka so I'd look familiar to myself in the mirror. What would Mrs. Bettleheim make of a babushka, with its ancient peasant associations? Would she complain to the landlord? I didn't belong in the building anyway, it was too posh for me even in its decline.

Finally dressed, I left the bedroom. A paper airplane hit me on the shoulder. I jumped back before I realized what it was, then saw there were paper planes all over the room, caught in branches of all the house plants. Dan ran over, explaining that he didn't expect me to open the door just then, and Bob looked up from where he sat cross-legged with Adam on the living room rug. He was surrounded by scraps of folded paper, the airplane design book open at his side; he looked exhausted, his face betraying a kind of loosening, a hint of sag. I could see for the first time how he'd look in his fifties. When he saw me, he straightened and smiled with those even California teeth. Today we both looked old.

"We've been trying all the designs, Mom," said Adam. "Dad says it's the best Christmas present we ever got him."

Both kids were flushed with enthusiasm and I tried to match my tone to their faces. Although they bought the book for Bob, he'd had time only to leaf through it. We had tried a few of the designs without him the night before I saw Tom Siegel. I asked the boys if they were having better luck this time than they'd had with me.

Bob gestured toward the book. "I thought the ones you tried were impossible. But we have the good designs down now and we're starting an assembly line."

"Adam was throwing them out the window, but John called up for him to stop," Dan said.

Adam forestalled me. "John thought it was funny, Mom. You want to watch me make a loop? Dad just showed me how."

I smiled at his delight. "Two loops and then I need breakfast. I'm starving."

Adam threw the plane toward me; I retrieved it and threw it at Dan. Passing Adam on my way to the kitchen, I rumpled his hair. Light brown, more like Bob's than mine, it was thick and straight. "You need a shampoo," I said. "Your hair feels like hay." He ducked away, as shy of being touched as ever.

I was famished, a hunger headache beginning. By the time Bob came after me, I was already on my second bowl of Cheerios. He poured coffee from the big pot on the stove and flopped into the other chair across from me.

He said he'd wanted me to sleep as long as I needed and asked if I felt better for the rest; I thanked him warily. We hadn't talked yet about the papers he'd given me to read at the hospital the afternoon before; I asked why he'd given them to me.

He hesitated, and I spoke impatiently. We'd been together a long time, and I knew when he had a plan cooking. "Come on, Bob, you're telling me something but I don't know what."

He rubbed his eyes with his knuckles, like a child, and sat up straight. His voice was very low, unlike him, forcing me to listen carefully. Each sentence came out separately, unattached to its neighbors on each side. "Mona."

I put down my spoon; I wasn't going to like what came next.

"Mona, I know you want to believe in Chou." Another gap. "But it's not enough. Not enough time. Not a good enough promise." He sighed behind his hands. "I think we've got to look at every other possibility."

I felt like throwing up; I didn't want to hear him. "You think I shouldn't take the treatment?"

He shook his head bleakly. "No, he's offering the best there is. I'm saying it's not enough, we have to do more. I've been reading everything I can lay hands on since you went into the hospital. From Laetrile to faith-healing."

I pushed away my bowl, sorry I started talking to him. I knew Chou didn't offer enough. But the hope of ten years was better than the threat of two. Bob was always ready to look for an alternative, some further option. I wasn't ready yet.

"But why those papers? You didn't give me anything on Laetrile or faith-healing, you gave me articles on character and personality. What the hell is the message? What am I supposed to do?"

"I thought the articles made sense. Some of them fitted you."

I'd seen the fit myself. Some of them matched me in a way I couldn't help but see. But I wanted him to tell me that he understood I didn't really have anything to do with making the lymphoma. Having it was bad enough, I couldn't add the feeling it was my fault. Now I could barely get the words out, speaking as low as he had, looking down at my hands. "What good does it do to read how I'm the kind of person who gets this in the first place? Or is feeling guilty supposed to be good for my character?"

"I'm not saying you're doing this on purpose." His voice was strained, trying for patience, what I called his you're-an-idiot-but-I-understand voice.

"Unconsciously? You think I'm doing this unconsciously? I'm responsible but I'm too stupid to know it?"

I jumped when Adam called for help from the other room. Bob turned his head without moving the rest of his body, calling back. "I'll be there in a minute! I'm talking to your mother."

He poured himself more coffee and slowly stirred in a spoon of sugar. I stared at my bowl of cereal.

"You think it's better to say I'm doing it unconsciously? So you can blame me and then tell me you're not blaming me at the same time? With that superior voice?" I leaned forward, mimicking. "I understand you better than you do yourself, honey. I read minds."

He looked stonily back at me. "You're not even a little funny."

"I know. I just figured it out." I knew I should stop but I always pushed too hard when we fought, was always taken by surprise when my words drew blood. "Maybe you think I should start psychoanalysis to change my character. We'll call it the Bob Richards cure for cancer. Maybe you'll win the Nobel Prize."

Without warning, he slapped my face. I threw the tepid coffee from my cup at him, and he grabbed my wrists, pinning my hands together. It was like one of our old fights, when we were first married. The boys were calling him again, and he shouted at them without letting go of me.

"I said I'd be in when I'm ready! Go play in your room if you can't get the planes!"

Enraged, he hissed at me. "We've been together eleven years, by now I can't remember what it was like before you! I'm not saying you're responsible for this any more than you're responsible for the size of your tits. If anybody's to blame for this, it's me. I should have seen it, I should have felt it in bed with you, I should have known that something was wrong. When Denton said it was all right, I stopped thinking for myself. If anyone's to blame, it's me, so don't give me crap about the Nobel Prize."

Releasing me, he took a towel from the sink and began sponging off his jeans.

"Mona, if Chou could guarantee a cure, I wouldn't bother you with this. I know you want to believe in him and leave it all to him. But his treatment is dangerous and he isn't offering a cure. I'm saying if that's the best conventional medicine offers, we better go outside it."

"I don't want anyone mucking around in my head. I've told you that before."

"But it's different now. You can't turn down any chances anymore."

"Bob, I can't afford four hours a week dredging up my childhood." I was surprised at the finality of my voice; I didn't feel definite inside.

Wiping his jeans as though my fate depended on their getting clean, he spoke exhaustedly.

"I'm not saying analysis. But I know there's a connection between what kind of person you are and getting this fucking lymphoma. We're all one system, not mind in one place and body in the other with a couple of wires connecting them. If being one kind of person makes you vulnerable to this disease, changing yourself might make you less vulnerable. Shit, you know the possibilities, you're a neurobiologist!"

"So I'll get cured by changing how I think?" We were glaring at each other again.

"Even terminal patients sometimes get complete remissions," he said distantly.

"You still want a miracle?"

"If you could make it happen, it wouldn't be a miracle." He shook his head as though to clear it. "You don't even need to cure yourself, you'll be getting Chou's treatment, all you need is to add to what he does. Chou offers a chance of ten years at best. Why depend only on him?"

He stood up again to rinse his cup, neat and methodical. "I'd better look in on the kids. I told them I'd take them to the Museum of Natural History; we'll have lunch there too. Mona, if I could get inside you and change for you, I would. Could you at least think about what I've said?"

Putting my arms around him, I pressed my face against his chest. "I'm sorry, Bob. I'm still getting used to the whole idea of having this."

He leaned back against the counter, resting his chin on the top of my head. "I never thought anything like this could happen to me," he said.

"To me." The gulf between us widened again.

As I stiffened, he caught himself and changed the final pronoun. "Could happen to us."

Without answering, I walked out of the kitchen. There was no point in saying anything. Bob might say he wanted to share the years he had left, split them down the middle and give me half, but those were only words and fantasy. To him, he'd said, he didn't understand how something this terrible could happen to him. As though he were supposed to be exempt from pain.

The boys' door was shut; Bob knocked and they told him to come in. Dan was buried in a book as usual, and Adam was building a rocket base from Lego.

"I'm going to change now. I spilled some coffee. If you guys get your coats, we'll go to the Museum," Bob said.

Dan looked from his set face to mine. "Are you coming, Mom?"

I hesitated, yearning to go with him, but I didn't have the stamina, I couldn't go. "I don't think so, sweetheart. I'm going to do some work here. But I'll be waiting for you to get back later."

His face fell, and he looked suddenly delicate. His hair was a darker brown than Adam's, but his skin was pale like Bob's. Today he was pouchy beneath the eyes like Bob too. Adam didn't interrupt his Lego, but he was always less dependent on me, the younger one who was more private, who kept more inside himself. I was sure they knew that more was wrong than they'd been told. Bob said I thought I had a poker face when anyone who looked at me could tell my state of mind; and I looked sick now even to myself.

I took Dan in my arms, and kissed his hair; still hugging me at nine, he came to my shoulders. They really knew so little about me. I felt cardboard myself sometimes, an empty façade. When I left Brownsville, I threw away my childhood with my past. I'd remade myself out of a vacuum. But you had to pay for everything you did. The children were real but Mommy was a robot. I watched my body kiss them good-bye from a long tunnel, wanting desperately to promise my children my protection.

Locking the door as the elevator descended with them, I wandered back to the kitchen to reheat coffee, and carried a mug to the back room, my office. Six feet by eight, it was meant to be the maid's room for people who didn't think maids needed living space. People like Bob's mother, always complaining her cleaning woman didn't work hard enough, when she'd never washed a floor in her life. She was almost as self-satisfied as Mrs. Bettleheim and she'd raised a child who believed in her fairy tales. Terrible things didn't happen to nice people. No one but a child had the right to feel so safe in this world.

I turned the pages of *Science* without interest as I sipped my aging coffee, putting off reading the rest of the papers Bob had left for me. I really wanted to pull the covers over my head and go back to sleep.

It was strange; I wouldn't have had children if Bob hadn't insisted. I was preoccupied with work, too intent on being independent. I didn't even play with dolls when I was little. No, Mona was going to grow up and be somebody special.

Really, I was afraid I couldn't love them enough, and afraid I'd ruin them. When I was pregnant the first time, with Dan, I was afraid my body couldn't even make a baby right. I took one Valium in my third month, and called the doctor in a panic, afraid the baby was going to be a monster from one pill. And after Dan I had to have a second child, had to have Adam. I couldn't stop at one, alone with two adults, at their mercy, with no one else to turn to. I still worried that Dan was too sensitive, Adam too reserved, but I worried less each year. If I were really doing so much wrong, I'd see it by now, or their teachers would call me. In their school, the teachers kept track, a child couldn't get lost.

Reluctantly, I opened the first paper on remissions, read the summary and discussion, and went back to the beginning. Two hundred cases, all documented, with medical records, some terminally ill. Sudden shrinking of the tumors without treatment; some literally disappearing as a doctor watched. There was no simple common factor, but the reports were tantalizing.

A man with an inoperable brain tumor decided to travel around the world and realize a dream of thirty years that he'd long before given up as hopeless. Returning two years later with no sign of tumor, he went back to traveling. A woman, chained to a bedridden husband, whose cancer disappeared at his death. Another man, very religious, with a complete remission after his entire congregation prayed for him. Almost all the cures involved a basic change in everyday life, fulfilling some profound wish the person had lost hope of ever satisfying. Some of them said that they'd felt their lives were over years before they became ill, that they felt alive again only when they decided to give themselves the present of their craving. In the reports of prayer, they talked about an experience of being loved that none of them had ever had before.

I went back out, looked at the plants in the living room, and began to water them. These were miracles, of course, extraordinary examples outside of normal medicine. My grandma would understand them; my grandpa too. I wasn't even sure whether I had a hopeless wish or not. Cutting a few dry dead branches from one of the bamboos, I was aware of how quiet the apartment was now that Bob was out. I wanted to live in the country, that was one wish; it was one disagreement between us. But I doubted that moving would make a miracle.

I rotated some pots for better light, and carried the Dracaena farther from the window. A week ago, a rat came out of anesthesia while I operated, squealing with high-pitched cries of fear and agony. I spent months perfecting my anesthesia techniques so that no animal would ever wake in the middle that way; but I sometimes took too long implanting all the electrodes.

I had to operate if I was going to ask the questions I'd been trained to study, but I hated what I had to do. That was definitely a hopeless wish: how to find the answers I wanted without using animals. If I let myself think about it more, I'd have to stop my work. I'd never understood why no one else was bothered by the misery of the laboratory animals.

But Bob was right, I didn't need a miracle. Everyone made cancer cells each day, and the body usually destroyed them. My body hadn't, had let them grow and spread and almost take me over. Chou's treatment would bring the number of deranged cells down, but my body had to kill the rest to get a cure.

The phone rang and I picked it up. It was Bob calling from the Museum. He still sounded strained.

"Hi. I called to tell you I phoned my folks last night. I put it off until we saw Chou. They may call back this morning. I forgot to tell you."

I envied him. I had no one to call.

"They wanted to fly East right away. I told them no. Not unless you agreed first."

He was waiting for my answer. He wanted to see them. One

thing to live a continent away, to phone once a week, another not to have them now. What are parents for if not times like this? But they weren't my parents.

"Did your mother fall apart?"

He stammered. Was he protecting her? "Not so much, not as much as I expected. But stunned. Of course. They both sent their love and said you should take care of yourself, not worry about other people."

I answered sourly. "That sounds like them."

"Come on, Mona. Get off it."

"I'm not up to talking about it with them."

"I told them that. They just want to let you know they care. Look, let them give you a little comfort. Even if it's not what you want, take what you can get for once."

"I may be asleep when you get back."

He hung up.

I started to dial the lab at school to find out how my animals were. But I couldn't keep my eyes open. I staggered into the bedroom, and lay down on the bed. This was my private world, inside my head, where I could go back to the part of me I'd cut off. Even Bob didn't know about it; I'd never told him. I comforted myself in an old familiar way, rubbing my body inside my panties until I climaxed. Soothed, I curled up under the warm covers.

I was six years old and it was summer. I was sitting in my grandpa's room, crowded with his desk, his books in five languages, the wardrobe closet, and the giant geranium he grew on the table near the window. In its pot filled with star-shaped moss, the geranium stretched almost to the ceiling and made red flowers all year. I loved looking at the moss through a magnifying glass we'd bought in Woolworth's, pretending I could run free between the soft green tufts. I could smell the one gardenia plant too, its scent mixing with the odor of rubbing alcohol he used before giving himself insulin each morning.

My grandpa grew up in Warsaw, the last of his father's children. "My father died when I was younger than you," he told me, "and his younger brother married my mother. It was the law from the Talmud, and I think he even loved my mother. But he'd spent twenty years in the Army of the Czar and was good for nothing when he came out. No decent woman would have had him anyway. But my mother had no choice."

"And they had children too?" I asked, knowing the answer to the fairy tale.

"Three who lived, added to my father's five. My mother was a saint, and she loved us all the same. But he cared only for his own. Even though we were his brother's children. Many nights my mother would go hungry to feed one of us."

"Was she beautiful?" I asked. She had to be, I knew, not just because it was a fairy tale. My grandfather was so handsome that people turned to stare at him on the street even now. When he married, he and his wife looked like Polish stage performers. They passed for Poles and went to Polish coffee houses.

"I had to work when I was only six, the same age as you are now," he said, "to keep from starving. At night, I'd try to read, although my eyes were closing on me."

"But you couldn't read," I recited. "It wasn't allowed."

"That's right. Only Yiddish and Hebrew. No Polish or Russian or German." He grimaced. "Such fools they were in the shtetl. As though great writers can ever be condemned. As though we could shut out the goyish world."

He looked too sad for me to look at him. I spurred him on to the better parts. "And you came here to America?"

He held me in his lap in the soft armchair, looking out the window to the crowded street. "I came here first when I was only sixteen, and I stayed a year. They said the streets were paved with gold, but it was worse here than in Warsaw. My older brother paid my passage back to Poland. That was where I met your grandmother, your mother's mother that you never saw. She was so beautiful. And spoke five languages herself. Then the Army would have taken me, so I came back across the ocean with her in 1912. And here I am. Forty-six years and I've never been outside New York."

We both heard the door to the apartment open. I got off my grandpa's lap; if my father was home, he didn't like to see me sitting there.

"Where is everybody?" my father called. "Helen, where are you?"

"Go say hello to your father," my grandpa said, pushing me away from him. "It's later than I thought; I have to go to shul."

My father ran into me when I came into the living room. His eyes were shining with excitement. "Where's your mother?"

"I think she's shopping. For supper."

"I have a surprise. Come downstairs. Or look out the window first."

He propelled me to their bedroom, pushed the window up, and stuck his head out, leaning over the sill. Then he pulled me over to look out with him. I was afraid; I wasn't allowed to stand by a window open so wide.

"Don't squirm," he said. "Look down there."

He pointed to the street, and turned my head so I was looking where he looked.

"I don't see anything," I said. "Just a car."

"Our car. I just brought it."

He pulled me back and crashed the window down, dancing with impatience. His black hair fell over his eyes. He took my hand and ran for the door, almost falling over my grandfather.

"I just got a car. Almost new. A steal." His enthusiasm overflowed. "My first car since before the war."

My grandfather stopped in his tracks, white-faced. He tried to speak but his voice came out in a croak. He tried again but now my father glared at him.

"I'm the head of this house. If I want the car I can get it."

My grandfather put up his hands, palms outward, looked away. "I meant nothing. I said nothing. It's downstairs?"

My father opened the door, but stopped himself from bounding down. I could see he was disappointed with us.

"It looks beautiful from the window," I said, placating him until my mother came. It was going to be an awful fight. Where did he get the money?

He pushed me ahead of him on the stairs, gesturing to my grandfather to hurry up. He was taller than my grandpa by two heads, and as handsome in his own way. No beer belly on him like on so many of the other men.

When we got out on the street, there was a crowd around the car. "Clear out!" my father shouted, laughing. "Make way for the new owner!"

Isaac clapped, enviously, I thought, and then the other men. Now I really looked at the car. It was black and sleek, shiny with polish, the windshield glistening. No rust. No dents. My mouth went dry and my hands damp. I ran my hand along the fender.

"It's really ours?" I whispered. "It's the most beautiful car I ever saw."

My father hugged me quickly and opened the door; my grandpa climbed in back, wiping his forehead with a handkerchief. He wasn't supposed to walk so fast, the doctor said. I sat in front next to my father.

My father pointed out the shiny black trim on the seats, the fabric upholstery, the radio, the clean ashtrays front and back. He rolled the windows up and down and honked the horn. He pulled away with a roar, the neighbors waving.

"We'll look for your mother," he said. "Pick her up in style."

He turned the corner sharply, throwing me against the window. "I used to drive a Packard like this," he said. "Once I worked as someone's driver for a month. He found me trying to climb in when he parked it outside a store, and he hired me."

"What happened?" I asked, excited as always by my father's stories.

"He was in with Murder, Inc., not one of them but connected. A lawyer. They caught him raking money off the top and tied him to a cement block in the East River. Lefty Kaiser stopped me on the street and told me not to go to work for him that morning. It was nice of him. I used to play pool with his kid brother."

"How'd you get this car?" my grandfather asked from the back.

"Just tell me if you like it," my father answered. "Don't worry about the details."

"It's very nice," my grandfather said. "Very fancy."

"Did they kill him before they threw him in the river?" I asked. "Was he dead already?"

My father shrugged. "I don't know. I didn't think it was smart to ask. But it was a beautiful car. A 1937 Packard."

He braked in front of the butcher's and pulled over to the curb. There was plenty of space, there always was. He honked at some women in chairs who looked at him suspiciously, with squinty eyes; I didn't think they knew who he was in the car. He sent me out to get my mother.

The butcher's was my favorite store, with halves of cows hanging from giant hooks on the white ceiling. I even loved the smell of it, and the sight and sound of the axes used for chopping through bone. I stopped in front of the first counter to say hello and ask how they were, the way I'd been taught. I knew them since I was a baby; my mother said they used to save lamb chops for me when rationing was on; they knew my father was in combat fighting Germans.

The vegetable stands were along the other side and extending to the back, wooden crates of fruit and lettuce. I found my mother at the back, feeling oranges. I plunged right in; there was no way to tell her gently.

"Daddy's got a surprise for you. He sent me to get you; he's outside."

She looked at my flushed face, saw I'd say nothing more, and put the oranges back into the crate. Picking up her shopping bag, she walked out ahead of me.

My father was standing in front of the car, leaning on it nonchalantly, smoking a cigarette. He looked like the hero in a movie.

My mother put the bag down while still ten feet away from him, and walked slowly closer. He kept smoking, looking suddenly nervous. I hoped she wouldn't make him take it back: we could ride so far in it, even out of Brooklyn.

She gestured to the car, without saying anything, and he nodded.

"I just got it," he said.

Then she walked around it slowly while he walked with her. She still didn't say anything. My grandfather was still inside, huddled down as though he wanted not to be noticed.

Finally my mother spoke. "How did you get it?"

My father hesitated, and stammered slightly. "A poker game. I won it. Helen, I knew I was going to win before I sat down. I told you so many times, I know when luck's on my side of the table. I dreamed last night about this poker game and some kind of big winning. At work today, at lunch, this guy walks in, a big rich jerk, the boss's cousin, and he sees us playing poker and asks if he can play. I tell him we're all serious players. Then he gets mad, says he's not used to people like me telling him he's not good enough. So I get this flash, that this is it. I didn't even remember the dream until this bastard says I couldn't say he's not good enough. So I get this taste in my mouth that I only get when I'm gonna win, like sour apples. So I pull out a chair and tell him to sit down."

"And he played until you won his Packard?" my mother asked.

"You expect me to believe you won this car in one single lousy poker game at lunch? You think I'm such a fool I'll believe you that the boss's cousin lost a Packard at lunch over poker? He'd have to be such a moron they'd never let him drive!" She was shrieking now.

My father turned white, like her, and began breathing in heavy snorts. "What the hell are you talking about?" he shouted.

My mother backed off, lowered her voice. I had the feeling she changed the subject. "You played with him until you won his car? You used the money you should bring home to gamble for a car?"

"I was winning," my father said. "I was gambling with the money I won gambling. It was like the time in the army that I won all those thousands. He kept saying he'd win it back if we kept playing, he wouldn't let me stop."

"What if you lost?"

"Helen, it's not like that. After the first game I was using money I won. Not bread money. I don't hardly ever gamble with bread money."

She stroked the smooth black fender, then looked sharply at him. "You're telling me this guy is such a jerk he let you take his car away from him?" My father nodded.

"Look," she said, "if you won this from the boss's cousin, what if he complains to the boss?"

"What's he going to do to me?" my father said. "The jerk insisted on playing with us. Helen, he won't complain anyway, no one shilled him, he wanted to play."

"So he doesn't complain," my mother said. "The boss is gonna like you making a fool of his cousin, his family? You think he's gonna be so glad to see you tomorrow?"

"I'm not giving it back! I fight for this country for two years, and when I come back I get nothing! The bastards back here get rich on the black market and all I get are a couple of lousy medals and pictures in my head I can't forget. And big deal: I can get back my old job driving a lousy truck. That bastard thinking he's too good for me owes me his goddamn car!"

"You could go back to night school."

"I'm too old. It's too late for me to listen to some crummy teacher. Helen, can't you hear what I'm saying?"

My grandpa leaned out the window. "Helen, even if he gives it back, the man will feel a fool."

My father turned around; I think he forgot my grandpa was there. "Yeah, that's right." He turned back to my mother, and spread his hands, grinning at her. "Then he's a double shmuck. He'd put a contract out on me if I'm that dumb."

"The car is here, Helen," my grandpa said. "Why don't we go for a ride? Mona, sit in back with me, let your mommy sit in front."

Still white-faced, my mother climbed stiffly in. My father shifted into gear, not looking at her. We drove for hours, out on the Belt Parkway toward Long Island. He got lost coming back, and refused to ask directions; I fell asleep against my grandpa and they carried me upstairs.

Now I was thirty-four, and somehow it was all connected. I lay in the bed, with dreams and memories all mingled. When the phone rang, I reached for it without thinking.

"Mona? It's Doris."

I wanted to hang up, and go back to dreaming. My throat was dry and my voice shook. But they were Bob's parents.

She rushed right in; it was just like her. "Listen, Mona, I know you're very self-sufficient and very competent, and very able to do whatever you have to do. But there are times to let other people help a little too. We told Bob we'd be happy to fly East if you let us. We could stay at a hotel and just be there, near you but not on top of you." She sounded suddenly embarrassed, and retreated to a phrase from Bob's internship. "Sort of on call."

I was still confused, between worlds, trying to remember who I was. "That's very sweet of you, Doris. But I can't really imagine what good it would do. I'm hoping to go back to work in a week."

Jeff cleared his throat. "Hello, Mona. I'm on the other phone. How are you feeling?"

A void. I began to answer, then without in the least expecting it, began sobbing so hard I had to put the phone down on the bed. I tried blowing my nose, and picked up the phone again. Jeff interrupted when I tried to speak.

"Mona, honey, we're flying East this afternoon. We'll be at the Hilton tonight. If we wait for permission from you, we'll be here till hell freezes over."

He hung up, and I slumped over with my face in my arms. The

pillow and sheets were wet. I let go completely for the first time since the diagnosis, howling and keening with all the air in my lungs, open and exposed to agony, pleading wordlessly with God to let me live, as though I were three years old again and still believed in His mercy, but knowing all the time I howled that there was no mercy and I was totally, horribly alone.

9

MY UNCLE OBBIE LIVED ACROSS THE STREET FROM US, IN THE same brownstone as Isaac and Rose. My mother's older brother by thirteen years, balding and paunchy, Obbie was grown and married while my mother was still a child. Like my father, he drove a truck, but he was steward for his branch of the Teamster's Union: an important man. I knew he sometimes helped my father get a job.

It was late in the afternoon; I met Obbie with Isaac while I was walking back from Hebrew school; it was spring and I must have been just seven. Obbie insisted I come inside with them, promising he'd phone my mother to tell her where I was. "Aunt Fannie baked apple pie," he said.

She always baked two pies together because they went so fast, and she always complained that the oven burned one and ignored the other, but no one else noticed. I was already on my third slice: Fannie baked better than my mother and my mother hardly ever baked now that she was singing professionally.

Isaac sat next to me, sharing the pie and drinking black coffee. My uncle sat across from me against the wall, tilting backward in the kitchen chair, smoking a cigar and talking about the union. I drank my milk and listened, putting off going home.

"All I have to do is call Marty on the phone and tell him it's me and I'm sending my cousin over for a job." Obbie snapped his fingers in the air. "Like this, you got a job."

Isaac cut more pie. "So you're a big shot. Just watch out nobody breaks your arms for opening your mouth the wrong minute. They're still crumbs, even if they're union."

Obbie puffed dreamily, engulfing us in heavy smoke. "The real big shots don't even know what the inside of a truck looks like no more. They all got clean nails and Caddies and big mansions on the Island. Fancy. And all the girls go out to ladies' lunches. Very refined." He tapped ashes onto his plate.

"So they're just like bosses. And meanwhile they're out on the Island. It matters to me how they live?" Isaac drained the last of the coffee from the thick white cup, blew his nose into a white handkerchief, and sat looking at what came out.

"At least I make a good living. Better than pushing a pencil around." Obbie blew a smoke ring into the air above me, and I started to push my chair back from the table, feeling sick from the smell.

Fannie turned from the stove, and reached over Isaac for a piece of pie. She stood, broad-hipped in her housedress, chewing with her mouth open. I looked away, afraid of throwing up. "I wouldn't mind a fancy lunch," she said. "Lots of silver spoons, a tablecloth, somebody else doing all the work and me sitting like a lady getting waited on."

She winked at Obbie, and turned to me. "I hear your mother's still singing at bar mitzvahs."

I tried to answer without looking her in the face. Not until she finished the pie. "She's going out again Saturday night. My Aunt Malkah's sewing a dress for her."

Isaac snorted. "Why not borrow a dress from Fannie? You got a closetful of dresses, right, Fannie?"

It was true; Fannie went shopping every week, even though she took back almost as much as she bought. Obbie said when he died Fannie could open a dress store from her closets.

"So I like to shop. It's such a sin, Isaac? I like to look good when I go out."

Obbie leaned over to pat her bottom and grinned at me. "Your aunt's a good looker when she wants to be, Mona."

I knew that too. When she put on make-up, she looked completely different. They went out at night almost every week, more than anyone else, and even to shows on Broadway. Sometimes when they were going out, Fannie would cross the street to where everyone sat outside our building, and the men would whistle and joke with her. In her dresser drawer, she had eye-shadow, and mascara, and lots of different rouges and lipsticks, and jewelry too, shining rhinestone necklaces and earrings. My mother had been singing at bar mitzvahs for several months, and getting more calls with each appearance. She said now that she was entertaining, she had to ask Fannie to show her how to make her face.

"My mother says a lot of people like the way she sings. She says they clap a lot and ask for more."

"But she can't buy her own dresses?" Fannie asked. "Your father's sister has to make her one?"

I blushed. My aunt was making the dress from a picture in a magazine; maybe I shouldn't have told them. "My mother says this way she can buy really good fabric. Malkah sews very well."

Now I was more embarrassed. My mother said Fannie's dresses all looked like horse blankets, she wouldn't go to her own funeral in one of them. She said Fannie had no eye for a good cut, for all her store-going.

Obbie put the cigar onto a saucer and edged out from behind the table. He took the cover off a pot barehanded and picked out some stew with a spoon. "So my sister's an entertainer. A real singer. When she was a little girl like you, Mona, she used to tell us how she was gonna be famous when she grew up. She used to prance around in her underwear singing all the hits; Momma was always telling her she was gonna be late for school. But she got serious when Momma died. It's years since I heard her sing."

I nodded. She never even sang to me.

Smiling, he took more stew. "So what are you gonna do with all the money she's making?"

I didn't know how to answer. My father had been fired in the fall and couldn't get a job for months; he'd even had to sell the Packard. Obbie got him work in January, but he was mad, said he couldn't keep running interference.

My father told my mother he couldn't take orders from anyone, not after the army, even if it got him fired. And she was saving her money to buy a garage with him, like he always said he wanted. But my mother told me not to talk about any of it. She said we'd let everyone know when we could show them the garage and not a second sooner.

Saving me from an answer, Isaac stood up and stretched. He was still wearing his shiny business suit. My father said bookkeepers wore suits and thought they were better than other people, but they didn't make more money. "Maybe my Rose is done washing the kitchen floor," Isaac said. "You spend time shopping and she spends it cleaning. So who's happier?"

"Yeah, but at your house, Rose cleans the ashtrays before I finish my cigar," Obbie answered. "And then she tries to give me pneumonia by opening all the windows." He coughed delicately in imitation of Rose.

Fannie wiped her mouth with the back of her hand. "Don't talk about her," she said. "She's my best friend. A very unselfish woman."

She walked Isaac over to the door and unlocked it for him. I thought again about her being best friends with Rose, with Rose so clean. My mother said Fannie didn't even bother sweeping under the rugs. And my father hated eating off her plates, he always wiped them on his napkin, just to make sure. I didn't understand the way Isaac was over here all the time either. I thought of when my grandpa didn't speak to them for months after Fannie bought the encyclopedia from the door-to-door salesman. My cousin Richie was eleven and sick with whooping cough, and she gave the books to him to cut the pictures out. They still had the encyclopedia on a shelf in the foyer, but any time I looked something up, the middle of the explanation had a square cut out.

Richie was ten years older than I, so I was a baby when it happened. It was during the war, and Obbie was rich working overtime; now Richie had left school and joined the navy.

Isaac and I walked downstairs together; he wanted to buy something at the drugstore.

"So your mother's a singer now," Isaac said. "And what are you going to be when you grow up, an actress?"

I shook my head. I knew I was going to be something all by myself, not just married, but I didn't know what. "I don't know."

"You read all the time. I always see you with your nose in a book. You going to finish high school? Go to college?"

Too far off to think about. "I don't know."

"I wish my Hannah studied like you. But she takes after Rose. I got a sister who's a schoolteacher. A real scholar in Philadelphia: Irene. But Hannah doesn't get on with her so well, Rose neither." He sighed. "You marry, and you say good-bye to the people you grew up with."

Isaac was a pessimist, my father said, always looking on the bad side. I thought of Rose's mother; Hannah said she went crazy when Rose was little and was put away. I met her once at Chanukah, a little white-haired lady in a flowered housedress too big for her, but she spoke only Yiddish and I didn't understand a word. Then she pushed someone's baby carriage into the street with the baby in it, and was sent off again. Hannah said she wasn't worth much.

"When Rose was in the orphanage, did they celebrate Chanukah?" I asked.

Isaac stared at me. I realized my question came from nowhere. "Of course they did. It was a home for Jewish children. And most of them had family outside, like Rose. Just one parent and too poor to keep them. But they sent a Chanukah present, and if they didn't, the home gave them something. That's why she cleans so much."

I didn't understand what he meant. After a while he went on. "She never had anything of her own. She shared a room with fifty other girls and the bigger ones stole anything pretty. So she keeps everything clean now because she's so glad to have it."

I understood at last. My grandpa talked about how he had nothing when he was growing up, not even shoes. They all did. My mother said that after my grandpa lost his business they were so poor that she had only one blouse to wear to school. She took it off every night to wash it, and ironed it when she got up in the morning. Not like me: I had five blouses, one for each day of school.

I kissed Isaac good night and crossed to my building. It felt late, my father would be home soon and we'd have supper. I wondered again why he was later than the other men. I hoped at least they didn't fight tonight; it scared me so. Sometimes I thought they fought more since my mother started singing, and sometimes I thought it was the same.

A long time passed while I slept. When I woke, I was calm, drained of feeling. I splashed cold water on my face and covered it with make-up for when the boys came back. In the kitchen, I settled on American cheese and two slices of bread, and ate quickly, trying not to gag.

I dialed Ellen's number while heating a can of soup, fighting my feeling she wouldn't care or want to know me now; I knew that much about myself, that I'd never keep a friend if I paid attention to those feelings. I listened to the ringing at the other end and watched my body stirring soup, impressed at how well it moved the separate bones and muscles in spite of how it felt inside. When Ellen answered, I'd have to explain who I was.

When she didn't answer, I hung up and sat a while longer, looking blankly at the cookbooks wedged onto the lucite shelf, spattered with cooking oils, stained, the favorites with torn bindings, covers missing. The spice jars were dusty, the tops speckled with soot coming in the kitchen window from the incinerator. I liked to cook, I always said, not clean. This was a working kitchen, overrun with spatulas and tongs, vegetable peelers and measuring spoons, and oddities like the never-used poaching rings picked up through the years at notions counters. It was straight out of a woman's magazine; all it needed was the smell of cookies and a freckle-faced little boy with a glass of milk.

I saw three paperbacks from Bookmaster's on the counter. Bob must have left them too. Two books on nutrition, one on vegetable juices. I leafed through, looking for indices, references to experiments, some indications of the reasons for their prescriptions. Here it said that mice with leukemia lived longer if they got vitamin C; later in the chapter, that yeast shrank tumors in cell cultures, in the test tube. But there were no references.

I couldn't go to the scientific journals, there were too many, it would take years to sift through. Anyway, science moved too cautiously. Wishful thinking or not, I wanted possibilities.

I flipped pages, uncomfortable even in the solitude of the apartment. These books were like pornography to a minister, to be carried with hunched shoulders in a plain brown wrapper. If my professors saw me, they'd take back my doctorate. I searched for names, to see if there were any I recognized, someone I could meet for a consultation. You don't take prescriptions from a book. But all the addresses were on the other coast, in California, guru country.

I opened the book on juices, decorated with line drawings, dedicated to the doctor who'd lost his license on two continents but saved the writer's life. "The vegetable must be absolutely fresh and without brown spots." Then the cell walls broken down in a special machine, not like my orange juice squeezer, a special machine that sucked out the juice inside each cell, not just between cells. I thought of my first class in physiology: the chemical balance inside each of the trillions of cells of the body was like the balance inside the first one-celled creatures three billion years ago. And the fluid around each cell now was like the salt water the first creatures floated in. We carried the primeval ocean in our bodies, in the space around each cell, outside the cell wall, the dike.

An old science-fiction story: men left the solar system to explore the planets of other suns; and they began to die. The salt water around each cell needed the moon and the lunar tides the moon created. Without tides, the body fell into chaos, the waves of our internal ocean surging unchanneled, lethal.

The writer prescribed four glasses of carrot juice a day, the residue of two pounds of raw pulped carrots, advising readers not to be concerned about their skin turning orange, and added one beet a day, a clove of raw garlic and a quarter glass of onion juice, but admitted, "Many people find this difficult to tolerate at first." I grimaced. Did people really do this?

Warming my hands around the soup mug, I went back to the living room and looked out the window at the toy sleds on the toy hills of the Park. An inch-long German shepherd collided with a doll sled and the doll flew head-first into the snow. I wondered whether Bob came back for our sleds while I slept. Everyone stored them in the basement; José would know.

I tried Ellen from the living room; I could have dialed the wrong number before. While I waited, McCrae staggered out of the hall closet, and stretched in front of me, wagging her stubby tail. She knew I was thinking of going out. I bent to scratch her, and she rolled over on her back, exposing her belly and her neck, bending her front paws in submission, licking me through twelve long rings, until I gave up.

I lay back on the couch, and stared into the leaves of the avocado. Bob grew it from the pit and it was taking over the living room, flopping eight feet in all directions. It was a memento of California, and he couldn't bear to trim it.

He said he felt guilty: as a doctor he should have known I was sick. Was it easier for him to be a doctor who missed a diagnosis than my husband? As a doctor he was negligent, but potentially powerful; as a husband, he was simply unimportant, without special knowledge. Maybe negligence was preferable to unimportance. But how should he have known? After the first node, my cancer grew inside, not on the surface. It was my body and I didn't know.

The first time she met my parents, Bob's mother brought leather-bound picture albums from Los Angeles with her. They held snapshots of her little angel, her precious pearl, her only child born after ten years of trying to conceive. She brought an entire album of him playing in the sandbox in their garden in embroidered little sunsuits, smiling into the sun with blissful assurance. He'd really grown up believing he could control what happened to him.

I could feel connections too. Even if I wanted to call Bob an idiot, even if I'd never admit it to him, I felt the connections. It wasn't my fault I was sick, but it wasn't just a random event. Lots of people ran away from their parents. Lots of people moved away. Bob moved to New York from the Coast, but he didn't get sick. There had to be more.

I saw the burning car in my mind's eye. "Seventy percent of our patients lost a parent or parent-figure in the four years before diagnosis." I sighed; McCrae licked my hand, then jumped onto the couch to lick me better, lying down on top of me, belly to belly, treating me like her puppy, grooming my neck, my nose, the invisible fur behind my ears, offering me her concentrated love. I scratched her as best I could and kissed her black clown nose.

When I married Bob, he stood for everything my childhood wasn't. I wondered if it was murder to make yourself over, erasing the voices of the past that lived within. I'd tried to rub out whatever in myself came from my parents, and then they died in Utah, leaving nothing of themselves but buried fragments in my mind.

Pushing McCrae off me, I walked with her to the boys' room. Leaning against the door of his cage, Kevin stood on his hind legs to say hello, his pink nose twitching rapidly. I unlatched the door and he ran up my arm to my shoulder, licking my ear delicately with his soft pointed tongue. He snaked his tail back and forth in his version of a wag; I scratched his belly; and he purred against me and ground his teeth in joy. With his white glistening fur and pink ears and feet, he looked even more like a stuffed doll than McCrae did, and he smelled more like baking bread than like an animal. Only his scaly tail was ugly, and betrayed him: not the figment of a designer's imagination or even an exotic creature from a distant land, but a rat.

He was our third pet rat, our third white lab rat, rescued by a student from his fraternity house. The boy brought Kevin to my office in a shoebox stuffed with newspaper, reminding me shyly I'd told my classes I kept pet rats. When he reached into the box, Kevin squeaked in terror, burying himself deeper yet in newspaper, trying to hide from uncouth fraternity sophomores. Only his bottom stuck out, white and shivering.

Everyone in the family had worked at taming him, and he ran loose in our apartment all day. No one could shut a drawer or drop into a chair without a final check for Kevin's safety. Curious, he came to the door when the bell rang, sat purring in any lap offered, and stayed up all day to be with us, although he was naturally nocturnal. We put him into his cage only at night, to keep him from crawling into bed with the boys: restless sleepers, they might crush him.

Kevin rotated on my shoulder to ride backward, in his favorite position, tail down the front of my t-shirt, head alertly turned to look behind us, watching where we'd already been. We walked together to the kitchen, as Crae trotted by my side. She was an Airedale, a rat-catcher by nature, but she was just a puppy when Kevin moved in and, like the animals in the old pictures in *Life* magazine, they got along. I took two dog biscuits from the pantry and offered one to each of them. Crae ran off with hers but Kevin sniffed disdainfully and turned away. I'd forgotten it was the brand he didn't like, and I gave him one from the other box. He held it with both paws and nibbled happily.

The first time I met Bob, it was over the body of a dying rat, a rat I was trying to save. I was a graduate assistant to my thesis adviser on a hyperactivity study. Bob came into the lab with a friend of his from my department, idly looking around, and found me bending over an animal I'd just operated on. I'd taken out brain tissue with a suction pump, closed the wound, and finished sewing the scalp over the hole when he stopped breathing. Too much anesthesia; his breath had been raspy from the ether almost from the beginning. I cleared an airway down his throat with a straw and breathed into his mouth while pressing on his ribs, like a lifeguard with a drowning victim, too caught up in getting him to breathe again to be embarrassed, although even then a bit of me thought I might look funny. I was sorry they were there but I couldn't risk the time to throw them out.

Later Bob took me for coffee in the cafeteria, and I explained to him that each rat operated on was a rat I'd already spent a week training, an investment of my time, and I couldn't have them die if I could help it. He told me I looked just like the woman scientist in a sci-fi movie, except he'd never seen any of them do mouth-to-mouth resuscitation on a rat.

When I fell in love with him, I confessed that I couldn't bear to sacrifice my animals when I was done with them, but packed the survivors into cartons to carry to a stream at the back of the campus. It felt like murder to do otherwise, I said, and I had to give them a chance to live, although I'd probably be kicked out of school if anyone else found out.

So we carried cartons at midnight down a rocky hillside to the stream while Bob muttered about my setting off plague and I answered that a few more rats wouldn't matter to a city already overrun. Anyway, they were white rats, not wild ones, and even more, I couldn't kill them.

I sat up and reached again for the phone; I'd put off calling Phil at the lab as long as I could. We'd been doing research together for three years, and published seven joint papers; married like me, Phil was in some ways closer to me than Bob was.

Bob had told him I had the flu; much as I dreaded the call, I wanted to tell him the news myself. He answered on the first ring, before I was ready. I'd half-hoped he'd be gone for the day.

"Mona! I was going to call as soon as I finished here! How are you?"

I swallowed. I'd been rehearsing this all week, all the careful evasions. I realized I'd never be ready, even if he hadn't answered for a hundred rings. It came out straight and ugly. "I've got a malignancy."

"What?"

"A malignancy. I've got a malignancy."

"Oh Christ."

There was a terrible silence; I couldn't think of anything to add. I was trying not to cry, but our silence went on endlessly. In faint crosstalk on the line, a man with a commanding voice ordered airline tickets from an agent. I hoped they couldn't hear us too. In the silence, Phil was mourning for me. I was witness to my funeral. No wonder Bob wanted to make these calls for me.

I started to explain to him; I'd made it worse by being so abrupt. "I'm starting an experimental drug treatment. The doctor's talking about it giving me ten years."

"You mean there is a treatment?"

"Yes, that's what I'm trying to tell you."

I spoke impatiently. His surprise jolted me; in the last week, I'd learned you could always find a treatment if you phoned enough people, even if the treatment was lethal. I'd already forgotten Blake's telling us there was nothing to do.

"Mona, from the way you sounded, you were saying good-bye."

He asked me to wait while he found a place for the cage of rats he was holding, and I listened to him moving in the background. It was like a game of bad-news good-news.

Did I make it sound worse than it was?

When he came back, his voice was muted, not like itself. He asked a lot of questions, pushing the way he always did, but still in the same strange voice, and I reached for whatever facts I had about the treatment. I thought I'd be working again in another week, and we talked about the study we were running and how Phil would manage the routines until then. Twice he asked what more he could do, and I couldn't answer. I just wanted to get away and hide.

I wondered if I could have managed not to tell him, and worried about his passing on the news. He sometimes talked too much. Then he asked if this was confidential, and I realized how well he knew me and why it was we worked so well together, and I told him to tell anyone else that I had a bad flu.

We ran out of words again and I was going to ring off when he asked in the most tentative of voices if he could ask me something.

"What?" I asked, feeling trapped and tired. Was he going to ask how it felt?

"I wondered if you thought about taking off from work. Traveling maybe." He sounded apologetic. "You always talk about going West."

"See Naples and die?" I was suddenly furious.

He tried to backtrack, placating me. "I didn't mean it that way. I just was thinking I didn't think I could work if it were me. I'd leave for the Caribbean and dive every day."

He was lying. You only did that when you ran out of hope. My voice was hard. "You don't know what you'd do in my place."

This time I hung up without waiting, thinking I might never bother about politeness again.

Crae whimpered by the door and I put on my boots and coat to take her down. José was on the elevator and we said nothing to each other. I'd have kicked him if he so much as grimaced opening the door.

The owner of the German shepherd McCrae hated came into the lobby with his dog as I got out. I held Crae tight against the mirrored wall while he dragged his bitch past; both dogs were growling. The last time they'd fought, Crae threw the shepherd into the air and onto one of the tufted couches; we'd had to separate them with an elevator pole. Bob said I was too proud of McCrae's fierceness.

In the street, I kept her on the leash even though she knew how to heel. I told other dog walkers I was the only New Yorker in history to get a ticket for an unleashed dog in the Park at seven o'clock on a Sunday morning, and they laughed; and I said no one else ever got a ticket for dirty license plates, and they laughed and thought I was joking; and then I thought, but didn't say, that I was the only graduate student in the history of Baltimore to be assigned a probation officer after running a light.

I was coming back from the lab at one in the morning and I ran a yellow traffic light. The judge put me on probation because it was the law, he said. And every two weeks I'd put on my only dress and drive down to the main police station and sit on a hard green bench with the other criminals, waiting my turn. My probation officer was Southern, and not much older than I was, and he didn't know what to do with me any more than I knew what to do with him.

"How are you today, Miss Mona?" he'd say, playing with his wireless glasses and doodling on a yellow pad. I figured he called me Miss because I was a grad student, not a simple bum, and Mona to keep me in my place.

"Fine," I'd say, worrying about chain gangs and the Ku Klux Klan if I didn't answer right, and then he'd check my name off in his notepad and tell me to come back in two weeks.

Bob said I got traffic tickets because I looked guilty as soon as a cop came into sight.

"How can I look guilty inside my car from half a mile away?" I asked.

"No one else gets a ticket for dirty license plates. You must do something to catch their eye."

I didn't answer, remembering that I dropped to twenty miles an hour as soon as I saw the patrol car, and crossed the entire city at a crawl, with my eyes on the rearview mirror, watching them watch me.

I wouldn't even get the car inspected by myself; I made Bob go.

The light turned green and I started across the street, hoping to avoid the bag lady. She was heading in my direction, working her way down the line of cars trapped by the light, muttering into windows. Everyone on the West Side knew her, she'd even been in the *Times,* distinguished from the other shopping bag ladies who raided garbage cans by the polka dot bandana she tied over her face like a desperado.

Adam asked me why she hid behind the bandana. "Andrew says she has no nose," he said. "Bugs ate it."

I asked Ellen if anyone had ever seen her face. Maybe Adam's friend was right. A kind of syphilis. "Just tell Adam she's crazy," Ellen said.

She stumbled toward the curb now, too near to me. Her long skirt was wet with slush, her skinny arms held the shopping bags in the air to keep them dry. The driver in the nearest car stared at her, and she stopped long enough to curse him. She was usually harmless, limited to curses, but last summer she attacked the man who walks through the Park with a parrot on his shoulder. McCrae growled, and I held the leash with both hands, but she didn't even look at us.

This part of the Park was empty, too flat for sleds. I waved to a few people on the other side of the Park road; they waved back. I hoped to see Ellen if I walked around the football field. It was almost four.

I knew Bob's parents would arrive in a few hours. A good hostess would make sure she had food in the apartment. She might clean the bathrooms. I wondered about the question of etiquette: how sick did you have to be before you had no duties as a hostess? If I could be walking in the Park, should I be shopping in the grocery? But I hadn't invited them.

I knew I'd have to go home without meeting Ellen if I didn't see her soon. I began counting breaths as I walked, deciding I'd find her before I left if I reached one hundred before coming around the field. It was an old habit, resurrected again for the latest crisis. Seeking signs and portents.

Children did that; it put me at age eight or so.

When I was preparing for my graduate orals, I became obsessed with traffic lights. I'd pass if the light turned green before I stopped my car, fail if it stayed red. I'd crawl up to the red light in first gear, ignoring all the cars behind me, willing the light to turn green, counting on being able to move slowly enough to give it time to change. It was a good choice of omens, offering some control on my side. And I passed.

I was almost around the field now, breathing faster. Ninety, . . . ninety-four, . . . ninety-seven, . . . ninety-nine, one hundred. Where was she anyway? No one was ever there when you really wanted them. So much for omens. I sat on a bench, suddenly very tired, and watched McCrae sniff the markers left by other dogs in the snow.

Long ago, when I was young and my father was alive, we'd walked one afternoon in snow like this. We'd moved from Brownsville and it was Sunday, his only day off. My mother was cleaning in the frenzied way she sometimes had and I was doing homework in my room. He knocked and asked hesitantly if I would like a walk. We hardly ever spoke to each other by then, and I took the question as the gesture of truce it was. The sun was brilliant, and the single private homes we passed looked rural in the whiteness. We were the only people out, and we walked for miles through a deserted land, immobilized in a fairy-tale trance, until we came to a storybook railway station, hidden behind a screen of hemlocks out in the middle of a field. We looked at the wooden station for a long time without saying anything, holding gloved hands, until my father reached down and made a snowball to throw into the sky. I made one too, and we started throwing them at each other, ducking behind the trees, running back and forth across the tracks until our coats were splattered and damp.

A black form shot across the inner road. Ellen's retriever, Tinker; in a minute, Ellen came out from behind the hemlocks and crossed too. I felt a gush of relief.

"I ought to leash her but it's too hard," she said. "Did you see her run across the road? I was looking at the kites those kids are flying over on the East Side, and she just took off. I guess she spotted McCrae." Ellen bent over and kissed me on the cheek. "How are you? Should you be out in the snow? Bob told me not to call."

Embarrassed, I held her hand for a few seconds before letting go. She was holding herself in. Like me. "I was looking for you; I thought you might be out here."

Her eyes were wide in her thin face; she looked tired. "Can you come back with me for coffee?" she asked. "Are the boys with Bob?"

"They're all at the Museum, looking at dinosaurs. We had a fight."

"You had a fight? Now? How could you fight now?"

I shrugged, calling McCrae to follow me. Ellen was single, living alone, had never lived with anyone for more than a few months. How could she understand the tangles you got into after eleven years of marriage? She pivoted to look at me, so suddenly that Tinker stumbled against her legs.

"Mona, if I can do anything for you, just ask me. I know how hard it is for you to ask, but we've been friends a long time now. And I really care about you." Her voice broke and I thought again that I couldn't manage this.

The words slipped out before I knew what I was going to say. "Ellen, do you know anything about people making themselves sick?"

Then I heard myself, that wasn't what Bob said, he just said there was a connection. Not that I made myself sick.

"You mean psychosomatic? Like ulcers?"

"I don't know what I mean. But more deliberate. Something you do to yourself."

"Like getting into an accident?"

"I don't know. Yes, more like that." Like when I put the match in the oven all those years ago to make a wall of flame.

We both bent to leash the dogs, fumbling with the catches in the cold. Ellen dropped to her knees to get at Tinker, and Tinker tried to lick her. Still busying herself with the leash, Ellen asked the next question without looking at me.

"Is that what you feel? You've gotten sick because you want to?"

I was sorry I started talking. I didn't know what I thought. I lied, changing Bob's words, making him say what he never said. "Bob thinks I'm punishing myself. He says we could make a miracle if I could change my feelings. Cure the cancer."

She flinched at the word "cancer." I knew it was a weapon. My right to say it. She was still kneeling in the snow, staring at me.

"Are you serious? If we had that kind of control, no one would ever die."

We crossed the avenue, and crunched in snow down the side-street block of brownstones. No doormen in the brownstones, so the streets stayed unshoveled longer. I was used up by all the walking, grateful that her apartment was only half a block away. She waved at dog walkers across the street; and I waited as she searched for her keys in all her pockets. Who ever said it was easy to control the body? But my grandma would agree. If you changed the feelings, you sometimes got a cure.

One key for the hall door, two for the apartment, pushing her door partly open and reaching inside to undo the police lock as well. She parted the flowered curtains at the windows, but it was still dim inside and she turned on lamps. It was always dark inside, on the ground floor and blocked by other buildings from the sun, with gates on all the windows. But she had use of the little garden in the back and in summer we drank coffee at a wooden table next to honeysuckle vines.

We hung our parkas over the bathtub; I sat down while she measured coffee into a percolator. The kitchen was just an alcove; I could see her clearly, her dancer's body, all legs and grace.

"You're telling me not only that you've given yourself cancer but that you can cure yourself by the right thoughts?" she asked.

I was curled up on the old velvet couch, the desk and bookshelves crammed with papers behind me. My voice caught and I had to clear my throat. "I don't know what I think. But it doesn't feel like an accident. It almost feels like something I've expected all along. Like here it is at last, what I've been waiting for."

She carried over coffee cups, went back for cheese and apples. One reason her body was so beautiful: no cake ever. And of course no kids. No one but Tinker and a walk around the Park every day. She sat across from me in the lumpy blue armchair and sliced an apple. Her voice was hard and grudging.

"Actually, I've heard of somebody who's doing what you're

talking about. A doctor in Atlanta. Someone I dance with just took her mother down to see him. He has people go into a kind of trance and then picture killing their tumor. Like the tumor is an octopus and you're shooting it with a laser beam."

My hand shook, spilling coffee. One thing for me to have my private thoughts, another to have someone in Georgia paid for doing it. I felt like a child crawling toward a large hairy caterpillar: fascinated and appalled in equal quantities.

"It works?" I asked.

She shrugged, and carefully pared apple core from each slice. "He says it does. My friend said she wasn't there long enough to tell."

"Can I have his name?"

"I can get it for you tonight."

She poured out coffee and sipped quietly. I always forgot she drank it black. I added two spoons of sugar to my own cup before remembering the books all said sugar was poison, food for the cancer. I decided to ignore their imprecations for the moment; the sugar was keeping me from falling over.

When Ellen spoke, her voice was gentler than before, patient.

"What about chance, Mona? Luck? Things just happen sometimes without anyone making them happen. Somebody has to get sick."

I shifted in the armchair, remembering my father's photographs of Auschwitz.

"You know that line of Einstein's?" she added. " 'God doesn't play dice with the universe.' I've never understood why he hated the idea so much."

I drank more coffee, and ate an apple, hardly listening anymore to what we said. I could see the numbers in my first statistics course. Throw a thousand pennies, ten at a time. Predict how many heads and tails you'll get before you begin, calculating by the mathematical formulas of the laws of chance. Then count. A thousand pennies in groups of ten gives you one hundred groups. The mathematics predicts that 65.62 percent of the groups will be half and half or sixty–forty; 23.44 percent will be seven one way and three the other; and only two in one thousand twenty-four throws all heads or all tails. You can't predict what any single penny will do, and you can't ever predict the outcome of a particular toss, but you can predict the pattern. By the mathematics of chance. And that's the way it came out when we did it. Not exact but close. And the more we tossed the pennies, the closer our results came to the mathematical predictions.

God played dice with the universe and out of it came order. The right number of pennies came out heads, the right number of women my age got cancer. Whether or not there was meaning in my being chosen, or whether it just happened, I had to find ways of fighting back. When I left Ellen's, I counted cracks in the shoveled pavement. If they came out even, I'd be cured.

10

IT WAS SUMMER, AUGUST, THE MIDDLE OF A WEEK-LONG HEAT wave. We were lucky, my mother said, the apartments on the third floor were baking under the roof, and the apartments on the court trapped hot air all night, but we faced the street: we had a breeze through the bedrooms toward morning.

It was three in the afternoon; a fireman had already come from the firehouse on Stanley's block to open a hydrant in front of our building. Soon the Bungalow Bar truck would drive by with ice cream, and maybe, a little later, the truck with a merry-go-round on it, or even better, the Whip. I liked the Whip more, but it came less often.

The youngest kids were running through the water naked; the rest of us wore underwear. When a bunch of boys started peeing in the gutter, each one trying to go the farthest, Hannah and I walked away with Sheila.

We were floating old popsicle sticks along the stream the hydrant made against the curb, but the water was running slowly, with so many hydrants open, too slowly to push away all the garbage in the gutter. I bent to push my stick around a dam of candy wrappers.

"Don't touch the water," Sheila warned. "It's got number one in it from those boys. You know what?" she added, looking sideways at me through her hair, "Sammy's big brother told me that we had you-know-what's too, but God cut them off because we were bad." Her eyes were round and worried, almost black against pale creamy skin. Her skin was delicate; if you slapped her, she got big welts.

I was seven, and only two years older than Sheila; if I were still older, she wouldn't dare ask. "That doesn't make you into a girl," I answered, jiggling the dam with another popsicle stick. "It just makes your voice squeaky. My grandpa told me, he listens to opera all the time on the radio and he said they used to make a special kind of singer that way. It's got a name but I don't remember it."

We heard the bell of the ice cream truck around the corner. Hannah ran across the street to her apartment, to get money from Rose, and Sheila and I ran back to the card table where our mothers were playing Mah-Jongg. My mother felt my head. "You're sweating, but you're not dripping like usual," she said, and took the coins from her purse. "When you get it, I want you to sit down here where I can see you so I know you're not running around. That's all I need, for you to get sick when I have to sing tomorrow."

I heard the women asking about her singing as I left. "I got an offer in the Catskills for next week, if I wanted," she was saying, "but Sam said it was too far. He can't even boil water, and my father's no better, the three of them would starve if I was gone."

I knew that wasn't the real reason: if we had to, we could stay with my grandma, or she could stay with us. I'd like that: with my grandma without a husband, and my grandpa without a wife, I always hoped they'd get to like each other more and marry. But my father said he didn't want his wife gallivanting at a night club, even if it was at a kosher hotel. She said it was her money that would buy them a garage, but then he slammed the door and walked out. My grandpa said she was lucky he didn't hit her.

When I sat down again with my Dixie Cup they were talking about something else. They couldn't be very interested in Mah-Jongg today; when the game was good, they didn't say two words. I wiped sweat from my face; maybe it was too hot for grown-ups to concentrate. Walking around the table, I looked at everybody's tray until Shirley shooed me away. My mother said I could start to play next year; I already knew the tiles.

"So my mother-in-law says to me, 'When are you going to have another baby? I'm an old lady already and I only got five grandchildren.' "

Shirley put down a four-wind. "I felt like telling her I had my Stevie only because Nate forced me."

"All they ever think about is babies," Sheila's mother said. "Even my own mother's asking me about another before it's too late. She says the Nazis killed so many, we have to make it up. 'For God,' she says, not for her."

Their faces tightened; no one said anything until Annie started again.

"That doesn't bother me. When you get old, that's all you have to think about. Grandchildren. But you want to hear what my lunatic mother-in-law called me about last week? She phoned to tell me she couldn't eat at my house anymore because I wasn't kosher enough! The nerve of her! I said to her, 'Momma, I keep separate plates and silver for the dairy and the meat, in different cupboards; and separate pots, and even two dish drainers and different towels for drying, and I wait six hours after we have meat to let the children have a glass of milk. What do you want from my life now?" She looked around expectantly, eyes glistening. "You want to hear what she said? She's making up new laws every year."

They all looked up from their tiles waiting for the rest; her mother-in-law was famous. Once when she was visiting, and Annie was at the grocery, she tried to throw out half the sheets and put the special ones on the bed that you can get only on the Lower East Side: with a hole in the middle for making babies. Annie caught her carrying out the old sheets, they had an argument right in the hall; and Mrs. Goldstein came out of her apartment yelling that Annie had no respect for age, until Annie's mother-in-law turned on her, and told her to stay out of it with her curses. Mrs. Goldstein got red as a beet, but Mr. Goldstein ran out in his slippers, and took her back inside with him before she answered.

Now Annie started to giggle. "She said to me, she said, what I had to do for her to eat in my house, was get two different garbage pails. One for meat and one for dairy." She spread her hands helplessly as all the women laughed. "Can you imagine putting two pails on the dumbwaiter every night for John to unload in the basement? He'd come upstairs and spit in my face."

"What did you tell her?" Shirley asked.

"I was mad, I asked her if she thought we ate out of the garbage pails. I told her, even if she could get a rabbi crazy enough to go along with her, I'd get three to tell her she was off her rocker. Even the Chasidim don't use two garbage pails. And you know what my husband says? He says I should humor her, she's his mother." She stopped, her face screwed up in disgust. "My son's wives should only humor me half so good when they get married."

I finished my Dixie Cup, licking the last of the ice cream from the inside. An ambulance barreled down the street, its siren yowling, lights flashing. When it stopped in front of Hannah's brownstone, I realized she'd never come back out.

I ran around the table to take my mother's hand. Everyone was standing up to see, people inside the buildings leaning out of their windows. Two men hurried from the back of the ambulance with a stretcher; my mother raced across the street with me still clutching her hand.

They waved her back, but she interrupted them, her words jumbled in a rush. "Who's sick? What's the matter? Who called you? My sister-in-law is in this building."

"Could you let us pass please, lady? It's an emergency. And if your sister-in-law is Mrs. Klein, maybe you could show us up?"

It was Rose then, not Fannie or the couple who lived on the top floor. I ran up the narrow stairs ahead of my mother and banged on Rose's door, shouting that the ambulance was here. Hannah opened it; she'd been crying but she wasn't crying now.

"It's OK," she said. "I heard them from the window. My mother's got a gallbladder attack."

The men came through behind me, my mother on their heels, and I pressed against the wall to let them pass. Rose lay on the blue couch in the living room, with Fannie standing next to her. Hannah ran back to her mother, and I watched the men roll Rose onto the stretcher, while Fannie told my mother the story.

"I knocked to ask if she wanted something from the grocery, I knew she wasn't feeling so good," she said. "I heard groaning. When I looked in the kitchen, she was stretched out on the linoleum, bright green. So I called the ambulance."

Rose was still groaning. I couldn't understand how the men could be so calm; I was grateful she wasn't my mother.

"Why didn't you call anybody?" my mother asked, stuttering a little. "We were all downstairs."

One of the men walked back to us, interrupting. "Lady, we're taking her over to Beth Israel now. You want to sign this paper? It just says she's wearing a wedding ring and no jewelry."

"Did you call Isaac?" my mother asked, ignoring him. "Hannah," she called, "it's all right, a gallbladder isn't so bad. Your mommy will be all right."

"I called him already; Rose even talked to him." Fannie was trying to read the paper; she turned to the man. "You sure I'm not signing something I shouldn't? That's all this says?"

He looked bored and impatient; I wondered if he was waiting for a tip. "That's all it says, lady, it's in plain English."

Rose moaned again, and Fannie signed. Rose's face was at the level of my eyes as they passed me; Fannie was right: she did look green. Fannie bent to kiss her on the forehead, and Hannah tried to follow them down the stairs. My mother stopped her, holding her by the shoulders. "They don't let children in the hospital," she said. "You come with me until Isaac gets home. You can have supper with us."

Hannah went to wash her face; while we waited for her, Fannie brought a bucket and scrubbing brush out of the kitchen. My mother stared; Fannie looked embarrassed.

"She was in the middle of the kitchen floor," she said. "I couldn't leave it in the middle. I didn't do as good a job as Rose, but I finished while we were waiting for the ambulance. Hannah was sitting with her anyway, there was nothing else for me to do."

My mother began to giggle, and Fannie looked offended. She turned back to the kitchen, speaking over her shoulder. "If you'll excuse me, I'll just start to wax in here. It's so hot, it's already dry."

My mother followed her, but she didn't turn around.

"God bless you, Fannie," my mother said, bending to kiss the back of her neck; I'd never noticed before how much taller she was than my aunt.

When we left the apartment, my mother was still smiling.

A month later, at the beginning of February, Bob's parents had come and gone. I'd had the first round of chemo, and I'd have the second in another few days. Now I was lecturing to one hundred fifty undergraduates in a lecture hall built for three times that number. Most of them were clustered toward the front rows; a few diehard recluses were scattered toward the empty rear. My voice echoed slightly. I was teaching introductory psychology, organizing the course around brain function. My classes were always disappointed by the lecture schedule I gave them at the beginning of the semester; I taught so much more biology and so much less Freud than they expected. But my enrollment went up each term.

I was winding up a lecture on placebos. "If you tell people that a sugar pill is a powerful drug, about one in three will get pain relief. Another third will feel side effects from the same inert pill. Not necessarily the same people."

Rising from my chair I walked to the blackboard, careful not to trip over the microphone wire. It was easier to lecture from behind the lectern the whole time, but I was too tired to stand. I didn't like using the microphone either, but I couldn't project my voice without breaking into coughing spasms. Most of the nodes had shrunk after the first treatment, but I was still filled with cancer.

I chalked in the statement, and turned to the lectern for the last few minutes, glancing briefly at my notes. "When my younger son was three, he complained of toothache. When the dentist couldn't find anything, he gave him a placebo, telling me he'd know the pain was imaginary if my son felt better." I paused, for emphasis, getting ready to sum up.

"But the most interesting point is that placebos work even when there's a clear physical problem. You tell the brain that the pill is effective, and the brain produces its own drugs to do what you expect the pill to do. If it's supposed to be a painkiller, the brain makes its own opiates to kill pain; if it's expected to make you sick, then the brain goes ahead to make you sick: headache, dizziness, nausea, diarrhea, whatever. The brain has far more control than we believed even fifteen years ago. Then we had almost no idea of how any of this worked, no idea of the mechanisms, like the opiates, or the other enkephalins, and, in self-defense, we were likely to dismiss the whole idea as impossible."

Listening to myself talk, I wondered what they'd think if they knew how far I stretched these bits of science in my private life. I'd begun to meditate an hour each night, pulling out forgotten childhood memories to find what in them connected to my cancer, sifting my constructions of the past to mend what weakened me. Bob had lost interest in making love since we got the diagnosis; I had time for my memories at night.

I glanced at the clock and finished the lecture. "Did you ever notice that you start to feel better just before the doctor sees you?" About a quarter of the class nodded.

"Did your mother tell you that always happens?" I smiled and a girl giggled.

When the bell rang, most of the class stampeded out, but about ten students clustered around me with questions. Last time, I'd brought in a EMG feedback monitor Phil and I had in the lab, and I'd trained two students in muscle relaxation in front of the class. They loved demonstrations, and they learned better if I could show them concrete events. But I wanted to sit down now and rest.

I broke free as quickly as I could, and crossed the hall to our lab. As soon as I shut the door behind me, the noise of the changing classes vanished, lost in the web of soundproofed walls. My soul expanded in the quiet.

Phil was lying across a workbench, his head and shoulders hidden in the machinery of our main recorder. Each time we hooked it up this week, our EEG's came out flat, as though the animals were in coma; he was trying to find the latest short circuit. I'd wanted to call the company, but he insisted that he could fix it before they'd send us a technician.

As I sat down, I knew not to ask Phil how the repair was going; he'd tell me when he finished. We grunted hellos at each other, and I went back to the graphs I'd been drawing of our last results. The graphs didn't tell me anything different from my numbers, and told me less than my statistics, but I still thought better with a picture in front of me.

We were doing something different from our other work, repeating another lab's experiments instead of asking our own questions, making sure we could get their results before breaking new ground.

Some of it was old work, over ten years old. Implant electrodes all over a rat's brain, train him in a Skinner box or maze to make a right–wrong discrimination, and record his brain waves each time he performs; while he's trying to decide which response to make, but before he acts. He learns the discrimination: to go left, not right; to pick black, not white; to press triangle, not circle. As he learns the correct response, the brain waves evolve until they make one pattern before he makes the right choice, and a different pattern before he makes a mistake. Before he responds, not after.

We could look at the brain patterns and know what the animal was going to do *before* he did it. We were reading his mind.

That was the old work; it still gave me shivers. In the next step, we recorded the general patterns of the brain once more; we also imbedded microscopic electrodes into individual brain cells.

The total brain pattern was the simple sum of billions of single cells firing at the same moment; but our new recordings showed the individual cell to be unpredictable. Pattern A always preceded a correct response and Pattern B always preceded an error, but any given cell might fire in Pattern A only half the time, and in Pattern B, one time out of three. The numbers were different for each cell, but the point was the same: we couldn't predict which cells would take part in making the pattern of the moment, even though we knew the pattern would somehow appear.

We'd been taught the brain was like a complex wiring circuit, the same neurons connected to each other always. Like dominoes, in a fixed arrangement, each one would flip the next in line. But it seemed the brain cell did the equivalent of flipping a coin instead: heads, the cell fired; tails, it didn't. If the cells went on and off randomly, how did you get the right number firing each time: how did you get the pattern? I knew the mathematical explanation but the meaning in the reality eluded me.

Phil spoke teasingly to my complaint. "Each neuron is exercising free will. Within a master plan." He was still on his back, head lost in the machine, circuit boards lined up in order at his side. "This is the physical evidence of free will."

I drew on the yellow pad in front of me, broad sweeping curves punctuated by slashes. The illusion of freedom. That was exactly what I was obsessed with. You struggled over your decisions, like those nerve cells, to go or not, to do or not, and in the end your sense of choice was made irrelevant by statistical prediction; your choice was subordinated to a master pattern that was itself fixed. Like my insurance company, paying five thousand to two hospitals in two months for my diagnosis and treatment. They didn't know I'd be applying for payments when they did their tables, but they knew someone would, they knew just how many women my age would be ill. They knew just how many of us had to get sick and each one diagnosed meant one less woman still to be heard from this year.

I knew I was crying an ancient lament behind the ponderings of intellect: Why me? But the question was still real: how did you go from randomness, from chaos, to lawfulness?

"Phil, if each neuron adds its bit to the total pattern, and the pattern is fixed, then each neuron must act on the basis of what the others do. If not, you couldn't keep the totals right."

He slid out from under the recorder, wiping soldering flux off his beard with the sleeve of his lab coat. He was hooked.

"The math says they act independently," he said.

I shrugged. "That's just an assumption. Maybe it's a wrong assumption."

"Do you know the old science-fiction story about this? Group mind of the photons?" He shifted from the workbench to his chair, swiveling it around to face me, sliding down onto the back of his neck, his feet on my desk. His beard was so bushy it looked religious, part of a taboo on shaving, but he was raised a Christian Scientist in Cincinnati. "A physicist is troubled by the question of light," he said. "Theory says with a perfect mirror angled forty-five degrees to a beam of light, half the photons will pass through and half will get reflected. Which ones do what is random but the pattern has to come out half and half. He's got the same question you do. How do chance events end up giving a fixed pattern?"

I put my feet up on my desk too, the soles of our shoes inches apart, facing each other across the narrow space. In some ways, we were more intimate than if we were married. Phil stopped and pulled a joint from his pants pocket. I raised an eyebrow; he gestured to the machine. "You know I picture circuits better if I smoke. A little."

He took a drag before going on. "So the guy decides the photons have got to be talking to each other. When they get to the mirror, they must be divvying up into groups, Group A goes through, Group B bounces off. He builds the perfect mirror and the smallest pinhole in the world, it only passes one photon of light at a time." He grinned widely, with thick red lips, barbaric, showing the chipped front tooth of his high school football team. He'd look right with the gold earring of a pirate.

"He sets up the equipment, angles the mirror just right, and sends the first photon through the pinhole. The first photon reaches the mirror, realizes he's got to decide: bounce off or go through. This is it, which way is he going to go. But he can't make up his mind because he doesn't know what the others will do. So he slows down to think about it. He's been traveling at light speed, a hundred eighty-six thousand miles per second. When he slows down, all that motion turns to heat . . . he blows up the East Coast." He leaned back and took another drag as I laughed.

"You know the physicist at Stanford who says maybe the photons really do have a group mind?" I asked.

"I know," he said. "We read the same articles." His voice deepened, and he hesitated. "Do you know Jung's work on synchronicity? You know Koestler's *Roots of Coincidence*?"

I shook my head; I'd read some of Jung, but I'd only vaguely heard of Koestler's book.

"Koestler says we call something coincidence to avoid noticing connections that have nothing to do with cause and effect. Coincidence is just a label so we can forget about it. I read the book when you got sick."

"Why?"

"The day after you told me, an old friend called from Michigan to say he had a lymphoma. I never knew anyone with a lymphoma before."

He was sitting upright now, feet on the floor, his fingers tapping nervous rhythms on his knees. "I've been keeping a diary ever since. Remember in college philosophy that you could never prove cause and effect? I've begun to wonder if cause and effect is always an illusion, with no connection to the real world. When you press a button and the light goes on, it's just coincidence; that's the way the light switch works, it's the way the brain works, it's why the sun rises every morning. Coincidence."

I looked at him narrowly, wondering just how stoned he was. "Give me some examples."

He reached inside the jacket hanging over his chair, taking out a small diary. "If I don't keep it with me, I forget to write them down," he said, turning pages. "I'm just going to read a sample day, I'm not picking out only the best ones."

I lay back, listening. "From last Tuesday. My car drops the front U-joint driving in, I get towed to a station. While I'm waiting for an estimate, I leaf through magazines. I read an article on San Diego, a city I've never visited. That night, my brother calls to tell me he's just won an office pool for a week in San Diego." He looked up at me, unblinking. "That gets four stars on the coincidence scale."

He read on; I tried to listen critically. "That night, before I go to sleep, I'm reading an article on ants. I think my son could really use new ants for his ant farm, it's been empty for months. It's a pity they don't ship queen ants by mail. Four o'clock in the morning, my daughter has a nightmare. I pad into her room to tell her it's just a dream, I come back out in the hall, and there's a giant ant, looks like a queen, in the middle of the carpet. In January. We don't have ants. So I put it in the ant farm." He grinned at me suddenly. "If she hatches a colony, I'm going to have to go back to praying. I'll tell my mom she was right all those years I laughed at her."

"Are they all that dramatic?"

"No. Like the day after, we go for pizza, and you tell me about making your own pasta, and my wife says when I get home that she's just signed up for a class in pasta making." He hesitated again, then looked sharply at me. "Jung called it synchronicity, Koestler calls it acausal phenomena. But they don't mean things just happen randomly either. It wouldn't make sense to talk about as random: it's too common. Jung says if you pay attention to it, you make it happen more. You get to be a focus for the effect. It's as though nothing in the universe is really separate, everything in the universe is one interwoven network and my reading about San Diego resonates with my brother's winning the office pool."

"That's modern physics," I said.

"Jung worked with a physicist: Pauli."

"Are you getting more of them, whatever they are?"

He nibbled at his upper lip. "I'm writing more down. I see more of them. I think I'm getting more, a lot more. But I wouldn't admit it to anyone else yet. I just thought you should know about it."

He put out the joint, put it back in his wallet, poured the ashes down the sink, and leaned back in his chair with his eyes closed. His face was relaxed behind the beard now, the lines at his forehead smoothed, his shoulders down, no longer hunched. The lab was quiet again, and I leaned back too, aware of the rhythm of his breathing. I'd read Jung on coincidence, what he called synchronicity, remembered his writing that the more attuned you were, the more it happened. The prepared mind has events happen around it. Maybe we shaped reality by our expectations. . . . That was straight out of the last book I read on quantum physics. The physicists said matter was just one of the forms energy sometimes took; maybe everything was really mind-stuff.

Pauli was a physicist; a Nobel Prize winner; that's why Jung was working with him. When I looked at Phil, I saw he was drifting off.

"Calling on the physicists to defend the idea of magic," I said. "And having them say that's what they were talking about all along."

He nodded, muttering agreement, and I shut my eyes too. When we were in college, DNA was hypothetical, continents didn't move, and the brain was like a telephone switchboard, always limited to running in the same circuits. Now DNA was remade in the lab, California was drifting into the Pacific trenches, there was a black hole in the center of our galaxy, and the brain might turn out to operate like a slot machine. Maybe Carlos Castaneda really was a sorcerer's apprentice, maybe he wasn't making up Don Juan. Maybe he really did run his Volkswagen on magic instead of gas.

I sat up to look at my watch; it was time for the animal room. I removed my notebook from the desk along with a pair of plastic gloves, and went through to the back.

When I opened the door, the rats all froze in their cages in instinctive alarm. I took an old lab coat from the hook over the door and buttoned it shut, sniffing the air. It was smelly, a day overdue for cleaning cages.

I used to imagine students cleaned the cages, but they didn't anymore, and I wondered if they ever had. My adviser in grad school was always complaining about the good old days after the big war. Three wars back, he meant my father's war, when to my youngest students Vietnam was already history. But scraping rat shit off cage floors didn't match my ideas of professorship. I sneezed, took off my gloves to blow my nose, and looked around, flipping on the overhead lights.

Rats were nocturnal; for some of our research, we reversed the day-night cycle so they'd be awake when we were. I'd be in here under fifteen-watt red lights the rats hardly noticed, making my notes more by touch than sight. But it didn't matter for what I was doing today.

By now the rats had gone back to their small noises, their chitters, gnawing the compressed nuggets of food, pulling on the piping of their water bottles. Each animal was alone in his cage, so that they wouldn't disturb the electrodes sticking out of their scalps by pawing at each other. I looked through the Plexiglas front of the first cage and a curious animal peered back at me. When I opened the door, he froze again, and I reached under his warm belly to pick him up. I cradled him against my body while I looked him over, grateful the rats didn't bite me.

Some people were bitten, others not. Sometimes I half wished one would bite, particularly one I was taking away for brain biopsy. It would balance better.

The rat peed right through the coat, and shat small ovoid pellets. A frightened animal. But at least he looked healthy, without puffiness around the scalp incisions, without reddening of the skin. The next two rats looked healthy too.

But the fourth animal was chasing his tail in a blurred circle of motion. When I tapped on the Plexiglas, he leaped into the air and went for my face, his claws straight out. I jumped back reflexively, he lost interest, and he began again to chase his tail. He was damaged, probably in the amygdala. I'd have to kill him and take brain slices for slides to see what had gone wrong. I made notes before moving on.

The surgery for sinking electrodes was simple, now that the technique was well established. I was grateful that few animals were damaged. It was so unlike my first summer fellowship in school, when I had to find the lethal doses of a new convulsant drug, dropping the rats into jars and slapping the covers on fast, while they tried to scramble up the straight sides, clawing at the glass, screaming as I marked the time to the first convulsion, and the second, and so on until they were broken-backed and dead. Murderer. I pushed the image from my mind for the thousandth time. If God existed, he ought to make me pay for that summer. That fellowship was a plum; I was so proud when I won it, before I knew what it would mean.

I went on with the weekly routine, mechanically weighing out food, while thinking about what Phil said. I was beginning to sweat with effort. Take a container of oxygen. Open it in a vacuum. Each molecule moves randomly, but you can predict the overall movement of the oxygen. The drunkard's walk, it's called, because the first mathematical proof was put in terms of the random stumble of a drunk on a street corner.

And if we knew more, if we were God or a good enough computer, able to calculate the trajectory of each molecule as it bounced off its brothers, we could predict the movement of individual molecules too. Not just the general pattern. If we knew more, if we were smarter, we'd see there was no chance, no randomness, only cause and effect. If we were God, we could predict each stumble of the drunk on the sidewalk, each turn of the penny as it fell through the air. The world was a giant clockwork set up by an unknown hand and left to run by natural law: that was the old physics. If we knew enough, if we could measure everything we'd need for the equations, if we could figure out the equations with our poor brains in the first place, not a sparrow could fall without our predicting it.

I finished weighing out food, sweating and icy, unable to go on to change the filthy litter. I should have asked Phil to do the work. I leaned against the door, starting to black out, then slid to a crouch with my head between my knees. If I passed out in here, no one would know it.

When my head cleared enough for me to stand, I stumbled out and back into the lab. Phil was still in his chair with his eyes shut.

"I'm not stoned," he said. "I'm contemplating circuits."

"I don't care. I feel sick, I have to lie down." I collapsed onto our cot, our luxury, imported from Phil's basement for cat naps. I curled up with my legs against my chest, too cold to remove the lab coat, sweating and nauseated.

Phil covered me with a blanket, I opened my eyes; he was bending over me.

"It's all right. I was just doing too much."

"A month ago, you told me you were almost dead, and now you're scraping shit off cages. I didn't know you were in there or I'd have told you to get out."

He turned away, and took orange juice from the lab refrigerator. I gagged at the smell; there were bodies on half the shelves, embalmed with formaldehyde, waiting for brain sections.

He handed me juice in a paper cup, watching while I sipped. I handed it back to him when I was done, feeling the warmth of the blanket beginning to penetrate.

I could hear my grandma chortling as she rolled out noodles on the kitchen table, on the clean towels. I could see my grandpa rubbing his callused hands. The betrayal of the Age of Reason by this century's science. The chaos of the twentieth century, of the new physics of Bohr, and Heisenberg, and Planck, of whichever of them said he was sorry he'd become a physicist, and of Einstein, who spent the rest of his life trying to disprove what they helped show in 1927. The universe is not like a machine, not a giant clockwork. When the physicists looked closely, they found chaos. A slot machine without reasons. God plays dice with the universe. At the level of the atom, cause and effect vanishes, events are truly random, there are no causes. We can predict the pattern but never, never, never any individual event. Not because of ignorance or stupidity, but in principle. At this level, there is only chance. Even to God. Out of chaos comes the world.

Maybe memory worked the same way. A throw of the dice. A gamble. Group mind of the photons. Connections across time and space without cause, without effect, and yet somehow made. Physics said space and time were illusions anyway.

My grandfather was speaking of the mysteries of the Kabbalah, the sacred book of holy numbers.

"Kabbalah can be studied only by the most religious. Only a few scholars are selected in any generation. The knowledge is too much for men; they go mad or die young."

11

I WAS GOING TO BE EIGHT IN A MONTH. HANNAH AND I WERE walking back to school after lunch; I was dragging out the half-block walk as much as I could. I'd been putting off asking all week, but I'd run out of time. Today was Friday and my mother was sure my Uncle Jake would be with us at my grandma's again on Sunday.

We stood at the corner, waiting for the light to change. Hannah was humming a hit song to herself and tapping out dance steps; she never minded coming late to school. We were alone, everyone else was already across the street and on line. The great carved doors hung open as Miss Malone herded the classes in. She was huge in her black satin dress, and she patrolled the lines with her ruler high in the air, ready to slap anyone who was out of order. She'd get us when we crossed.

I was still trying to find a way to begin. "Hannah, you know the men who sit in parked cars by Lincoln Terrace Park?"

"The perverts?" She stopped dancing and grinned at me before mimicking her mother, hunching her shoulders, pursing thin lips, and shaking a long finger at me. Her voice moved slowly across the words, drawing out the vowels. "Do-on't answer when they call you over. Do-on't go near them. Do-on't even look at them."

As if any of us would be so stupid.

She stopped clowning as she took in my expression, and went on in her normal voice. "Why? You didn't let one of them start up with you?"

The light turned green and we started to cross; I couldn't wait anymore. "Someone else. In my family. Do you think that makes it different?" I didn't believe him, but that's why my uncle said it was all right.

She stared at me, as serious now as I was. A garbage truck bounced toward us on the uneven tar, and the driver honked and waved his arms impatiently. I was terrified he'd get out to ask us what was so important that we had to stop in the middle of the street. Trying to smile innocently at him, I nudged Hannah to move on, but I had to pull her by the arm before she moved.

"A grownup or a cousin?" she asked.

I was afraid to say too much even now. I couldn't let her know who he was. "A grownup. But not a real relative. He married someone in my family."

We reached the pavement as the truck clattered past. The last children were going in; with her back to us, Miss Malone began to lock the doors. We'd have to go around to the side. We turned the corner, with Hannah looking down, concentrating on stepping over the cracks, her face impassive. I couldn't tell what she was thinking, and I noticed for the first time how sharp her chin was. When she spoke to me, her voice was intense, but she didn't look my way.

"Did he just show it to you?"

I wanted desperately to lie, but it was too late. And we'd have to separate in a few seconds; we were in different classes. I kept my voice low even though no one was near us.

"He just wanted me to touch it. And I won't tell you if I did or not. Do you think I'll get sick?"

"How am I supposed to know?"

I sniffled suddenly; if she didn't tell me, there was no one to ask. "Because you're always saying you know so much more than me, that's how."

Miss Malone was behind us, her tread heavy in her laced shoes. I risked a look over my shoulder; her face was quivering with distaste at our slowness. She raised her ruler in anticipation; I took Hannah's arm and hissed at her. "If you tell anyone what I said, I'll make you sorry."

She tried to pull away, but I was stronger. My fingers would leave bruises on her arm; I never lost a street fight. She whispered her answer.

"You won't get sick unless he's got a disease. But I don't know if he does or not. That's all I mean. You don't have to get so mad."

I let go and we ran for the side door, with Miss Malone just a few steps behind. I hurried to my own place in line; to my surprise, she turned away.

I was third from the front, third shortest out of forty, and the youngest in my class. My teacher smiled at me, but I didn't smile back. How could I tell if Jake had a disease or not? I'd heard somewhere you might not know until it was too late to do anything, and all your teeth fell out and you went crazy. Jake might not even know himself.

We were saluting the flag and singing "The Star-Spangled Banner"; I looked at the palms of my hands, inspecting them for breaks in the skin. I always had scrapes and cuts; I counted three just scabbing over. The germs could have gone right in.

If you had to cover toilet seats with paper because you never knew what you might get from other people, how many germs did I have from touching Jake?

If only God spared me this time, I'd never go near Jake again. I couldn't ignore him, because he was my uncle, but I'd stay at the other side of the room.

By the end of March I'd had my second and third rounds of chemotherapy. I was doing much better than Chou expected, the nodes half as big as when I began treatment. Chou said I was lucky the drugs helped so much; I didn't tell him what else I did beside the chemo.

Bob was out in the Park with the other dog walkers; it was almost eleven and I was getting sleepy. I'd been filing my nails, propped in bed against the pillows, letting my mind wander. Jake was still alive, a shrunken old man weakened by two heart attacks and cirrhosis, living quietly with his wife in a retirement village on Long Island. Two blocks from a synagogue, and four from a kosher butcher, I hadn't seen him since my wedding, but my Aunt Malkah told me about him when I called at Rosh Hashanah.

I hated doing my nails and usually put it off until they were broken and ragged. Filing lulled me into letting down my guard, my mind wandering into paths I'd rather barricade. But now I used the manicure deliberately, part of the nightly ritual, to help me remember. I had to face the ghosts in order to exorcise them; anything that weakened me helped the cancer.

I looked at the clock again, but the hands had hardly moved. Bob might be out another hour, anything to avoid coming home to bed. He stayed longer in the Park every week, out with the dog walkers while I lay here with my memories. I had no idea when he'd be back.

Grudgingly, I reached for the tape cassette on the night table. I'd postponed it as long as I could, but the tape was a new part of the nightly ritual. Maybe Bob would be back by the time I finished.

I shifted from the bed to a straight-backed chair, so I wouldn't fall asleep in the middle of the meditation, and began to breathe rhythmically, trying to relax down toward my toes, my eyes open but unfocused while I waited for the voice to begin. Ellen had gotten me not just the name of her friend's Atlanta doctor, but his taped instructions.

Dewey spoke slowly, in a warm Southern drawl, with long pauses I didn't expect, stopping in the middle of sentences and between words that ought to go together; the first time I heard him, I thought the tape had snapped.

We were alone in the room and he understood how hard it was for me to do what he wanted, but he insisted serenely that I try. I was here to relax, he said, as the first step to fighting my cancer. I had to relax before I could go on. "Begin with the muscles around your eyes," he urged, ". . . around your . . . mouth, . . . your . . . tongue, . . . inside . . . your throat . . ."

Erect in the chair, trying to keep all my attention on the exercise, I began to relax, then caught myself thinking about Bob. Even monks in a Zen retreat daydreamed on their meditation mats; it was unnatural for the mind to stay focused on one idea. I took a deep breath, listening to the tape again. "Now . . . . . . your . . . chest," he said.

I had so much cancer in my chest, it might break out if I didn't hold it in; but he persisted and I tried to let the muscles go. That whole part of my body felt numb.

It was heavy, but numb, without features or feeling. I wanted to get up and walk, but his voice was inside me, commanding me. I tried again to go beyond the blankness and feel my chest; and I felt the corrosion before I saw it. Then, as though I were a camera closing in, I saw the rotted back of the breastbone, riddled with holes, like wood infested with termites. Backing off, I opened eyes I hadn't known were shut, then hurried after him as he moved down my body, already past the diaphragm and belly and at the pelvis. I let muscles go again, and felt hot contractions moving up from my vagina; if I were a man, I'd have an erection. Tears were running out of my eyes, and the soles of my feet ached.

Dewey's soft voice continued: hypnotic, explaining, insistent. Relaxation was only the preliminary: we were together to fight the cancer. Soon, I had to make a picture of the tumors, forcing myself to look at them in whatever form made sense to me, in whatever imagery.

"Remember," he intoned, "the cancer cell is weak, confused, much weaker than the normal cell. If the host is normal, cancers are killed. We kill thousands of cancers in our lifetimes. Cancer cells are weak," he murmured once again, "you can kill them."

I was light-headed with power, convinced again by his conviction, immersed in his words. "Only normal cells recover from drugs or radiation," he said, "the cancer dies. Visualize your cancer, visualize your treatment. Use any pictures that make sense to you."

He stopped in one of his longest silences, getting ready for the last command. "Now picture your own body's immune cells, too many to count, like stars in the sky, your own army, surrounding any cancer that survives treatment, and destroying it. Cancer cells are weak. You can kill them by yourself."

I crossed my legs, uncrossed them, scratched my back, elated and anxious at the same time. I wanted to do what he said because I believed him; but I wanted to run away.

"Look at the cancer," he urged. "Look at it now. I know how hard it is." I tried to relax again, and shut my eyes, willing myself to see, imagining the twisted passageways of blood vessels. The cancers were unmistakable, monstrously deformed imitations of the normal cells, with parts that ought to be there missing altogether, and other parts misshapen.

They were scavenging the corridors for drifting molecules of food, pulling food out of the reach of my own cells with pale fat tentacles that flowed back into themselves when they were done, greedy mutations trying to pass themselves off as mine while they destroyed me. I searched for my own immune cells, and finally picked out a few patrolling clusters of small gray forms; I armed them with machine guns that spit fire instead of bullets.

The amoebae retreated before the guns, hiding in back passages, peering out fearfully from under pitted ledges, and they sizzled with their bodies to the walls as the soldiers found them. I smelled burning flesh.

Flakes of charred flesh dropped through the air, and an oily layer of poison began to film the walls, ready to form new tumors as soon as the patrols turned away.

I backed off, and fell against a pile of baby shoes just outside the cave, next to a soldier's helmet engraved with a swastika.

I opened my eyes; my heart was pounding and I felt like gagging; I'd gotten the cancer and the army mixed up again, with each other and with the Nazis. I didn't know whose side I was on.

Chou said his patients felt inseparable from the cancer, felt that they themselves were walking tumors; but he was talking about people who knew they were sick, while Dewey was talking about who got the disease in the first place. Dewey said his patients welcomed their cancer at some level of their being, and that was why their bodies didn't fight it off at the beginning. He talked about the benefits of being ill, and being taken care of, of not having responsibility because you're sick.

I thought he was simplifying, seeing only the surface of the issue; even Chou was aware of more. Something in me hadn't fought the cancer off; why I couldn't was unclear, but it wasn't because being sick was easier. By going back to memories, I was trying to change the parts of me that hadn't fought, even though I wasn't convinced that changing myself could so directly be mirrored in my immune system.

But Dewey called for an even more direct approach, through the imagery I called up while listening to his tape. He said that I could make my immunity stronger simply by strengthening those visions. Not myself, just the visions.

I shut my eyes for the third time, concentrating on sweeping up the poison, funneling a ray of light through my eyes, onto the walls, killing off every remnant of tumor. The phone rang, interrupting me; it was Bob's answering service.

"She said she's got bad chest pain, and does she have to go into the hospital. She was screaming into the phone."

The operator was calm and unconcerned, her voice flat, letting me know she thought the patient was a hypochondriac. Maybe she needed someone to talk to, not an ambulance. But the call was labeled an emergency and I had to pass the message on.

I scribbled a note for the kids, and taped it across their bedroom doorknob. They hardly ever woke, and I'd be back soon; if they needed help, they could ask the night man on the elevator. Hurrying out, I put my coat on in the hall, glad to escape the memories of Jake and the smell of charred flesh, the unexpected echoes of the concentration camps.

When I reached the street, the wind off the Hudson River engulfed me. Trees along Central Park West were swaying in the stronger gusts, and a few fallen branches were scattered on the pavement. Barbara was leaving the Park as I crossed, her face muffled in a scarf, her head down against the wind. Her dogs lagged behind, trying to carry off a four-foot limb blown onto the path, and she turned around to call them.

I wondered about passing her without speaking. We used to

spend hours walking our dogs, talking our way through endless turns around the oval football field. Everyone talked on the dog walks; that's what we came for. That's why I couldn't come out anymore. I'd told Ellen I was sick, but no one else; I couldn't bear to have them all know, but I couldn't lie. And even talking about the weather felt like a lie with people who didn't know.

Barbara saw me and slowed down while I hesitated in embarrassment. She stopped in front of me, so close I could see the fine lines about her eyes. She was still in her twenties, but her skin was dry. She said her skin needed the damp air of her English childhood, not New York pollution.

"Have you seen Bob?" I asked. "He has an emergency call." I was abrupt; I heard myself only when it was too late. One of Bob's complaints about me. I flushed. At least I could have said hello.

"He's in the oval," she said, "with your friend Ellen." Her voice was belligerent, her blue eyes unblinking behind sandy lashes. With the rest of her face still hidden in the scarf, she could have been an Arab woman for all I could read of her expression. I didn't answer, trying to judge whether her tone grew out of my lapsed friendship or whether it implied a question about Bob. We'd made love only twice in the last two and a half months, and I'd begun to wonder if he was screwing someone else. Before I could think of what more to say, her dogs ran to me.

Jumping up to lick my face, they threw themselves against me, their paws high on my chest. I tipped over backward, falling on the path, and they stood on my body, whimpering with pleasure, while I tried to hide behind my hands, unable even to roll over. Barbara shouted Cockney curses, hauling at their collars and kicking them; a small, round woman, but muscular. Her mother worked in a London factory. I began to giggle helplessly.

By the time she pulled me to my feet, I was crying, the icy tears running down my cheeks. "It's all right," I said. "They surprised me. I forgot how heavy Labradors are." I found a balled-up Kleenex in a pocket and blew my nose while she apologized over and over and tried to brush me off with gloved hands.

I wiped my eyes, still on the edge of hysterics; my legs were trembling. I knew the drugs Chou gave me stripped away the muscles and made me weak, but he said my moods were from the chemo too, that my rages and crying jags came from his drugs.

Barbara was watching me intently, no longer belligerent. She was a dress designer, with an eye for detail; she must have seen how sick I looked. Unless she knew something about Bob and wondered how much I knew. I wanted to ask if Bob and Ellen were alone when she saw them, but she spoke before I did.

"How come you're never out anymore?"

Was she asking about me or giving me an opening to tell her we were splitting up? Seeing only half a couple in the Park usually meant they were getting ready to separate; if that's what she thought, she wasn't totally inaccurate. My voice came out more harshly than I expected.

"I'm writing a book. No time."

I flushed again; now I sounded insulting. It was a rotten lie anyway; half the people around here were writing books. "I've got to get Bob. It's really urgent."

Turning my back, I started up the little hill toward the playground. I wouldn't have noticed the incline if I weren't anemic. Now it was too little blood to carry oxygen, instead of cancer cells pressed in lumps against my diaphragm; at least I could take a deep breath without coughing.

A man came out of dense bushes; I jumped and let out a strangled shriek. But he kept his distance and his voice was carefully obsequious, apologetic. "You got a cigarette, ma'am?"

This was the first year men were calling me ma'am. I shook my head, making vague gestures with my hands. "I don't smoke."

"Everybody don't smoke no more," he sighed, tipping sideways with a mock salute. Drunk. "Go with Jesus anyway."

His voice had a tinge of Southern drawl. Baptist probably. I'd clipped two articles about faith healers last week; he'd probably know some himself. I saluted back, remembering a derelict who began speaking to the Virgin Mary last summer while I sat at the other end of the bench. Maybe he really saw her.

I was almost at the oval, able to hear voices carried by the wind. As I cut through the last stand of hemlocks I saw Bob with Ellen at the other end of the field.

Bob's hands were deep in his pockets, and his whole body tilted toward Ellen as they spoke. I kept walking, watching them without their knowing. Even the little sex we'd had was mechanical on his part, as though he were doing me a favor.

He leaned closer to her; I waved my arms and shouted, unable to stand it if they kissed. Even though I knew he couldn't be that stupid. Even if they were screwing. They turned, Bob started running toward me, and Ellen and the dogs followed. Everyone in the Park ran but me and two eighty-year-old ladies.

"What's wrong?" Bob's voice carried thinly on the wind.

"An emergency call." No point shouting more; the wind was against me, blowing in my face. Until now the trees had protected me. I waited for him to come nearer. "Miss Kleniam. Your service didn't sound worried, but she says she needs an ambulance."

"Oh Christ! That's the fifth call today."

He didn't look guilty. Were they really just talking? With the hours Bob worked, he could fit in ten affairs without my knowing, without going to my best friend. He'd always said an affair was too much trouble. But he was joking with me then; that was before.

"Who is she?" I asked. He had very few young patients, but sometimes a younger woman brought in a parent. Not that there weren't enough nurses at the hospital if he wanted a woman. I glanced at Ellen, but she was keeping back.

"She's been nursing an old mother for years; her mother died last month; she's depressed, but I can't get her to take what I've prescribed, and she won't accept a referral to a shrink." He ended the clinical recitation, and made a face. "Wasted her life and stuck with it now."

"She sounds very attached to you."

He looked down at me, annoyed. He knew I was suspicious of everyone. "Mona, she's a fifty-five-year-old virgin. She doesn't even have a cat to talk to."

He turned his back to say good night to Ellen, and stalked off without another word to me. I told McCrae to stay. He'd be on the phone a long time; now that I was out, I didn't want to go back.

Ellen's cheeks were red. Maybe it was the cold, not shame. "Are you staying out?" I asked.

"A few more minutes. I'll keep you company."

"I'm not a middle-aged spinster." It came out sharply. I meant it to be light. I didn't want her taking pity on me.

She flashed a look, then shrugged. "Bob said you've been doing those Dewey tapes I got for you. I'm glad they're useful."

Her voice was formal now, like mine; careful. Bob said he walked on eggs around me. I went back over what I'd said and admitted to myself that I sounded prickly.

"Is that what you were doing? Talking about me?" I didn't know I was going to say that either. I smiled to make it softer, but she didn't smile back.

"Bob was talking about your treatment."

I didn't answer. Was he complaining to her?

"He said it's hard on you that he can't work shorter hours. He's so involved in taking care of you; that's all he talked about." Her voice warmed, as if at the memory, and she tossed her hair girlishly. Was she hoping to marry Bob if I died? She wasn't a fifty-five-year-old spinster; she was thirty-two and single.

Gary came out of a side path with his poodle. When he saw us, he lit a cigarette. Ellen roused herself, smiled politely at him, and pecked me on the cheek.

"I'm going to go in now. Take care."

Gary was one of the few dog walkers I didn't like. At least I wouldn't be tempted to tell him about myself. Now he blew smoke in my direction and began talking without even a hello, as though he'd seen me just a few minutes ago instead of more than a month before.

"I was talking with Bob tonight about the patient who shot the doctor's wife in the elevator," he said.

His round face was boyish, naive, guileless, his gaze direct, his eyes wide and blank. He never had any idea what he was saying. I suddenly felt exhausted, and I sat down on the nearest bench before I answered. "It's one way to get rid of your wife."

"That's funny. That's what Bob said."

I wondered just what Bob had meant. If he was trying to shut Gary up, he'd been too subtle.

"Can we talk about something else? I could skip hearing about it."

When he sat next to me, the wind blew cigarette smoke at me. The smell was unbearable, nauseating, and I moved back to get away from it. He was probably wondering what was wrong with what he'd said, turning it over in his head and ticking off possibilities. Gary needed a primer to identify the emotion in a sentence.

I shivered, ready to go back as soon as I felt able to walk, surprised at how comfortable I was with him. For all my annoyance, I didn't mind his awkward pauses and general ineptness tonight. With Gary, I didn't have to worry about my own blunders.

"John and Maxine broke up," he said. "Did you hear?"

Maybe he was fishing for me to say something about Bob, maybe even Gary knew something was wrong between us.

"I heard. John's taking the cat."

I watched his face as he fell back into his own thoughts; he was good looking, but neuter, like a store mannequin. He lived alone in the neatest apartment I ever saw, and hardly ever dated. Did he push sex off into folded underwear and labeled drawers and the computer programs he invented for IBM? His chest was hairy, I knew that from the summer, from sunbathing afternoons on blankets in the meadow. Black curly hair, thick. Apelike. I could pull on it. If he ever yanked on my hair, it would fall out.

I shook my head, then called McCrae. Gary stood up with me, ready to leave too. "You look tired," he said. "But I like your hair short. The other way was messy."

I almost kissed him, glad to take a compliment on any terms. If he made a pass at me, I'd fall right into his arms, so pleased at being wanted it wouldn't matter what I thought of him.

My watch said it was close to midnight. The few people still in the Park had shepherds and huskies and Dobermans, but even they'd be leaving soon. We separated at the corner, and I walked slowly down the block to my building, conserving strength.

Nick was on the door; he asked if I was all right, and took my arm to walk me to the elevator. I must look worse than I thought. The elevator shift had changed too: José was on. I said hello when I got on, but he only nodded sourly. I'd heard he had too many kids, a new one popping out every year. I felt sorry for his wife, but at least he noticed her.

As we went up, I let myself imagine that Bob was off the phone, waiting for me. When I opened the door, the couch would be empty. I'd turn and see him standing naked, prick extended, pointed upward, ready to pierce me through my clothes, he was so hot with desire. I could feel his arms engulf me, and I felt weak with longing to be held.

But Bob was still talking on the phone, lying on the couch looking up into the leaves of the avocado tree. McCrae ran to him as though they'd been separated for days, and sat in front of the couch, wagging her tail so hard her whole rear end vibrated. Bob sat up without interrupting his sentence, before her enthusiasm outran her training and fifty pounds of dog jumped on his belly.

I was so disappointed I started to cry, and turned away to the boys' room so Bob wouldn't see me. Dan was on top of the bunk bed, Adam beneath, each of them hidden inside a sleeping bag. The room was a mess, model airplanes all over the rug, and parts of an erector set half made into a robot.

I tried not to bother them about cleaning up; but last week I fell over a cap gun and went into a fury, throwing it down the incinerator chute in the hall. They were awed by my rage, watching me big-eyed from the door as I stalked back in and threw the toys still on the floor at the walls. The plaster was studded with fresh pockmarks.

Chou said the chemotherapy made everyone in the program irritable. Each time we saw him, he asked Bob, not me, how I was acting, as though I couldn't even judge how it affected me. Maybe he was right; I couldn't remember how I used to feel; and last week it felt quite normal to throw toys at the walls like a two-year-old.

I walked to the window to close the curtains, although the morning light didn't seem to wake them. Kevin stood up at the door of his cage to say hello. I took him out, he nestled against me with a purr, and we walked together toward the kitchen.

Behind me, Bob's voice changed timbre as though he were talking to another doctor. He saw patients all day and even part of Saturday; when did I come in?

I placed Kevin on the counter with a cracker, put a tablespoon of yeast in the blender with V-8, and added a few drops of soy sauce. I'd started by mixing the yeast just with a spoon, making damp lumps on the side of the glass that left me gagging. The taste took getting used to even without the lumps.

But yeast was good for me, all the yeastie microscopic organisms filled with vitamins. I looked at the label on the jar again, calculating. With four tablespoons a day, I got 6000 percent of the minimum daily requirement of B_2 and B_{12}, 8000 percent of B_6. My cells were floating away in vitamins.

I turned off the blender, drank while trying not to notice. It got better as I got used to it, but it would never make the best restaurants. I pulled off my sweater, hot again, feeling the walls of the kitchen closing in. It was a true New York high-class apartment: when the maid cooked, in the old days, she didn't have to be comfortable. A roach ran out from behind a counter, and I squashed it with a napkin. I had to call the exterminator again, and I had to show the super the plaster coming down in my office. Among the many have-to-do's I'd let slide.

Bob came up behind me. "Sorry I was on so long," he said. "She called the ambulance before I got upstairs. I was trying to cancel the call."

Now that he was with me, I didn't know what to do. "It doesn't matter. I didn't think you'd stay on unless you had to."

He pulled the juicer onto the counter, and began scraping a bunch of carrots. Another part of my diet. "I'm glad you had some time outside."

We sounded like strangers on a first date. I watched him insert the carrots, organic carrots from the health food store near us, watched the catcher fill with rich orange juice. Two glasses from a pound of carrots, the rest a dried mass of unusable cellulose. It seemed like a waste of most of it, even though I knew it was an illusion. What was left couldn't be digested anyway, except by a rabbit, and I wasn't even sure of that.

He handed me the glass of juice; I drank it easily. It was sweet, delicious, one of the few sweet things I had now that I ate no sugar. Bob watched, his face drawn, aged five years in the last two months. His step had no spring in it anymore, only determination.

"I saw my old analyst today," he said abruptly. "I decided it was time to talk to someone about what's going on between us."

I blushed, I could feel myself blushing. "You mean about sex?"

"He said I should have called him sooner. I told him I thought we could work it out."

If he called his analyst, maybe he wasn't in someone else's bed. Or maybe he was anyway. I knew he didn't want to break up, not when he kept making me concoctions of carrot juice and yeast, not when he pored over reports of new experimental treatments the way he did. But it wasn't just sex, he hardly touched me for any reason.

I leaned against the counter, then away, remembering the roach. Did Jackie O have roaches on Fifth Avenue? "Did he say anything useful?"

"He said to try not to be so serious about it. A few other things, too, just for me, private."

Once he would have reached for me, not stood there woodenly like an awkward fifteen-year-old. If I sat on the countertop and spread my legs, would that excite him? I looked involuntarily at the window; the bamboo shade was up and the people across the street could see us. Anyway, I really wanted to lie in bed with him.

I picked up Kevin, holding him warmly against me. McCrae trotted in from the living room, wondering what she was missing. I wasn't going to make the first move. "I won't break if we make love," I said, "if that's what he meant."

I carried Kevin back to the boys' room, then began to wash up.

He probably found me repulsive. My hair was streaked with gray, and thinner every day. I couldn't brush it anymore; clumps came out on the bristles. As though I'd aged twenty years in two months. When I'd always looked younger than I really was. When we walked outside together now, I held his arm for support, keeping him down to a slow promenade so I wouldn't gasp for breath. I felt like his aged mother. Or my own.

I started to cry over the sink, my face buried in my hands, trying to be quiet to keep Bob from hearing me.

When I came out he was reading, or pretending to read. I didn't look at him, and crawled under the covers on my side. But I got out of bed to turn off the lights when he went into the bathroom.

By the time he came back, I was half-asleep, curled on my side with the blanket over my head. I heard him stumble against the bed frame and felt him rock the bed climbing in, but I didn't move. He reached for me, and pulled himself against me, his belly at my back, his prick erect and hard against my closed thighs; I felt myself beginning to rouse.

I shifted one leg so he could reach inside to stroke me.

"You're awake," he whispered.

I grunted and he put a hand around me, against my breast. I creamed and wriggled around to face him, wanting desperately to kiss, ready for his tongue inside my mouth while he penetrated me. But he moved so that my lips brushed the side of his face. He wouldn't kiss me since I started chemo, afraid he'd make me sick, insisting the mouth had too many bacteria. It was safer to blow him than kiss him, he'd said, but he didn't really mean that either, even right after a shower he didn't like me blowing him, he said it worried him. He'd like it better if we could make love through plastic.

I nibbled him under the chin where tomorrow's whiskers were beginning to come out, conscious now of our being two separate people. His hands fondled my breasts, but the rhythm was mechanical and repetitive. He sketched an embrace near my naval; it was rapid and distracted. I was cooling down.

I opened my legs, hoping he could penetrate before I turned off; if foreplay didn't work, fucking still might. He sat up and turned away to fit on a Forex; another hedge against infection, and one Chou suggested. The Forex was icy against me, and made me flinch. When he tried to enter, I was too tight. He reached down to guide himself in, I felt his touch, felt him freeze for a second, and felt him go soft.

"What's the matter?"

"Shhh."

"What's wrong?"

"I don't want to talk about it."

"Should I touch you?"

"No." He sounded definite.

He lay against me without moving, his body tense and his prick soft. I wanted to go to sleep. I had to teach in the morning. I started to drift off.

"Mona?"

"Mmm." If I didn't answer, he'd go away.

"I'm sorry. I love you. I'd fake it if I could."

I was awake now, but I still didn't answer. There was nothing to say, and I wasn't going to touch him again. After a while, his voice went on; ashamed, miserable, almost inaudible.

"I felt a node. When I touched you. I feel them everywhere." His tone sharpened into bitter self-contempt. "When before I didn't feel any of them. I'm a Monday-morning quarterback."

I moved away and turned around to look at him from a distance. He was rigid on his back, his silhouette outlined against the backdrop of city lights through the window. He turned to face me, then turned away to look up at the ceiling again. "I'm sorry. It doesn't do any good telling you, does it?"

"Are you sleeping with Ellen?"

His whole body jerked, and he sat up, staring at me. He sounded shocked. "Jesus! No! Is that what you think?"

He looked as though he meant it, as though it were the truth. I knew his soul was naked. But what he'd said still hurt. I had enough trouble feeling I was all cancer, like the evil witch of fairy tales, shedding poison as I stalked through the forest. I couldn't take care of him too. Not now. My voice was cool when I spoke. "All right. That's something anyway. But you're right, I don't want to hear confessions."

Now it was his turn not to answer. I went on, keeping down the anger. "I won't bother you about sex. Let's try to forget it and go to sleep, OK?" I turned over again and shut my eyes, too exhausted to care anymore. In the middle of the night, I felt him get out of bed, and when I woke to the alarm in the morning, I saw he'd spent the rest of the night on the couch.

THE PARK FORSYTHIA HAD ALL TURNED YELLOW, REFLECTING back the feeling of sunlight even when overhead clouds threw them into shadow. From the bedroom window, I watched a flock of Canada geese drop honking to the waters of the reservoir, mysteriously threading their way through the skyscrapers of Manhattan to rest here on their migration north. Like the skyscrapers, the reservoir was man-made; man-made like most of Central Park itself, from mosquito marsh. But the geese found the water as they flew up the Atlantic coast from Cape Hatteras, taking just what they needed from the city: survivors.

They flew so high that the lines of the flock were black smudges in the sky, like wisps of smoke somehow broken free of furnaces and incinerators. On the water, they were loud; their calls raucous; and even this April the sight of them brought me out of myself for a moment of peace.

I turned my back, forcing myself to continue the work of remembering. Jake was haunting me this morning, his image plaintive and compelling. It would be easier if my parents were alive; then I could ask them if they accepted what I remembered as true.

All I had were fragments. What I put together was a construction, a creation, in its way a work of art. Memories were not facts, they were the ashes of facts, distorted attempts to make sense of a child's perceptions. But memories were all I had.

Jake was short and dumpy, his teeth crooked. He was bald, the dome of his head shiny under the bulb of my grandma's kitchen, only a fringe of pale brown hair remaining; and he always smelled of cologne. His eyes were soft and brown, and easily filled with tears, and in his wallet he carried pictures of all the brothers, sisters, cousins, aunts and uncles who died in the Nazi extermination camps.

The lone survivor of his family, he'd been brought here before the invasion of Poland as the betrothed of my father's sister, not knowing when he boarded the ship that no one would be coming after him. Sometimes he brought me dresses from the factory where he worked; beautiful dresses, more than we could afford ourselves, and he'd tell me how I reminded him of his youngest sister.

I fought with Hannah about Jake at noon on Friday; we had assembly that afternoon and didn't speak again, although we sat side by side in the honor guard.

The next Sunday I spent the morning going from my bed to the bathroom, sick with spasms of nervous diarrhea. My mother said it couldn't have been anything I ate because I didn't eat enough of anything to get sick, and she gave me hot water to drink with lemon and honey in it. By mid-morning, she stopped her vacuuming to feel my head while I lay face-down on the bed, and told me I could stay home with my grandpa if I had to. The diarrhea passed after that, and I gave the bathroom up to my father the next time he knocked on the door, so he could dress.

I was doing a jigsaw puzzle at the kitchen table when my mother walked in. I knew it was time for them to leave; even her powder and lipstick were on. She held out my crinoline and taffeta skirt, and my stomach turned over.

"I don't see why you shouldn't come if you feel all right now," she said. "Then I don't have to worry your grandma about you being sick again."

I knew she never changed her mind when she sounded so decided; and maybe Jake wouldn't bother me this time. I stepped numbly into the slip and skirt, drew off my pajama bottoms, and took the cotton panties she gave me. When I was done dressing, she looked bleakly at my limp hair.

"Nothing we can do about it," she murmured, and combed it out to make new braids. She hurt me when she pulled on the knots, but I said nothing to annoy her more; I could tell by the lines around her mouth that she had a headache already. When she was done, she took me by the shoulders in warning.

"I'm bringing you like a lady, Mona. I better not catch you fighting with your cousin like last time. You understand?"

I shut my eyes and promised to be good, ashamed again at shaming her before my father's relatives; unable to explain what came over me with Karen while we played in my grandma's bedroom, unable to understand it myself. My father came to the kitchen doorway, handsome in his blue suit, and looked at me approvingly. "I never thought you'd look so pretty the way you doubled up this morning. You ready for the bus?"

"What if I get sick again?"

"You won't," my mother said. "You never get sick once we get started."

She took my winter coat from the foyer closet and kneeled to help me with the big black buttons; I began to count the blue dots on the linoleum. She made a face. "Ugh. You didn't brush your teeth, did you?"

I blushed, embarrassed. "I forgot. With my stomach."

My father held out my mother's coat, commanding, his voice deep. "Let her be, Helen. It's enough."

He watched her put on her gloves, her face pinched; tapping his foot impatiently, he moved to the hall door. When my grandpa came from his room to kiss us all good-bye, my mother kissed his cheek with her arms around his neck, her voice childish. "You'll be all right by yourself, Poppa? You sure?"

Patting her shoulder, he exchanged looks with my father. "I need time by myself too. Anyway, I'll listen to the opera all afternoon on the radio. Mona, from you I want a special hug."

He bent over, and I too put my arms around him, wanting desperately to stay home with him, even though I hated opera. I buried my face in his neck and tightened my hold for a moment. "I'll miss you, Grandpa," I muttered, quite unlike myself, and he looked questioningly at me as I let go. But my father was waiting, and I turned my back on my grandfather before he could ask me anything, ran past my parents, and clattered down the marble stairs two at a time. When we reached the street, my mother gave me a red LifeSaver from her purse.

We didn't speak on the three-block walk to the bus, our heads down against the March wind, and I was quiet as we rode to the El. Once on the train, I stood as usual at the front window of the first car, where I could watch the tracks unfold before us, but today I stood there so they wouldn't ask me why I didn't. When we rounded the big curve, I didn't tip my body to help keep the train from falling off the track onto the street. If we did fall, I wouldn't have to meet Jake.

At my grandma's, the hall was dark, the light bulb snatched again, and the hall reeked of pee. My father growled low in his throat when he smelled it, and followed close behind my mother as she climbed the dark stairs in her stiletto heels. I tried to hold my breath, but I was gagging anyway, the smell of pee mixing with ancient dirt, roaches, and the grease of chicken fat and lard the different tenants used for frying. It smelled even worse than our building on a Friday afternoon. I pushed my mother to one side so I could run up the stairs; as I reached the landing, my grandma's door swung open. My Uncle Jake scooped me up in a bear hug, laughing; then swung me around into the kitchen and my grandma's waiting arms. Jake in the flesh was only Uncle Jake.

I felt wonderful during dinner, the nausea all gone, and stuffed myself with knishes and kasha varnishkas while my grandma beamed with delight. But I started worrying again when she began to ladle out the dessert prunes. Now Karen and I would be banished to the bedroom while the grownups played pinochle in the kitchen. Although Jake would be playing too. My father was looking forward to the game all day; as far as I knew, that was why we came again so soon. Even if Jake wanted to bother us, he'd be busy with my father.

"You be good with your cousin," my father whispered, handing me a deck of cards. "No fighting like last time." He began to clear dishes from the table; my mother looked up from her prunes, annoyed at his hurrying her.

I followed Karen into the bedroom, sorry I didn't have my cardigan along. It was freezing here in winter. Together we unfolded the extra blankets at the foot of the bed, and wrapped them as shawls around our shoulders. I would have liked to get under the covers completely, but we weren't allowed to with our clothes on. Karen shuffled the deck and dealt; and I began to forget about Jake. She was ten and I was still seven; she played a better game of gin rummy than I did, but I loved to play so much I didn't mind.

When Jake pushed open the bedroom door, he was drunk again, like last time. He was probably losing to my father. He stumbled over to the bed, sat down next to Karen, and put one arm around her shoulder. She tried to move away but he pulled her tighter against him, his fingers gripping her hard.

"How's my maidele? Who's winning?"

Looking at the cards she held, he unbuttoned the top buttons of her blouse to slide in his hand. Karen turned red, and stopped struggling, but she wouldn't look at him. His hand moved back and forth across her new and tiny breasts, the pearl buttons of her blouse all opened now. Karen stared fixedly at her cards, drew from the deck and discarded, and somehow I took my turn next, but I saw only his hand playing with her body and the curly brown hair above his knuckles. Was this new? Or something I'd never seen before? I hadn't noticed before that Karen was growing breasts either. Hannah said I didn't see half the things that went on around me.

He held my eyes with his, his voice conspiratorial. "Uncle Jake is playing with his little girl. Mona knows it's just a little game, right Mona? Mona likes games."

Pulling up her blouse, he slid his hand under the elastic waistband of her skirt. I watched, shivering, unable to look away, the smell of his whiskey fusing with the image of his hand between her legs.

This was very, very bad. My father would kill me if he knew. Karen turned her head at last, her mouth against Jake's ear. "You're drunk."

He hesitated, his hand still inside her clothing.

"Someone might come in," I whispered. "I might scream."

"You would make such a fuss over a little cuddling by your uncle? Maybe you want to play again with Uncle Jake yourself? You want to play with your Uncle Jake?" His hand free again, he touched the zipper of his pants.

My mind felt as frozen as my body, the thoughts splintered, the kitchen miles away. If only God would strike him dead. I was shocked to hear chairs scraping distantly against the floor in the next room; the game was breaking up.

Swaying slightly, he got to his feet and looked down at us. "Mona, my little sweet maidele, you shouldn't let yourself get so excited. Since when is a little friendliness from your uncle a capital offense?"

His voice and face surrounded me, gigantic, huge, a nightmare form filling the air. I choked on the stench of whiskey, my stomach turned upside down, my body floating unconnected to me.

Jake left the room, and Karen reached stiffly for the deck; I thought she was crying, but I kept my eyes on my cards, unable to look her in the face. I tried to follow her lead and play on as though nothing had happened, and we finished the game without either of us caring at all who won.

I left Karen on the bed, and I went to the kitchen to sit near my mother. Jake was drinking a glass of tea at the table and telling my father how well the dress business was doing, while my mother and aunt knitted. On seeing my face, my mother felt my forehead, and asked if the bedroom was getting enough heat.

When she tucked me in that night, I asked her to stay a few minutes longer. I still heard Jake's voice circling around me, cajoling me to touch him. His eyes were sad and liquid; I couldn't bring myself to hurt him. And I was curious; that's what I couldn't ever admit to anyone. If I told my mother, she'd send me away, to an orphanage or reform school. There was a reform school near the El, with stone walls topped by barbed wire; I might go there.

I clutched my mother's hand and gazed up at her face. She was still pale with headache. As I watched, she pressed her knuckles against her forehead.

How could I explain it didn't seem so bad at first, the time before, even though I knew it was, that I knew it, but knowing seemed very far away? Karen wasn't curious; she just wanted him to disappear. Jake was her father. I gagged.

"Are you sick again?" my mother asked. "If you're nauseous, go right into the bathroom."

"I'm not sick."

She shifted on the narrow bed. "You haven't been yourself all day."

If I told her about Jake and Karen, she'd think I was lying. But I couldn't ignore it. I had to know. Unless it happened all the time. When a girl started to grow up.

I went rigid under the blanket, my nails digging into her hand. Was that why no one wanted to talk about your body changing? My mother unwrapped my fingers, rubbing her palm. "Mona, I have things to do. I can't sit here all night."

I had to think of how to ask her. I picked a flower in the wallpaper near my head and stared at it. I wasn't Jake's daughter and I was still flat-chested. So it didn't have to do with getting bigger like Karen. He was acting like one of the men sitting in parked cars by the playground.

"It's Uncle Jake," I whispered.

She pressed her forehead again; I knew she couldn't stand him even though he was always nice to her. "What about him?"

I whispered again, barely hinting at the truth. "Do grown-up men ever get too close?"

Her voice hardened. "Mona, what are you talking about?"

"He put his hand in Karen's underpants when we were playing cards." It was out. Maybe she didn't hear me. I stared at the rose on the wallpaper while she stared open-mouthed at me.

"What did you say?"

It was too late. "He touched her."

She turned on the lamp next to the bed; I pulled the covers over my head.

She pulled them off. "Are you telling me something you saw?"

I nodded. I'd die before I'd tell her the rest.

She hesitated and threw a look over her shoulder to make sure we were still alone in the room. "Has he bothered you?"

I shook my head no. It was almost true.

"You're sure? You're telling me the truth?"

I nodded vigorously, praying for forgiveness.

"Maybe he was just fixing her clothes."

She was willing me to say that's all it was, that I was wrong, dirty-minded in my innocence. I saw Jake's hairy knuckles. I heard his voice. I shook my head again, but I couldn't speak. I was sorry I'd started.

She smoothed her skirt over her knees and picked lint off the flannel blanket before saying anything else. "Jake drinks too much, Mona. When people drink too much, they sometimes do things they don't really mean. You stay away from him, and if you don't like the way he's acting, you tell him I said to leave you alone. But don't tell your father. If anyone has to speak to him, I will. And you mustn't tell anyone else. You understand?"

"Uh huh." She was finished. Silence. I mouthed a question. "Karen?"

"That's your uncle's family. If his wife can't keep him satisfied, there's nothing I can do. And maybe you're imagining a little bit too. You go to sleep now. Jake won't bother you with your father around." She stood up, but she didn't move away from the bed. "Mona? There's nothing else I have to know?"

"Nothing. Uh uh."

She kissed my forehead, and I curled up under the blankets with my knees bent to my chest, leaving just a little air space around my nose. If Karen didn't like it, maybe it wasn't so bad. I muffled my sobs in the pillow. Dirty-minded and a coward both. I went over the conversation again. What else could I do?

The next day, Hannah asked me how my Sunday was; I told her it was fine.

I opened my eyes, aware of a foul taste in my mouth. My throat was dry, the muscles strained, as though I'd been screaming aloud. My old address book sat near me on the night table. I could phone Jake now and shout curses at him. I didn't even have to tell him who I was; I could call anonymously. Enlarged images of his face flitted past me, confused forever with the smell of schnapps and cologne. But the Jake I remembered was gone, twenty-seven years in the past, not the Jake still living. It was too late to go back.

I turned the pages of the address book, passing Karen's number in New Orleans. She was a social worker, unmarried, an expert in family therapy. We hadn't spoken since my parents died, although I owned one of her books. What could I say to her after all this time? I'm sorry, Karen, my mother said it wasn't our business?

My parents' listing was on the facing page, slashed through by a large black X I'd scrawled after the accident. My fingers punched the numbers for their old apartment as though independent of the rest of me, the phone began to ring in Brooklyn, and I listened, no longer knowing what I even hoped.

A woman answered; I hung up without speaking.

Jake was giving us money that winter. God knows how much he slipped my mother all those years after the war. My father had been fired again, just like the year before, for socking a customer who called him a kike; he stayed out of work for months, until Obbie found him a job. Obbie said everyone knew he was a troublemaker.

No married women had jobs. If Jake and my grandpa hadn't helped, who would have paid for us?

I needed to get out, away from myself. Adam was going to be eight in four days and wanted an amateur magician's set. I could walk over to Broadway and buy it today. My own birthday was in three days. Bob said my present was waiting, and I was sure the boys had something for me too; but my birthday wish couldn't be satisfied as easily as Adam's. I hoped I could keep from crying.

Our birthdays were back-to-back, Adam born two weeks early, the day after I turned twenty-seven. Bob and I had celebrated at a local Mexican restaurant; I had contractions all through dinner, the cook joked that his chili would bring on the baby, and I went into labor during the night. We'd been so close then, and now we were so far apart.

I thought he was still out bike riding with the boys and I could come and go before they got back. Crae jumped off the bed, anxiously wagging her tail as I put a sweater on, and the phone rang.

By the time I reached it, it had stopped ringing. But I picked it up anyway. Bob's parents were on the line and he was already speaking with them. They were all talking at the same time. I held the phone, ready to tell them I was there when they slowed down. My watch said it was almost one o'clock, much later than I'd thought; they'd returned while I was meditating.

"Did they come yet?" Jeff asked, and I realized they must be talking about birthday presents.

"I just got in. I'm on my way down again to find out. Five packages, right?"

"Presents for Mona and Adam, two boxes for you, and something for Dan so he doesn't feel neglected," Jeff answered. "And wait until you open yours. They don't make them like that anymore. It brought back a lot of memories, sending them out to you."

I was going to tell them I was listening, and ask what they were talking about when he coughed, his voice deepening into somberness.

"How's Mona?"

It was time to hang up or cut in, but Bob answered before I could decide.

"I told you the other day. Doing all right." His voice became guarded, pushing them off. As though he were hiding something. Crae trotted over and collapsed against me on the floor.

"She's finished the fourth cycle of treatment?"

"Yeah."

"The doctor still thinks there's a chance?"

"Mom, I keep telling you the same thing. Hold on a minute. Kids, go into your room, I want to talk privately. You can say hello when I'm done, I'll let you know."

I couldn't do anything now, I was trapped. Whatever he was going to say, I had to know it. I brushed my hair back from my face, held Crae's warm body against me, and tried to breathe silently while the four of us waited for the boys to leave. Doris was the first to go on.

"You keep telling us she's doing all right, but you sound terrible. So what aren't you saying? Bob, baby, we can fly east in an hour if you need us."

"And have another blow-up like last time? You just about conducted funeral services here, you gave Mona hysterics."

"It wasn't that bad."

"Mom, it was just that bad. We need people who believe she's going to be all right, not mourners."

I shifted position and pushed Crae back as she stood to lick my face; whatever he was holding back, he hadn't said it yet.

"Bob, what then are you keeping from us?" Jeff asked. "Maybe we sound so worried because we hear something in your voice. Mona's never been that close to us, I have to say she's a hard person to get near, but she's your wife and the mother of your children. We think about you all every minute of the day."

His wife and the mother of his children; not Mona, not me. My breath caught in my throat and I swung the receiver up away from my mouth; I had to keep them from knowing I was there. I'd thought he cared for me more than that. Not Doris, she never had room for anyone but Bob and Bob's attachments. Jeff took a deep breath; I heard him light the next cigarette. He was pleading when he spoke again.

"Please try to put yourself in our shoes. We're three thousand miles away because the two of you for reasons of your own that I'll never understand choose to isolate yourselves from your family. I know Mona doesn't see any of her relatives, so it's not that you're tied by her. So there you are, all alone in the East, and we have no idea what's really going on. We try not to bug you, we don't phone more than once or twice a week. But I'm asking what the hell is going on with you!"

"Dad, I don't want to talk about it. Mona's responding to the treatment."

Doris began to cry, but Jeff simply continued to wait for Bob's answer, as though Bob had not already spoken; I could feel the pressure of his expectation. The silence lengthened as we waited together, the force of Jeff's will palpable across the continent, until Bob began to answer at last, picking his words gingerly, his voice harsh with emotion.

"The drugs affect her mind so she's . . . different. She accuses me of not caring about her, and . . . she looks half dead between the cancer and the medicines, and . . . she goes into tantrums like a two-year-old."

He stopped, his voice trembling. When he began again, he was almost inaudible. I knew I should stop listening but I couldn't.

"It's like lying in bed next to a corpse. And I keep having this flaky feeling I'm going to catch it from her . . ." He stopped again, while the words went on circling in my head, bouncing off the inside of my skull, and then he was louder, the words tumbling out of him.

"All right. Are you satisfied? She's doing all right, she's responding to the drugs, but she's sick all the time, and half crazy, and it's going to go on like this for at least another year. Worse, because the more treatment she gets, the sicker she's going to be from the drugs. And every time she gets a treatment, her resistance goes down so much we have to watch for her hemorrhaging from a bruise, or getting pneumonia because someone sneezed in the elevator with us. And I have to pretend to the kids that everything will be just peachy if we hang on."

"What about we fly in again? It's been three months. At least we can take the boys off your hands."

"No."

I was having trouble tracking, their voices fading in and out. I wanted to push his words away; more than that, I wanted them undone. No wonder he hardly ever wanted to make love, no wonder he'd gone soft the last time he touched me. Who would want to touch a leper?

Doris was still crying, talking through tears. "Please don't blow up at me like last time. But you know I have a friend whose mother did very well with Laetrile and diet."

"Shit."

"But she did! Without poisons to drive her crazy!"

"Mom, I'm going to get off now, but I'll make you happy, OK? We're going to see a Laetrile nut this week, partly to get you off my back, and mainly because I'm not as stupid as you think. I'm tired of hearing about your friend's mother. I want to see for myself."

He was shielding himself again, his voice calming as he sealed himself back up; a pseudo-WASP, but he'd learned the role well. The son of a bitch even managed to be polite. I just wanted them off so I could get away.

"I'm going to call the boys in to say hello and then I'm going to ask for the packages in the lobby," he said. "Listen, I appreciate your concern. But I don't want you here now. Not yet. Maybe we'll see you in June. If Mona's willing, I'd like to rent a cabin in the Sierras."

I put the phone down carefully; if they heard the click, they'd think it was interference on the line. Crae came back onto my lap and I held her against me, rocking back and forth, my fist locked against my mouth to keep from moaning. Like lying next to a corpse. I knew I shouldn't have listened. But it still wasn't fair. He was the spoiled brat, not me.

Still on the floor, I began yawning uncontrollably, my body desperate for oblivion, while Bob's words went on and on inside me. I was yawning so widely my jaw crackled and my eyes watered; I had to go to sleep for an hour, I couldn't stay up.

In bed, I fought sleep off until I found more Valium in the night table, then pulled the covers over my head and reached for darkness.

Dan woke me about an hour later, calling through the bedroom door. "Mom, are you awake yet? The mail's in and Dad just got a present from Granddad and Grammy. You want to come see?"

Struggling upright, I was glad it was Dan who came for me. We used to joke that Dan was my son and Adam, Bob's; long ago, when we were whole. Between sleep and Valium, I felt calmer than I'd expected, under control; but I could face Dan more easily than anyone else.

I told him I'd be right out and began applying make-up; I seldom wore any, but today I had to hide behind a mask. The marriage contract said for better or for worse. He was stuck with me and I with him.

When I reached the dining room, the three of them were standing at the table, their backs to me. Of the two cartons in the room, one was already gutted; Bob was ripping open the second with a steak knife.

I leaned against the doorway, contemplating him, wondering how much the caps on his teeth cost. They'd spoiled him, and he was still spoiled.

He pulled a package from the carton, and unwrapped a diesel locomotive. "The Southern Pacific! My second engine. After the Santa Fe." Turning it in his hands, caressing it the way he ought to hold me, he was talking as much to himself as to the boys. He still didn't see me, and I was in no hurry to announce myself. The arrogant son of a bitch had never been sick in his fucking life.

He unwrapped another car, a brick-red boxcar with Union Pacific in silver letters across it, and then a small caboose with a whistle on top.

"It looks like the little red caboose in the story," Adam said, tooting the whistle softly. "You know, 'the little red caboose always came last.' "

"Did you ask your parents to mail these?" I asked.

Bob jumped, he hadn't seen me watching. "I thought I might make a train layout in here. On a table. We don't use this room much, and it's almost empty anyway."

I looked toward the window, where I'd planned to add a convertible couch so he wouldn't have to sleep on the sofa every time he had a cold. There was still room for a layout. He could have his own bed in here and his own train set to play with, just like when he was a little sweet boychik.

"It's fine with me," I said, my voice too flat.

Bob searched my face for a moment, then turned back to the boys. "I left them in my folks' basement when I went away to college, and I thought it would be fun to set them up with you guys."

Walking away, I went to the kitchen for lunch. I had to eat, even if I wasn't hungry now. Sitting on the stool by the small table, I leafed through a catalogue of children's toys while their voices murmured in the dining room behind me. They were both too old for most of the toys in the catalogue; and I knew what they wanted anyway. A magician's set for Adam now; and a chemistry set for Dan in July, when he would be ten.

We were planning a sleep-over for Adam and five of his friends from school, with pizza and an ice cream cake. A smaller party than other years, and other years I'd baked the cake myself; but at least I wasn't getting chemo on either of our birthdays.

I began heating water for tea, wondering what else Bob's parents had sent. If Chou was right, I had nine more birthdays left. Or I could be hit first by a bus—like anyone else.

"Are you all right, Mom?"

Dan stood at the door of the fridge, his face worried.

I swiveled to face him. "Why? I feel all right."

He shrugged, shifted his feet uncomfortably, and looked down at the floor. "I don't know. How come you're in here when we're out there?"

"I guess I feel like it."

He reddened, hearing my answer as more flippant than I'd meant it. I wanted to put my arm around him, but I felt shy. He tilted his head, watching me sideways in a gesture he'd had since he was a toddler. "Mom, are you and Dad getting a divorce?"

I held my tongue, keeping it from blurting out too much, shutting in the spitefulness he shouldn't hear. I managed a neutral question.

"Why are you asking?"

"You stay away from each other. You never used to."

I made a face, exaggerating the grimace for his benefit; I had no intention of telling him about it. "No, we're not getting a divorce. We're not even thinking of it, Dan." Reminding myself that he was not yet even ten, I spoke to the child within him, softening my voice as best I could, explaining simply in the way I used to. "Married people can have trouble with each other without getting a divorce. We're not even thinking of a divorce."

He looked less strained, but still unsure. "Would you tell me if you and Dad change your minds?"

"Yes, but we're not going to. Forget about it."

My voice was brisk and apparently convincing; in any case, he looked relieved at last, and began rummaging in the fridge.

I wondered if I should have taken his question more seriously, but I couldn't treat him as a confidant. I smiled, remembering how seriously at three he'd announced that he'd be alive long after I was dead. And how I'd wanted to clobber him.

The bell rang; I heard Bob let Ellen in. I came out to the hall and she handed me a large bouquet of daffodils.

"I'm not finished," she said. "I hope you like this." From her purse, she extricated a small box, gift-wrapped with a dainty pattern. When I opened it, I found a thin gold bracelet on the purple velvet.

"It's real gold," she said. "It's supposed to be good for your biomagnetic fields. And I thought the engraving was beautiful."

I began to cry; I didn't deserve such a wonderful gift from her. Not knowing what to do, I admired the bracelet in the mirror near the door. Its delicacy made me feel delicate myself, ethereal and at the same time lithe. I wanted to wave my arm sinuously in the air, like a houri in the Arabian Nights. I would have known she was a dancer from her choice of bracelet alone. I thanked Ellen over and over, and called the boys to see.

"I was going to call you later," I said finally. "Are you leaving for the road tour this week?"

"Tomorrow. And I wouldn't really call it a road tour. We're just playing three colleges. But thank you." She smiled in mixed pleasure and embarrassment and turned to Adam. "I didn't forget you either, but they only had the game I wanted at the downtown store; they'll deliver it."

Thanking her shyly, he vanished; we walked toward the kitchen, and Ellen saw the trains. "For Adam?"

"Mine," Bob said. "I asked my folks to send them."

"Bob's father gave him trains for each birthday," I added. "Along with the rest of the toy store."

He threw me an angry look and turned back to her. "I started acting up in school when I was ten, and I broke some windows. My father was never home, he was always working, but he decided he had to make time for me somehow. Even if he had to get me out of bed at midnight, we'd work on model layouts. We even made a mock-up of the Sierra Madres from papier-mâché, with lakes way up in the mountains."

"I had a dollhouse like that," Ellen confessed, "that my father built with real electric lights. You lifted up the roof to reach in, and when the roof was down and the lights on, it looked absolutely real. My mother and I crocheted rugs for the floors, and wallpapered most of the rooms, but we never quite finished." She bit her lip, her face hardening. "I'd always dreamed of having girls to pass it on to. But my mother threw it out when she moved, after my father died, when I was in college."

Two weeks ago Bob said he wasn't sleeping with her, and I believed him. But they looked like a movie couple together. "Are you going to set the trains up in here?" she asked.

As she reached for an engine, Dan reappeared quietly, and whispered in Bob's ear. "Ask your mom," Bob said.

"We were wondering if we could give you a present now. One of your presents. While Ellen is here. Because we have two."

His face was so eager, I had to say yes. He ran out, and came back immediately with Adam and a huge box, red-wrapped like a valentine, with cut-out hearts and stars they'd pasted to the wrapping paper, and ribbons. I knew what was inside; the same present they'd bought for the last four years. I screwed my face up as I did each time, pretending wonder and puzzlement.

"Whatever can it be? I can't imagine!" I turned the box over, shook it gently, listened for an imaginary ticking. "A box of mushrooms? A wallet? A painting?" They shook no's of delight. "A briefcase!"

They beamed, their voices entwined.

"No, no. You're crazy. Open it up. Let Ellen see."

I unwrapped slowly, savoring their faces, still throwing out guesses. There were so many ribbons on the package it was like unwrapping a mummy. And then, of course, it was the yearly box of Swiss chocolates, a gift they first gave me because Dan said I loved chocolate and I'd never buy it for myself.

I examined the candies meticulously, picking up one chocolate after another before settling on a rich vanilla cream; even Bob wasn't going to worry about my eating sugar just now. Then I handed the box around for the others to take their first choices; every year we agreed they were the most delicious candies ever made. I smiled at them all, even Bob, glad that the boys had asked to include Ellen this year.

After she left, Bob came back into the kitchen to speak to me. "What's wrong?" he asked. "You were nice this morning and now you're pissed at me again."

"I listened in on your call. By accident."

His face paling, he sucked in his breath. I tried to speak through stiff muscles; my mouth felt so rigid I was surprised I could talk at all.

"I heard everything you said."

"You weren't supposed to hear any of it," he said softly.

"Obviously."

He reached for the chair and dropped onto it, drumming his fingers on the table.

"Like lying in bed next to a corpse," I whispered.

He smacked the top with his fist. "Shit! That's like holding me responsible for dreams. I said it, and I'm sorry you heard, but you weren't supposed to be listening. Don't shake your head at me like that!" he shouted. "Try to remember that I do still sleep next to you! And go to the hospital with you and spend half my time reading about lymphoma treatments!"

"But I heard everything you said. You can't undo what you said." I felt shriveled inside.

"Mona, I was telling my parents precisely what I wouldn't tell you. They were asking to help and I wanted help, like when I was a child and they could kiss away the hurt. If your parents were alive, you'd cry to them yourself." Leaning toward me, he gripped my shoulders. "We're going to pull through this shit somehow. And this weekend, you get my birthday present, and dinner at a Mexican restaurant, and ballet tickets. And you smile at me! You've said shit-assed things about me, too, you know. Like accusing me of fucking Ellen. Remember?"

I nodded, but words could wound more easily than they could heal. I knew he loved me, he took care of me so well, but it wasn't what I wanted. I'd believe him only when he touched me the way he used to.

13

WE WERE NEARING THE END OF THE SPRING SEMESTER. I'D TOLD Phil that I had to stop research for at least six months, that I felt going on in the lab as I'd been doing helped the lymphoma. I couldn't risk ignoring my feelings anymore; I had to stop and see if I really felt a weight off me. Phil knew I hated using animals, but he'd never expected me to really stop. He said I had to do what I felt I needed, but I knew he found my feelings inexplicable.

Today I staggered in with a heavy stack of exam papers. Phil was already marking tests at his desk, scrawling red-inked comments on the ruled pages. Looking up at me, he made a wry face.

I dropped limply into my chair with the exams in my lap and handed him the paper on top. One of my students had been writing gibberish on his exams all term; when I spoke with him he denied any problems; the dean refused to intervene unless the student asked him to.

Scanning the paper, Phil frowned, his eyebrows forming a black hedge across his forehead. "It's not a language problem? He speaks English?"

I shook my head. "I have to flunk him. Do you think I can warn his parents about him?"

Phil put the paper back in dismissal. "You'll be sticking out your neck even though you're tenured. You keep saying you're trying to make breathing space around you. Why ask for trouble?"

I stared at the paper again, but it was never going to make sense, with words scrambled crazily together, and nonsense scrawls crammed wildly in the margins. I knew the sensible course was to let it drop, but I couldn't. I didn't even like the boy, but teaching was more than lecturing from the front of the room. Looking at Phil's set face, I felt myself sinking under obligations.

Sighing, I dropped the rest of the exams on my desk and began pulling books from my bookcase to take home with me.

"I calculated the last set of results this morning," Phil said. "You want to see them?"

I looked sharply at him, hoping he wasn't going to pressure me again. Each time I went to the animal room, I felt the rats' terror rip into me; I'd even dreamed of that first summer and its screaming broken-backed rats. I was sure that doing what I hated gave the lymphoma strength. The cancer gave me leverage to do what I couldn't by myself. But I wasn't walling out my feelings so much now, and I felt worse about the animals since I'd decided to take time off.

"I'm not asking you to change your mind," Phil said bluntly. "Whether you and I stop working together for six months or forever, these results are still half yours."

Shamefaced and guilty, I fingered the gold pendant Bob had given me on my birthday; inscribed with shamanistic symbols of the Plains Indians, it had power. "Of course I want to see," I said. "I'm sorry."

He carried over a new graph, bright with colored penciling; when he bent over me, his beard tickled the back of my head. We'd been a team for three years, spending half our days side by side; in the fall, I'd move to my official cubicle in the teachers' room. Even if I kept a desk in here, we wouldn't be a team anymore; I'd thought it would be worse to stay.

"Significant at the point-oh-one level," he said. "The neurons function to maintain the overall pattern."

Scanning the numbers, I was aware of the warmth of his body, of the comfort his nearness gave me. Bob and I had made love a few more times; as the nodes shrank he could touch me again. But Phil and I were a couple too. Good decisions shouldn't feel this terrible.

My words were stiff. "Phil, I have so many questions I could run experiments for three lifetimes. The problem has nothing to do with my interest."

Without answering, he rested his arm lightly on my shoulder; dwarfing me, he was like a bulky black-haired giant from a fairy tale. He reached over me for the graph, and went back to his desk.

From my bookcase, I took out Bartlett on visual memory, Carlos Castaneda and the sorcerer Don Juan, Wickelgren on coding, Heisenberg on the uncertainty principle. I had to leave soon; Bob and I were going to see a nutritionist in Brooklyn later in the afternoon, but I had enough time to make some notes. Scrawling even more than usual, I began outlining on a yellow pad. Bartlett: Give people visual patterns to memorize, pictures resembling real objects, but more abstract; then ask them to draw what they remember over and over at different intervals of time. The remembered figures are abstracted, conceptualized, with details that don't fit taken out, forgotten, and the resemblance to real objects strengthened with each new drawing.

Another example: Have people remember random lists of nouns, then ask them to recall the nouns in any order; what was called free recall. People remembered by categories no matter how the nouns were given, putting together groups of animals, or flowers, or furniture. We made patterns, we made sense of what we remembered, even if it no longer fit what we really saw or heard, or what happened to us.

Show people a picture of two cars colliding. Tell half your group the cars are crashing, half that they are bumping into each other. The group told the cars are crashing remembers broken glass even though it wasn't in the picture; and the group told the cars are bumping remembers no glass. Our experience was always a construction, never the raw materials themselves; and our memories were even more an artificial construction than the original perception was. That was part of the meaning of Zen meditation or what Don Juan told Castaneda when Juan made him an apprentice sorcerer: stop your interpretations, stop seeing what you think you ought to, stop remembering what you think makes sense, stop deciding what you must have seen before it happens. See without preconception and you see magic. As Don Juan said, you enter the crack between worlds.

I looked up, feeling Phil's eyes on me. "I'm outlining for a course in memory. A new course. I'll have time if I'm not doing research." Shoving my chair back, knowing I was going to be late, I spoke apologetically.

"I'll bring back *The Roots of Coincidence* as soon as I get myself a copy. I keep rereading different sections."

He shrugged. "It doesn't matter. I can buy a copy too. Let me carry those out to your car, OK? I need a break before I set fire to these exams."

We walked to the parking lot together, without saying more; I felt sadder with each step. Phil put my books in the back seat with my exam papers; I rolled my window down and searched his face. "Phil, I feel as though we're getting a divorce."

Bending, he kissed me gently on the mouth. "We'll still have lunch together, we'll still be teaching in the same department," he said. "I'll see you tomorrow."

Waving, I drove slowly across the lot, and out the narrow exit road with its bumps across the middle to keep us to ten miles an hour; my heart began thumping as I drove. Once I picked up Bob, we'd leave for Brooklyn, the first time I'd be back since my parents died. I'd been telling myself all week that a doctor's appointment in Brooklyn Heights had nothing to do with returning to Brooklyn, but I'd only been trying to fool myself.

As I turned onto the highway, a truck honked me from behind, almost on my tail, although I hadn't seen him approaching. I waved him on and kept to fifty the rest of the way, concentrating on my driving while sweat trickled from my armpits.

Bob's office was just a few blocks from our apartment; limp from the drive, I stopped long enough at our building to ask John to carry in my exams. The day was beautiful, the first day of sun after half a week of May showers; leaving the Audi, I walked to Bob's office. It was almost two, our appointment was at four; the streets would fill soon with children leaving school. We were lucky to live where we did; both boys had several friends within a few safe blocks.

A few minutes after I took a seat in the gilded lobby, Bob came out, looking very doctorly in his gray suit, and we walked slowly to the car.

"We've got a new dent," I said. "Since yesterday. Left rear."

He bent to look, and stood up shrugging. "It's six years old. We're lucky it still runs."

Holding the door for me, he didn't see a beggar coming up behind. Turning, Bob collided with him, and pushed him automatically. The man staggered backward on the cobblestones until Bob caught his sleeve to steady him.

"Jesus, mister, I wasn't gonna hurt you."

"I didn't see you. It was an accident."

The man began to brush off his baggy khakis, shaking his head groggily. His head was matted and he stank; under all the filth was someone younger than I was. He caught my eye, but spoke only to Bob. "I could use half a buck for a drink. To quiet my nerves."

Bob looked him up and down, assessing him, before reaching for his wallet. "Here's two bucks. For honesty. Get some food too."

He thanked Bob and started up the block while I watched him from the car. Bob walked around to the driver's side, turned and shouted, "Hey, you!"

The man was already halfway up the street, surprising me when he turned. "Yeah?"

"Don't try to panhandle me every time you see me now."

Absently scratching his crotch, the beggar nodded; Bob smiled ruefully.

"He's been out here every warm day this spring," he said. "Sometimes he feeds the pigeons."

"Is that why you gave him money? You never like it when I give to a beggar."

His face was closed, impassive, the lines from nose to mouth clear in the afternoon light. "Maybe I'm changing. I have more sympathy than I used to."

Unable to talk about it anymore, I leaned back against the seat, closing my eyes against the image of the derelict. His eyes had been mournful, brown and sad; I wanted to take him home and feed him.

Bob turned at the corner to take us to the West Side Highway, driving too fast and throwing me sideways as he swerved sharply around a woman with a baby carriage in the middle of the block. Manhattan was filled with jaywalkers in the spring, everyone ignored the lights.

"Ten points if you hit her," I ventured.

"That's a New York joke," he said bleakly. "Today I'd rather be in California."

I looked away, not knowing what to say. I was bad at putting feelings into words, even worse than at believing the words he offered me. In other years, we reached each other with our bodies; but now my body was exactly what he turned from.

In silence, I gazed at the Hudson River as we followed its length down Manhattan. It was often rough and choppy, more an extension of the ocean at New York Bay than a true river. But today it was flat, waveless, with patches of iridescent silver too bright to look at long, like bits of overexposed photographs. It was always lighter here than anywhere else in Manhattan.

Bob asked if I was jittery, and I said yes, leaning forward to twirl the radio dial until I found Baroque music. I was afraid of crossing to Brooklyn, afraid of the ghosts, afraid of the memories of the years in Brownsville, before we moved. Bob had wanted to go back to Brownsville with me even when my parents were alive and I'd always refused. I didn't even know if my building was still standing, or whether they burned it in the riots of '68; or whether the whole block had been razed for housing projects.

Bob spoke quietly, his voice contemplative, trying to reach me. "It was odd, setting up the trains last month with the boys. I held the engines, and I could remember exactly how I used to feel, but it was only memory."

He put his warm hand on mine for a moment. "Neither of us is a child anymore. We were children long ago."

I blinked back sudden tears, and leaned out my window to let the wind whip my face. In my nightly remembrances, I'd reached the time of my grandfather's illness and Selim's prayers; meeting the derelict the day we left for Brooklyn was like stumbling on Selim in a waking dream.

Closing my eyes against the wind, I wiped them with the back of my hand, and let the memories crowd through.

* * *

I'd spoken with my mother about Jake in March. In April I was eight, and my grandpa went to the hospital with pneumonia. It was the first ambulance on the block since Rose's gallbladder attack the August before.

I was sick too, in the bed next to my grandpa's in the room we'd shared since my father came back from the army; I was afraid I'd made my grandpa sick, but my mother told me we had different germs, that I had a plain virus while he had pneumonia.

The bedroom was gray in the afternoon light, and I lay in bed watching him gasp for breath, wondering if I'd see his spirit leave through his mouth if he died while I watched. My mother paced back and forth on the squeaking floor, returning again and again to the window to peer out between the branches of my grandfather's potted geraniums, searching for the ambulance.

Selim crouched between our beds, crosslegged on the floor, rocking back and forth, bending so far forward that he banged his forehead on the flowered rug, pleading with Allah to save my grandpa. He kept calling him Joseph, his real name, and I became so confused in my own fever, I thought he was praying for someone else.

I don't know how old Selim was; I could never tell his age. Maybe he was fifty to my grandpa's sixty-odd. His face was lined and leathery, his skin as darkly brown as any I'd ever seen, Arab skin, burned by generations in the desert sun. I thought his name was Salem, the same as the town that burned the witches.

When the ambulance came, my mother ran downstairs to guide in the stretcher crew. My grandpa ws delirious, calling for his long-dead wife, my mother's mother; he reached up with both arms as Selim bent over his bed. Sobbing, Selim stooped to meet his mouth, and the two covered each other with frantic kisses.

When the stretcher crew came into the bedroom, they had to tear him off my grandpa's body; and in the hospital he sat in the open ward as long as the nurses let him, praying hour after hour, rocking again, and trying not to wail too loudly. When my grandpa got well, Selim told me his prayers were responsible.

Years later, when my grandpa was really dying, I asked him bitterly why his Allah didn't answer this time. We were both older then, and tired, and he was so thin the veins stood out in his arms, at his wrists, in his hands. He looked brittle, like a dried stick, and he stared at me, appalled. "Allah's will cannot be questioned," he said. "Who knows what mercy He hides behind this death?"

I knew such answers from the Hebrew school, from the fables that those sad-eyed men told wishfully and unconvincingly. The angel visits the house of the rich man, the rich man refuses him food and lodging, and in return the angel rebuilds the collapsed wall around his stables; the angel is given food and shelter by the poor but God-fearing man, and kills all his cows. The class was silent as the tales were told, ten of us trapped in that dim green room with plaster ceilings corroded by plumbing leaks, watching the concentration camp survivor tell his tale of mercy. "And then the angel revealed to him that there was treasure beneath the fallen wall; by repairing it, he kept the rich man from finding it and becoming richer. As for the poor man, it was fated that his wife should die; for his goodness it was changed, to cows."

By then we were too well trained by years of questions turned aside to ask the obvious. Was a death required of all? Why not the treasure in the poor man's home, the plague in the rich man's?

I looked back at Selim, and said no more. He was musty, his clothes grimy with sweat and dirt, the lines at his wrists black and crusted. My grandpa was dying, the house was sold, Selim hated the new owner and hardly ever came to work. Soon he would be fired.

When he came for a meal, my mother made him take a bath before he ate, ran down to the basement to wash his clothing in the machine, and dried them in the oven, scrubbing down the kitchen chair with Lysol when he left. His eyes were huge and luminous in his brown face, and innocent. I spooned stew onto his plate and watched him empty it, his hands shaky with exhaustion and emotion.

Later still, he disappeared.

Bob jarred me out of my reverie by angrily honking the car ahead. Cutting around it, he followed the looping entrance ramp onto the Brooklyn Bridge. I searched for the metal sign at the halfway point, marking the boundary line with Manhattan, but I couldn't find it.

In Brooklyn at last, we drove a few more blocks along quiet

streets, lined with renovated brownstones of the last century, the stonework steam-cleaned, the wood trim neatly painted. Window boxes sprouted red geraniums. The Heights.

Bob stopped. "His nurse said to use a parking garage three blocks down. Do you want me to drop you?"

I nodded, weakened by memories and fear of the examination ahead. "I'll meet you inside."

Without waiting, I turned to the brownstone and found the doctor's entrance under the stairs, his name by the bell, E. M. Schabtau, M.D. Inside, the white walls of the corridor curved at floor and ceiling to create a space without edges: architect-designed and expensive. I stepped through an arch into the waiting room and confronted a huge fish tank embedded in the white wall. Next to it was the receptionist, behind glass like the fish; she peered out a little window to ask my name.

"His assistant will be with you in a few minutes," she said. "She conducts the first section of the interview."

When I'd called for an appointment, they mailed me eight pages of questions that embraced equally the details of my mother's pregnancy, my current sex life, and everything I ate or drank for seven consecutive days; I'd wondered who waded through it all.

I checked my purse once more for the forms, then surveyed the other patients. Three of them seemed healthy enough, but I was riveted by the last, a gnarled old man held up in his chair by his frantic wife. His skin was yellow, and he was more dead than not, falling forward when she let go of him. She pulled him upright, moaning to herself; I averted my eyes, staring at the fish instead. She had no right to bring him here, not where I could see him. I looked from the corner of my eye: he was propped against the wooden chair back again, eyes shut. Was he going to die here? In front of our eyes? His wife read the paper in her hand, still moaning, then looked around helplessly, speaking to the room at large.

"How can I feed him seeds and nuts? Not even a little gefilte fish? Or some plain boiled chicken? This man says I can't even make him chicken soup."

Another lady, large and bright in a loose dress, leaned forward eagerly, happy to instruct her. "That's only for the first six months. Then you can add a little fish, a little chicken." Her eyes flicked to the moribund figure in the chair, once more beginning to sway forward; she licked her lips and looked down at her ringed fingers. "You waited a long time to bring him here."

The old woman gazed at her husband, and took his mummified hand to warm against her breasts. "Our doctor says only a miracle can save him," she whispered. "So I thought, what is there to lose, I heard this doctor Schabtau speaking on the radio, we'll go see him." She searched the paper again, tears running down her face. "But seeds are for birds to eat, not people."

I stumbled to the aquarium, trying to shut them all out, closing my universe to all but the guppies and the angel fish. Didn't Daniel tell me the guppies hatched live young and ate their babies?

My name was called; and I turned to face a nurse in a starched uniform, her hand out for the introduction. She was elegant and flat-chested, her voice slightly accented. Swiss. "I'm Miss Lahman. If you follow me, we'll begin."

As we turned to leave the waiting room, Bob hurried in. His eyes swept across the seated figures, stopping momentarily at the slouched old man; then he held out his own hand to Miss Lahman.

Single file, we followed her down the corridor to a small office, already crowded with a metal desk and plastic chairs. She told us where to sit, took my forms, and scanned them quickly, probably to see if I'd really answered all the questions. I was embarrassed, partly because I'd lied in places, and partly because I sounded like a pig even though I'd listed only half of what I ate. The forms came just after I'd finished the fourth round of chemo; I was always ravenous while the drugs wore off. Chou said it was a side effect, like when you smoked grass, but I was still ashamed to list it all. Not three bowls of Cheerios, but one, not cheese ravioli and half of Phil's eggplant parmigiana at lunch, but a cheese sandwich.

Miss Lahman's hair was perfectly cut, her cheekbones high; even her collarbone was elegant. She would have made me feel fat and wondering about the hem of my skirt coming down in back anyway; but now I was ten pounds overweight too. I'd known three other Swiss women, all flat-chested, hipless, and fashionable. I tried consoling myself with the image of her being commonplace in Geneva, but it was hopeless.

She put down the papers and turned to me, asking again many of the questions I'd already answered, watching my face with each reply before writing it down. "And your sex life?" she asked at last. "How is that?"

She looked from my face to Bob's in the long silence that followed. I wasn't going to tell anyone like her what it was like. "Fine," I said, when Bob remained mute.

"Enough? Not too much?"

"It's fine."

"No changes since you became ill?"

"It's fine."

Giving me up, she faced Bob; he was watching me. He shifted in his chair uncomfortably, between choices, then spread his hands. "It's less. At first, Mona was too sick, and then . . ." His voice trailed off.

"How often?"

"Um. Once a week. Maybe."

It was less, but I wasn't going to say it.

"How do you feel about the change, Mona?" she asked.

"It's fine. It'll work out." I'd kill her if she didn't stop. She had no right to call me Mona either.

"You understand, I have to ask these questions," she said, leaning forward earnestly. "We believe in treating the whole person here, no matter why you come."

"Holistic medicine," I answered, but she missed the irony of my tone. She nodded, relieved at my understanding, and smiled. Her teeth were too large.

After another silence, she looked at her watch. "Why don't we meet Dr. Schabtau?"

We followed her again, Bob in the middle of our file this time; I comforted myself with the image of her toothy smile. Opening the door to Schabtau's office, she stood aside and gave our names; he was seated behind a large chrome desk, nibbling something from a china plate.

A balding man in his fifties, tanned and glowing with health, he could have been a testimonial to himself. His walls were filled with pictures of Switzerland, but he said he was a Hungarian emigré, trained at Lausanne. We talked about his work awhile.

When I told him I was getting chemotherapy, he pursed his mouth regretfully. "Poison. Drugs may kill cancers, but they are poison to the body as well."

He pushed back his chair, and stalked around the desk to where I sat, standing over me like the Calvinist he might have been, swollen with the word of God. "Of course these drugs sometimes work, but the approach is stupid. You don't want to administer poisons, you want the body to fight for itself. As it should have done at first, at the beginning." He glared down at me, his eyes flashing fire. "You eat sugar, don't you?"

When I flinched, he nodded in comprehension, his judgment confirmed. He turned away, pacing across the burgundy carpet. "If I treat you, you eliminate all animal protein for at least half a year. You give up all meat, all fish, all dairy. You have no coffee, no tea, no alcohol. No sugar." He turned back, his voice softer. "When I examine you and we take hair samples for laboratory tests, I'll know exactly what vitamin and mineral supplements you will require."

Returning to his chair, he hunched forward and looked at me. "Unfortunately, at this time I cannot legally give you Laetrile. However, you can receive it from an excellent physician in Mexico City."

Bob finally stirred behind me. "Are you saying that you would insist that Mona discontinue her medical treatment?"

"Her drugs. Yes."

I felt shock even after all he'd said. I knew what he was going to say when I asked the next question, but I had to be sure. "What about radiation? I'm due for radiation at the end of the summer."

"Absolutely forbidden. If you received radiation, I would not treat you. Radiation completely destroys the body's own defenses."

"You're very sure of yourself," Bob said. "Just how many patients with lymphomas have you treated?"

A good question. Schabtau hesitated, and stood up, offering us the plate; it held apricot kernels. "We get Laetrile from these, as you know."

Bob shook his head, in rejection, but I accepted a handful. Schabtau replaced the china on his desk, and began again to pace the carpet, crunching apricot kernels. "Actually, I've never seen a lymphoma before. But I've had two patients with Hodgkin's disease. Very similar."

I knew he was a fraud now. All cancers are different. "How did they do?"

When he answered, he was less assured. "The disease is diminished in one patient. Not in the other as yet. But she'd had radiation before she came to me. I have many more patients with solid tumors," he added hurriedly at the sight of our stormy faces. "Most of them live longer than expected and I've had a few remissions. Of course, few patients come to me until they give up hope of a conventional reprieve."

"But I would be your first lymphoma patient?"

"Yes."

The gall of this man. When I was on a working program. I wasn't dying right now, not like that old man outside.

"Stand up," Schabtau said. "With both hands at your sides. I want to try something."

I looked to Bob for support. He shrugged, why not? We drove all the way to Brooklyn for this visit.

Schabtau placed himself in front of me and put one hand on my left shoulder. Telling me to relax, he rubbed my chest just below the collarbone, then pressed behind my jaw, just under the ears. "Now close your eyes and raise your right arm as high as you can while I try to push it down."

When I didn't respond, he pushed my arm up. I raised it higher still, then resisted when he pressed down on it. But my arm was forced down; he was much stronger than I.

"All right. That was the control." He placed some stones in my right hand and faced me again. I couldn't help it, I was curious. This felt like magic. I pushed upward against him again, my eyes shut as he asked. I felt the pressure of his weight, felt him pushing steadily down, and heard him grunt with effort, but this time I was stronger.

Bob whistled. "What the hell are you doing?"

I opened my eyes to see. Bob was leaning forward on the couch, watching Schabtau closely as he substituted another set of stones.

"Push," he said. "Harder. As hard as you can." He wiped sweat from his forehead; his face was red with effort. "Now switch hands. Pick up your left arm."

Once again I was stronger on half the trials. But my eyes were shut most of the time. Was he really pushing with the same effort every time? When I opened my eyes, Bob was standing next to Schabtau, watching his hands and arms and face.

"What are you doing?" Bob asked again.

"It looks like magic, no?" Schabtau said. "I give your wife different chelating ions to hold, different minerals. They're immediately absorbed by the skin into the body and I can tell what she needs, what she is deficient in, by changes in the strength of her arms. In this case, I see instantly that she needs supplements of zinc and selenium, but of course, I expected that when you tell me she takes drugs."

He looked me in the face from a foot away, his eyes round and blue, like Lake Geneva itself in the painting behind him.

"You wish another demonstration? I want you to close your eyes once more. When I tell you, try to touch your nose with your left hand."

I shut them, feeling myself sway slightly, off balance. I peeked and saw him taking more stones from a box. Blind again, I felt him press the stones against my body in a rhythmic pattern, now somewhere near my left hip, now my shoulder, now on my back. I tried to touch my nose each time he asked. Twice I couldn't do it. My hand wandered through the empty air, but I couldn't find it. I couldn't find my nose. I felt like the sick joke we all told as children, about little Charlotte with cerebral palsy, slapping her forehead with the ice cream cone instead of eating it.

"All right," he said, putting the metals back into small labeled boxes in his desk drawer. "I don't know how that works, perhaps on the principles of acupressure, but I do know they are excellent tests of vitamin and mineral deficiencies. We'll run samples through our lab, of course, but I wanted a clinical impression for myself." He offered his hand in farewell. "We'll send you the results and my suggestions within two weeks. Then of course the decision is yours. I wish you luck in either case."

He almost clicked his heels in dismissal, far more Swiss than Hungarian. I was stunned by the demonstrations. I was sure I was the same each time; yet I couldn't find my nose. My nose.

When we left the office, I looked to see if the old couple was still there; they weren't. Bob's face was pensive; he shook his head several times as though arguing with someone invisible.

"Did he really push as hard on my arm each time?"

"He rolled up his sleeve so I could watch the muscles of his forearm. If he was faking, he fooled me. Acupressure? Is that what he said?"

"Does it matter? He said he didn't understand it. Bob, I couldn't find my nose."

He shook his head again. "I saw."

We reached the parking garage, on the corner of the local shopping area. I turned to Bob as we pulled out. "Do you think we could drive toward Brownsville?"

In his surprise, he stalled the car, and we sat partway out on the street, cars honking at us, while we waited for the flooded engine to recover.

"Of course," he said. "If you're sure you really want to."

"I'm sure," I said, and took a map of New York from the glove compartment, searching for familiar streets to guide us; seeing for the first time that Brooklyn and Queens were both on Long Island, off the mainland of the United States, like Manhattan. As we began to drive, I found Kings Highway, Ocean Parkway, Pitkin Avenue, all names I knew in isolation, as separate streets unconnected to each other. I'd never learned Brooklyn's surface, knew only subway stops or views from the tracks of elevated trains.

From the map, I directed Bob toward Eastern Parkway, my stomach clenching more with each ten blocks. The streets were black and Spanish, progressively poorer as we drove east, until we came to the old dividing line at Howard Avenue. We were still a half-hour's walk from where I'd lived, but now it was territory that was once home.

We were the only whites around; I'd be afraid to step out if we got a flat. Bob turned off the engine, his face shocked, staring at the surreal landscape ahead. In front of us the streets were empty, no one moving across them, most of the buildings razed, the blocks reduced to brick-red rubble gleaming with broken glass. Farther on, a few scattered buildings were still standing amidst the rubble, their windows boarded up with tin and wood, havens for junkies and rats. One burned-out building displayed flat squares of painted plaster on the open brick, once the pastel walls of apartments. There were still curtains at a few windows, and a clothesline with fresh washing ran across a demolished courtyard.

I put my face against the window, tears running down my

cheeks. "We have to go back. It's not here. Nothing's left. It's all in my head."

Bob turned the car without answering. He was pale and tense. "It's not like Watts," he said, after a long silence. And then,"Are you sure your block is gone? We didn't go that far. It might still be standing."

I shook my head; I didn't want to know. I wasn't ready. With each block we drove, a chunk of memory broke loose. Until I saw the present, the past was still alive. Seeing what really was out there changed even the memory, tingeing it with the present and defiling it. I blew my nose as we headed west again, a new thought occurring to me. Schabtau might be a phony, but I couldn't touch my nose. And his diet might work whether or not he was a phony. Magic is everywhere.

"HERE . . . AND FOURTEEN-CARAT GOLD FOR THE RING. DIAmonds are my birthstone," she said.

"Like Mona's," my mother answered.

We were in the waiting room of the hospital, my grandfather upstairs with pneumonia. It was still April, a week since the ambulance had come for him. My mother held Fannie's hand under the floor lamp, absently turning it so that the facets of the diamond made moving rainbows of the light.

"So it's a birthday present?" she asked. "Obbie gave it to you for your birthday?" She let go of the hand reluctantly; Fannie too seemed reluctant to let go.

"You want to see, Mona?" she asked, stretching out her arm. "Maybe someday when you're all grown up, your husband will give you a diamond like this."

I touched her fingers tentatively, staring at the blue-white jewel. I decided I didn't like diamonds: they were cold and hard and not at all romantic. Not like the tiger's eye I once saw in a teacher's ring at school. I was sorry my birthstone was a diamond if that's what I had to have if I ever got jewelry for a present.

When she was satisfied I'd looked long enough, Fannie dropped into the armchair next to me. She took another LifeSaver from her purse, and offered me the pack; I picked off the green one at the top for an orange underneath before returning the candy to her hand. Her knuckles were red and chapped from washing too many dishes; but the ring still sparkled in the light. My mother lit another cigarette and Fannie began her story once more.

"He took me out to dinner at the chinks, and we were going to go to a movie, maybe even to the Fox downtown, and then right in the middle of the table, he puts down this little white box and he doesn't say anything. Just grinning like a monkey. I tell you, when I opened it I let out such a shriek that everyone stares at me, and the waiters come running to see if I got a cockroach in my soup. I told Obbie, 'I know you love me, but who ever expected a diamond?' "

My mother crossed her legs again, elegant in her high heels and shiny stockings and pulled down the hem of her skirt; then she buttoned her cardigan. There were five cigarettes in her ashtray. In the silence, I stood up and walked across the brown linoleum to the wall clock. The little hand was almost at the five and the big hand was on the ten. I called to her across the room. "Is it time to see Grandpa?"

"A few more minutes," she answered. "But I told you, you have to wait down here."

"I know," I said, glaring at her. "I'm not a moron. You told me at least ten times."

She glared back at me, her face pinched, and brushed her hand across her forehead. "Mona, don't push me now. Try to act decent for a change."

"I just wish I could see him," I muttered. They kept telling me he was getting better, that they'd even send him home soon, but it was different when they wouldn't let me see him for myself.

"It's a good thing Sam's working again," Fannie said, a few minutes later. "Of course, we'd pay all the hospital bills if we had to."

My mother didn't answer and Fannie looked over at her; when she went on, her voice was sharper. "I wish your father would be a little more thankful to Obbie for his help."

My mother was staring into space; answering Fannie, she looked as though she couldn't quite remember what they were talking about. "You shouldn't pay so much attention," she murmured. "You can't change either one of them. Even when Obbie was in the eighth grade, when Poppa wanted him to become a teacher, he'd go to the pool hall in the afternoon. Poppa says he'd drag him out by the ear, and the next day he'd be back at the pool hall until Poppa got him. They always fought."

She spread her fingers to check the nail polish she'd put on before we left, and took a file from her pocketbook, an odd smile on her face. "Or his swimming off the pier by the East River when Poppa warned him not to, and his friend Heschie getting his leg crushed between two steamers. Poppa almost killed Obbie that time, hitting him with his belt and my mother screaming to stop it."

Fannie stood up to walk around the chairs, stretching in her Persian lamb coat. "It's just that your father doesn't appreciate him," she complained. "Obbie makes a good living, he's a good husband, and he tries to be a good son, but Poppa acts like he doesn't notice. Obbie says he'd never turn his back on our Richie the way Poppa did with him up there in that hospital bed, no matter what Richie did."

My mother's face soured, and Fannie backed off, her hands outspread in front of her. "I'm sorry, Helen. I take it back. I'm upset in here myself. I don't like hospitals."

My mother's voice was low. "Poppa was tired the other night; I told you he didn't mean anything by it. It hurts Poppa too that they don't get along better." Lighting another cigarette, she blew smoke into the air. "He doesn't get on so well with Sam all the time either, if you want to know. If I didn't insist . . ." She took in my listening face, stopped herself, looked up at the clock.

After two quick puffs, she ground her cigarette into the ashtray and stood up. "It's time. Mona, you stay with Fannie. When Fannie comes up, you wait for me here. You can finish your homework while you're waiting. I'll tell Grandpa you're down here."

She stooped to kiss me, and I lifted my face, a mirror to hers, reflecting back her own fear and anger and envy. Both of us had tight pale mouths, white faces, large eyes. But I was dark like my father, and she looked like her dead mother.

I didn't watch her while she waited for the elevator but opened my notebook to my homework. I was the smartest in the class; the homework was so easy it didn't even distract me. I decided to write all the answers with my right hand instead of my left to make it interesting for myself. When I wrote with my right hand, I was Noma instead of Mona, and I lived in a real house with trees around it, in a small town that had very few people. And nobody ever shouted.

Noma had her own room too, and a sister who liked all the things she did. When they went outside they had a yard with swings and a seesaw all to themselves, and a little forest to hide in that their mother and father and grandpa didn't know about. And when it snowed, everything was white, and there was no garbage underneath.

Tightening my hold on the pencil, I concentrated harder. Sometimes, I could almost believe that I'd turn into Noma if I could get my letters perfect. For a moment, I forgot where I really was, and became Noma, stretched out on the grass watching a squirrel jump toward me, holding a nut in his paws and chittering. The grass was almost as high as my head, hiding me within it, and the uncut tops waved delicately in the breeze, just like in the picture book I'd brought from the library, when I was Mona.

Fannie touched my shoulder, making me jump. "I'm going up now," she said softly. "Your mommy will be down soon." I put my arms around her soft body, and she hugged me before leaving. Looking around, I saw the waiting room had filled up while I daydreamed, with people talking in every corner, and women crying.

That was the season of Jake, of my grandfather's pneumonia and Selim's prayers, of my father's losing one more job before Obbie found him another. Most of my mother's savings from her singing were used up while my father was out of work, even with Jake helping us, and even more money vanished in my grandpa's hospital bills. I didn't know how many of the bills Obbie paid; even this much I'd only pieced together now.

But the memories were spiraling in toward the center; no matter that the reconstructions were made slowly and half against my will. Jake and Selim were already in the past again, enigmatic as they would always have to be, but no longer reverberating nightmarishly, now down to human form and size. Isaac and Isaac's murder of Rose on a bright October afternoon lay ahead whenever I could face them, and after Isaac, lay the center of the spiral.

June had begun in the two weeks since I'd seen Schabtau. Today was Friday, my last class over at noon, and I had some time before my appointment at Memorial for my sixth treatment. On my way back from the college, I parked the Audi outside our apartment building, and stopped inside for the day's mail.

Schabtau's report had finally been sent, packed in a thick manila folder on the marble table near the mailboxes, the envelope too large to fit with standard letters. Carrying it out, I crossed to a bench by the Park and opened the envelope to the roar of bulldozers ripping up the concrete of the playground behind me. The chain-link fence had been removed already, while a billboard announced that a new playground was to be constructed on the site from funds donated by a private citizen in honor of his dead mother.

Hunched against the noise and dust, I read Schabtau's recommendations: twenty pills a day of vitamins and minerals; six glasses of carrot, beet, and spinach juice; and the incomprehensible diet sheet. No meat, no fish, no eggs, no cheese or milk. Like the old lady in his waiting room, I wondered if you had to eat seeds like a bird.

Schabtau had said chemo was poison, but I felt stronger than I had in months; and for the first time, I couldn't find any nodes of lymphoma on myself. Still, I thought Schabtau's diet might be worth following along with Chou's treatment. Later in the day, I'd be vomiting again, locked in the bedroom for the weekend, the shades down because the sun hurt my eyes. I needed yeast at the Health Food Store on Broadway; I decided to walk there while I could.

The store had been owned for years by a dour old man who turned it dry and dusty; two years before, he'd sold it to an actor and his wife, and retired to Florida. They'd renovated thoroughly and exorcised his ghost, hanging pots of ivy from ceiling beams, jamming the aisles with wooden barrels of fruit, and adding books.

Ron worked in the store intermittently, leaving most of the work to his wife; the bulk of his time went to auditions. He looked different almost every time I saw him, depending on the role he was trying out for. Today, he looked grubby and slightly desperate, someone you'd hurry past if he wanted the time at a street corner.

I asked if he was going to an audition, he said he was, and I told him I couldn't understand how he changed the way he looked so drastically from day to day.

To show me, he touched muscles in his cheeks and near his mouth, deliberately relaxed them, and became ten years younger, handsome, and reliable.

"It's a TV shot, a soap," he explained. "It's work, even if it's a soap; my agent says I should try for it." He tensed the muscles once more, changing back into a failure. I clapped and he bowed deeply, with a flourish.

"What's for today?" he asked. "More carrots?"

"Carrots, yeast, and some new vitamins." From Schabtau's diet.

Ron ran a kind of clinic here; I spoke on impulse.

"You know anyone on a cancer diet?"

His face lost all expression. If he'd had any doubts about me before, he didn't anymore. He leaned back against the shelves, and crossed his arms over his chest.

"You really interested?"

"Yeah. Personal reasons. In my family." We were both talking like the punk in his soap opera.

"I have two customers I know about myself. Both terminal cancer. They gave up on them. They went down to this guy in Missouri and he put them on a whole diet. Juices, no animal protein, apricot kernels, coffee enemas, raw onion and garlic. The works. One of them even had his fillings taken out because some dentist told him mercury keeps the body from fighting back."

He made a face and a quick gesture toward his nose.

"I can't imagine a dentist working on either of them, you can smell them coming a block away. But they're well. Almost two years. And them I know myself."

I tried to sound casual. "What's his name? The doctor?"

"Clark. Everyone in the business knows about him. And I also know about a guy in Brooklyn, but I don't know if he's so good. I never met anybody who saw him."

"Schabtau?"

"You know him?"

"I've heard of him. And heard him on the radio. These customers. They really had cancer? Diagnosed?"

"Definitely. Yeah. But I didn't see them before, only since. I don't have the store that long."

"What's he doing in Missouri?"

"He comes from there. Baptist Sunday-school teacher. One of the women told me he was going to die himself, and then somehow he found this diet, and got cured and started taking other people. It's sort of his mission."

"Home remedies from Baptist Missouri."

He didn't smile. "If I had cancer, I'd try it."

The bell rang as another customer walked in; I left Ron a list of what I needed and retreated to the back of the store while he began to recommend tryptophan for insomnia. Once he'd given me pantothenic acid and PABA for shin splints I'd gotten jogging, before I was sick. At least he knew two people on the same diet, even if he didn't know Schabtau.

I picked out another copy of *The Roots of Coincidence* so I could return Phil's, and found a guide to meditation I'd wanted for months. When I first saw Einstein's *Relativity* in the occult section of a midtown bookstore, I'd laughed. But now I understood the filing system. On these shelves, *Relativity* was next to *Life After Death.* Picking two vegetarian cookbooks by their covers, I saw Ron was alone again. At the register, I asked about the paper hex signs hanging from the rafters.

"A friend brought them from Pennsylvania," Ron said. "Amish country. I had a guy in last week, drunk, giving me a hard time. I pulled down two of the signs, and did an exorcism number." Bellowing, he rose on tiptoes, his arms extended toward me. "Beware! The devil is present in this room! Flee before you fall into the pit!"

Unclipping the signs he dropped his voice to normal. "I figured he'd think I was nutsier than him, but he rolled his eyes so I saw the whites and ran like hell."

I ran my fingers gently over the patterns. "Are they real?"

"Supposed to be. At least if you're Amish."

"Do you have extras?"

He handed them to me. "If you want, get them Xeroxed next door."

I ran my fingers back and forth, fascinated by the patterns. "Is it supposed to work if you make a copy?"

"So far as I know, the strength is supposed to be in the design itself. My friend took a class in witchcraft and that's what he told me. Just bring them back when you're done." He looked embarrassed. "It sounds funny, but I feel safer with them up."

Next door, I had twenty-five copies made; if I was going to use them against the evil eye, I'd buy enough. Holding my books and Schabtau's papers, knowing that in an hour Chou would be calculating my dose of chemo as much by intuition as by science, I wondered if the hex signs would have stopped Mrs. Goldstein. If my mother had the hex signs when Mrs. Goldstein cursed her, would my brother have lived?

When I returned the originals to Ron, I told him Bob would pick up the rest of my order later in the day. I put the copies in the envelope from Schabtau and carried them and the books in a cab to Memorial.

When I reached Hematology, I looked around for familiar faces. I'd never spoken with most of the other patients, but I knew many of them by sight. The clinic was open for lymphomas and Hodgkins' only one afternoon a week and two mornings. I didn't know who came in the mornings but I'd begun to know who came on Friday afternoons.

The lady who knitted from her wheelchair had finished her third sweater for her youngest grandson, and the boy on crutches had ended treatment and gone back to college to wait out the five years he needed before he could consider himself cured. I never saw the little girl with a brain tumor again, and a nurse told me that one old man I talked with on my second visit had died: pneumonia as a complication of the chemo.

We were linked by a common bond, all of us drafted into a war of annihilation. I shared my reading on vitamins and touted Dewey to two women in their thirties who'd fallen out of remission and were told they had only a year to live.

In turn, Mrs. Nettlebaum told me of the nutritionist she saw who ordered meat three times a day and steak for breakfast. I heard of where to go for illegal Laetrile injections; who'd heard of whole-body irradiation; who had looked into heat treatment at Roswell Park, where they raised the body temperature to 107 ° in the hope of killing off the fast-growing malignant cells.

Bob was going to be late; he'd warned me he had a meeting with the new chairman of the cardiology department at his hospital. A shake-up was in the wind, the new man wanting to bring in his own people, the old staff powerless within the hospital hierarchy to stop him. The last time a shake-up occurred, one senior professor arrived to find his desk moved from his office to a closet cubicle, his books locked in and a new key put on the door. He'd had tenure, so he couldn't be dismissed, but he gave up trying to work under fire after a year, and moved to Pittsburgh and another appointment.

Bob taught part time. He said it kept him more alert with patients. If the chairman didn't take to Bob, he'd have to scramble for a part-time slot at another hospital.

I scanned the waiting room, but it was almost empty. Sighing, I began walking to a seat when my number was called for the routine blood test.

In the corridor, a nurse put a thermometer in my mouth and attached a blood pressure sleeve.

"No emergencies today," she announced. "The doctors are zipping through."

I nodded glumly; I hated waiting around for Chou, but I'd rather wait than see him without Bob. If Chou was depressed today, I'd feel hopeless even if everything he said was good, his tone more powerful than his words.

The nurse sneezed, blew her nose on a Kleenex from her pocket. I backed away and she apologized. "It's allergy," she said hoarsely. "Those damned roses in the vase at the main desk. Every spring, the patients look at me like I'm Typhoid Mary. Not that I blame you," she added. "What do you do about your kids getting colds?"

I shrugged, too anxious about seeing Chou alone to pay her much attention once she said it wasn't a cold. "Lock them in the closet until my blood count goes up."

She smiled, making notes on my chart before leading me down the hall to an examination room. "So it's a stupid question. Your pressure's a little high, by the way."

"My pressure goes up every time I come here."

Her hand on the doorknob, she paused. "But you look terrific. Nothing like when you first came."

Thanking her, grateful she'd noticed, sorry I hadn't been more friendly, I shut the door. Changing into the hospital gown, I perched on the examining table, nervously feeling my neck and groin for nodes. They could pop up overnight, Chou said, the disease was unpredictable; that I hadn't felt any this morning didn't mean they weren't there now. At least the nurse had said I looked good.

I heard Chou's voice in the corridor, and stiffened. "She has to be admitted immediately. With her white count down to eight hundred, I guarantee she'll spike a fever from her own gut bacteria by tonight."

Off the table, peeking out the door, my heart thumping, I saw his receding back. Was my count eight hundred? I couldn't go into the hospital just like that, I needed Bob; and they had to let me say good-bye to the boys.

Minutes passed before he came back, but then he went into another room. No one came for me. Peering through the partly open door, I saw the nurse with allergies hurry by; I stepped out to intercept her. "Do you know my count? I heard Dr. Chou getting ready to admit someone."

Patting my arm, she tried to soothe me. "Relax. Not you. Your count's fine."

I went back to the table and stared at the white walls, trying to calm down. There was nothing to look at but a metal desk, a chair, the sink and a scale. I'd been waiting twenty minutes and Bob still wasn't here. I picked up one of my books, began leafing through it. On my third visit, I waited two hours in a cubicle like this, learning only later that Chou had had an emergency bone marrow to do, and an admission for acute lymphocytic leukemia. If I could only concentrate while I waited, I could work on my outline for the course in memory. But I couldn't even read a mindless paperback here.

I leafed through, only half attending, the cookbook looking more like a chemistry test, one-third of the pages filled with tables for balancing protein requirements. Corn plus milk. Bulgur plus soy beans. I didn't know what a soy bean looked like. Or bulgur. I looked bulgur up in the index: it was a kind of unrefined wheat. The tables said grains and beans had to be eaten together for complete protein balance. A quarter cup of beans for each serving of grain. The only bean dish I knew was baked beans. I followed an asterisk to the bottom of the page. "Beans may cause gassiness until you become accustomed to the diet."

How would the kids feel about farting in class?

I tried the other book, by a mellow lady from Berkeley. When she began, she didn't know what a soy bean was. But she insisted it was easier than it looked, and that you could balance your foods over a whole day, didn't have to with each meal. Eat beans for dinner and fart at home. We could open all the windows and blame it on McCrae.

In the next chapter, she wasn't quite so mellow. I had to bake all my own bread. Mix, knead, wait an hour, shape, wait an hour, bake an hour. Four hours per loaf. I didn't have that kind of time. I wondered if I could buy my bread at the Health Food Store.

I checked my watch; another ten minutes gone. Bob might still be with the new chief of his department at the hospital, and not just careless of the time, of Friday's midtown traffic. With a pencil, I started marking possible recipes, but I didn't know what anything tasted like. Bulgur-lentil pilaf with raisins and pine nuts. But it wasn't for fun anyway; and no one else had to try it, they could still eat hamburgers.

I heard Chou's rapid walk outside, heard him pause before knocking. As he opened the door, he smiled widely; he looked rested, and his gait was bouncy. His mood would be up today, his presence reassuring no matter what the news. But I still wanted Bob with me; I could never remember what Chou said.

Skimming the chart on the desk, he spoke to me while reading. His voice had a slight lilt even when he was down; I thought he'd grown up with Chinese, with tonal changes part of the language. "Where's Bob?"

"Late. Aren't doctors always late?"

His smile was gay, his almond eyes opaque in the fluorescent light. "So my wife says. But you always have patients who need you. What are you reading?"

I hesitated; I hadn't told him about seeing Schabtau. "Vegetarian cookbooks. I saw a nutritionist two weeks ago."

He flushed for the moment, his voice suddenly sardonic. "Did he tell you to stop chemo?"

I nodded, embarrassed in front of him, as though it was me

who'd made the suggestion. I cleared my throat. "Would you object to my following his diet?"

Shrugging, he turned to the sink to wash his hands, scrubbing them forcefully, pulling at his fingers. "Did someone tell you that a friend of their Aunt Sadie got a food cure? Without all those nasty drugs? It's always a friend of Aunt Sadie's or a second cousin of Uncle Harry's, and people like me are keeping the truth from the world."

I wanted to put on my clothes and run.

"I wasn't considering stopping chemo," I said carefully. "But there's a lot of medical literature lately about diet. Even about cooked beef being a carcinogen. I just wanted to know how you felt about it."

My hands were shaking as much as my voice. What if he said he wouldn't treat me? But that was crazy, he wouldn't do that. I stuffed the books into my purse, my head down so I wouldn't see his face.

When I looked up, he was controlled again, his voice cool. "Sorry. I don't care what you eat as long as you get a decent balance. I just saw a twenty-year-old man with Stage II Hodgkin's; I could save him but he doesn't believe in drugs. You got the backlash. Now tell me how you're doing."

I never knew what to answer; I always felt like saying I was fine as though it were merely a polite question. But not now. Today, I needed to tell him how wonderful his medicines were. I tried to remember my list of details. I'd been rehearsing my answer all day, but couldn't remember any of it now. "No more nodes that I can feel," I said finally. "Even in my elbow. And I can climb two flights of stairs without panting."

I was very proud of that, and took the risk of a small joke. I wanted him to smile with me this afternoon. "Next week I'm going to jog."

He looked sharply at me before smiling; the tension still between us vanished. Then I lay back and he began to prod my body, jabbing my chest with outstretched fingers, drumming to feel the outlines of liver and spleen. His touch was heavy today, as he prodded to feel what maybe wasn't there. I winced in pain, and smelled mint on his breath. Last time it was cinnamon. My heart was pounding so loudly, I could barely hear his voice.

"All neck nodes gone," he said. "And the one in your wrist is pin-sized. Your liver and spleen feel normal. For the first time."

He looked up abstractedly, his fingers still feeling their way around my thighs. "Have you cut down your work yet? Spending more time at home?"

"A bit," I answered, never understanding why he always asked. "I've stopped research for now."

Bob opened the door, saw Chou over me, and stepped quietly into the room. He was pale, his face thinned down, almost ascetic. He waited for a moment, watching Chou intently, then bent to put his coat and briefcase on the chair. I smiled up at him, to reassure him that all looked well; grateful that he'd come in time.

"How's your wife doing with chemo?" Chou asked. "Still problems?"

Bob looked guarded, glanced at me, and smiled tightly. "The chemo's beginning to feel worse than the lymphoma."

Straightening, Chou arched his back, stretching out the kinks, wincing. "Still irritable? Depressed?"

"Still irritable. Edgy all the time. Unpredictable. And she cried for two days when she stopped the prednisone this time."

I started to interrupt, but Chou cut me off with a wave of his hand. "Everyone's affected by the prednisone, Mona. You don't have to feel ashamed of it. It's a steroid, it affects the brain directly. You know that from your own work."

I shrugged, angry at them for ganging up on me. Chou moved to his desk, still talking patiently.

"Most patients get depressed and irritable; some people get paranoid; a few get manic. Last winter, one of my patients accused his wife of poisoning him; another, in a manic episode, tried to put all his savings into a wacky scheme for making paper clothes. Luckily, he lives in a small town and the bank manager called his wife. The drugs are toxic; if we had a choice, we wouldn't use them. Bob, if Mona seems worse with this next cycle, call me and I'll prescribe Mellaril."

"I won't take it."

"You will if I prescribe it," he said shortly. "From what you've both told me, you can't judge your own mood. It would be a small dose, not dangerous."

Looking down, he began to write prescriptions for Bob to fill at the basement pharmacy while I went on to the chemo room for my two injections, double-checking the dosages against my total body weight and surface. He'd made an error once, a minor one, an error of addition in which he'd ordered more pills than I could take in the days allotted; the pharmacist had refused to fill it and made Bob wait until he could locate Chou and read the prescription back to him. But the total dosage, while restricted to a certain range by the evidence available, was decided by him on each visit, depending on the change in nodes from the time before, and the reaction of my bone marrow to the drugs. A matter of clinical intuition.

"A question," Bob said. "We're planning to travel out West this summer. Any reason not to?"

Chou thought a moment, began to speak, and altered what he was going to say. "If Mona's count is over two thousand she can go. But stay within three hours of a major hospital. If you should get sick, you can't risk a longer drive."

Bob looked toward me quickly, to see if I'd acknowledged Chou's words. He wanted to vacation near his parents in the Sierras and I was fighting for a tour of Arizona and Utah with the boys. We hadn't been West since my parents' deaths.

I wanted to explore places I hadn't seen since then, while I still could, and not spend the summer visiting with his parents in a cabin.

Chou handed Bob the scrips and leaned back in his chair, his eyes bright. "No one has asked me how Mona's doing," he said.

My heart skipped a beat, and I felt a wave of nausea. Chou grinned at me, his voice lilting again. "You're doing very well. Very well. Better than I ever expected. Almost no nodes on examination. We'll plan one more round of chemo in a month, after the one today, and then we'll schedule the radiation." He paused dramatically, enjoying himself. "You may be in a complete remission by the end of chemo, before we begin radiation."

I'd been sitting on the table as we talked; with his words, the blood left my head, I saw black spots in front of my eyes. If I understood him, he was saying I might not die.

"A complete remission means no sign of disease?" I asked.

He nodded, his eyes fixed on mine.

"You think I might have no sign of disease even before the radiation?"

Bright with tension, he repeated himself. "Before radiation.

The radiation and the chemo after that would be extra, insurance."

"You're saying I might be cured?" I was whispering.

He rocked back and forth on his heels, his face intense and youthful. "I think some patients are getting cures with this regimen. I think you may be one of them."

"More than ten years," Bob said.

Chou turned to him. "Mona's natural life span."

I started to cry and Chou walked quietly out the door, shutting it gently behind him. Bob and I ran to each other.

Standing in the middle of the cubicle, I clung to him and he to me. Holding me so tightly that I hurt, he picked me up and danced around the room, planting kisses on my head and neck.

I was giggling uncontrollably, giggling and crying all at once. Five months now since the diagnosis; I'd forgotten what it felt like to have this kind of hope. The tie on the gown undid and Bob ran his hands across my bare back, caressing my skin, nuzzling me, crying and laughing with me. His body was hard against mine, his penis erect and hard within his clothing. He kissed me full on the mouth, not thinking of germs, not afraid of hurting me, not afraid of catching my lymphoma either; and I clung to him, our tongues searching, entwined, each of us wanting to swallow up the other. He loved me, that was what was wrong all these months, he loved me and he couldn't bear to have me die.

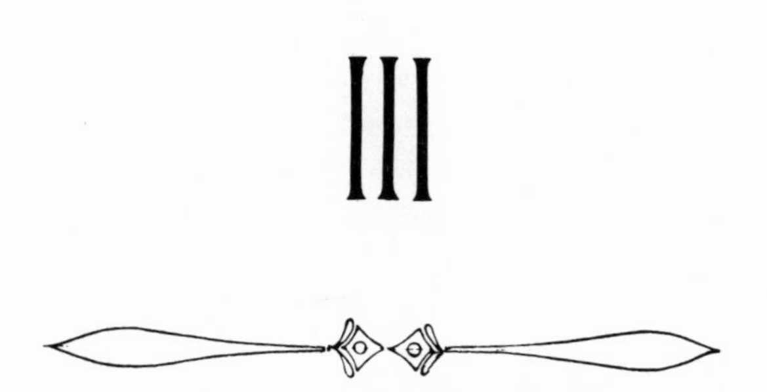
III

I WAS SICK FOR THE USUAL THREE DAYS AFTER THE CHEMO, BUT this time I hardly cared; throwing up was a small price to pay for a possible cure. Chou hadn't promised a cure; he only thought I had a chance, but even a chance was infinitely more than he'd ever offered before.

Ten years was long enough for me to go on living as though I had some future, but I'd forgotten how it felt not to have an inexorable execution date. In the next few days, Bob and I began to let ourselves say we might do something in a year, or two, or five, sounding like normal people for the first time since the diagnosis. I even caught myself thinking of the boys finishing college.

We couldn't tell them the news when we hadn't ever told them that ten years was the most we could hope for. But they knew we'd seen the doctor, and they knew right away that everything was changed. Although the chemo left me as sick as always, Bob told me that the mood of the apartment was lighter; and the boys sounded less frightened when they came to the bedroom to ask how I felt.

Four days later, I was well enough to celebrate; we had dinner at a restaurant in Chinatown. Neither child said anything about the change during the drive, but I saw Dan look from Bob's face to mine and nudge Adam when he thought I didn't notice.

At the table, Adam methodically dropped the broad, flat Chinese noodles into his bowl of wonton soup, his round face pensive. He spoke suddenly. "How come you and Dad look so happy?"

I turned to Bob, hesitating before answering; he took over gingerly. "We look happy?"

Adam nodded and dropped his eyes once more, as if adding noodles to his soup in the right pattern really mattered to him. Dan stopped eating to watch Bob's face.

"We look happy because Mom's doctor said the treatments are going better than he expected," Bob said.

"What does that mean?" Dan asked tensely. "She wasn't doing so well before?"

Bob's answer was matter of fact, dry; Dan and Adam were too perceptive to fool with, and he wanted to drop the subject quickly.

"It means she'll probably need less medicine than the doctor thought at first."

The boys exchanged looks. Each appeared to find the other satisfied; and only I knew the effort that went into Bob's simple words. After a brief pause, Adam asked me to show him once again how to eat with chopsticks.

When we left the restaurant, I insisted on a movie. Later in the week my blood count would drop; for the moment, it was high enough for a crowded movie to be safe; we decided on an old film in the Village, *Creature from the Black Lagoon.* I ate popcorn throughout the film, loving the struggle between good and evil, so black and white and definite, thinking how satisfied I'd be to get my visualizations so crisp.

After the boys went to bed, sorry only that they had school and couldn't sleep late the next morning, Bob and I showered together, soaping each other slowly and ceremonially. Unable to wait, we made love in the shower, Bob entering me as I braced myself against the corner wall. During the night, we made love again, and again the night after, with the shades up so that we could see the sky from our bed, a starless sky made pink by the diffused lights of the city below. By the end of the week, my bottom was so sore I could hardly sit, as though I were a virgin bride.

The college year ended a few days later, just as Phil and I finished writing our final paper. I was taking the summer off, and in the fall I would have my office on another floor; we took his car and went out for a final sad lunch at the Italian restaurant we'd eaten at each Wednesday for the last two years.

At the end of the meal, I handed Phil the box I'd been holding on my lap, my surprise gift for him. It was a locked diary, to be opened only with an engraved key. *For Coincidences,* the key said. Phil turned it over in his huge hands several times.

"I brought something for you too," he said abruptly. "Stay here. It's in the trunk of my car."

I sipped coffee and looked around the dim restaurant; for whatever reason, it catered to faculty and administration, but not students. When Phil came back, he carried a bulky package wrapped in brown paper; it was so big it blocked his view, and he stumbled against more than one chair while threading his way back to our table.

"I won it," he said, his eyes sparkling in anticipation. "You have to promise to keep it in your new office. To remind you of me."

Propping the bundle against my chair, I began to tear the paper, oblivious to the crowded tables around us, pulling off endless bits of tape, feeling for the shape inside.

Phil stood watching me. He smiled mischievously. "I've been told to tell you my little girl thinks you don't deserve it, and she'll take it if you don't like it."

By now, the people at nearby tables were watching too. I finally unwound the last layer of paper. A five-foot stuffed animal faced me.

"King Kong. In memory of my lesser moods," Phil said dryly.

I giggled, and circled around the creature to give Phil a hug. When I reached him, he put his arms around me, and what began lightly shifted unexpectedly. We began to kiss frantically: on the mouth; the neck; around the eyes; all kinds of emotions pouring out at once. It was almost impossible to pull away; when we finally separated, I was shaky, my heart pounding. I felt the other customers staring after us as we left.

Phil held the door for me; I inched past him with King Kong in my arms, more aware of his body under his clothes than during all our years together.

The drive back to campus took only a few minutes. I mulled over what had happened. It wasn't that I'd never thought about going to bed with Phil. We spent too much time alone for either of us never to think about it. When Bob stopped touching me after I got sick I imagined having an affair with Phil. But that was just inside my head; we'd never kissed like this before.

In the parking lot, Phil stopped next to my Audi. When he reached for me, I raised my mouth to his. We'd been taken by surprise in the restaurant, not knowing how much we needed to acknowledge what we felt. Now we kissed long and thoroughly, with the intimacy we'd never allowed ourselves before, both admitting the end of our private world.

While I retrieved Kong from the back seat, Phil came around

to open the door and help me out. "I'll see you in September," he said. "Let me know if you change your mind about the lab."

I smiled, and shook my head firmly, turning to wave once as I drove off. I didn't know what I was going to do once I stopped working with animals, but the decision to stop had been too hard to make to go back on now.

After dinner, I brought Kong out, wondering what Bob would make of it; of course, he understood. He'd worked intimately with other women over and over in the course of his hospital years; watching his face, I remembered the painted wooden train someone had given him at the end of his internship. A nurse on a cardiac-arrest team; I'd never been able to remember her name.

During the next week, the few remaining nodes disappeared, and my original elation changed slowly to fear that Chou was too optimistic. I'd turned to other treatments because Chou didn't promise enough; I'd have expected to lose interest in them now that he thought he might have a cure. But the chance of a cure with chemo only made me more desperate not to miss out. Now I had to do more for myself. Not less.

Chou had said I was doing better than he'd ever expected. He assumed it was his drugs; if I told him about the other treatments, he'd probably shrug them off. But Schabtau's vitamins, Dewey's visualizations, and my own efforts to understand myself were all mixed up with his medicines, all confounded into one mass, with no way to disentangle them. However good the chemo, I had to assume I was doing better than Chou expected because of what else I did.

One morning, when everyone left for the day, I took Ron's hex signs from my folder. Feeling silly but determined, I planted them in all the rooms, beginning with our bedroom: two under the pad of the waterbed and one behind the headboard; one behind my favorite Utah photo, in Canyonlands. I slipped one behind the kitchen calendar; one behind the pegboard; another on the door of my medicine cabinet, behind a new list of vitamins and minerals. More went under couch cushions, on the assumption Bob never picked them up; on the underside of chairs; and beneath the convertible couch we'd just bought for the dining room. With a few still left, I slipped one under the mattress of each boy's bed.

I felt peculiar, united to my grandparents and Mrs. Goldstein, and, at the same time, half crazy. I had no idea what Bob would say if he found them, was sure only that I didn't want Dan or Adam to know. But the apartment felt safer when I finished.

After that, I broke out the new cookbooks, determined to follow Schabtau's diet more strictly than ever. The boys ate hamburgers whenever I gave them a choice, but Bob was willing to try everything. As I chewed black bread from the Health Food Store, and kasha and onions, or dipped whole scallions into salt, I felt as if I were returning to my father's childhood on his farm in Poland, with some part of myself making up for years of deprivation.

The day before my seventh and last chemo, the second week of July, I went off to Bloomingdale's. I'd bought no clothes since the diagnosis in January, not wanting to decorate a body that I hated; now I was ready for a shopping spree. Applying gray eye shadow and liner at home, face make-up and lipstick, I looked strange to myself, but better looking than I was used to. Even José smiled debonairely, while John tipped his hat at the door and whistled for a cab without my asking. In the cab, I felt like a child on holiday, sorry only that Ellen was rehearsing for a show and unable to go out with me.

Of course, Bloomingdale's overwhelmed me right away. Getting lost, I wandered through the lingerie department and impulsively bought several pairs of panties. One was held together by pink ribbons to be untied deftly at the last moment by one's lover; I had it wrapped separately to take with me on vacation in August.

For all my efforts at home, I wasn't quite in fashion, my skirt a bit too long, my shoes too narrow, and my make-up simply a decade out of style. A saleswoman asked me superciliously if I needed help; she was barely older than my oldest students and I turned her down. But I stopped to watch a make-up demonstration, a free promotional, then volunteered to have a new face made for myself.

Under all her glitter, the saleswoman was about my own age, and eager to explain her work. Remaking my face in stages, she showed me how to lighten the shadows under my eyes, how to accent my cheekbones, and how to apply eyeliner only to the end of my upper lids for the current year's look. When she was done, I gazed at her creation in the mirror, admiring the mannequin reflected back at me, disliking only the new raspberry lipstick, and thanked her; she was proud of the results and pressed her samples on me. For the rest of the afternoon, the saleswomen were more attentive than usual, responsive to the expert make-up; I enjoyed myself, and remembered how different it was going shopping with my mother.

When the boys came home from day camp, Dan, two weeks short of his tenth birthday, surveyed me. "You look like someone else," he said. "Is that all from make-up?"

"Do you like it?"

"You look like someone in a magazine."

I turned to Adam and he shook his head in an emphatic no. "You look pretty but you don't look like you."

But Bob was pleased, smiling as I spooned out lentil soup at dinner, teasing me that I didn't quite match the peasant food. At night, I was still made-up, unwilling to wash it off because I wasn't sure I'd ever go through the trouble of applying it myself; and I'd put on my new black panties. Admiring me, he stood at the side of the bed.

"Bloomingdale's?"

I nodded, glowing in his appraisal. "She said my boyfriend would love them."

As he rolled into bed toward me, I thought again that the problem all these months was fear. Later, falling asleep, I hoped we'd still make love if Chou's treatment turned out not to be a cure. Still later, anxious about seeing Chou the next day and sleeping badly, I woke and padded into the bathroom to wash the ruined make-up from my face. Wide awake, I moved to the living room, and sat under Bob's avocado tree watching the sun rise over Central Park, enjoying my memory of the day before and allowing myself to return to childhood yet again.

My father's sister Malkah was married at the beginning of May, just after my eighth birthday, just after my grandpa recovered from pneumonia and came home. My mother had a choice of dresses for herself that she and Malkah had made for her singing appearances, but I had nothing for a wedding. My mother announced that we were buying something special and took me on the subway to a store I'd never seen before.

At her insistence, I was wearing my best school dress and my best slip, embroidered with a pink ribbon and a row of lace; she wore her finest street dress, and a white hat and gloves. The entrance to the store was small, with wrought-iron carvings around the doorway; and a doorman let us in. Passing by him, I hesitated; my mother's face was rigid, her head held higher than I'd thought possible.

Inside, the ceilings were high and arched, like churches I'd seen in movies. It looked nothing like May's, the floor almost devoid of shoppers. A woman in a black dress glided over to ask what we wanted; she had an English accent and blond hair pulled into such a tight bun it pulled the skin of her face taut too. She awed me into speechlessness, and I took my mother's hand for protection.

Raking us with her eyes, she led us to a private dressing room, with its own door and mirror. I hung my clothing on a hanger and waited in my slip as she brought one dress at a time to the room, each so encased in a stiff plastic wrapper I could hardly make it out. My mother dismissed the first with a shake of her head; when she hesitated over the second I reached out to see it better. The woman twitched it away as if my hands were dirty, and my mother, her face tighter than the blonde's, hatchetlike, dismissed it too.

"The fabric would look right on a horse," she said caustically.

The woman brought other dresses, each more expensive than the last, and I became frantic at the prices while my mother criticized their stitching, their color, or their cut.

The dress she finally chose was hand-made, of pink organdy with a heavy satin sash: a dress for a princess. It cost forty dollars, twice what she'd planned to spend, only ten less than my father's salary for the week. I cried on the subway, hating the store, the woman, the dress, and my mother for taking me; and afraid of what my father would do.

Eventually, she slapped me, not caring whether other people on the train stared. "Everybody at this wedding is going to see you in this dress and say, 'Oh, that's Helen's daughter,' " she hissed. "And nobody's going to feel sorry for us! You understand me, Mona? You're going to wear this and act like you belong in it!"

When we got home, my father was asleep on the couch, the newspaper on the floor next to him, folded open to the racing page. He woke, and my mother took the dress from its cardboard box to show him, picking up the newspaper while he slowly turned the dress in his hands.

"Forty dollars!" he said, looking from the price tag to her face as though waiting for her to say it was a mistake in printing. But all she did was hold the newspaper open in front of her, so that we could see the penciled circles around the horses' names. My father dropped the dress onto its box and disappeared into the kitchen; I heard him drinking water from the tap.

When I put it on for Malkah's wedding, I was disappointed that I didn't look transformed. It seemed to me anyone could see I was still Mona. I was afraid my mother would be angry with me for looking so much like myself, and I stood stiffly to one side as the dancing began. But then my father asked me for the honor of the first dance, and guided me through a long and elaborate waltz.

Bob found me sleeping on the couch when he woke at seven; he covered me with a blanket, helped the boys get breakfast before the camp bus came, and left a note that he'd meet me at the hospital as soon as he could get free of the afternoon's meeting with his chairman.

By the time I reached Memorial, I was as nervous as ever: Chou could always take back on one visit what he said on the last. But he found no nodes when he examined me, not one, and he repeated his expectation of a complete remission before radiation began.

Bob was late, locked into his departmental meeting; the new chairman liked long Friday afternoon conferences. I took two prescriptions to the basement pharmacy to be filled before getting my injections, hoping Bob would come soon.

When I came back, I asked Chou's secretary to tell my husband I was already in the chemo area. Smiling widely, she assured me she'd tell him as soon as he arrived. "I hear you're doing great," she said. I grinned back at her, remembering how suspicious I'd been when she praised Chou after our first meeting.

I made my way through the crowded hallway to the back, a smile still on my face, and I registered with the nurse at the chemo desk.

As I turned away from her, I saw Mrs. Nettlebaum in a chair against the wall, looking healthy in her tweed suit, her cheeks pink beneath china-blue eyes. She was number twenty-three on the protocol to my number twenty-eight, in the final phase of treatment, on the chemo I'd get in the fall, after the radiation; and she'd been in a complete remission for months. I eyed her gray hair, wondering if I could ask where she got her wig, hoping she was still in remission; and I told her how well she looked.

"I feel wonderful," she said happily. "I even went horseback riding last week. I only feel terrible when I get chemo. My husband says I should stop but I tell him Dr. Chou says I have to finish."

"Are you still on the diet?"

She grimaced. "I never thought I could hate steak so much."

"The nutritionist I saw wouldn't take me if I took chemo."

"Mine doesn't like it either," she said with a shrug, "but I told him they could both pretend the other doctor doesn't exist. He said to me, 'All right, my dear lady, we'll all close our eyes and try to be happy.' After all, what matters is getting well," she added. "Who cares why?"

I smiled in agreement, about to tell her my own news, when I saw David come out of the chemo room, a nurse holding his arm. We'd begun treatment the same time, and I was the sicker one then, but he hadn't done as well, he was nowhere near a remission. He groped for a chair, his face beaded with sweat, his hands shaking, and the nurse handed him a box of tissues and a bag to throw up in, telling him solicitously to call her if he needed help.

Closing his eyes, he leaned forward in the chair with his face in his hands. Mrs. Nettlebaum stopped talking; we opened our magazines. After a while, David began to talk, his voice still thick from the drugs, telling us he'd thrown up the week before even though his chemo had been canceled because his blood count was too low.

"At the George Washington Bridge, like always," he said. "My wife was laughing, she said she couldn't help it, I was right on time, I always throw up then." He shook his head bemusedly and blew his nose. "I keep telling myself, it's not just the drugs, it's my brain too, my brain makes me sick because it expects it."

A nurse called Mrs. Nettlebaum; she made a face and stood. "Off to the wars," she murmured.

I checked my watch, wondering how much longer Bob would be, and David closed his eyes again. With them still shut, his head resting against the wall, he spoke in a low shy voice.

"You know what I did last week? I saw a psychic healer."

I stared at him in surprise. David was an electrical engineer. "A what? A psychic healer?"

"We got his name from my wife's cousin. Chou says I'm doing OK, but we figured what the hell, I could do a lot better. I told him I wasn't a believer, but he said it didn't matter."

He leaned forward to retch into the paper bag; I averted my eyes until he stopped. "He just had me sit in a chair," David said. "He put one hand on my head and the other on my shoulder and he prayed. I got all hot and tingly, like pins and needles. He said to call him when I saw my doctor, tell him if anything was changed."

Watching his beaded face, I listened to his thick hoarse voice. Psychic healing seemed a lot easier to take than chemo. "Did it make a difference?"

He answered slowly, his face thoughtful. "I don't know. The doctor just told me all my nodes are down, he told me just now when he examined me, before he sent me over here. It's six weeks since the last chemo, nothing should have shrunk since he sent me home last week."

His voice sharpened sardonically. "Of course, Chou said the disease is unpredictable, with its ups and downs, even though I've never once gone down before with no drugs, you know that crap, what they always say. I'm not saying I believe it either, you understand, but who the hell understands any of this?"

I understood completely. "What's his name? The healer?"

"Lindgren. Herb Lindgren. I have his card if you want it."

It was a white card embossed only with the name and telephone number; I copied it to file at home. My files got odder every week, with clippings from *Science,* and *World Medical News* and *The New York Times,* and pieces on Schabtau and Dewey, on yeast cures and prayer. David excused himself, running for the bathroom, and I leaned back in my chair. Mrs. Nettlebaum was eating meat three times a day while I ate none. Maybe it was all luck, maybe it didn't matter what you did. Or maybe it all mattered. Other societies believed in laying on of hands; my own grandma made wax statues to heal. Or maybe it didn't matter exactly what you did but only how fully you concentrated on it.

My name was called just as Bob came into sight at the other end of the corridor. I waved to him and followed the nurse, lying down on a cot in a back cubicle while she put the I.V. into my arm. As soon as the drip began, I could feel the drug burning in my veins. It was poison, but more toxic to the lymphoma than to me. The nurse brought tissues and made sympathetic noises as I began to sneeze spasmodically, my eyes running and my nose in full flood. This medicine had its full effect in the first half-hour after injection, while the pills I took at home had their effects over the next ten days. The two nurses began talking gaily about their summer vacation plans and I shut my eyes and ears against them. I'd asked Chou again about our trip; again, he'd said to stay within three hours of a major hospital. I'd have to check the maps.

With my eyes still closed, I practiced the visualization. It was a good time, the chemo at its most powerful. I thought the two methods worked together, not as a simple summation, but synergistically. The lymphoma cells were weak, weaker than my own body; it was the mass of them that made them powerful, but none of them alone. Singling out a clump of lymphomas hiding under a ledge around a bend of fat, I began raying them with light. They tried to scatter, but I caught them all, and they disintegrated, without smoke or smell or any sign they'd ever been there. With half my mind, I was pleased; sometimes I still had trouble killing them without leaving around bits and pieces, dangerous fragments from which new monsters could grow.

My toes and right leg twitched spasmodically, out of my control, and I felt heat running up and down my leg. The books I'd seen on psychic healing said the healee often felt heat or tingling, what David had described; I hoped it meant healing when it began during a visualization.

The nurse checked the I.V. in my arm and took my pulse, asking about my vacation plans. I told her we were going West, thinking the trip seemed almost stupid if we really had to be three hours from a major hospital; it made more sense to stay around New York. But I wasn't going to miss any chances I had even with Chou's hope of a cure; these last months I'd learned to postpone as little as possible. To live in the present, not in a mythical future, not in the what-might-be, like most of the people I knew. It was the one gift of the lymphoma.

The nurse freed me from the I.V. and helped me to sit up, telling me to wait a few more minutes before standing. When she was satisfied, she steered me out to the waiting row of chairs. Bob strode toward us, taking me from her, his face anxious.

My voice was hoarse, my sinuses and the lining of my nose still on fire. "I need a few more minutes. I can't talk yet. But Chou said everything's fine."

As the full force of the drug hit me, I stopped thinking coherently, my thoughts splintering ahead of me and disappearing before I could remember them. The worst of that would pass quickly, but I'd told Chou I was sure I couldn't think normally for weeks after taking the injection. He'd never heard that was a side effect, but he was curious and asked a lot of questions. "We don't have enough experience with these drugs to know everything they do," he'd commented. "They're all too new."

When I felt more steady, Bob took my arm; we plodded slowly toward the elevator and out. One of the medicines damaged peripheral nerves, numbing the soles of my feet; I walked on invisible pillows. We got a taxi at the door, and I settled back, hoping not to throw up in the cab. Bob handed me the box of tissues the nurse had given him; the sneezing spasms stopped by the time we reached our building.

"How did the meeting with your chairman go?" I asked.

"He still doesn't like me any more than I like him," Bob answered. "I'll tell you about it tomorrow."

In the elevator, I leaned against the wall, ignoring José, trying to pull myself together for the boys. The way I felt now, I couldn't believe we'd ever be flying West.

I heard McCrae barking as we reached our floor. When Bob unlocked the door, she ran out, circling us frantically and jumping up. Bob fended her off me; and she satisfied herself by putting her paws on his shoulders and licking his face as he bent down.

Adam stuck his head around the corner of the living room, then rushed over. "I didn't hear you, my door was shut. I made a robot with the erector set, by myself. Dan's playing with Mike downstairs."

Pulling back, he looked me over. "Are you too sick to see? You look terrible."

"I feel terrible, but I can stay up that long." I managed a quavering smile, hoping I didn't fall down on him.

His voice was deliberately careless as he led me to his room. "You'll be sick tonight and tomorrow and by the next day you'll feel better? And this is the last time for a while?"

"I'll feel better and this is the last time for a while."

He lifted the robot, a five-foot monster a few inches taller than himself. "If it had a motor, it could walk right through walls," he said. "I still don't understand why medicines should make you sick."

Bob answered behind me. "Because they're very powerful. The same reason you can't take more than a spoon of ampicillin when you get a sore throat."

"Then why can't Mom take less? So she doesn't feel sick?"

"Because they're lousy medicines," I said for the fiftieth time. "They can't tell the difference between me and the germs. They need glasses."

He grinned at my joke, reassured by even feeble humor. I blew him a kiss and ran for the bathroom, without the time to shut the door before throwing up in the toilet. Then I lay down in our bedroom on a camping mat; for the next three days, just thinking of the waves the waterbed made would start me retching.

16

I CALLED DAVID'S HEALER A WEEK LATER.

"He just came from work," his wife said softly. "He's watering the lawn; I'll call him."

Whatever I'd expected, it hadn't included the watering of lawns. But I had no time to wonder about my surprise; a man came quickly to the phone, his voice deep and colored by a strong New Jersey accent. I told him I'd gotten his name from David Kolenberg and asked for an appointment for a healing.

"Hold on while I get a pencil," he said. "My little girl is starting school in September and she gives all the pencils to her dolls to practice writing."

When he came back, his voice was still warm but more businesslike; he took my name and number. "Don't tell me the problem," he said. "I get better results if I can meet you first without knowing."

He gave me an appointment for the next evening, sooner than I'd expected, and I embarrassed him by asking his fee.

"I don't have one," he said. "I'll accept a contribution afterward, if you want to make one, but healers don't ask for money."

When I hung up, I remembered that my grandma too had taken contributions, but charged no fee; she said it was bad for her to ask for money. I wondered how Herb earned his living.

At night, after the boys were asleep, I told Bob about the call.

"Why now?" he asked curiously. "When Chou says you're going into a remission?"

I was defiant, shamefaced, and defensive, all the professors who'd trained me making yowling noises at my back.

"Because now I don't need a miracle. All I need is a little boost."

"Mona, I'd pray to the devil if I thought it would help."

I smiled at him weakly. Calling Herb made me feel as though I were going back, not to Brownsville, but beyond it, to the shtetl my grandfather had fled, and to the farm my grandmother had abandoned. I'd been afraid Bob wouldn't come with me.

"I once prayed to the devil," I said slowly. "I never told you. After Isaac killed Rose. And after the trouble with my father. That winter. Hannah and I prayed to the devil for help."

But I cut off my confession, not ready to face it yet, and turned toward the kitchen.

"Do you want anything before we go to bed? I'm going to have some cereal."

The following evening, the boys stayed with a sitter while we crossed the bridge to New Jersey. An unknown state to me, I was surprised when we turned onto a wooded road after ten minutes. We drove through a small town filled with Victorian houses, many on an acre or more of land, and continued north past lush front yards and bits of undeveloped woods; we even passed two farms. Then we were in the town Herb lived in, more a working-class town than the others; even so, any of the houses would have cost a fortune in New York.

A little girl was bicycling outside: the pencil snatcher. We parked in the driveway, and she told us her daddy was inside with someone else. Bob rang the bell; Herb's wife came to the door. She was wearing an apron over slacks, and invited us into the kitchen, offering tea while she cleared the dinner dishes.

I liked her immediately; we talked about children until a burly man in baggy chinos walked in. Herb.

"The people I'm with now said they'd be pleased if you watched their healing," he said. "They've been here before."

My grandma may have been a healer, but she didn't talk about it, and I only witnessed a healing once; out of my depth, I couldn't imagine how Bob felt. But he said he'd like to see, and Herb led us to a small den behind the living room. It was crammed with books, another surprise, many in boxes on the floor. He introduced us to an elderly couple, and began without further ceremony.

The woman sat in a straight chair, her eyes closed. Herb stood behind her, with one hand on the top of her head and the other on her right shoulder. She was wearing a crucifix, and held it while he prayed.

I thought she was about seventy until I realized she was gnarled because of arthritis, the joints of her hands so swollen she could hardly bend her fingers.

Herb shut his eyes, and began to pray, calling on Jesus and Mary to intervene. The room was bright, and in the light the woman's face relaxed. After a few minutes, Herb asked if she felt anything.

"Tingling," she said. "Starting in my legs. Now in my fingers too, and I feel heat in my middle."

He went back to praying, calling on St. Michael and St. Luke, and several others I never even heard of; his intensity was palpable, his belief in what he was doing total. "Do you feel anything now?" he asked, sweat pouring down his face.

"It's stopped," she said cautiously. "I could feel the angels' presence and now they're gone."

He straightened up, taking his hands from her body, and opened his eyes. "I felt them go," he agreed. "Tingling over?"

She nodded, and he turned to her husband. "You see any aura this time?"

The man shook his head regretfully. "The two of you can, but me, I don't see a thing."

I watched the woman. She was holding out her hands, and flexing the fingers; the swellings had gone down. As I stared, they shrank still more.

I looked at Bob for verification. He was hunched over tensely, his gaze flicking from Herb to the woman, absorbing it all. "I've read about healings like this," he murmured. "I never thought I'd see it."

Going to her, he asked to feel her hands. "How long have you had arthritis?" he asked.

"About five years." Her purse sat next to her on the floor; she bent to take out a handkerchief and wiped tears from her eyes. "This last year I couldn't even do housework. My husband had to help me. But I've seen Herb three times now and each time I'm better. Did you see the way I just bent over? He says if I prayed more, I wouldn't need him."

When they left, Herb asked if we'd mind if he had some milk and cake before working with us. "This uses me up," he explained. "I can't get enough to eat after a healing."

We sat around the kitchen table while his wife put their little girl to bed. The kitchen was bright and modern, with yellow counters and hanging plants at the windows. The living room walls were hung with crucifixes.

"We're Catholic," he said. "But it doesn't matter what faith you are."

"I'm Jewish. I'm not sure it'll work if you pray to Christ."

He took a big piece of layer cake. "Christ and Mary are set up better for intervening, but I can ask Moses and Abraham too. You don't even have to pray, you can heal without it. But it works better for me if I pray."

I saw Bob decide to ignore Herb's comments. "What kind of people do you see?" he asked.

"Mainly in the neighborhood, surrounding towns. I've only been doing it about three years, so not that many people know me. You're the first from Manhattan."

He wiped his mouth on a paper napkin, and poured another

glass of milk. "What do you do anyway? You look like you're used to telling people what to do."

"I'm a doctor," Bob said. "A heart doctor."

Herb's head shot up; he looked embarrassed. Bob gestured toward me. "My wife is a scientist, a professor of neurobiology."

When Herb just stared at me, I told him I studied how memory worked. He put his elbows on the table and leaned forward with intense curiosity. "How?" he asked. "What do you do?"

Now it was my turn to be embarrassed. "I give animals different drugs and hook them up to machines that tell me what parts of their brains are working when they try to do things they've been taught. Sometimes I don't use drugs, sometimes I take out small sections of the brain first."

"And they walk around after you do that?" His voice was amazed.

"My partner and I use very tiny electrodes; they're put in permanently with surgery. It's not so hard."

He shook his head. "I have enough trouble taking apart a carburetor."

"You're a car mechanic?" Bob asked.

"Yeah, I own my own garage."

"That's what my father did," I said.

"And you're a professor?"

I shrugged. "Sometimes I think he had more fun taking cars apart. But it's not so different from trying to understand the brain. They're both machinery."

"Can I ask how you got into healing?" Bob asked.

Herb leaned back in the kitchen chair, just the way my uncle Obbie used to. I began to feel very relaxed. "My kid, my little girl, fell out of the swing one day; she landed on her head, and she wasn't breathing. I started praying over her, like I never did in my life, even though I was brought up very devout, and I had this impulse to put my hands on her body while I prayed. She started breathing; when the ambulance came, they said it was a miracle she was alive. I didn't tell them about her not breathing, I figured the doctors wouldn't believe me.

"Then about a year later, I was under a car, fixing a U-joint, and the lift slipped. I was pinned under, with a concussion. They got me out, I wasn't hurt bad; when I came to, I saw things different. Like I can see an aura around you now if I turn off the lights so it gets dim in here. And I kept getting this impulse to help people who were sick. I told my priest and he talked with me a lot, and then he sent me to see some people he knows, at a monastery. They instructed me, they said I was a natural, that I ought to do it, that it was a gift from Jesus. But I told you, it doesn't matter about being Jewish. In the end, we're all under one God, even the Australian aborigines."

He stood up at last, drank a glass of water, and told us he was ready if we were. In the den, he surprised me again by doing the same test Dr. Schabtau had done, having me raise my arm while he pressed down, giving me different pills to hold each time. "You got something wrong with your blood," he said. "A kind of cancer."

As he went on with the test, he had Bob write down the supplements he wanted me to take. Not knowing that I'd seen Schabtau, he made essentially the same recommendations. He told me that the pills I'd held were vitamins and minerals, that the test was called the MRT, the muscle response test, and that the MRT was better known than I realized. I asked where he'd learned about it, and he said he'd been studying everything he could find for the last three years, and meeting with other people like himself. "It's like fixing a car," he said. "Sometimes you get it working even if you don't know why, but the more you know, the better your chances."

Then he had me lie down on the couch; he placed his hands on me. He put one hand on the top of my head and the other on my naval, commenting that my abdomen felt odd to him, diseased. I wondered if Chou was wrong about a complete remission.

"I'm touching you at two chakra points," he volunteered. "Where different energy concentrates in the body."

I was totally lost; I listened blankly. "It's Hindu," he mumbled. "I used to think it was a lot of crap, but it isn't, it works."

He looked about to pray, but stopped himself. "I'm going to do an exorcism too; I usually do with cancer."

He was suddenly didactic. "Lots of people get cancer because they're possessed, and possession weakens them."

I made no response; by now, I was too stunned for any kind of answer; I didn't even look at Bob. Herb began to pray, and I felt the tingling that David and the woman before me had described, what I'd felt while visualizing in the chemo area; but the tingling wasn't confined to my arms and legs, it suffused my whole body. Faintly, from far away, I heard him calling on Mary and Jesus, and a pantheon of saints, and then on Moses and Abraham and Isaac, asking them to heal me, asking them to heal me out of their love and mercy; and then his voice changed, became commanding, and he ordered the spirit within me, the spirit possessing me, to go back to the pit, to the pit where it belonged.

I felt my arms and legs twitch, as out of control as if they belonged to someone else, and a spasm ran from my abdomen up to my head. Sweat was pouring out of me, drenching the couch, and I felt incredibly light, as though I were floating in the air. Then, still far away, Herb thanked them all for their help; and he removed his hands.

When I sat up, Bob was gaping at me, his pupils dilated in a white face.

"You look different! I never saw how assymetrical you were before! Mona, your face straightened out when you had those spasms." He turned to Herb. "Do you have a mirror? She has to look in a mirror!"

I gazed at myself in the mirror Herb brought over, unable to see what Bob saw. But I felt profoundly lighter, a weight gone that I couldn't yet identify, something so long a part of me I hadn't known it was there. I looked profoundly relaxed, and a decade younger; Bob kept staring as if I were a ghost.

He asked Herb if there was any chance of a drink, and Herb offered beer, clucking his tongue sympathetically. "I was nervous too," he said. "I never did anything like this with two big shots like you."

On the way out, Bob dropped a contribution on Herb's desk. He told me later that he'd left the amount he charged his own patients for a first consultation.

That night, the first of the Brownsville dreams began. My parents were waiting for me, I knew that as I climbed the stairs to their apartment, but inside I couldn't find them. I searched the apartment, calling forlornly, sure there was a room I'd missed, a room I knew was there although I'd never seen it.

Unable to believe in Herb's exorcism, I couldn't disbelieve it either. Something had happened, even if I didn't know what to make of it.

The summer I was eight my parents were happy. My father had gotten a raise at the new job Obbie found for him, and we were saving money again to buy a gas station. When he took my mother to look for a Persian lamb coat like Fannie's, I wondered if he'd been gambling, but my mother didn't ask. I decided she was content to let him gamble as long as she could put a deposit into the savings account each week.

One September evening, I came back from Hebrew school to find them in the kitchen, sitting over a notebook filled with numbers. My mother looked up at me, her eyes shining.

"Your father got another raise. His boss made him shop foreman."

"Go tell Grandpa we're getting supper at Ratner's," my father said happily.

I looked toward the stove where I could smell beef simmering; my mother followed my gaze and stood to turn off the gas. "Go on, Mona. Tell Grandpa we're celebrating."

In the restaurant, over cheese blintzes and vegetable cutlet, they talked about buying the garage within two years. My father put his arm around my mother's shoulders; when we left they walked ahead on the street, holding hands.

Later in the month, my father came home past the usual time, slamming the door and calling for my mother. I was reading at the kitchen table; looking up, I was afraid he'd been fired again. But when he faced me, I saw he was grinning, his face sweaty. "Mona, how would you like to see the garage I'm gonna buy? Your daddy's gonna be an independent businessman."

My mother came running from the bathroom; he picked her up and kissed her full on the mouth in front of me.

"I talked with the guy on East Eighty-ninth Street," he said. "He wants to sell out soon and we might be able to make a deal! You want to see the place?"

She pulled back, her mouth tight. "We don't have the money yet."

My father looked squarely at her. It was what he called his

honest poker face, for when he was bluffing. He hesitated. "I got a little more cash than you know about."

I tried to shrink into the hard-backed kitchen chair, to become invisible.

Pale, my mother leaned against the wall. "How much cash?"

He looked down at his brown shoes, and up again, like a small boy caught throwing spitballs by the principal.

"Over a thousand," he whispered. "I won it at the track. Five thousand dollars."

My mother's eyes rolled up to show the whites, and she slid gracefully to the floor. It wasn't at all the way she'd fainted when she got the letter from him in the hospital during the war.

Bending over her, supporting her head, cradling her in his arms, he talked frantically. "Helen, it's OK. It was a fluke, a hundred-to-one shot. I knew it was gonna happen, I had one of my special feelings, so I put fifty dollars on this horse. You don't have to worry. I went with Obbie the other night, with your brother, when you were singing at that fancy affair on Eastern Parkway."

I peered at my mother, my heart pounding. My father called on me, pleading. "Mona, you remember? I left you with Grandpa."

"You said you were going for a drive with Obbie," my mother whispered. "That's what you told Poppa."

"So? I had to drive to the track, didn't I? Listen, Helen, you knew you were picking a bum when you married me."

Her head against his shoulder, my mother giggled suddenly; she saw my horrified expression, stopped, tried to cover her mouth with her hand, and then giggled again. Leaning forward, her face mischievous, she kissed him with her arms around his neck, and murmured words I couldn't hear into his ear. I was blushing, but couldn't get away without going right up against them. I finally sidled past and shut myself into the bathroom; it was the only private place in the house. Sitting on the toilet lid, I thought about five thousand dollars. Five thousand dollars was a fortune. We were rich. We could buy anything we wanted with five thousand dollars.

When I realized he might have the money with him, I ran out; my grandpa had just come home from prayers. My mother's face was flushed; she looked dazzled.

"He won it on the horses, Poppa. It means we can buy a business."

I came up behind them, too excited to be quiet. "Do you have the money with you?"

My father reached spasmodically for the windbreaker he'd hung over the kitchen chair. From the inside pocket he withdrew four fat white envelopes, held shut with large paper clips. "I was waiting for someone to ask me," he smiled.

Sweeping my books from the table, he spread out bill after bill, until he covered the entire surface; but he still had more and made a layer on top of the first, and then another. "I got mainly fives and tens," he said. "So I could have a real fat wad."

"They're not new," I blurted.

He raised his head sharply. "Of course not, Mona. They just reuse the cash they take in. All this money other people lost."

"What was the name of the horse?" my grandpa asked.

"Lucky Man. Hundred-to-one odds."

"So on this you will build a business," he said, his face pensive. "God works in wondrous ways." Leaning toward the table, he brushed the bills with his fingertips. "Never have I seen so much money in my life." Then he turned and embraced my father.

17

I'D TRIED TO CUT AWAY MY CHILDHOOD, AND PRETEND I'D MADE myself from air, without roots in the past. As my memories closed in, I felt the wall against the past grow weaker, and the exorcism, whatever it meant, eroded it still more. In my dreams, my parents no longer turned their backs, but waited in the Brownsville apartment for me to find them in the room I'd shut away and lost.

I saw Chou at the end of July for a final examination before I left on vacation. He said I looked fine, but he was depressed, and added he couldn't be sure of the remission until he got the results of the lymphangiogram when I came back. He depressed me with his own mood; I was glad to get away. But I met David as I was leaving. "I've seen Herb," I told him.

He was thinner, his skin sallow; he looked tense and sad. "How was it?"

I hesitated, uncomfortable at revealing all of it, but wondering how much David had chosen not to tell.

"I got the tingling you talked about. He did an exorcism too. You didn't mention that."

He looked down at his shoes. "I was too embarrassed. It felt like something happened, didn't it? Or did it for you?"

"My husband said my face changed while he was praying. As though it was twisted before, very subtly, and then straightened out. And I felt different."

I waited for his response, but he didn't make one.

"Herb said not to worry, I'd be all right," I said finally. "Do you know how good his predictions are?"

He shrugged, his voice strained. "I wish I did. But he didn't tell me I'd be all right. He just told me to try praying."

He rang for the elevator, then turned back to me, stammering. "Did you know that Mrs. Nettlebaum had a recurrence?"

I backed against the wall as if he'd threatened me. No wonder Chou looked depressed. "Oh God. She was well when I saw her here two weeks ago."

He was miserable in his white shirt, a sorry messenger. "In her chest. She's getting more radiation. Chou said he could buy her time, that's all."

"But I thought she was cured. Chou told me he thought he had a cure. In June. At least for some of us."

David looked blank, surprised. "I saw him an hour ago; he said she's not the only early recurrence. He looked awful himself; I didn't want to ask too much." He grimaced shakily. "Some news I'd rather not have."

When I got back, I phoned Bob at his office, unable to hold in the news. Offering the homely platitudes I was learning to live by, he said we had to wait it out, there was no point planning for the worst until we had to; but he was grim at dinner.

Later we talked about postponing our trip and getting the lymph-angiogram now, but I was afraid I wouldn't feel able to go if the news was bad. The radiation couldn't start until the fall no matter what; I needed time to recover fully from the chemo. We agreed to act as if Chou were right and I was well, and began packing.

* * *

Now the plane slowed, its landing gear down for the glide into Los Angeles airport. When we got out, I looked for Jeff and Doris at the gate; Adam recognized them first. They'd aged since January.

I pecked each of them on the cheek, fending off Jeff when he tried to wrap his arms around me, and we made small talk about the flight while waiting for the luggage. I knew they still hoped we'd stay with them, and not go on to Utah.

Doris bridged the awkwardness by giving Dan and Adam their presents; sure there'd be presents, I was glad I'd warned them not to ask. The boxes held radio-controlled robots; they began running them on the airport floor. I turned away to get a seat, pretending not to see the annoyance of people trying to get by, glad of anything that made the meeting easier.

Later, after dinner in a Japanese restaurant, we sat in their living room, still arguing about a cabin near them in the Sierras. It was nine p.m., California time; midnight in New York, and midnight to my body.

Jeff stirred a whiskey and soda, and reached for some potato chips across the bar top. "I don't see how you're going to traipse across Utah when you're sick and weak."

I bridled once more, and moved the potato chips from him to me. "I'm not sick; I'm in remission. I may not be in great shape, but I can certainly travel in a car."

Jeff looked over me to Bob, shaking his head in bewilderment. "Bob, you're the doctor. Is it really safe? I thought Mona's supposed to take it easy."

Bob sipped his vodka before answering; he hated to argue with them. And I knew he'd go again to the Sierras if he could; I was the one insisting on Utah.

"Mona's doing very well," he said again. "As long as her count stays reasonable, there's no reason not to go. If we have to, we'll fly out. But we're planning to stay on main roads, and near the car when we camp."

"I'm sure you'd fall in love with the new cabin if you only looked at it," Doris murmured.

"I'm not staying in a cabin again," I repeated. "Since my parents died, we've stayed in a cabin every summer to give you and

Bob and the boys time together. This year, I'm going to travel."

I knew they'd never understand me, and I was sorry to fight them even as I argued. I wondered if they'd understand better if I told them I wanted not just to travel but to see the place where my parents died. But I thought that would frighten them more, it meant driving into more isolated territory. I couldn't believe they'd never taken risks, couldn't believe they'd always opted for safety. Jeff must have gambled: he'd built his construction company from nothing. But they couldn't seem to give way now, and I used my trump card to end it.

"I don't know how many more summers I have to see this country again."

They both looked down, and Bob caught my eye, warning me not to threaten his parents again. Jeff still had all his hair, but he'd gone white since January, and deep lines led from his nose to mouth, while Doris was fifteen pounds heavier, her belly sagging through an expensive sundress in spite of her years of yoga. I drank the rest of my club soda in a gulp and said good night, announcing I'd see them in the morning.

As I crossed to the guest wing at the back of the house, I was yawning but distracted, longing to be gone. I'd been here seven or eight times since my parents died, in summer and in winter. But I felt as though I'd been told about my parents for the first time each time I slept here.

In bed, I tried to visualize lymphoma cells, not knowing if I even had lymphoma left, but unable to dare stopping until the lymphangiogram. I couldn't concentrate, it felt like a parody or a child's game of pretend, without real connection to my body.

Their voices murmured in the living room; I wondered how late Bob would sleep in the morning. But I knew I'd stay up with my folks if it were I. If they were alive.

Alone in bed, I admitted that Bob's parents would embrace me as their daughter if I let them; the aloofness was all mine. I thought Doris was a pampered child, but she offered what she could: I was the rejecting one, not they. I knew Jeff was right when he complained to Bob; I was hard to know, I did push them off.

Too tense to sleep, I pulled the map of the Southwest from my duffel bag, once more following the road my parents died on, from its beginnings near Capitol Reef to Bryce Canyon. One hundred fifteen miles, all of it winding, part of Route 12 was even unpaved, with rockslides and flash floods common at the northern end; at Capitol Reef you were to ask a ranger if it was passable.

Bob and I had been in Utah three times when the boys were very little, including the summer that my parents died. We'd driven from Zion to Bryce to Canyonlands on the main routes that were themselves no more than two-lane roads; we'd seen Route 12 but passed it by.

I'd been entranced by Canyonlands, identifying with its bleakness and awesome labyrinths even as they frightened me. On our first visit, Dan was almost three and Adam just over a year; Adam developed diarrhea and an oozing rash from the 110° heat. We left for the cool mountains of Colorado but came back the following year, in September, haunted by visions of the eroded cliffs and statued rocks.

The heat in September was bearable, and we camped in the campground with its pit toilets and single water pump. A thunderstorm began one afternoon, bolts of lightning searing the scarlet rocks above us and ricocheting down the inclined slickrock. As we ran for the safety of the car, a group of old people roared past on motorcycles. Their bodies were thin and muscled, their faces spare; playing with the storm, they followed one another up a steeply tilted rockface and circled laughing in the rain.

Later Bob and I sat outside the tent while a full moon illuminated monstrous shapes eroded by wind from the soft sandstone. A coyote began to howl, and we packed up at three in the morning, depositing our sleeping children in the back of the station wagon, and drove straight north for five hundred miles to the greenery of Yellowstone. Awed into panic by Canyonlands, we drove away at eighty miles an hour, hated Yellowstone, and returned two weeks later for a last hungry look at the twisted rocks before flying home.

When I planned the trip with my parents, I mentioned Canyonlands only in passing: it wasn't country to recommend to a pair of middle-aged Brooklyn Jews. Although I wondered at the time if that part of Utah looked like Moses's desert.

No, the path I traced for my father followed interstate highways from Denver to Las Vegas to Los Angeles; when they detoured to see Bryce and Zion, they were supposed to follow a main connecting road. I couldn't imagine what he was doing on a back-country track so far from anywhere he had reason to be.

After the accident, I searched the map over and over to find what they were doing there. They crashed near the town of Escalante, but the police knew only that they'd been driving south. If they had a purpose on that road, no one knew what it had been, or whether it had been fulfilled.

By now, I knew all the towns along the way; from Escalante, with 638 people, to Grover, with none. East of Escalante, lay one hundred thousand square miles of wilderness: of red rock, coyote, and canyons, but no people; and west of Escalante about three thousand square miles of ranching country before the next town, except for dotted settlements along the single road to Bryce.

I had more people on my block.

Shivering suddenly, my fingers icy, I groped through my duffel bag, feeling for the five hex signs at the bottom. Tonight I wanted them around me in this alien house, whose owners loved my husband and would love me if I let them.

I turned off the lamp in case Bob surprised me, slipped two hex signs between the foam pad and the plywood underneath, and taped a third behind the headboard. Bob knew nothing about them; if he knew, he might even agree: he'd seen Herb's exorcism. But putting them out might seem like an oblique insult to his parents, even though I'd placed them in our apartment too; I'd insulted them enough by my refusal to stay beyond the night.

When Bob finally came to bed, I was still wide awake. Undressing, he sat on the edge of the bed, and confessed he'd begun looking forward to our trip. We talked a bit about his parents' disappointment; then he slipped under the sheet blanket and put his arms around me. I tensed, and he whispered that we couldn't be heard, the boys were across the hall and asleep.

While he waited with his hands behind his head, I changed into the sheer black camisole he'd bought me right after we married; my Bloomingdale's ribbons would wait for another night. Crawling in beside him, I lay across his chest; he stroked me in the silky fabric.

"I haven't seen that in years," he murmured.

He reached under the camisole, and I tried to kiss him, but he retreated, still unwilling to kiss three weeks after chemo. I made him enter me quickly, no longer aware of the noises we might make; as I came, I had a fleeting image of the unlocked door. Before falling asleep at Bob's side I laughed aloud, remembering Phil's wry description of his ten-year-old son who stumbled in on him one night, apologized, and turned back to ask if he could watch the mating.

In the morning, Bob's mother made pancakes while his father smoked cigarettes and drank black coffee. When we drove away, they waved from the driveway; they looked defeated and shrunken. Bob said he'd promised to phone them from Utah.

An hour later, we were in the California desert of the San Bernardino mountains, sagebrush and tumbleweed sparse on the rocky slopes, and ancient lava beds black beneath them. Beyond the ghost town of Calico, the land flattened; the road was straight before us all the way to Las Vegas. Our map showed dinosaur tracks half a mile into a dirt road on an Indian reservation; the boys clamored for the detour, but we would have stopped even if they hadn't asked. It was 109°, and a dry wind seared my skin when I got out.

Dan and Adam began searching for the tracks while Bob and I made sandwiches in the wind. The paper plates kept blowing off the open tailgate, and the wind threw oil against my shirt when I opened a can of sardines. Adam stomped back for his sandwich looking sulky. "We can't find them. I bet it's a fake."

Toweling off sardine oil, swatting at invisible gnats, I too began to look, crossing back and forth on the uneven rock surface. With half my mind, I wondered what Navajos did to tourists found wandering on reservation land, not knowing what the rangers meant when they warned that reservations had their own laws; then I stumbled on a row of ancient lizard tracks, and bent to touch them. Adam ran over at my shout, but he was unimpressed. When he turned away, he saw the first dinosaur track.

Bob and Dan hurried to us; together we followed the footprints for a hundred yards, until they disappeared under a layer of sandstone more resistent to erosion, not to be worn down for another millennium. From the distance between tracks, we guessed the creature to be twelve feet long, ambling his way harmlessly among the lizards. The land was drying out, the ancient sea receding into desert, and the age of dinosaurs passing. As we walked back to the car for cameras, I thought that each up or down step I took on the uneven surface carried me back and forth in time. Adam looked disdainfully at me when I told him.

"It's not a real time machine. If it was real, you could see what was happening at each stop."

I made a face at him, thinking that children didn't know enough to appreciate the real mystery. But they were excited; when they clambered back into the car after lunch, Dan announced he'd write about the tracks in his diary that night.

As we drove on, playing ghost and twenty questions, and an endless game of buzz that reached six hundred forty-five before Bob missed, I read the map once more to see if there was any way to avoid passing through Las Vegas. Dinosaur tracks might make me feel the immensity of time, but we were still on the road my father would have taken if he'd lived. He'd stopped gambling long before the accident, after the final gamble my mother never forgot; they might have passed through the city without stopping, but the feel of the town and what it might have meant to him was something I wanted to keep at bay.

It was October, just before Sukkos, the harvest festival. At Hebrew school, they were building the straw Sukkah that all the classes would visit for traditional gifts of fruit. The Sukkah was decked with leaves and branches, with ears of corn, and grapes, and oranges hung from the rafters; and it sat on the roof of the building. It looked out of place above the brick façade, but my grandpa said it was the best they could do in the city.

They gave us special ticket books this Sukkos, to sell for money to be donated to the poor. Hannah and I were working together, the way we did every spring when we sold tickets to plant trees in Israel. We'd started in my building right after Hebrew school, and we'd each sold half a book by the time we reached Mrs. Goldstein's landing; everyone had bought a ticket.

Hannah was teasing me about my new boyfriend when she dared me to ring Mrs. Goldstein's bell: we usually skipped her. I knocked, unable to turn down a dare, hoping she wouldn't hear, hoping she was out even though I smelled cooking, hoping Mr. Goldstein would answer instead.

When she opened the door, she looked us over without smiling, wiping her hands on her cotton apron.

"Would you like to buy a ticket for the poor?" I quavered.

She turned away without a word, and disappeared into her living room.

"Are we supposed to follow her?" Hannah whispered. "Because I'm not going in there."

"I don't think she'd let you. No one ever goes inside."

For all my fear, I was curious, and I stepped over the threshold to peer around. Witches were supposed to have cats, and Mrs. Goldstein didn't, no one had a cat except the butcher and the grocery man. Witches were supposed to sell their souls to the devil too, but I didn't know if Jewish witches believed in the devil. Or had cats. In fact, I knew hardly anything about witches; I didn't even know if it was a sin to ask Mrs. Goldstein to buy a ticket from the Hebrew school.

Taking two steps, I craned my neck and peeked around the doorway to the kitchen; there were pots on the stove, but I heard her coming and jumped back before I could see more. She counted out fifty cents in nickels and dimes from a fat black change purse; I thanked her and turned to follow Hannah down the stairs.

"Wait!" she called. "I have a cookie for you."

She brought a cookie from the kitchen; I gazed fearfully at it in her freckled hand. It was a chocolate sandwich cookie, and it looked just like the chocolate sandwich cookies my mother bought at the grocery. If I didn't take it, she'd curse me.

"Thank you!" I said again.

She nodded sharply and shut the door in my face; I started after Hannah. We were outside before either of us broke our silence; even then, Hannah looked over her shoulder before speaking.

"Are you going to eat it? What if it's poisoned?"

I stared at her in surprise; for once I felt superior. "I'd have to be crazy to eat it, stupid. Do you think it's safe to put it in my pocket?"

She reached into her blouse. "Wrap it in my handkerchief. I'll throw it out when I go home. So your mother doesn't even have to know you knocked on her door."

It was almost suppertime; I didn't know if my mother would let me out again, and by the next day people would tell us they'd already given money. We still had half my building to go through, the whole wing on the other side of the courtyard, and the ground floor on my side. We should have gone on, but I wasn't ready yet, not after facing Mrs. Goldstein.

Following my glance, Hannah answered my unspoken question. "The building next to mine has Gypsies. I'm not allowed in there." She lowered her voice. "My father says they kidnap children and sell them."

"Why don't we split up at your building then?" I asked. "Just your building so we can go faster. I'll go to my Aunt Fannie and you try the new lady on the third floor."

She agreed, and we crossed the street together, pushing open the heavy wooden door to her brownstone, a door that always stuck, and walked down the narrow hall to the stairs.

"I'm going up to my place, I need to make number one," Hannah said. "You go to your aunt's and I'll get you after I stop at the third floor."

Glad to get an easy sale, I knocked on Fannie's door; behind me, Hannah clattered one flight up to her apartment. Fannie opened the door immediately and I stretched to kiss her.

"Since when do you have to knock?" she asked. "The door is never locked; you should come right in."

"Would you like to buy a ticket for the poor?" I asked, becoming instantly official; I wanted her to know I came on business. She turned to get her purse, and the screams began above us: short, sharp, high-pitched screams. At first I didn't even know whose voice it was.

Fannie pushed me aside and ran for the stairs, reaching them just as Hannah bolted down. Hannah's face and hands were bloody, her white blouse smeared red; there was blood on her skirt, on her knees, on her socks and shoes. Her eyes unfocused, she tried to dodge past Fannie, but Fannie held her, shouting over her screams, demanding to know where she was hurt. Hannah clawed at Fannie's face and kicked her; I saw she'd left blood on Fannie's apron.

If Hannah were hurt, Rose would be with her, so it couldn't be Hannah. Rose must have had an accident. Fannie slapped Hannah's face to stop her shrieks; I darted past them both and raced up the stairs to help.

The apartment door was open; they were in the kitchen. Isaac sat at the table, huddled in his old brown coat; and Rose lay on the floor, spreadeagled on her back, her eyes open, her mouth twisted in terror. Her dress was soaked with blood, blood had puddled on the linoleum, a heap of sodden towels lay across her stomach.

Isaac looked dully at me. "I tried to stop the bleeding with the towels."

I knew Rose was dead even though I'd never seen anyone dead before. I stepped toward her anyway, and then I saw the bread knife in front of Isaac on the table. The blade was red, the white tablecloth red beneath it.

I backed off, my eyes riveted on Isaac. He went on explaining, pleading with me to understand, his voice hoarse, as though he'd already explained a thousand times.

"I told her to stop and she wouldn't. I was cutting the pumpernickel, and I told her she had to stop."

He raised his right hand in front of him, turning it back and forth as though it were on exhibit; I was too frightened to move.

"This hand killed her," he said. "This hand and that knife." He moved his chin a fraction of an inch, in the knife's direction.

Then he wrapped his coat around himself again, nodding his head in despair. "I killed my Rose."

I retreated, afraid to turn my back on him; each step of mine an eternity long. Rose lay on the floor, unmoving; I saw Hannah's footprints on the linoleum. When I reached the door, I turned at last and ran.

I felt as though I'd been with Isaac forever, but hardly anything had changed downstairs. Fannie still held onto Hannah, still not knowing; Obbie stood with her, his pants half on, pulling up his suspenders. She must have told them it was Rose as I reached them, because Obbie ran past me suddenly, jumping the stairs two at a time behind me.

"It doesn't matter," I told Fannie. "Rose is dead."

She let go of Hannah and ran after Obbie; I sat down on the floor, thinking dimly that I'd said nothing about Isaac, nothing about murder. I knew I never would either; what had passed between us was mine alone.

Hannah shuddered, and spoke to the air. "My father killed her."

Unable to say anything, I held her against me. I wondered if he'd put his coat on after he killed her; if he was cold and trying to keep warm. Above us, Fannie began to scream; neighbors poured in; Obbie shouted for the police. Women tried to move us from the hall but Hannah wouldn't budge; I wouldn't leave her, and someone threw a blanket around us both. Every so often Hannah spoke again, the same words. "My father killed her."

My mother came from nowhere to bring us a glass of whiskey. "Rose is dead," I said. "Hannah found her."

She said she knew, and rubbed my hands with hers. My father came down, his face haggard; he too had blood on his hands. Isaac must have stabbed her in the stomach, where the towels were heaped.

"He's still in the kitchen," my father said. "Like he's stuck to the chair by Rose."

My mother held her hand to her throat, her voice a whisper. "He says he killed her?"

"He says when she laughed at his pants, she said he looked like a clown." My father shook his head. "I have to wait with him. Obbie and me will wait until the police come."

After a while, my mother and Fannie got us both inside. Fannie wanted Hannah to climb into the bathtub, but she wouldn't take off her clothes, and they had to content themselves with washing off her face and hands. A policeman asked Hannah what she knew, and she told him to ask Isaac, to ask her father. Fannie told him to leave Hannah alone.

When I insisted, my mother stood at the door with me to watch them take him away. They'd handcuffed him and he looked smaller, like a child. He was still in the old brown coat, and his pants and shoes had clotted stains. Hannah was inside with Fannie; she didn't want to see him and he'd asked specially not to have to say good-bye to her. His head bowed, he didn't say anything to me either.

Later, the ambulance took Rose's body, but by then we were across the street in my apartment. The doctor visited and gave Hannah a shot to make her sleep; my mother sat with her while she lay on my bed in her bloody clothes. Her aunt came from Philadelphia in the middle of the night in a friend's car, and my father carried Hannah down without waking her. I was asleep in my grandpa's bed; I didn't see her go.

It wasn't the end; they talked about it over and over. I was glad they didn't understand either.

"She wanted to know why everyone but him was making money since the war," my father said. "Like she always said, but worse. She wanted him to get a raise, and he said they'd fire him first, he took too many religious holidays."

My mother was knitting a sweater for me for winter; we were in the living room, and I was pretending to do homework. I was afraid my father was going to cry again, and I was careful not to look up.

"He couldn't make her understand, Helen."

My mother's voice was soft, defensive. "She was raised in an orphanage. She wanted security. Sam, if everyone killed their wife for nagging there'd be no one left."

But he insisted, refusing to back down. "She went too far. She told him she'd rather see Hannah dead than married to a fool like him."

Isaac put out his hand, turning it slowly in the light. That hand and that knife killed her. He'd only stabbed her once, and then she bled to death. And he was sorry.

My grandpa spoke from behind the newspaper. "So he killed her?"

Isaac explained to me again. "I told her to stop and she wouldn't. And then she said I looked like a clown in my pants. Like the clown I was."

My mother giggled hysterically. "Can you see him wearing his tallis with the other murderers?" No one answered; she blew her nose into her handkerchief.

He'd done it and he tried to stop the bleeding with her kitchen towels. She must have yelled at him for getting them so dirty.

"She didn't mean it," my mother said. "She was just saying what came into her head."

Isaac shook his head; she'd gone too far. I wondered if she'd been so angry because my mother had just shown Rose her new Persian lamb coat the night before. Isaac looked out at me from mournful brown eyes; brown eyes and an old brown coat. If only he'd been glad he killed her. She was dead anyway, it didn't matter to her if he was glad. Whatever they might say about repentance.

The remembered voices blended imperceptibly into a song on

the car's radio. I opened my eyes, my ears popping as I swallowed, and saw we were climbing on a mountain road. Bob said we'd all been asleep when he reached Las Vegas; and he decided to drive straight through. We were almost at Zion.

We spent the next five days exploring Zion, and then drove on to Bryce. I was more jittery each day, and the boys more cranky. It was our second morning at Bryce; we'd gone horseback riding, then stopped for breakfast. The stale smell of cooking permeated the air of the restaurant, and a tour bus had just unloaded its camera-laden occupants to compete with us for the waitress' attention. Adam complained that his pancakes were doughy; Dan kicked him under the table, and I told them both to be quiet.

They weren't acting like themselves, fighting in the car and complaining on the trails; they'd disappointed me. I was disappointed in Bryce too: it was more crowded than I'd remembered.

Sipping my bitter coffee, I glared at the mobs around us; the restaurant felt like a New York luncheonette at noon.

An hour later, we parked near a trailhead, and crossed the grassy plateau leading to the edge of Bryce Canyon. The plateau was green and studded with wildflowers; and then it ended, abruptly. Below was a wide amphitheater of red eroded spires, narrow stone towers rising five hundred to a thousand feet from the canyon floor.

Adam began to whine again, complaining of the heat and bugs. To keep myself from shouting at him, I walked ahead, and began the hike down the yard-wide trail. A crowd of tourists stood at the rim taking pictures, but no one followed us down. We'd looked from the edge the day before; today we were going in. I called back a warning that the trail was slippery.

Slippery and steep, it dropped five hundred feet in the next mile. We were winding through the first of the sandstone spires in minutes, the people above no longer in earshot, and in a few minutes more, barely visible. The green plateau was high above, irrelevant among the orange rocks. If we walked for an hour, we'd be at the bottom of the amphitheater, at the floodplain made by melting snow in spring.

Bryce was smaller than Zion, drier, and much stranger, its rocks red and jagged to Zion's blue-gray serenely rounded surfaces. I wondered what my parents would have made of this landscape; they'd found my travel lust incomprehensible.

"A tree is a tree," my father had once said, and I'd stalked from the room in a rage. He'd been afraid of unknown places, the idea of travel linked with chaos, with the war in Europe or with his terrified arrival at Ellis Island when he was ten.

When we returned to the motel room after an early lunch, the boys watched TV while I pored over the maps once more. I knew we could drive east from Bryce and be in Escalante in two hours. I wanted to see where they'd been killed without more waiting. The boys began arguing about which show to watch; I shouted at them for the tenth time that day, and Bob finally came out of the shower.

"I want to go to Escalante now," I said. "It's on the way to Capitol Reef and Colorado anyway. Or Canyonlands."

"You're not going to see anything," Bob answered. "You don't even know exactly where it happened."

"What if I go to the police station?"

He shrugged without answering, and sat on the bed to put on socks.

"Someone might remember. People don't move around much out here."

"Daniel, let Adam alone," he said. "You won't be satisfied unless we go, will you?"

"My father was a very good driver. I want to know what happened."

His answer was toneless. "You got the report. A truck went out of control and your father went off the road."

"I'll go myself then. You can stay here." I marched from the room and paced seething around the motel building several times. We'd been through the argument before. In New York he'd said we would go; he was just delaying.

When I came back, Bob was packing a duffel bag. "We're ready to leave," he said. "But if you can't find more out, will you finally be able to let it rest?"

I nodded calmly, more sure than I'd been in New York. "As long as I see where it happened."

We checked out and began driving, everyone quiet with private thoughts. I could feel the boys' eyes boring into my back. "Do you understand why I want to see where Grandma and Grandpa died?" I asked. "We're so near where it happened. Don't you want to see for yourself?"

"Will the car still be there?" Adam asked.

"No." Bob's voice was definite. "There won't be anything to see. But your mother is hoping she can talk with someone who knows more about it."

"It's kind of gruesome," Dan said hesitatingly. I turned around to face him.

"If Dad and I were killed somewhere, in an accident, wouldn't you want to see where it happened?"

He contemplated an inner vision; after a moment he answered carefully. "I don't know. It might hurt too much."

I picked my words as carefully as he'd picked his. "It hurts me more not seeing. Even after all this time, I can't completely believe they're gone. I need to be able to say good-bye."

His face was uncomprehending; he was too young. I looked at Adam, but he'd withdrawn, pressing his nose against the glass to stare out at the distance. Bob nudged me with his elbow, asking me to be quiet. I turned and looked out the window too.

The land dropped as we left Bryce and became steadily more arid, the grassland giving way to sagebrush. This was ranching country, but overgrazed, the growth sparser every season, turned into desert by the cattle.

"The map shows a campground with a lake just outside Escalante," I said. The boys began looking forward to a swim. I was glad to see them cheer up.

A half-hour later we turned onto a dirt road, forded a small river and corkscrewed around a hill. The lake was before us, large and miraculously blue against the parched earth, but the campsites were totally unshaded in an open field, scorching under the sun. Only one site was taken, a small van parked before the picnic bench.

The ranger was spraying herbicide outside the rest rooms; he explained that keeping down the weeds discouraged rattlesnakes, even if it made the campsites barren, and he warned us not to walk through brush on the way to the lake.

Bob volunteered to take the boys swimming; I followed the ranger back to his office. We talked a bit about sights to see; and then I explained my mission.

"That would be state police," he said sympathetically. "No idea who that would be so far back. Sheriff is new too, but I'll give you directions to his office."

At the lake, I called to Bob. "I have directions to the sheriff's office. He's new but he might know something."

The boys were splashing in the water, looking happier than they had in days. "I can go myself. It's right in town. There's no reason to drag everyone along."

Bob toweled himself off, swatting at the sand gnats, and gave me a worried look. "You sure you want to go alone? It's probably going to be a big disappointment."

"I'd rather."

He objected again, not liking to leave me to myself, but I overrode him. "It's the first time the boys look happy. When I come back, I'll swim too."

The water had risen by the time I forded the river to get out. If it rose much more, we wouldn't be able to leave, and I wondered distractedly why it was up without rain. My hands were wet with perspiration in the air-conditioning, I felt sick to my stomach, and my throat was scratchy. I hoped I wasn't getting a cold, that it was all nerves.

Escalante had one main street, with two general stores, a café, a fast-food stand, and a bank. I turned onto a dirt road and drove another mile in search of the sheriff's office. When I found it, I had to sit in the car awhile to nerve myself up.

My memories were at the center now, up to what happened after the murder. I finally understood why I felt so responsible for the accident, that my guilt was part of the past, rooted in what happened after Isaac left for prison, rooted in my wish to cut my father out of me when it was over. But the accident was real too; I had to lay that ghost to rest before I could come closer to him.

I thought the sheriff was out until a lean balding man appeared from a back room. When I told him what I wanted, he shook his head regretfully.

"I'm sorry, ma'am. I wasn't sheriff then."

"Is there any way to find out exactly where it happened?" I insisted. "Any record of that?"

"I doubt it, ma'am. Five years ago?"

He went back out, called to me to give him a few minutes, and returned with a large map and some notes.

"We did have a record of it. Truck crossed to their side of the road, and your dad swerved left and went over the edge. I can't tell you exactly where, but it was along this stretch. There's twenty-seven miles between Boulder and us, and it was somewhere in there."

Unfolding the map at the desk, he showed me where we were, and made a box around a section of road to the east.

"It starts to be rough country out there," he said. "Road winds a lot, and there's drop-offs on both sides. But my guess, it was just plain bad luck. Note I have says truck driver lost his brakes in the heat, he just couldn't stop."

"But he lived," I said bitterly.

He gave me an odd look and handed me the map. "I'm sorry, ma'am, but that's all I got. You could take a look out there yourself, but drive careful. It's not country for an Easterner."

I thanked him and turned to leave when he called me. "Make sure you got water with you. We get more traffic than we used to, but it can still be a long wait if you break down."

I drove off quickly, before I could think; but I hesitated when I reached the main road again. I'd promised Bob I was just going to the sheriff; but it was only about twenty more miles to the accident. My father had already driven the worst part of the road when it happened, the unpaved part outside Capitol Reef. I could see him frowning at the wheel, his head forward over hunched shoulders, sorry he'd come, desperate to be home, driving too fast so he could be done with it. It was my business anyway, no one else's; I turned left and started out of town.

The road forked a few miles later, and a marker said the dirt road on the right was Hole-in-the-Rock Road. On my map it wound for sixty miles through red rock, all of it country that Butch Cassidy once hid out in, taunting the lawmen with his disappearances. My father would have liked that road, liked to follow in Butch Cassidy's path. I was tempted to take the turn, but I'd already broken my word to Bob by coming out here myself; and if I broke down, no one would know: you were supposed to tell a ranger before going into back country.

Ten miles farther and the road curved sharply to the right; I parked at the graveled look-out along the edge and stepped out to survey a new landscape. The terrain beneath had suddenly turned from cattle country to canyonlands, bare rock in reds and blues rolling up and down in sea-like waves to the horizon. The road cut sharply through the rock, breaking the natural lines of canyon and plateau, a narrow black ribbon teetering on razor edges. It was an immense space, austere and barren, like a spectacle of Mars. *Planet of the Apes* was filmed in this landscape, at Glen Canyon to the south; so was *The Ten Commandments.* My parents must have been overcome.

My throat had really begun to hurt; I drank water from the canteen, telling myself it was just dryness. My blood count was low; if I got sick, we were a long way from a hospital. Shivering, I turned down the air-conditioning in the car. After the congested roads of New York, this empty space was overwhelming. I hadn't seen anyone else in half an hour.

I turned on the radio for company, but all I got was static; the odds against my parents and the truck colliding must have been enormous.

I clutched the wheel, following the twisting ribbon through corrugated landscape; the road was like a roller coaster. I slowed to thirty, then twenty, looking for where it happened, looking for a sign of the wreckage or the fire. There were so few plants, the rocks themselves might still be scorched.

A truck came toward me from around a hairpin turn, too fast for the narrow road; he honked and I moved to the edge to let him pass. But the road dropped off fifty feet on both sides; we needed rails. Then I was climbing again. I couldn't believe they'd built a road through this.

At last I reached a valley, and houses ahead; a village. A ramshackle general store sat at the side of the road. I pulled over and walked in. This was the town of Boulder.

The woman looked at me strangely; maybe I looked as frantic as I felt. I ordered two Cokes and asked if I could refill my canteen; I was so thirsty I'd finished all my water on the way.

She took my canteen to a sink at the back while I gulped the sodas. I knew I must have passed the site of the accident without knowing it. I wasn't ready to let go. I told her my parents had been killed near the town, four years before.

"I remember," she said gruffly. "We don't get many accidents like that out here. There wasn't nothing anyone could do for them; you could see smoke for sixty miles. At least they were thrown clear."

In her dress and apron she looked like a farmer from another age; at the counter I saw an open Mormon Bible. When she volunteered no more, I prodded her. "Did you see it?"

"I saw the smoke and went down there in my pick-up truck; but they was gone by the time I got there. State Police got them out real fast. It was the first New York car I ever seen. Not that there was much left."

She knew; she'd seen it. Taking out the map, I spread it on the counter. "Can you show me where it happened?"

She narrowed her eyes, her mouth pursed, remembering; then she took my pencil and marked an X. It was behind me, about four miles; one of the many turns and twists along the ridge line. High and up. He'd always been afraid of heights.

I'd missed the spot, for all my careful driving; I'd passed it without seeing. But I couldn't stop there even if I found it on the way back; the road up there was all hairpin turns.

My legs were shaking and I felt lightheaded. I wasn't ready to drive back. Thanking her, I turned to leave, thinking I'd find a place to stop farther down the valley.

She spoke unexpectedly, her voice quiet. "There's a cemetery a few miles on."

Thanking her again, I began to cry. I was mortified by my tears, sure I was too emotional for her Mormon taste, but I couldn't stop myself.

I drove off slowly, drinking from my canteen, glad the road was easy here, wondering how I'd ever make it back. My mind was wandering and I went too far before I realized, turning around in someone's driveway while their dog barked at me frantically. The cemetery was unmarked, no more than a small group of sun-baked graves behind a wire fence to one side of the road. The wooden gate was unlatched, and I walked in hesitantly, trying not to intrude, reading the markers as I picked my way among the mounds. They were all Mormon, family plots of three and four generations, holding too many small children. Plastic flowers decorated many of the graves, some fitted into plastic cups that had been blown over by the wind. I paced through, reading Mormon benedictions: he was a good husband, she bore ten children. Then among the newer plots, one with a marble monument, the only one: for Mosiah Smith, sergeant, 3rd Army, 80th division, 1912–1945, killed in action.

Staring at it, my head swimming, I knew this was why my father had taken this road. This was the sergeant who'd saved his life and died in the foxhole on top of him. On the road from Denver, it must have looked like only a minor detour. Having come so far, in country so alien to him, he must have seen the town of Boulder on the map and come to pay respects. He was here on his own, I had nothing to do with it. He'd died on his own, and I hadn't killed them, I wasn't responsible.

Sitting on the dry hot sand, I wondered if he was destined to drive out here from the beginning, to see Mosiah Smith and die himself. The sergeant had been waiting for him since 1945; he was thirty-three when he was killed. I began to cry again, for Mosiah Smith, and for the man who'd been my father beneath him in the foxhole, a man I'd been too young to know.

Shivering in the sun, I cried for us all until I was sodden with tears, wishing I could tell him at last that I loved him.

By the time I staggered back to the car it was almost six o'clock. I could hardly drive, crawling at fifteen miles an hour, veering to the edge of the road and back, passing the scene of the accident with a final farewell. By the time I made it to the campground I knew I had a raging fever.

They were sitting at the picnic table, having dinner. When I didn't move, Bob ran to the car and pulled open the door.

"I didn't know it was so late," I mumbled. "I think I'm sick."

I collapsed with my head against the steering wheel; he carried me out. "You're burning up," he said.

From his pack he took a thermometer and a stethoscope, part of his first-aid kit. I lay uncaring on the sand.

It was cooler, then too cool; I began to shiver. "You have a hundred and four," he said. "Dan has a sore throat; you must have caught the same bug."

Dan began to cry; ignoring him, Bob put aspirins in my hand for me to swallow and held his canteen to my mouth to wash them down. He sprinted for the ranger's office and ran back. "I have to drive down to his house. He's gone home."

Dan and Adam were looming over me, both crying. I didn't care anymore, couldn't help any of them. I asked for a blanket and they covered me with sleeping bags.

When Bob came back with the ranger, the two of them bundled me into the car. I heard Bob ask him to ship our gear to his parents' home, and I tried to tell him we should pack up ourselves. But I wasn't making sense, or else he wasn't paying any attention to me. They wrapped me in the sleeping bags, and I asked if the heat could be turned on.

"I radioed the hospital at Salt Lake City," Bob said. "It's three hundred miles from here, so we'll drive back to Bryce and get a private plane. They have an airport and a Cessna for sightseeing; the pilot will be ready for us by the time we get there."

I didn't follow the rest of the trip, knew vaguely only that Bob was speeding terribly, driving through small towns with his hand on the horn as if he were an ambulance. Every so often I'd croak for water and the canteen would appear. I thought it was wonderful we had so many canteens.

I don't remember the flight either, have only a flash of being carried onto the plane in the dark. At Salt Lake, an ambulance was waiting, a real one, and Bob held my hand. But I was tossing around by then, delirious. When they admitted me, the intern said it was good Bob drove so fast; if he'd been an hour later, I'd have been dead.

18

I LAY ON A STRETCHER IN THE EMERGENCY ROOM OF THE HOSPITAL while they debated what drugs to give me. Bob was there some of the time, and the boys, and my parents, and Isaac; I kept telling them all that everything would be all right.

Isaac was in prison, awaiting trial; Hannah was still with her aunt in Philadelphia. We were buying the garage at the end of the year with the money my father had won on the horses. Fannie and Obbie knew, but no neighbors; my mother said it was to be a secret until we owned the garage, that people would envy us too much. But my father was so excited he walked to the garage every Saturday just to watch customers drive in and out.

The day we got the news I'd just come in from Hebrew school. My mother was on the phone, her face ashen; gesturing for me to be quiet, she turned her back. I put my books on the kitchen table, afraid my grandpa had had a heart attack.

She was talking too low for me to hear, but she wasn't screaming; I decided my father had been fired again. When she got off, she was icily calm, retrieving my father's Camels from the cupboard and heating a pot of coffee before telling me what the call was about. She poured herself a cup, adding milk and sugar with great care, then sat down and puffed a smoke ring in the air. She never smoked before dinner or drank coffee, never used milk just before a meal of meat.

Her eyes glittering, she looked straight at me. "Your father's been arrested. With my brother. With Obbie."

I felt as though the floor had given way beneath me. I wanted my grandfather, but he was at shul. We were alone. Staring back at her in mute terror, I was afraid to ask if they'd killed someone.

She stubbed out her cigarette and lit another, sitting upright in her chair as though she'd break if she slumped. She began to tell me what they'd done, choked, put her face in her hands and sobbed once. She stopped herself with an effort of will, and went on speaking from behind her hands.

"They're thieves. Both of them. My brother and my husband."

She sobbed again, her chest heaving, the backs of her hands wet with tears. I still didn't understand what they'd done, and I was still afraid to ask. Isaac looked up at me from the kitchen chair, the knife in front of him. At least they hadn't killed anyone.

She moaned into the room's silence. "When Poppa comes home, I have to tell him."

I wondered if they'd robbed a store, or broken into a rich person's house; finding my tongue at last, I asked only if they were in jail, like Isaac.

She stared at me as if I were responsible, her face hard, her mouth twisting, and answered indirectly. "That was your father on the phone, he wants me to get him bail. I guess I have to, don't I? Poppa will tell me it's part of my obligation as a Jewish wife."

She was talking to me as if I were adult, as if I understood when I didn't. Standing to wash her coffee cup, she poured out more instead, her voice bitter. "Mona, when you get married, I hope you pick better than me."

Then Bob leaned over me and said I had pneumonia; he wanted the doctor to start penicillin. A stranger in a white coat pulled him away; when I called for Bob, the stranger said they had to use other antibiotics, that they needed stronger medicines than penicillin. He said a doctor on the staff had died that winter because they hadn't used strong enough drugs, a doctor on chemo like me. The antibiotics he was going to give me were dangerous but necessary; he felt he had no choice.

I told him to go ahead, I was waiting for my grandpa; someone began an I.V. The boys bent over the blankets to kiss me good-bye while tears ran down their cheeks, and I ran to my grandpa when he came home; my mother told him what had happened.

"The two of them?" he repeated. "They've been stealing all year?"

"That's where Fannie's ring came from, and both our coats," my mother said grimly. "And our garage money. Sam didn't win nothing on the horses."

She poured coffee into his special cup; holding the cup with both hands, he stared into it. "That's a lot of money they took."

She gazed at him reproachfully. "I can add too, Poppa. At least they didn't arrest them here, where everyone would see." Turning suddenly, she ran into the bathroom.

He sighed and finished the coffee before making his calls. Curled up in the living room armchair, I listened to him arranging bail, crying into my balled up sweater so he wouldn't hear me. When he finished, he told my mother through the bathroom door that he'd go to the police station for her, that it wasn't for a woman to do.

Fannie knocked as he was leaving, as my mother was tying his scarf. Fannie's face was red and puffy; she put her arms out to my mother, but my mother pushed her away. My grandpa stopped long enough to ask her what she knew.

She shook her head dolefully. "Nothing. Obbie never told me nothing."

My mother grunted, her voice acid. "Didn't you wonder how he got you all your presents?"

Fannie stared at her, narrowing her eyes. "So what about the down payment on your famous garage?"

"He said he won it on the horses. He's won before."

"I bet he talked Obbie into it," Fannie said accusingly.

My mother's knuckles were white against the back of the chair. "No one ever talks Obbie into nothing!"

I whimpered and Bob took my hand. Then he was gone; I shut my eyes again.

My father was home on bail; I knew that meant he wasn't going to jail yet. I listened to them through the bedroom door.

"We started with pilfering. Small things. There's always pilfering. Then we took some machinery off the docks. We said it never got delivered . . . peanuts. Everyone steals off the docks."

"Not everyone," my mother said.

He answered softly, but he didn't relent. "More people than you know, Helen. In this country, everyone steals a little."

"This was with Obbie?" she asked.

"Helen, he's been stealing for years!"

She kept pushing, her voice more frightening than Miss Malone's at school. She sounded as though she hated him.

"He cut you in?"

He hesitated for the first time. "We talked about it for a long time. He's never done big jobs. . . . Helen, I want that garage. I don't want no bosses telling me to wipe my nose every day."

I knew he shrugged as plainly as if I could see through the wall. "When he got me this new job, it looked easy to heist a truck. The whole truck. He's got the union contacts. Where to sell it. It was all taken care of. I don't even know that part of it."

But there was no hard evidence; they were denying everything. It was after midnight and I began to fall asleep.

"The boss says he'll drop the charges if we give back the money."

His voice was flat and stubborn; I came out of sleep, not sure if he'd really said it. In the living room, my mother laughed aloud. He overrode her laughter, implacable and at the same time patient, as if she were stupid.

"Helen, with this behind me, I'll never get a job again. I can't give the money back."

I was in an intensive care unit; I tossed on the bed while a nurse changed I.V. tubes. Bob sat with me, and his parents, and the boys; then my own parents came back. My father was talking again, telling her he couldn't return the money. He'd hijacked the truck to buy the garage; if he gave the money back, he'd have less than before. He'd have nothing.

Slumped in the chair, unshaven, he looked like Isaac. Defeated. I crept away, unable to bear watching him. I counted all the pennies that I'd saved since I was six, but I was old enough to know I didn't have enough. And I knew even then that we couldn't ask Jake for the money.

I was crying; Bob told me not to cry, he was with me, my fever was going down. But my father stayed away more; when he was at home they fought. He told her the money was in the bank, in his name so that she couldn't get it. Her mouth a tight line, she said it didn't matter what he did, we were living off her money anyway. She took every singing job she could get; even if he didn't go to jail, I was sure she'd leave him.

Hannah moved back, with Isaac's sister from Philadelphia; Irene let us play together after I recited the names of twenty Presidents. We stayed outside in all kinds of weather: Irene wouldn't let me into the apartment and I didn't want Hannah at my house. I told her nothing, I knew my mother would die if I told anyone; and Hannah wasn't curious. Pale and withdrawn, she had no curiosity left.

My mother grew thinner, drinking endless cups of coffee with her cigarettes; both my parents stank of tobacco. My father's eyes were darker, with blue circles under them; when he didn't shave, the blue matched the color of his cheeks. He was impatient and shouted at me for making noise the way he had when he first came home from the war.

One night he took out his pictures of the camps again, of the living skeletons in the tiered bunks, too weak even to lift the rifles he'd given them to shoot the guards. Of the pile of baby shoes and gold teeth outside the gas chambers. I thought of Isaac in prison, saw them lead him praying to the execution room.

My father turned the photos over slowly, the muscles in his jaw jumping, a sheen of perspiration on his forehead. My mother was out. I was supposed to be asleep, but I'd gotten up to use the bathroom, and tiptoed over to see what he was looking at. His voice harsh, he sent me back to bed; I thought he was thinking of how it would feel to be a prisoner.

The next afternoon they were both gone when I came home from school. My grandpa met me at the door; I was sure my father was in jail, my mother saying good-bye to him. I asked where they were but he wouldn't tell me, and for a moment I even wondered if my father had killed her, like Rose. Finally he said my father was with my Uncle Obbie, and my mother out, by herself.

He made me hot chocolate, and my mother came home while I was still blowing on it and thinking that everyone but her made it too hot. She was wrapped in her coat and scarf even though it was warm out, and she sat at the table without removing them. Her eyes were red.

Across from her, my grandpa held her hands in his; she gazed hopelessly at him.

"He wouldn't take it. He laughed at me, he said it wasn't worth a tenth the money. He laughed at me, Poppa."

My grandpa wiped her eyes gently with a napkin. Her voice was beseeching.

"I felt like a beggar, like garbage."

Without raising his head, he ordered me into the bedroom. I stood up obediently, but turned back at the threshold.

"You can't pretend I didn't hear anything. It's too late."

She shivered in her coat, her eyes huge and wounded; I felt transparent to her gaze, as if I weren't there.

"I tried to give your father's boss my wedding ring. My wedding ring and everything I've saved from singing. He laughed, he said it was peanuts; he wants all the money back or your father goes to jail."

She traced a pattern on the table with her finger, her tone bitter beyond words.

"He said next time Sam shouldn't send a stand-in."

My grandpa sucked in his breath. "A crumb."

"A bastard, Poppa. A fourteen-karat bastard. I told him Sam would kill me if he knew I was there."

"Daddy didn't know?" I was appalled. She'd gone alone.

"Mona, I can say a lot of things about your father, but they don't include sending his wife to beg for him." She smiled for the first time, sardonically. "I may have married a thief, but I didn't marry a coward."

When I woke again I was still in intensive care, but my fever was down. Bob stayed with me as long as the nurses allowed; he said his parents were at a motel with the boys. I was still confused; that night I became delirious again, tearing out the I.V. tubes and wandering down the hall to find my father. I asked at the Hebrew school, but they were too busy; it was near Chanukah and they were preparing for the eight days of celebration.

The teacher's cheeks flushed as he told the tale of victory over the Syrians two thousand years before; his voice grew louder.

"The evil king Antiochus refused to let the Jews pray to Yahweh, the true God; his scum entered the holy temple and defiled it with statues of the pagan gods. The priest Mattathias and his five sons rebelled, and Judas Maccabeus, the eldest, led the rebel army to victory."

He stared into the distance as if he could see their army coming; picking at my nails, I tried to shut them out. I was sure my father was going to go to prison. His voice dropped dramatically, but no one seemed to be listening; most of the class was glassy-eyed with boredom, and the daily dice game at the back was unchanging in its rhythm.

"A tiny rebel army, they won against the mighty forces of Antiochus, and drove them out of Palestine! Wishing to thank Yahweh for their great victory, they began to cleanse the temple, ready to dedicate it afresh with the burning of oil in the holy menorah."

He paced the room, his burning eyes fixed on mine. "They had oil for one night, for one night only, but . . . miraculously . . . the oil burned . . . and burned . . . and burned. For eight days. Yahweh's miracle."

I averted my eyes, tearing at a cuticle with my teeth. Behind me, a boy belched; I giggled uncontrollably. Christmas was coming too, it always came near Chanukah. Eight days of oil wasn't impressive against weeks of Christmas songs on the radio. And God hadn't made the miracle when the Maccabees needed Him, when they were still fighting.

Mr. Solomon generally ignored belches, but this time he called to the boy. "You do not believe Yahweh made such a miracle?"

It was Jacob, the worst troublemaker in the class, the only one of us ever to talk back. I couldn't, I felt too sorry for our teachers.

"If God is so powerful, why doesn't He make miracles anymore?" he sneered.

Mr. Solomon shrank into his black coat; his pants were shiny like Isaac's, his eyes as mournful beneath the yarmulke. When my father slumped in his chair, he looked like him.

"Many of us who survived the camps feel it was God's doing," he whispered.

Jacob was defiant; instead of stopping, he uttered the unspeakable. "Then why did He let six million die?"

Turning his back to the window overlooking the playground, Mr. Solomon began crying. "God's ways are mysterious. Perhaps it is a test."

Even the boys playing dice stopped. If we could have, we all would have run. This wasn't to be talked about here, this wasn't to be talked about at all.

Jacob pushed on, although his voice trembled. His stepfather was a survivor of the camps; he never knew his real father, who died in combat. I understood why he didn't believe in miracles. He came only because his mother insisted he be prepared for bar mitzvah when he was thirteen.

"My father says some people believe God is so weak He didn't even make the world. The Devil did."

Mr. Solomon flinched in the hushed room. Jacob continued, his words dropping into the abyss. "My father says God and the Devil have fought for the world since the beginning of time, since creation, but the Devil always wins."

Mr. Solomon's voice was pitched high with strain. "That is a Christian heresy. People have been burned at the stake for that belief."

He surprised me; I'd thought Christians burned only Jews. But Jacob's statement tore through me: a revelation. Even Job made sense if the Devil was stronger.

"Jews do not believe in the Devil," Mr. Solomon added, his face cracking like the reflections in a broken mirror. "Men make evil, you need no devil to explain it."

My father slumped in the chair, staring at his photographs; Isaac held out his hand in the presence of his dead wife's body; without warning I began to sob.

"Men have been free to choose what they do since Adam and Eve ate of the forbidden fruit," Mr. Solomon cried.

Opening my eyes, I told the nurse it wasn't Isaac's fault: if the knife hadn't been there when Rose taunted him, he never would have killed her. Mr. Solomon put his arms around me; I'd been his best pupil until October, and now I sat silently through class I asked him why my baby brother died, and he held me closer.

"Mona, my sweet maidele, I do not know the answers. Men have asked these questions since they fled the caves with wooden spears. It is why the animals are blessed; they live in ignorance."

I clung to him, my head buried in his narrow chest, and then I ran from the room. He had no answers; and I hated him, he'd let them come and take him like a cow into their cattle cars.

Bob held my hand and I smiled at him, but I told him I couldn't stay. When my grandpa came home, I had to ask him if the Devil was stronger than God.

When I woke again, my fever was gone. I stayed up longer, asking Bob questions.

He slumped exhaustedly in the room's armchair, watching me with red-rimmed eyes. His face was pale, his cheeks sharp and hollowed. "The boys gave you water and covered you when you thrashed around. Do you remember them saying good-bye in the morning? They didn't know if they'd ever see you again."

"I don't remember any of it," I said. "I thought my parents were in the car. I thought they were giving me water."

He'd lost weight, said he'd forgotten to eat at first and still wasn't hungry. Too tired to sit up, he was aging in front of my eyes. He'd lost his innocence completely, his childlike faith in his invulnerability.

"I've never been this tired," he said. "You don't realize how close you came."

A nurse told him it was time to leave; he said he'd be back as soon as they let him in again. When he left, I thought that I hadn't been frightened at all, I was too sick. Once I reached the campground, I'd turned over all responsibility to him; I'd trusted him to save me.

The next day my fever rose again; either the antibiotic wasn't working or I was having a reaction to it. They stopped it and started other drugs, equally toxic. I tossed in the narrow bed, the Devil standing over me, reciting my sins.

Bob plotted my fever and white count against the timing of the drug injections, hoping to see a connection, to see whether one of them was responsible. The doctors in charge said they could do nothing more; and they insisted that the antibiotics couldn't be stopped until my white count began to rise. I'd had pneumonia at the start, but my count was so low the normal bacteria in my body were giving me a fever now. Bob called Chou every day, but he had nothing different to offer.

After another week, my white count began slowly to rise, a few hundred blood cells at a time, and my fever slowly fell. They still let the boys visit daily, and I tried to stay alert for my short minutes with them.

On one visit Dan asked if I had cancer.

I was afraid to look at Bob, but from the corner of my eye I saw him freeze. I tried to buy time, asking Dan why he asked.

"Because you're so sick. And the nurses say it's from chemotherapy. Chemotherapy is for cancer, isn't it?"

I thought frantically, not wanting him to brood alone as I did over my father; when I turned to Adam, he too was waiting for my answer, his eyes boring into mine.

I tried to tell the truth and still deny it, my words dry and inflectionless. "It's not called cancer. It's called a nodular lymphoma, and it's a blood disease."

"Like leukemia?" His voice was shaky but he wasn't going to turn back; I hadn't deflected him.

"No. Much less malignant. Less dangerous."

"Isn't leukemia cancer?" This was Adam, his voice treble, high-pitched, hoping I'd say no.

Bob interrupted grimly, trying to get them past the words we'd bogged down in. "As far as you're concerned the answer is yes. Your mother's making a technical distinction that doctors make. We didn't tell you when we found out because we've been hoping you'd never have to know, that Mom will be well."

Dan's face crumpled; he backed against the wall, his hands balled into fists. "You were wrong! You should never lie! Don't you think Adam and I talk about what goes on? You think we're morons?"

It was too late to stop; I blundered on, trying to be honest and protective at the same time, trying to salvage what we could, afraid I was saying too much but unable to stop. If I weren't still weak, I'd have known to keep quiet.

"The doctor says even if I don't get cured, I'll live until you're a lot older. We didn't want you to know what you didn't have to know."

"How much older?" Adam whispered.

I looked down at my hands, not knowing what to say now, desperately sorry I'd blundered into giving him the opening.

"You'd be seventeen, Adam," Bob said gently. "That's what the doctors told us at the beginning."

"So I'd be nineteen?" Dan asked. Bob nodded silently.

Adam ran out, crying. "That's still not enough!"

Dan stood a moment longer, struggling to keep from crying too; he looked at me, then at Bob. "You're not lying? Not now?"

Bob's voice was exhausted. "Did I lie on the way here when I said Mom might die in the car? When I said you had to help me, you had to take care of her until we got to the plane? Do you remember how we all three slept in the same bed at that damned motel those first nights; how we held on to each other?"

"I'm on a special program, Dan," I whispered. "My doctor's hoping the treatment I'm getting is a cure."

He nodded slowly and turned for the door. "I better talk to Adam. I don't think he understands."

I was crying weakly. "Would you tell Adam I'm sorry?" I was hooked to I.V. bottles; I couldn't follow him. When he didn't turn, I called to his back. "Dan!" He stood still. "Dan, if I expected to die, I'd pull you both out of school and we'd travel for six months or a year, not just for a vacation. We wouldn't try to keep to our regular life."

He smiled quirkily, his mouth twisting. "So if you buy a travel trailer, I should know it's bad news?"

I smiled back as best I could. "Only if I take you out of school too. All right?"

"Yeah. All right. I think I understand."

Bob followed him out of the room. When he came back, his face was sagging. "I hope Adam will understand when he's older. My folks are with them now, don't worry."

"I'm sorry," I whispered. "It was all my fault for going on to the cemetery without you."

His face somber, he closed his eyes. "You said you were satisfied."

I told him again that I was satisfied, and he smiled at me for the first time. My eyes were closing too, I couldn't stay awake, but it was over, I'd told him the truth.

That night I dreamed that Isaac and my father were walking off together while Rose pointed at their baggy pants and jeered. I didn't understand, but I was crying when I woke, and I had the dream again and again in the next months.

IV

19

I WAS DISCHARGED FROM THE HOSPITAL A WEEK AFTER THE scene with the boys; Bob brought the floor nurses several bottles of champagne before we left. We flew straight back to New York from Salt Lake, and Chou scheduled the lymphangiogram for just after the Labor Day weekend, promising to call me with the results as soon as he had them. The boys were back in school, and Bob stayed home to wait with me.

As soon as I heard Chou's voice on the phone, I knew I had nodes, that the test was positive.

"I'm sorry," he said miserably. "I should have known you were too sick when you came in. I shot off my mouth in June, saying they'd be gone."

Helplessly, he searched for reassuring words, for something to salvage from the wreckage. I thought desperately that this was as bad as getting the diagnosis in the first place, that I couldn't possibly prepare myself for this kind of news.

"The nodes left are half the size they were at the beginning," he said at last. "We really shouldn't have expected better. And they ought to vanish with the radiation."

Listening bitterly, I was afraid to believe him again; he wanted a cure too much. Bob listened on the extension, as silent as I. I wasn't cured and the odds against my getting cured had just gone up.

"Are we back to ten years?" Bob asked finally, his voice low.

Chou coughed. "Presumably."

"And Mona will need more radiation than you thought?"

Chou withdrew, becoming formal in his failure. "That's Dr. Lee's decision. She and I will consult after Mona sees her."

"And after radiation, the same chemo you planned all along?"

"That's the protocol," Chou answered distantly. "Of course, exactly what we do depends on whether Mona's in remission then." He seemed as desperate as I was to get off the phone.

I'd spoken from the living room, Bob from the bedroom. When we hung up, we sat quietly together on the living room couch, his arm around my shoulders as I curled against him. Listening to his heart thumping in my ear, I thought it ironic that we'd moved in opposite directions. I'd hoped for good news, and I knew Bob had expected bad. He didn't believe in fairy tales anymore, and I didn't expect the worst as a matter of course. We went the next morning to the radiologist.

In the waiting room once more, I huddled in the green gown that barely covered my crotch. A nurse made Bob leave the area. I tried not to think about the radiation, or the fact that I still had a lymphoma, tried not to count off ten years, tried to stay a blank. Eventually I was sent to a cubicle and Bob was allowed to wait with me.

Dr. Lee showed up an hour later with two residents in tow. They took endless measurements with a tape, copying down each little number twice; outlined different shapes on my chest and abdomen; and began tattooing a few black dots onto their outlines. The tattooing was painless, but they turned me to and fro like a piece of meat and ignored my questions until Bob shouted at them; then they looked puzzled by his anger.

"We mark the body to be sure we place the fields of radiation properly," Lee finally explained, drumming the tattoos with her long fingers. She smiled sardonically. "The tattoos are permanent even if the lines fade with washing; we wouldn't want to overradiate an area in error."

Her assistants went on working as though mute; I wondered if they spoke English. Between the stretchers of comatose patients in the waiting room, the thump of X-ray machines and the silent team tattooing me, I felt unreal, like an actress in a film. At some point, I said that Chou had hoped for a remission, more to hear the sound of my own voice than because I expected an answer.

"Dr. Chou and I disagree about the usefulness of chemotherapy," Lee answered dryly. She knew my life depended on the last rounds of chemo after she was done; and still she spoke with so little feeling. I needed her and I hated her already.

The next three months were a nightmare: I lost hair, I threw up, I was exhausted all the time. The week my neck was radiated I felt as if someone had poured acid down my throat; and I was afraid. At night I screamed in my sleep, watching the bevatron machine descending over me on its boom, ten tons of murderous metal coming down on me while the metal door clanged shut, the technician scrambling for shelter before turning on the radiation. I couldn't even talk with Bob about it.

I tried to think of the radiation as healing light, but my resolutions failed whenever I lay down on the glass table in the X-ray room. I saw Herb twice more, and tried to pray myself, and at night I dreamed of Isaac and my father.

I was bald halfway up the back of my head; in October, I had the rest of my hair cut to an inch of my scalp and I bought a wig. When the radiation ended in December, Chou scheduled another lymphangiogram. I waited with Bob for the results once more, calmer this time, and surprised that it was impossible to be afraid of dying all the time. When Chou called, I made him repeat twice what he said: that the results were normal.

We saw him the next day, and he showed us the lymphangiogram films, to convince us that they showed nothing. I listened as he spoke hesitantly again of my having time, of my still having a chance of getting cured, wondering when I'd feel the relief I knew I ought to feel. The next week, I was still struggling with disbelief, and he began the remaining chemo.

My bone marrow was utterly depleted; I had no resistance. Although Chou gave me only four cycles of chemo altogether, I needed months to recover from each one, and the chemo lasted through the winter, spring, and summer. I was admitted to the hospital twice more with high fevers, and went on sick leave from the university until the fall. As the remission continued, Bob and I wistfully agreed I might be cured if only I survived the treatment.

When my hair grew back it was curly and gray; I used a dark rinse and kept it short, in a kind of Afro. And the remission remained.

I saw Chou once a month for the next year, then every other month, anxious for a week before each visit, and terrified as I lay under his hands while he prodded me for nodes. I called him in a panic the first time I had swollen glands with a sore throat; he saw me that afternoon as an emergency, and happily reassured me that they were normal, that normal people got normal neck nodes with infections.

But Mrs. Nettlebaum had another recurrence, and so did David, after only a short remission. The protocol was discontinued; Chou was depressed.

"It's not a cure," he said. "For most patients, it's not even more effective than the ordinary treatments. At the rate we're getting recurrences, almost everyone will have disease again at the end of seven years."

He sat at the metal desk after examining me and finding no disease once more. Slumping, his face defeated, he talked half to me, half to himself.

"Ten percent of my patients died of complications. For nothing."

Dressing, I flinched at his despair, afraid of being contaminated by it. I reminded him that my first doctor had told me that I had only two or three years left to live.

"You'd be dead by now," he repeated reflectively. "You were in my sickest group, the worst fifteen percent. You needed everything we gave you."

I ticked off other treatments coming down the line, the best bets of the moment: microwaves, hybridomas, purified interferon; he added that there were two new drugs being used at Memorial since my last visit. We both kept our files.

We shook hands as I left, buoying each other up; and I reminded myself that in his better moods he still was sure a third of his patients were cured. He bounced like a Yo-Yo, and I didn't dare bounce with him.

By the time I reached the street the sky was darkening, a summer storm approaching. I'd started treatment three and a half years before; I'd already had more time than Blake had said and I had time to wait, time to see what came along, what worked on other people. And maybe I was even cured.

At the beginning of September, we went again to Utah, the first visit since I'd almost died near Escalante. The four of us had backpacked for a week in Virginia the summer before and again over Easter; we'd been planning this trip to Canyonlands for months. We carried the lightest gear we could, tents that weighed less than three pounds, down bags, freeze-dried food. Most of our weight was in water, over sixty pounds in giant plastic bottles, about seven gallons.

The first day we hiked into Elephant Canyon and made camp late in the afternoon, climbing halfway up the rock wall to pitch our tents; we were safe from flash flood on a narrow sloping ledge twenty feet above the canyon floor.

The next morning we trekked on, passing the four-toed track of a bobcat in the sand at the floor, following a twisted passage between the towering walls until we climbed out. At the end, the passage was so narrow I had to take off my pack to squeeze through, pushing it ahead of me on the ground.

Beyond was a windsmoothed plateau, the middle level of rock, its floor cut by canyons like the one we'd just left, and marked by long rows of high rock walls above. I drank from my canteen and moved across the smooth rock to the next trail marker, a small stone balanced on three others.

For the rest of the morning, we followed the trail from cairn to cairn across the plateau, until it dropped into an open vast terrain of unearthly space. In front of us, flat orange plains alternated with narrow rows of standing rock, eroded into sharp-edged fins and isolated towers, some looking like ruined Mayan cities, others mere demented sculptures.

Wind blew, throwing sand in our faces, forcing us to tie red bandanas over nose and mouth before climbing down. We looked alien ourselves, hidden in wide blue terry hats and giant sunglasses, and now bandanas.

At one o'clock we stopped for lunch and a rest in a meadowlike flat field that looked immeasurably green from above, but faded into isolated clumps of gray-green sagebrush when we reached it. Over lunch, Bob made a paper rose from a napkin, and placed it as a centerpiece in our crumpled package of freeze-dried chow mein. When we finished, I packed the rose gently away, and lay down in the shade of a rock until the sun passed its peak; I got up again at three.

"You sure you want to walk to Druid Arch from here by yourself?" Bob asked. "I see rain clouds over the mountains."

"It's an easy walk," I smiled. "I'll get under a rock if it rains."

"It's about an hour's hike. If you're not back in three, we'll come after you."

I patted his hand. "Don't worry so. Boys, I'll see you later."

Daniel waved from where he sat; thirteen years old and half a head taller than I, his upper lip sprouting welcome hairs. Adam was eleven, still chunky and prepubescent. Grinning, he looked up from their chess game. "If you meet a Martian, bring him back."

I blew a kiss and started off, hurrying ahead of the rain, admiring the chameleons as they scuttled past me, stopping long enough to photograph a cactus growing from a crevice, a bird's nest hidden in a hole in the rock.

An hour later, I faced the Arch, a somber structure carved by wind and storm out of the sandstone, looking like an ancient megalithic ruin, one with Stonehenge. Clouds had masked the sky, sunbeams shafting through the few remaining spaces in pillars of light. As I tried to climb nearer, clouds came together overhead, lightning snaking from them in thin-tongued ribbons, striking rock less than a thousand feet away. Smelling ozone, I clambered down the slope to less open ground and crouched beneath a ledge, soaked and shivering, trying to squeeze all of myself into too small a space, covering my ears against the thunder. I hoped the boys were safe with Bob; I knew it would be hard for them to find a shelter large enough to hold them all. As I waited out the storm, I thought of the paper rose Bob had made at lunch, and I saw my father's roses falling on the bed again.

My mother stayed in bed that morning, her head under the pillows; it was Friday. In the kitchen, my father wore a suit and tie, and he'd shaved. For a moment I thought he was giving back the money; then I realized my mother would be up with him in that case, not hiding beneath the covers. My grandfather sat with him, both of them morose over coffee, but they paid me no attention and I took my own corn flakes.

"Obbie's got standing," my father said. "The union twisted the boss's arm; they don't want him on trial."

Putting his cup down drearily, he leaned back. "So I'm the patsy. I pay the money back by Monday or I go on trial."

"Obbie will pay it back if you pay," my grandpa said. "He'll stand by your decision."

"And I talked Obbie into it," my father said, rubbing puffy eyes with the back of his hand. "I know. I don't deserve him backing me up now."

My grandpa shrugged impatiently. "I'm talking about you wasting your life in jail, not about deserving."

My father nodded thoughtfully, and turned to me, saying he'd walk me to school. At the door, he told my grandpa he'd know by nightfall.

His eyes bright with tears, my grandpa hugged him. "Gae gazint," he said.

As we walked off, I wanted to tell my father that he didn't have to steal for me, that I didn't need anything and I'd never ask for anything again, but I was afraid to speak when I looked at his set face.

I kept thinking I had no more time; if I was to act, it had to be today. At recess, I asked Hannah if she'd ever heard of praying to the Devil. She shook her head in denial.

"Your father's coming up for trial," I said.

She glowered at me and clenched her fists, ready to fight. I hadn't mentioned Isaac since she came back from Philadelphia. I was whispering already; looking around the schoolyard, I lowered my voice still more.

"If you promise not to tell anyone, ever, not until you're dead, I have something to tell you."

Her green eyes were narrowed, slitted with fury. "It better be good."

"My mother says she'll die if I tell anyone. You promise?"

"Maybe.'

I hesitated. "If you tell anyone else, I'll throw you off the roof."

"If it matters so goddamned much to you, don't bother." She turned her back.

"Hannah, you have to listen!"

"You have one minute, you creep." She started counting seconds.

"My father's in bad trouble, I can't tell you what, my mother would die, but he's going to go to jail forever. And so both of them are going to jail, right? Your father and mine?"

She showed her first sign of interest. "Your father killed someone?"

"I can't tell you what he did. I told you only if you promised. Anyway, it doesn't matter, he'll be in jail for ever and ever."

"So?"

"Listen, there are miracles, right? Like the oil lamp at Chanukah? Like Moses crossing the Red Sea? Like when Mrs. Rubin's boy got polio and then he walked? Or the baby down the block everyone thought would die? It happens."

"So?"

"I heard in Hebrew school about praying to the Devil. Jews don't believe in him, but that must mean it's not such a sin to pray, because it's not against the Laws, because nobody ever prohibited it. It's not in the Talmud."

She hunched forward, her face screwed up in puzzlement. "Why the Devil? Why not God?"

I blushed, I was really afraid she'd hit me now. "Don't get mad," I warned.

She backed away a step, and asked again, "Why not God?"

"Because you have to repent to pray to God; and you have to ask forgiveness of whoever you wronged. My father won't ask forgiveness, he says they can shove it up you-know-where, and your father . . . can't . . . I mean . . . she's gone. Your mother's gone."

She eyed me morosely, trusting no one. "What if he repented now? My father?"

I had to be honest with her. "I don't know. I just know at Rosh Hashanah they say you have to ask forgiveness of the person you wronged. It's not God's business."

She was unconvinced. I had a flash of intuition. "Listen, haven't you prayed already? You must have prayed!"

Clenching her fists, she closed her eyes with a convulsive heave. "God might still do something. The trial hasn't started."

"Since it isn't forbidden, would you try the other way? To the Devil?"

The bell rang; Miss Malone began lining everyone up as Hannah considered my proposal.

"We're too young to be held responsible," she said finally. "Girls have to be twelve."

For the rest of the afternoon, I watched the time, desperate to begin, afraid my father had already made his choice. By four o'clock, Hannah and I were at the library; I'd taken my mother's card and told the librarian my mother had sent me for books on devils and witches. I'd used my mother's card other times; the librarian told us to go upstairs to the adult section.

The library was my favorite building in all of Brownsville, with ivy climbing up the red brick walls, and a wide winding staircase to the second floor. Whenever I pretended to be Noma, I went to a library just like it. But today we were alone in the room, and the thin white curtains at the long windows moved eerily in the slightest breeze. It was getting late, and I was afraid.

Trying to hurry, we spread books on the floor; it was lucky we both read at sixth-grade level. "They keep talking about crazy old ladies," I complained, "as though there really aren't witches."

"Well, we know they're wrong," she answered curtly. "Look at Mrs. Goldstein."

A few minutes later, she drew her breath in sharply. "I don't think this is for us. And I don't understand it anyway. It's about something called a Black Mass."

I shoved her over to read with her, more heavy-hearted by the moment. "It looks like you have to be Catholic for this. I don't even know what a consecrated wafer is, do you?"

She shook her head. "You have to steal it from a church. Mona, that's out, we can't do that."

"It says you need an altar too." I shut the book in despair, sure it was too late anyway. "I guess it was a dumb idea."

She stared at me with a crazy glint in her eyes. "Listen, I just thought of something. In the horror comics, don't they sometimes have people call up the Devil by drawing a chalk figure . . . five-sided . . . a pentagram?"

I shivered. I knew what she meant, we read the same comics. "But then you sell your soul to the Devil. And you always end up not getting your wish anyway."

She watched me through half-shut lids; we'd exchanged positions. "We're not selling our souls, we're just going to pray," she argued. "And you don't think anything is going to really happen, do you?"

I began replacing the books so the librarian wouldn't see what we'd read. "We can do it in my basement," I said at last. "All we need is chalk."

She shook her head. "Uh uh. The last time I was in your basement, those wild dogs attacked us. And your loony super chased us out the time before. We can use my basement. No one ever goes down there."

We left the library in thoughtful silence. When I reached home, my father was still gone; he'd never even phoned after leaving with me in the morning. I was afraid he'd run away.

My mother put off dinner for an hour, and ate nothing herself; my grandpa went back to shul, and I picked at my roast chicken, waiting for Hannah's knock.

She came at seven o'clock, her face white and stern, her mouth a determined line, her eyes green slits of fire. When I came to the door, she held out a box of white chalk; I told my mother I'd be back in an hour.

As we crossed the street, I wondered if it was more sinful to do this on Shabbes; I hoped God was too busy listening to prayers to notice us, even though I knew that was impossible.

We crept silently into her brownstone, down the dark hall that was forever to make me think of blood. The door to the basement was behind the stairs; Hannah reached for the handle, and pulled. Nothing happened.

"It can't be locked," she muttered. "You try."

I held onto the metal handle with both hands, and pulled with all my strength; the door swung out with a creak. A smell of damp and mold wafted up the dark stone stairway.

"Don't lean on the banister," she whispered. "It's rotted."

"You go first," I whispered back, as bravely as I could manage. It was pitch-black down there.

She started down with me on her heels. The door swung shut behind us. "If we can get to the bottom, there's a light bulb on a chain," she said.

I didn't answer, I was too terrified, and her voice rose in high-pitched panic.

"Mona? Are you behind me?"

"Of course I am," I croaked. "You think I'm not as brave as you?"

She exhaled loudly. "It's just so dark."

She got to the bottom and I leaned against the clammy wall, afraid of falling through the rotten railing, and afraid of falling over her. This was crazy, the craziest thing we'd ever done.

"Do the Gypsies ever hide down here?" I whispered.

She found the light bulb as I blurted the question; it was a dim light and left the edges of the basement still in darkness, but at least I could see her. I heard a sudden scrabbling in one corner, and I leaped down the remaining stairs to hold onto her. She was shivering.

"Is someone there?" she quavered. A shadow ran from the corner to a pile of coal. Not a cat.

I hiccuped in relief; it was a rat. I became more practical. "We better be quiet, so my Aunt Fannie doesn't hear us through the floor."

"The chalk line has to be solid," she added. "We better sweep."

"And big enough. Just in case."

Together we swept the floor with some old newspapers we found in a corner. Hannah raised her eyes from where she kneeled, just before beginning the pentagram.

"You still want to go ahead?"

My heart was racing, and I half hoped my aunt would hear and make us stop, but I'd committed myself. I kneeled next to her, for a moment furious with my father for making me go through with this.

"Just don't pick up the chalk. It's got to be a solid line."

The first piece of chalk broke as she began; she pressed too hard. We erased the line with our shoes, and she began again, mumbling to herself, and crying. We stayed on the outside of the lines while she made the five sides, careful not to let any part of ourselves fall across the perimeter. We backed away when she finished, and sat side-by-side on the narrow bottom step. The rat was still shuffling in the coal bin.

"I just remembered, you need a magic formula," I said.

She shook her head firmly. "We're praying, we're not calling up anyone."

Staring at the pentagram, she grimaced. "It doesn't look like much, does it?"

I was thinking that too; it looked little different from the chalked lines we drew for sidewalk games. I picked up a small piece of coal and threw it into the center. She asked me what I thought I was doing, but I didn't answer. I stared at the coal, concentrating. After a moment, she clasped hands with me. We both had sweaty palms.

"If we see something smoky in the center, we stop," I said. "OK?" In the comic books, that was the first sign of the Devil's coming.

She gripped me harder. "If we see something smoky, we run like hell. So don't close your eyes."

I had enough trouble praying down there without having to

keep my eyes open; I wondered if we could take turns praying so one of us could stand guard. I turned to ask Hannah, but now she was staring at the pentagram. I was afraid to interrupt. Please let my father be all right, I prayed. Please let my father not go to jail. I knew he wanted to keep the money; but I couldn't pray for that. I thought the coal moved slightly in the shadowed light; my hand closed convulsively on Hannah's.

"It's moving!" I whimpered. She pulled loose and bolted up the stairs; we hit the door together, ran partway down the hall, turned, and ran back to slam it shut. On the way out, I remembered we'd left the light on; but neither of us was going to go down again.

When I reached home, my mother was huddled at the table, a full ashtray in front of her. She raised her eyes blearily.

"He isn't back. He's gone and I don't know where he is."

Her face was swollen from crying, her eyes so puffy they were half-closed.

"Grandpa's still in shul. Why don't you come to bed with me tonight?"

I went straight to the bedroom, and crawled into the double bed with her without undressing. She cried with her arms around me. I lay with her, watching the coal moving, not knowing if it was a trick of the shadows, of the swinging bulb. Remembering the fairy tales where wishes always made things worse, I was afraid. But I'd wished my father to be all right, so he couldn't be dead no matter where he was. Half asleep, I wondered how long a devil stayed in a pentagram once you called him up.

When the phone rang, my mother ran for it; with her uncombed hair in tangles, she looked more like a witch than Mrs. Goldstein. She answered on the third ring, but the line went dead at the sound of her voice. Sure it was my father, she waited with the phone in her lap in the cold foyer, but nothing more happened, and she finally stumbled back to bed with me. In the middle of the night, she got up once more to undress.

It was morning when I woke again. My mother was deeply asleep next to me, and my father stood over us, his gaze somber and intent, fixed on her tear-worn face. His jacket was crumpled, his shirt open at the collar, his tie stuffed into a pocket; he was tipsy, I smelled the liquor on him; and he held a huge bouquet of roses. When he saw me looking up at him, he smiled gently and dropped a rose from the bouquet onto the blanket.

I reached slowly for it, unable to tell from his face what he'd done, afraid he was saying good-bye. Then he winked at me and bent to wake my mother. Moaning, she tried to burrow inside the covers, but he shook her until she opened dazed eyes. With a sudden movement, he thrust the whole bouquet at her.

"It's all right, Helen. Everything's taken care of."

She sat up, her face alert now, and grim. Looking at her, I was afraid to feel relief.

"Where were you?" she asked.

He hesitated, took a deep breath, and grinned crookedly, opening his arms wide. "I took all the money from the bank yesterday, and I bet it on the horses this morning."

We both stared at him as if he were insane; her eyes were wide with disbelief. "You bet all the money on the horses?"

He nodded, his grin fading as he dropped his arms. His voice was dogged, his eyes flickering from her face to the red roses.

"I told you I couldn't give it back and lose my garage."

"You risked it all?" she whispered.

"Obbie promised he'd take care of you if I lost."

My mother threw the bouquet onto the floor and began to dress on the far side of the bed, away from him. I'd never seen my father drunk, he never drank, he hated it, but I understood he'd had to nerve himself to face her. Wanting to feel happy, I couldn't; I wondered if he'd be a drunkard now, like Jake.

She buttoned her blouse with her back still to him; waiting, he watched her attentively. When she turned, her face was like stone.

"I'm going out," she said. "If I knew what you were planning, I'd have left you."

He flushed, but his gaze was steady.

"I promise you I'll never gamble again."

She looked him slowly up and down. "You had no right to do this without telling me."

"If I'd told you, I couldn't have gone through with it."

She watched him a moment longer, her face unsoftened, but she nodded in understanding. Then she took her old red coat from the hall closet and walked out. Clutching my rose, I wondered if Hannah's prayer had been answered too.

My father turned to me, forcing a smile, and repeated that everything was all right. I asked in a small voice if he really had enough money to pay back his boss, and for a moment he looked angry. Then he smiled again and asked if I wanted to count the money.

I shook my head; he kissed me and said he was going after my mother. When he left, I went to my bedroom and sat in my grandpa's chair with a library book about four children shipwrecked on a desert island without grown-ups. Reading, I listened for their return, and tried not to think. When my grandpa came home from shul I told him what my father had done. He sat down heavily on his bed.

"I prayed for him all yesterday and this morning," he said.

"So did I," I answered softly, in the only confession I was ever to make. He nodded thoughtfully.

"You're a good maidele. I hope you can forgive your father."

Above me, the clouds parted, the red rock glistening in the orange light as the sky cleared. Over the needles of eroded stone, in the heavens, a double rainbow formed, a small arc inside the large in a mirror image.

Hannah and I prayed in the dank basement, while my grandpa prayed at shul; my father placed his bets and won. I'd never know which of us saved him, or if either of us did.

My father was wrong and he was a hero; both views were true and I'd never reconcile them.

He dropped the roses on the bed and I saluted him. Bowing tipsily, he winked at me; then he straightened and saluted back; we acknowledged one another across the years.

Thanking the unknowable gods for granting me a glimpse of their existence, I turned for camp before I trespassed on my privilege. In the evening, I wore Bob's rose in my hair.